"Happy birthday, Maggie!"

I turned around and found myself looking into Griff Palmer's sparkling blue eyes.

Just a moment before, I had been thinking that Barry Carter was the greatest thing since talking movies. Now, as Griff kissed me lightly on the cheek, Barry faded right out of the picture. Barry was tall and lean, but Griff was taller and leaner. Barry was good-looking, but Griff was gorgeous. Barry was nice, but Griff was fascinating. Barry was the boy next door, but Griff was An Older Man.

Bantam titles in the Sweet Dreams series. Ask your bookseller for titles you have missed:

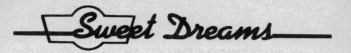

PICTURE PERFECT ROMANCE

J. B. Cooper

BANTAM BOOKS
NEW YORK • TORONTO • LONDON • SYDNEY • AUCKLAND

PICTURE PERFECT ROMANCE
A BANTAM BOOK 0 553 29983 2

First publication in Great Britain

PRINTING HISTORY
Bantam edition published 1994

Cover photo by Pat Hill

Bantam Books are published by Transworld Publishers Ltd, 61–63 Uxbridge Road, Ealing, London W5 5SA, in Australia by Transworld Publishers (Australia) Pty Ltd, 15–25 Helles Avenue, Moorebank, NSW 2170, and in New Zealand by Transworld Publishers (NZ) Ltd, 3 William Pickering Drive, Albany, Auckland.

Printed and bound in Great Britain by Cox & Wyman Ltd, Reading, Berkshire.

PICTURE PERFECT ROMANCE

Chapter One

My name is Maggie Devine, and I am *not* your typical American teenager.

At least I try hard not to be. I've always thought it was kind of neat to be a little different from everybody else. Not that I'm some kind of oddball or anything, but I don't think a person should have to follow every new fad the teen magazines splash across their covers to feel like part of the "in" crowd. "Just be yourself, Magic," my mother always says, and that about sums it up as far as I'm concerned.

Mom's the only person in the world who calls me Magic. I kind of like it, but I'm glad my dad talked her out of putting it down on my birth certificate. My mother isn't exactly a typical suburban housewife type. Dad calls her a free spirit, but a lot of people think she's a little weird. She's more into saving the environment than saving cents-off coupons, and though she's a pretty good cook, most of her favorite dishes are made out of things like seaweed and other stuff most people have never even heard of.

Richard Dunwoodie says that my mother is the last of the hippies, but I think he just says it to annoy me. It's amazing that Richard has managed to become so incredibly annoying in just sixteen years. But it's even more amazing that he used to think that he and I had some special sort of romantic relationship.

"You and me are going places, Red," Richard told me back in eighth grade.

"You and *I* are going nowhere fast," I said.

I absolutely *despise* being called Red! It's true that I have the same curly, carrot-colored hair as my mom, but identifying a person by her hair color is just too stupid. Besides, Richard and I had very little in common in eighth grade, and by the time we became sophomores at North Central High, we had nothing in common at all. Why he kept believing that someday I'd wake up and realize that he was my Prince Charming is a mystery I don't think I'll ever solve.

It's true that I hadn't had much success in the Prince Charming department at that point. I'd dated a few boys the previous year, but none of them made me feel like one of those heroines in the romance novels. You know what I mean: "The moment she saw him, her heart began to pound like a jackhammer, and she knew at once that this was the boy she had been waiting for all her life."

My friend Rose Sue kept telling me that I wasn't trying hard enough where romance was concerned, and sometimes I thought she might be right. It wasn't that I didn't want to fall in love, but you can't make that kind of thing happen until the time is right. Mom says you just have to let Mother Nature take her course, but according to Rose Sue, it doesn't hurt to give old Ma Nature a shove in the right direction.

"You've got to take the bull by the horns," she told me one day after school as we sat at the kitchen table and snacked on some of

Mom's leftover lentil chili. The May Carnival was only a few weeks away, and I still didn't have a date. "This is 1993, remember? You don't have to sit around like a Victorian maiden waiting for somebody to ask you out. *You* can do the asking."

In theory, I agreed with her. But at the same time, I guess I was kind of old-fashioned when it came to dating.

"There's plenty of time," I said. "I'm sure Lester or Jay or somebody will ask me to go."

"Lester or Jay?" Rose Sue wrinkled her nose as if they were two disgusting insects that might be found under some really slimy rock.

"Sure," I said. "What's wrong with Jay and Lester?" True, neither of them was ever likely to win the Mr. Excitement and Glamour Award, but they were nice enough guys.

"Nothing's *wrong* with them," said Rose Sue, "but nothing's *right* about them, either. You could do a lot better, Maggie."

I shrugged and cut a slice of Mom's home-baked five-grain bread. I guess I'm not bad-looking, and people tell me I'm fun to be around. There had to be at least one fabulous guy out there somewhere just dying to

4

meet a girl like me. Still, I couldn't seem to get all worked up about locating Mr. Right before the end of the month.

"The thing is," I said, "I don't really care if I go to the carnival or not."

Rose Sue gave me a skeptical look. "We're talking about the May Carnival," she reminded me. "The one *everyone* goes to."

"Maybe *not* everyone," I said rather sharply. Rose Sue's attitude was beginning to bug me.

"You're very weird sometimes, Maggie." Rose Sue sighed, taking another big spoonful of chili.

After Rose Sue went home, I found myself doing a lot of heavy thinking. I knew perfectly well that there were more important things in the world than having a date for the May Carnival, but at the moment I seemed to be having trouble pinpointing exactly what they were. What did I want out of life, anyway? I'd always figured on going to college, finding some kind of job, and maybe getting married and having a couple of kids someday. But didn't there have to be more to life than that?

"What's it all about?" I asked my mother

that evening as we washed and dried the supper dishes. I knew the question was kind of vague, but I had the feeling Mom would know what I meant.

She looked at me thoughtfully for a moment. "Living and loving," she said at last.

I waited for her to go on, but that was apparently all she had to say on the subject.

"That's it?"

"That's it, Magic," said Mom. "Work you care about and people to love." She smiled. "I guess it's kind of hard at your age to understand what I'm talking about."

"I guess it is," I agreed. I knew Mom was telling me the truth in her own peculiar way, but I wasn't exactly sure what that truth was. *Maybe it's better that way,* I thought. *After all, if you have all the answers before you're even out of high school, what are you supposed to think about for the rest of your life?*

After our conversation, I pretty much decided to call it a night as far as heavy thinking was concerned. Instead of trying to unlock the mysteries of the universe, I settled for looking at the newspaper before going upstairs to try and unlock the mysteries of my geometry homework. As usual, I turned first to the entertainment section. A new horror flick had just opened at the Triplex, and I was looking forward to checking out the review.

I should explain at this point that I am a total fanatic when it comes to movies, and I'm not talking about having a crush on some good-looking actor. A lot of my friends say they're into movies just because they see every film and buy every magazine that features the latest heartthrob.

What I love about going to the movies has nothing to do with seeing a hot new star on the big screen. But put me in a dark theater with a good film and a big box of popcorn and I'm in heaven. I love them all—old films, new films, foreign and domestic, color or black-and-white, comedies, dramas, you name it. For me, watching a good movie is like entering a different world. For however long it lasts, I'm not just an ordinary teenage girl. I really *am* "Magic" Devine, traveling to far-off lands and having fabulous adventures with the kind of people I've always wanted to meet.

Rose Sue says I'm a movie nut because I'm

trying to escape from reality, but it just so happens that I'm very pleased with my real life. It's just that something hard to explain happens to me when I'm watching a good film. It's as if somehow I'm sharing the problems and joys of the characters on the screen and experiencing them as my own. Their lives become a part of my life, and I leave the theater feeling more complete than when I went in. (Does any of this make sense?)

I said before that I love all movies. Well, I lied. Personally, I wouldn't mind at all if those slasher flicks stopped coming out. I'm sure a lot of hard work goes into all the special effects that make them so memorable, but there's just so much you can do with fake blood and guts before it starts getting monotonous.

Anyway, I love to read movie reviews and compare other people's ideas about films to my own. I had just finished reading the "Eye on Film" column and was about to turn to the comics, my second-favorite part of the paper, when I noticed a small ad in the lower left-hand corner of the movie page.

WANTED! TYPICAL TEENAGE GIRLS!

That stopped me cold. I lowered the paper and stared into space for a second before turning my attention back to the page.

Girls wanted for possible film roles. Apply in person at Fieldstone University Theater, Saturday 9 A.M.

I probably should have put down the paper and forgotten all about it, but I couldn't. As much as I hated to think of myself as a typical teenager, this seemed like a golden opportunity to get an insider's look at the magical world of moviemaking, and there was no way I was going to let it slip by. Maybe it would just be some dumb student film, and maybe I wouldn't get any farther than the front door of the theater, but I knew I had to give it a try.

I raced upstairs to my room and smiled at myself in the mirror over my dressing table. The girl grinning back at me looked remarkably like a typical American teenager!

Chapter Two

When I showed up at Fieldstone University a couple of minutes to nine on Saturday morning, I quickly discovered that I wasn't the only girl in town interested in getting into the movies. You would think they were giving away money or something the way people were lined up to get inside the theater. Most of the girls were older than me, college students who were very serious about becoming professional actresses.

The more I looked over the competition, the more I began to feel as if I were very much out of my league. I might have turned around then and there and headed home if the side entrance to the theater hadn't suddenly opened. A middle-aged woman and a handsome young guy, both carrying clipboards, stepped out and began walking slowly along the line. Neither of them spoke much as they looked us over, pausing only to jot down a note or exchange a few hushed words. I began to feel a little queasy as they reached me, but I forced myself to look straight into their eyes. My father always says that making eye contact is the first step in making people notice you, and he ought to know. Dad's a reporter for one of the biggest newspapers in the state. When you're competing with a mob of experienced reporters who are all trying to get the same scoop, you have to know how to get yourself noticed.

I don't know if the eye contact helped or not, but I was one of the dozen or so girls who was handed a number and asked to follow the clipboard people into the building. Inside, a man wearing a blue jacket snapped a Polaroid picture of each girl, handed out questionnaires, and asked each of us to find a seat near the stage. I filled in my name, address, and telephone number and answered the question about previous acting experience (*none*) before returning the questionnaire to the man in the blue jacket.

When all the forms were completed, they were passed up to the couple with the clipboards, who were now seated at a small table on the stage.

"Number One?" called the man in the blue jacket after a few very long minutes.

A dark-haired girl in a bright red minidress stood up and was ushered onto the stage. My attention started to wander as she quietly chatted with the people at the table. I was just beginning to fantasize about what it would be like to be a famous film star when the girl in the bright red dress suddenly screamed.

Instantly, all eyes were on the stage, but all we saw was a nervous-looking girl in a short red dress quietly stepping down from the stage and exiting the theater.

"Number Two?" called the man in the blue jacket.

A tall girl with straight blond hair jumped from her seat and climbed the short flight of stairs to the stage. This time I kept my eyes fixed on the proceedings and wasn't quite so startled when the blond girl let go with a horrible screech. I saw her shake the older woman's hand before making her hasty retreat.

"Number Three, please."

I checked the slip of paper in my hand for the thousandth time, cleared my throat, and ascended to the stage.

"Miss Devine?" said the woman behind the desk, glancing briefly at the clipboard before her.

"Maggie," I replied, before flashing my most pleasant smile.

"Maggie," she echoed. "I see you have no acting experience.

"That's true," I admitted. "But I really love the movies."

"Is that right?" said the woman. I nodded, suddenly feeling like a complete idiot.

"What kind of movies do you like, Maggie?"

I turned toward the handsome young man who had asked the question. I guessed he was in his early twenties, although his dancing blue eyes and the shock of wavy blond hair that tumbled down over his forehead made him look much younger.

"All kinds," I said, my voice coming out a little shaky. I cleared my throat and licked my dry lips.

"Any particular favorites?" he asked.

I usually love talking about my favorite films, but my mind had suddenly gone blank and I couldn't come up with a single title.

"It doesn't matter," said the woman, making a note on her clipboard. "We're looking for a certain type of girl for a crowd scene. We need several young women who have the right look and can scream well on cue."

"Scream?" I asked.

"Scream," the woman repeated. "Could you scream for us now, please? Just imagine you're terrified, and let us hear your best scream."

I glanced at the guy sitting next to her and was met by an encouraging smile. I returned the smile and closed my eyes. If you've never tried screaming on demand, you probably don't realize how tough it can be. I tried to summon up some horrible memory from my past to get me in the right frame of mind and was shocked to realize that, at least until that moment, I had been living an absurdly pleasant and unterrifying life. Here I was, almost sixteen years old, and nothing really terrible had ever happened to me. Tears of frustration began to well up behind my tightly clenched eyelids.

"You okay, Red?" asked the blond man behind the table.

That did it. I thought of Richard Dunwoodie and everyone else who had ever called me Red and the possibility that I would have to go through my entire life being called Red by attractive strangers like the blue-eyed young man. Suddenly a wail of pure anguish poured forth from my open mouth.

There was a long moment of silence before the woman with the clipboard finally spoke.

"Thank you," she said quietly. "That was very good."

"We have your number," said the young man, grinning as he nodded his approval. "We'll be in touch."

I sighed deeply and thanked them both before being ushered offstage by the man in the blue jacket. A dozen pairs of eyes watched in mixed admiration and envy as I walked briskly down the aisle and out into the cool morning air.

I was only home an hour when the phone rang.

"This is Griff Palmer," said the voice on the other end, and I knew at once that it was the handsome young man with the blond hair and piercing blue eyes.

"Did I—did I get the part?" I asked breathlessly.

"Sure did," he replied. "Congratulations."

"Thanks!" I could feel the blood pounding in my temples, and I knew it wasn't just because I was going to be in the movies. "When do we start?"

"Take it easy," said Griff with a chuckle in his voice. "You'll get a letter with all the details in a few days. I just didn't want you to have to sweat it out."

"I appreciate that," I said. *Not only good-looking,* I thought, *but considerate, too.*

"That was quite a scream you let out."

"Well . . ." I began, suddenly at a loss for words. How could I tell him that my rather intense response had been triggered by his calling me Red?

"Did you happen to notice the hair on Number Seven?" Griff asked, ignoring my hesitation. "I used the same trick on her. You should have heard her holler. I'll never understand why you redheads are so sensitive about your hair color."

"You mean you purposely called me Red

to get me to scream?" I asked in astonishment.

"Yep. Don't sound so surprised. A good director can find a way to get any response he wants from his actors."

For a moment I was angry with Griff, but the anger quickly dissolved. After all, I told myself, manipulating people's emotional responses is really what acting and directing are all about. And besides, he was *so* cute.

"Are you directing this film?" I asked, more interested than ever in the intriguing Griff Palmer.

"Not exactly," he said after an almost imperceptible pause. "More like a special assistant." I had a feeling that he was trying to impress me. Frankly, he wasn't doing a bad job.

"So," I said, which is something I usually say when I'm talking to handsome strangers and I'm not sure what to say next.

"So," said Griff Palmer. "I guess that's about it until we start shooting."

"Which will be . . . ?"

"Middle of June," he said. "It'll all be in the letter."

"Right," I said, wanting desperately to continue the conversation but not knowing what else to say. "The letter. Well, guess I'll see you then. In June, I mean."

"You can count on it," said Griff.

I sure will, I thought as I said good-bye and slowly hung up the phone.

The May Carnival came and went. Lester asked me to go with him, and we had a really nice time. He's no threat to Griff Palmer in the looks department, but not many high-school boys are. Anyway, my chance to get better acquainted with the gorgeous Mr. Palmer would be coming soon enough.

School ended uneventfully at the beginning of June. By the time I completed my last final, I was already thinking about coming back to North Central High as a junior in September. All in all, the past few summers had not been filled with the kind of fun-in-the-sun adventures they always show you in the movies.

Fortunately, this summer promised to be different. This summer I was going to be a movie star.

"That's not exactly what the letter says,"

Rose Sue insisted as she carefully read the document in question.

"Not in so many words," I grudgingly admitted.

"Not in *any* kind of words," said Rose Sue. I love that girl like a sister, but sometimes she really gets on my nerves.

What the letter did say was that I should show up at the Fieldstone University Theater at 6:00 A.M. sharp the morning of June 14, which is exactly what I did. Needless to say, I wasn't overjoyed about getting up slightly earlier than your average rooster. I knew I was going to have to make a few sacrifices if I was going to be a star, but I had hoped to begin making them at a more civilized hour.

I forgot all my complaints the moment I saw Griff Palmer waiting on the theater steps. He was talking to an older man with a balding head and a bushy gray mustache.

"Maggie Devine," said Griff as I drew nearer. "I'd like you to meet Les Gryphon."

"Les Gryphon?" I repeated, wondering if I had heard correctly. "The famous director?"

"I'm flattered," said the older man. "I don't think any of the other young ladies have ever heard of me before."

"That's hard to believe," I said. "You directed some of the greatest horror and suspense films of all time!"

"Better get on board with the others," said Griff, gesturing toward the big yellow bus on the driveway next to the theater. "We have to get to the canyon while the light's still good."

Reluctantly, I waved good-bye and joined the other girls on the bus. An hour later, we were standing under the hot summer sun that beat down on Stony Hollow Canyon, the vast natural chasm that is one of the state's major claims to fame as a tourist attraction.

If you're expecting to hear all the glamorous details about my day at this point in the story, I'm afraid you're in for a major disappointment. Hot, dirty, and boring? Definitely. Glamorous? No way!

Mostly what you do when you're a movie extra is wait. You wait for the makeup people to powder your forehead. You wait for the stylist to fluff your hair. You wait for the wardrobe person to adjust your costume. You wait for the camera crew to set up their equipment. You wait for the director to tell you exactly what he wants you to do and when he wants you to do it. And, before too long, you wait for the day to be over so you can go home, take a nice long shower, and go sleep.

I'm sure every movie director has his or her own way of getting the job done. There are probably some directors who sit down with the cast and crew in advance and explain exactly what kind of film they're making and what everyone's role in the film is going to be. Les Gryphon is not that sort of director. Mr. Gryphon does not explain anything to the cast. What Mr. Gryphon does is give instructions to his assistants, who then run the actors through their paces over and over until everybody on the set would rather jump into the canyon than repeat the same scene another time.

And that's when Mr. Gryphon instructs his assistants to have you do it all over again.

What we were filming at Stony Hollow Canyon that day were some scenes for Gryphon's new film, *Nights of Terror II*, a sequel to last year's box-office phenomenon entitled—you guessed it—*Nights of Terror*. Mostly what I remember about that morning is running around in the heat and screaming a lot.

"It's a dream sequence," Griff explained to me as we sipped lukewarm ginger ale during one of our few breaks. "Did you see *Nights of Terror*?"

"Part of it," I answered. "I had to leave when the bad guy's head exploded."

"It was pretty gruesome, wasn't it?" said Griff with a grin. "Not your cup of tea, huh?"

"Not really," I agreed. "I mean, Les Gryphon is definitely brilliant, but I could do without all that blood and gore."

"Personally, I've always loved horror films," said Griff, "and this could be one of the best ever. The picture's basically finished except for a few of the dream sequences that we're shooting on location. We decided to try using 'real' girls instead of trained actresses to get the kind of effect we're aiming for in this scene. We've been running behind schedule, but we're hoping to have the whole thing wrapped up and in the theaters by the end of August. A perfect summer movie."

"Right," I said, wincing at the knowledge that I was acting in exactly the kind of movie I generally avoided watching. "But why all the running and screaming? I mean, shouldn't somebody at least be chasing us or something?"

"That comes later. The editing and special-effects people will fill in the monster after we finish shooting. When you see the horrible creature that's been chasing you around the canyon, you'll know why you were screaming so much."

"I guess you guys know what you're doing," I said with a sigh, and took a sip of ginger ale. "I just wish Les Gryphon wasn't such a tyrant."

"What do you mean?"

I looked around and lowered my voice. "He's just impossible!" I said, giving vent to some of the frustration that had been build-ing up all morning. "I know he's a genius and everything, but that doesn't excuse the way he treats people. He's had us running around screaming our lungs out in this hundred-degree heat, and this is only the second break we've had all day! Did you hear him yell at that skinny blond girl when she tripped and fell flat on her face? The poor kid almost broke into tears!"

"He's a tough bird, all right," said Griff with another of his dazzling grins. "But if you think he's hard on actors, you should try having him for a father."

"What are you talking about?" I asked.

"Didn't I tell you?" said Griff. "Les Gryphon is my dad."

"But—but I thought your name was Palmer," I stammered, astonished.

"I changed my name when I started studying film in college. People can have some pretty unrealistic expectations of a film student who happens to be Lester Gryphon, Junior. Kind of like being Hemingway's kid in a writing class, I'd imagine. Anyway, Palmer was my mother's name, and my friends always called me Griff, so I became Griff Palmer."

"I'm so sorry about those things I said. If I had realized . . ."

"Don't worry about it," Griff said with a shrug.

I was about to apologize again when a bell rang to announce that it was time to get back to work. As I started to leave, Griff suddenly took hold of my hand and gave it a quick squeeze. Maybe he was just being friendly, or maybe he was reassuring me that I hadn't said anything wrong. I didn't know, and I didn't really care. I felt a warm flush of excitement at that moment and it didn't go away until we finished shooting much later that afternoon.

When it was all over, I climbed wearily back onto the bus and waved good-bye to Lester Gryphon, Jr., hoping that I hadn't seen the last of the handsome young man with the beautiful blue eyes.

Chapter Three

"So tell me," said Rose Sue the next morning as she settled back in the chair at the side of my bed. "What's it like to be a movie star?"

"I wish I knew," I said hoarsely. I'd woken up with a slightly sore throat, a throbbing headache, and assorted aches and pains in muscles that I never even knew I had before. I guess running around in a dusty canyon all day under a blazing summer sun while fleeing from an invisible monster and screaming in terror is not the best thing for a person's health.

"You're so lucky," Rose Sue sighed. "I can't wait to see you on the screen."

"Don't hold your breath," I croaked.

Griff had made a special point of warning each girl that her performance had only a slight chance of making it into the final cut of the movie. Griff said he wouldn't be too surprised if the entire dream sequence wound up on the cutting-room floor, and somehow I had the feeling that I wasn't going to emerge from this experience as a star of the silver screen.

Despite a vague sense of disappointment, however, my day as a movie extra taught me a valuable lesson about myself. As I said before, I've never been the kind of person who goes gaga over movie stars. The satisfaction I get from watching a good movie has very little to do with the so-called star quality of the performers on the screen.

"So what's your point?" Rose Sue asked impatiently after I explained all this to her.

"My point," I said, "is that I'm not really interested in becoming a movie star."

"Are you kidding?" asked Rose Sue. "You've always been a movie nut. As long as I've known you, you've been carrying on about great films and directors and actors and stuff like that."

"Exactly. But I've never really been interested in seeing myself on the screen. You know Alfred Hitchcock, the famous director?"

"The guy who made all those scary old movies?"

"Right. Hitchcock shocked a lot of people when he said that actors are cattle. Until yesterday I never really understood what he meant. Now I do. He was talking from the director's point of view. The actor's job is to do whatever the director tells him to do. A great actor may bring his own special magic to a performance, but it's up to the director whether that performance comes through on film."

Rose Sue sighed loudly, the way she always does when I start talking about movies.

"Do you think you can get to the point before lunchtime?" she asked.

"I think I'd like to make movies," I said. It was the first time I'd ever said it out loud, and I kind of liked the way it sounded.

"What do you mean, 'make movies'?" Rose Sue asked. "You mean like be a writer? Or a director?"

"I don't know," I admitted. "Maybe both. I just know I'd like to be the one *giving* the orders instead of the one taking them."

"That's the Maggie Devine I know," Rose Sue said with a grin. "But face it, Maggie. You don't know anything about making movies."

"I just spent a whole day working with Les Gryphon," I pointed out. "Besides, I've been watching movies all my life. I must have learned something after all this time."

Rose Sue looked at me in silence for a long moment. "So do it," she said at last.

"Do it?" I echoed. "Do what?"

"Make a movie! Isn't that what we've been talking about for the past half hour?"

"I suppose so," I said. Suddenly I was feeling a lot less sure of myself. "But you're right. I don't really know much of anything about making movies. I wouldn't even know who to ask for advice."

Rose Sue thought for a moment, and then a mischievous grin spread slowly across her face.

"That's the fun part," she said.

"I'm glad you called," said Griff. He leaned back in his chair and sipped a cup of hot black coffee.

"So am I." I could hardly believe I was sitting in the Campus Coffee Shop with Les Gryphon's gorgeous son talking about making movies! It had taken Rose Sue the better part of an hour to convince me to call Griff at his hotel, and I only managed to work up the courage by telling myself that he wouldn't be there. As it happened, my call woke him up. What surprised me even more was that he seemed genuinely pleased to hear from me and invited me to join him for breakfast. In spite of my aching muscles and sore throat, I knew it was an offer I couldn't refuse.

"I was thinking about you yesterday after the shoot," Griff said now.

"Were you?" I asked in what I hoped would pass as a casual tone of voice. I wondered if everyone in the room could hear the pounding of my heart.

"Sure was. You did a good job out there, Maggie. You showed a lot of talent."

"Thanks," I said, "but it doesn't take much talent to run around, look terrified, and scream a lot."

"You'd be surprised," said Griff. "Not everybody has a natural talent for taking direction."

"Following orders isn't exactly my thing, either," I said. "That's kind of what I wanted to talk to you about."

"I know," said Griff. He sighed as if he were hearing a story he had heard many times before. "You want to be a star."

"Actually, no."

"No?" Griff looked amazed.

"No," I repeated. "I think I'd like to make movies of my own."

Griff laughed. "So you want to be a film-maker!"

"Is that so funny?" I asked, a little annoyed.

"Not really," he said, almost apologetically. "In fact, it's kind of refreshing. It's just sur-prisingly ambitious for a kid your age. No offense, but I don't think you have any idea what making films is really all about."

"Maybe not," I admitted, kind of upset about being referred to as a kid. "But I'm willing to learn. That's why I came to you. I thought maybe you could tell me how to get started."

"There's only one way to learn filmmak-ing," he said, "and that's by making films."

"Didn't you say you studied filmmaking in college?"

"Sure. And I learned a lot, too. If you're really interested in filmmaking, you should read as many books and take as many classes as you can. But when you get down to the nitty-gritty, reading about how movies are made and actually making them are two very different things."

"Oh, sure," I said wearily. "I think I have almost a hundred dollars in the bank. I'll go right out tomorrow and start making a movie."

"I'm serious," said Griff. "It's true that shooting film can be very expensive, but why not start with video?"

"Video?"

"Make a videotape. Get hold of a camcorder, buy yourself a couple of blank tapes, and you're in business. You'll be amazed at how quickly you start learning about the art of filmmaking."

"I've never even held a video camera," I said. "I wouldn't know how to work one."

"It's not a whole lot harder than taking snapshots," said Griff. "I can teach you the basics in fifteen minutes." He paused thoughtfully for a moment and then picked up the copy of the *Fieldstone News* that he had been skimming when I arrived at the coffee shop. He flipped through the pages, found the classified section, and circled an item with a red pen he took from his jacket pocket. "Read," he ordered, thrusting the paper under my nose.

Video Competition said the ad. *Open to the public.*

"It's sponsored by the Fieldstone theater department," Griff explained as I scanned the rest of the notice. "You don't have to be a student. You don't even have to have experience. All you have to do is do it."

"Do it," I echoed aloud for the second time that day. There were a hundred reasons why I knew I should forget about the contest, and the fact that I couldn't possibly win was right up there near the top of the list. But at the same time, I knew Griff and Rose Sue were right. There was no way I was going to learn about making films unless I gave it a try, and this was just the sort of incentive I needed to get started.

"Do it," Griff repeated, reaching across the table to give my hand an encouraging squeeze. I was absolutely positive his hand lingered on mine a few moments longer than it needed to.

I gazed deep into Griff's sparkling eyes and slowly nodded my head.

"A video camera?" said my father that afternoon. "Are you going to start making home movies?"

"Not exactly," I said. "Actually, I'm planning to enter a video contest."

"That's great," said Dad. "What kind of video are you going to make?"

I looked vaguely around the room. "I'm not exactly sure," I said, which had to be the understatement of the century. As a matter of fact, I hadn't the foggiest notion of what I wanted to do. I had left my meeting with Griff brimming over with enthusiasm. I was going to get hold of a video camera, make a sensational video, win the contest, and live happily ever after with Griff Palmer. Not that I took the last part of that scenario too seriously, of course, but an adoring look and a congratulatory kiss from the gorgeous young assistant director didn't seem completely outside the realm of future possibilities.

Unfortunately, when I came down to earth, I realized I had no idea what my prize-winning entry would be about.

"Need an idea?" said Dad, who has an uncanny knack for reading my mind.

"Or two," I admitted. "Here are the official rules." I handed him the sheet of paper I had picked up at the university after saying good-bye to Griff. "I haven't had time to read them yet."

"Let's see," said Dad. " 'Open to all amateurs . . .' "

"That's me, all right."

" 'All works must be original and no longer than ten minutes in length . . .' "

"Ten minutes!" I interrupted. "That's not much time to tell a story in."

"Once you get started, I think you'll be surprised how long ten minutes can be," said Dad, looking up from the page. "The TV newspeople cover most major stories in less than four minutes, and that includes film coverage, live interviews, and analysis."

"But news is different," I insisted, although I saw his point. "I want to make a movie."

"Take it easy, honey," Dad said. "Nobody starts writing epic novels until they've knocked off a couple of short stories first. What category were you planning to enter in, anyway?"

"Category?"

" 'Entries must be submitted in one of the following categories," Dad read. " 'Drama, Nature, Musical Performance, or Documentary.' "

I peered at the rules over Dad's shoulder and considered the four choices. As a lifelong movie buff, my first inclination was to do a drama or a comedy of some sort. But the more I thought about it, the more I realized how complicated doing something like that would be. Even without any kind of fancy camera work, I'd still need a good script and some talented actors. I've always been good at writing, but I didn't know anything about writing a video script. And without good actors, I'd probably wind up with something that looked and sounded like an elementary school production. As much as I hated to admit it, I really wasn't ready to write, cast, and produce a drama, even one that was only ten minutes long.

How about Nature, then? I thought. *You don't need much of a script for a nature film, and you don't even need any actors!* All I'd have to do is take my camera into the woods and shoot some plants and animals doing their thing. What could be easier?

Who was I kidding? In the first place, I knew even less about nature than I did about writing video scripts. I'm the kind of person who starts to panic if I'm more than half a mile from an air-conditioned mall. And even if I were some kind of nature freak, I still wouldn't know how to capture it on videotape. I could just imagine the kind of nature film I'd produce with my limited know-how: ten minutes of grass growing while squirrels ran around looking for acorns. With my luck, one of the nasty rodents would probably sneak up from behind and bite me on the ankle!

All right, then: Musical Performance. There was a category I could really sink my teeth into. I love music, and I've watched enough rock videos to know what they're supposed to look like. But could I actually put together an interesting video of my own? *Probably not,* I decided regretfully. Without sophisticated technical effects, all I'd wind up with would be ten minutes of a band standing around playing their instruments in a garage.

Besides, half the entries in the contest would probably be in the Musical Performance category. Most kids think of MTV as soon as they hear the word *video*.

"That leaves Documentary," I said aloud.

"Excellent choice," said Dad, oblivious to the complex process of elimination that had just run through my mind.

"Actually," I admitted after a moment's reflection, "I'm not sure I know exactly what a documentary is."

"A documentary is just a true story," Dad explained.

"About?"

"About anything," he said. "The point is to tell an interesting true story without using actors or written dialogue."

"No actors and no script," I muttered. Suddenly, Documentary was beginning to sound like a very appealing category.

"All you need is a subject."

"Right," I said nonchalantly. After all, "anything" seemed to be a pretty broad field to choose from.

"And a video camera," he added. "And somebody to show you how to use it."

"No problem," I said, grinning at Dad with renewed confidence. All my troubles seemed to vanish into thin air. Now all I had to do was come up with ten minutes of prize-winning videotape.

To make a long story short, Dad borrowed my uncle Bob's camcorder, and Griff promised to show me how to use the thing, but coming up with a good idea was proving to be a lot more difficult than I had anticipated.

"A video?" Rose Sue said excitedly as we sat on my front porch the next afternoon. "What band are you going to do?"

"It's not going to be that kind of video," I explained, but Rose Sue wasn't listening.

"I can see it now," she said between bites of one of Mom's carob-chip cookies. She gazed off into the distance. "A slow love song. Close-up on the singer's face. Cut to a house in the country. Soft rain beating on the windowpane. Two lovers inside, kissing tenderly. Then back to the band . . ."

"Wait a minute," I interrupted. "I told you it's not that kind of video."

"Oh, I get it," said Rose Sue. "You're doing a heavy metal thing! Guys with long, curly hair stomping around the stage with lots of smoke and fire and stuff . . ."

"Wrong again," I said. "In the first place, I

wouldn't know how to shoot rain on window-panes or make smoke pour off a stage. And in the second place, *I'm not doing a music video.*"

"But you said . . ."

"Video isn't only rock 'n' roll on MTV. Video is anything you can watch on a TV screen, from a soap opera to a commercial to the evening news. It just so happens I'm planning to shoot a documentary."

"Meaning?"

I hesitated a moment, then shook my head. "Meaning I don't know," I confessed. "Meaning I'm up the creek with a borrowed camcorder and not a single decent idea in my head."

Rose Sue and I gazed at each other thoughtfully for a long time before she finally broke the silence.

"Richard Dunwoodie," she said.

"What about him?"

"I ran into him at the mall last week. He told me he's managing a new band. Maybe you could do something on them."

"Rose Sue, you're not listening to me. I don't want to do a rock video."

"I know. I'm not talking about a *regular*

rock video. I just thought maybe you could make some kind of documentary about Richard's band, something about what it's like for a new band to get started. You know —how they got together, how they pick their songs, what it's like to rehearse and look for jobs. Stuff like that."

I stared at Rose Sue for a minute and nodded, a big grin spreading across my face.

"Either that's the dumbest idea I've ever heard," I said, "or else it's positively brilliant!"

Rose Sue shrugged her shoulders and grabbed another cookie from the plate on the floor.

"Just mention me in the credits," she said airily, and took a huge bite out of the cookie.

Chapter Four

Meanwhile a major event was looming on the horizon. I was about to turn Sweet Sixteen.

As you might have guessed, my mom and dad are not the kind of people to make a big fuss about things like that. I mean, they love me a whole lot and they'd throw a big party for me anytime I wanted one, but a fancy Sweet Sixteen party with expensive clothes, corsages, party favors, and all that junk just isn't their scene—or mine, either, for that matter. Sixteen was a special kind of birthday, but I didn't feel the need to put a severe strain on the family budget in order to celebrate it.

Anyway, Rose Sue had decided to throw a big birthday bash for me. My parents were footing the bill for the refreshments, but Rose Sue was in charge of inviting the guests, providing the house, and generally organizing the shindig. It was Rose Sue's idea to invite Griff Palmer.

"He'll never come," I said.

"He would if you asked him," she said.

"He's a very busy person," I protested. "He doesn't have time for a kid's birthday party."

"Sixteen is *not* a kid anymore."

"Compared to Griff it is," I sighed. "He must be at least twenty-two."

"Don't you want him to come to the party?"

"Sure I do. I just don't think *he'll* want to come, that's all."

"You'll never know if you don't ask him," Rose Sue pointed out. "What do you have to lose?"

Just my pride and dignity, I thought, but didn't say it aloud. I couldn't bear the thought of his laughing at the idea of being a guest at a teenage birthday party. The practical side of me was convinced that Griff and I had no future together, but the romantic side practically swooned at the thought of dancing with Griff Palmer while my friends turned green with envy.

My practical side never had a chance.

"Nice to hear from you," said Griff when I called him at the hotel.

I got right to the point. "I'm going to be sixteen next week . . ." I began.

"Congratulations," said Griff. "A good age, sixteen. I remember it well."

"Uh—yeah. Anyway, my friend Rose Sue is throwing a party for me, and I was wondering if maybe—"

"I'd drop by?" he interrupted. "Absolutely. No problem."

"You'll come?" I squeaked. "Really?"

"Sure," said Griff. "I like to keep in touch with the younger generation. You kids make up a large part of the movie-going public, you know."

"Terrific," I said, although it wasn't exactly the answer I wanted to hear. I would have been a whole lot happier if Griff had said he was coming because he thought I was a beautiful, desirable woman and he was crazy about me. Still, I wasn't going to complain. Better to have Griff think of me as a member of "the younger generation" than not to have him think of me at all.

*　　*　　*

Griff wasn't the first to arrive at Rose Sue's house that Saturday night, but I knew right away that this was going to be one terrific party whether he showed up or not. Different people have different talents, and Rose Sue's genius happens to lie in putting together a guest list. When Rose Sue is in charge, you never know whom you're going to be partying with. She has a knack for putting unlikely people together in such a way that everyone has a good time, and she's always on the lookout for new faces.

Rose Sue's parties are lots of fun, and this one was no exception. The food was great, the music was lively, and the conversation sparkled. As usual, Rose Sue had assembled a group of people who all seemed to enjoy each other's company, and a major part of her talent as a party-giver was making sure that her guests had the opportunity to meet each other. Rose Sue is the kind of person who will grab you by the elbow and drag you across the room to introduce you to someone she thinks you ought to meet, which is exactly what she did to me that night.

"Barry Carter, I'd like you to meet Maggie Devine."

"Happy birthday, Maggie," said a tall, dark-haired boy, smiling pleasantly at me.

"Thank you," I said, returning the smile. Although we had never met before, I had seen Barry Carter run on several occasions at varsity track meets. I remember commenting on his good looks to Rose Sue at the regional finals in May, and I was sure it was no coincidence that she had invited him to my birthday party a few weeks later.

"It turns out you and Barry have something in common," said Rose Sue. "Barry's entering the Fieldstone video contest, too."

"Really?" I said. "Are you interested in film?"

"Not especially," Barry said with a shy sort of half-smile. His half-smile was a lot cuter than a lot of full-size grins I've seen. "I mean, I like movies and everything, but I'm not really into filmmaking. My main interest is anthropology."

"Anthropology?" I repeated. I turned to glance at Rose Sue, but she had hurried off to turn more strangers into friends.

"The study of mankind," said Barry. "I'm planning to major in it in college."

"I'm afraid I don't know much about anthropology," I admitted.

"Most people don't," said Barry, "and that's too bad. It's really fascinating stuff, all about how various people around the world solve the basic problems of everyday life."

"Sounds pretty heavy," I said. I had always thought of Barry Carter as a handsome boy with a charming smile and a strong pair of legs. It had never occurred to me that he might have more on his mind than training for the next race.

"It gets pretty complex," he said, "especially when you start getting into civilizations that no longer exist, like the Spartans of Greece or the Incas of Peru."

"I always wondered how people who write the history books seem to know so much about stuff that happened so long ago."

"That's where archaeology comes in," said Barry. "You'd be amazed at how much you can learn about people's lives by studying the places they used to live."

"Don't archaeologists go around digging up old bones and pieces of pottery and stuff like that?" I asked.

"That's the general idea," said Barry, "but

it's not as boring as you make it sound. Actually, it was archaeology that got me involved with videotape. A friend of my father's is working at the archaeological site over near the canyon—"

"Stony Hollow Canyon?" I interrupted. I'd always pictured archaeologists working in far-off places like Africa or Asia or somewhere. It was hard to imagine anybody digging around about an hour's drive from my front door.

Barry nodded. "That's right. There have been quite a few major archaeological finds made in this part of the country in recent years. Anyway, my father's friend invited me to observe the archaeologists at work, and I thought it would be a good idea to record it on video. When I heard about the contest, I figured I'd try doing a short documentary about archaeology." He paused while he poured two glasses of punch from the big bowl on the table. "What about you?" he asked as he handed me one of the glasses.

"Me?" I said. It wasn't exactly a brilliant response, but it was fairly typical of the kind of thing I tend to say to seventeen-year-old boys with whom I might be beginning to fall in love.

"What are you doing for the contest?" he prompted. "You know, the video contest."

"Oh, *that* contest," I said. "I'm hoping to shoot a rock group in action."

"Oh." Barry sounded a little disappointed. "A rock video."

"Not really," I said. "It's going to be a documentary. You see . . ."

But before I could explain, a pretty blond girl appeared at Barry's side.

"Hi," she said, her overly made-up eyes fixed on me.

"Hi," I said.

"Do you two know each other?" asked Barry. "Melanie Warner, this is—"

"I know," Melanie interrupted. "Devine and I were in gym class together last semester."

I nodded and forced a smile. For some reason, Melanie and I had taken an instant dislike to each other the moment we met. There was just something about her that rubbed me the wrong way. The last time I had seen her was at the track finals last month. Now that I thought about it, I remembered that she had been making goo-goo eyes at Barry Carter.

"Maggie was just telling me about the video she's making for the contest at Fieldstone," Barry told her.

"I haven't really started yet," I said, ignoring Melanie's hostile gaze, "but it's going to be a documentary about the making of a rock band."

"Sounds interesting," said Barry. "It's certainly different from my archaeology project, although I guess you could say we both dig rock."

It took me a moment to get the joke. Then Barry and I started laughing at the same time. Melanie looked confused and then added her own artificial chuckle, though I was pretty sure she had no idea what we were laughing about.

"Have you started taping yet?" I asked Barry.

"Yes," he said. "I've been shooting the excavation on and off for the past couple of weeks, but I haven't really given much thought to editing the tape yet."

"You're way ahead of me," I said. "I haven't even learned how to work the camcorder."

"It's really pretty easy once you learn the basics," Barry assured me. "If you'd like—"

"Excuse me, Barry *dear*," Melanie interrupted with the poorest excuse for a smile I'd seen in a long time. "I'm dying of thirst. Would you mind pouring me a glass of punch?"

Barry obligingly dipped the ladle into the large glass bowl, and while his back was turned the smile disappeared from Melanie's face. She flashed me a look that, if looks could kill, would have left me dead and buried on the spot.

"You were saying?" I prompted eagerly as Barry handed the glass to Melanie.

"I was just going to say that I could show you how to work the camcorder sometime if you'd like."

"That sounds terrific," I said. "I need all the help I can get."

While Melanie stared into her glass as if considering how to poison the punch and force it down my throat, Barry went on, "I'm planning a visit to the excavation one day

51

next week. If you're interested, you might come along to the site."

"Sort of a site-seeing expedition?" I quipped. It wasn't a great joke, but it got both of us laughing again. I noticed that Melanie wasn't laughing this time; instead, she was staring at somebody behind me.

"Happy birthday, Maggie!"

I turned around and found myself looking into Griff Palmer's sparkling blue eyes.

Just a moment before, I had been thinking that Barry Carter was the greatest thing since talking movies. Now, as Griff put his strong hands on my shoulders and kissed me lightly on the cheek, Barry faded right out of the picture. Barry was tall and lean, but Griff was taller and leaner. Barry was good-looking, but Griff was gorgeous. Barry was nice, but Griff was fascinating. Barry was the boy next door, but Griff was An Older Man.

"I'm so glad you were able to come," I said when I could catch my breath.

"It was nice of you to invite me," said Griff, his voice rich and resonant. There was an awkward moment of silence that was broken by Melanie clearing her throat.

"Maggie, aren't you going to introduce us to your friend?" she asked in a voice sweet enough to bring on an attack of diabetes.

"Sorry," I said. "Griff Palmer, this is Melanie Warner." Melanie extended her hand, and Griff shook it. She seemed extremely reluctant to release her grip. "And this is Barry Carter," I said when Melanie finally let go.

"Nice to meet you," Barry said. Was I imagining it, or was he trying to make his voice sound deeper?

"Griff is a filmmaker," I said. "As a matter of fact, his father . . ."

Griff gave me a warning look, and I let my voice trail off. I didn't think Barry or Melanie would have known who Les Gryphon was or have cared that Griff was his son, but I had to respect Griff's desire to separate his own identity from that of his famous father.

"As a matter of fact," said Griff, "Maggie just did some extra work in the film we were shooting out at Stony Hollow Canyon."

Barry turned to me with a look of surprise in his soft brown eyes. "I didn't know you were an actress."

"One of my many talents." I joked with a modest shrug.

"I'm in the Drama Club at school," Melanie announced. We all looked at her expectantly, but apparently she had nothing more to say.

"Maggie and I were just talking about the canyon," Barry told Griff. "There's an archaeological dig going on just north of there—"

"I know," Griff interrupted. "We ran into some trouble with those people when we first scheduled the shoot. It seems our original location was a little too close to their site, and they asked us if we'd mind moving farther into the canyon. I guess those scientist-types don't understand the time and budgetary pressures involved in making a major motion picture."

Barry's face flushed slightly. "I'm not sure that making a movie is necessarily more important than unearthing the remains of an ancient civilization."

I noticed Griff's expression harden for a fraction of a second before he flashed his boyish grin at Barry. "To each his own," he said. "Far be it for me to upset anybody else's applecart, insignificant though it may be."

"Now just a minute—" Barry began, his face still flushed with anger, but I put my hand firmly on his arm.

"Please don't argue on my birthday," I begged, looking first at Barry and then at Griff. Barry slowly nodded in agreement while Griff just shrugged. "Thanks," I said. Impulsively I kissed Barry on the cheek and saw the anger leave his eyes. But the fury in Melanie's glare made me shiver a little.

At that point Griff was glancing curiously around the room. I felt vaguely annoyed by his attitude, but I couldn't deny the powerful attraction I felt for him. I was still holding on to Barry's arm, which further enraged Melanie but had no effect at all on Griff. Suddenly I had the insane idea of using Barry Carter to make Griff jealous.

"Speaking of films," I said as Griff turned back in my direction, "Barry just offered to help me with my video project."

"Is that right?" Griff looked at Barry in surprise. "You know anything about filmmaking?"

"A little," Barry replied.

Griff grinned at me. "I'll be around for another week or two," he said. "If you need any *real* help, feel free to give me a call."

I could feel the muscles in Barry's arm tense under my hand, and I wondered what kind of game I was getting myself involved in. Who was I really trying to make jealous—Griff or Melanie—and what exactly was I trying to accomplish?

Chapter Five

As it turned out, I didn't need either Griff or Barry to help me learn the basics of using a video camera. The one my father borrowed for me was a state-of-the-art machine that anybody with two hands and half a brain could figure out how to use in about five minutes. By the time I finished reading the instruction booklet and taking a few practice shots of my dad doing a hokey soft-shoe routine, I was champing at the bit to start working on my video project. All I had to do now was convince Richard Dunwoodie to let me shoot his new band.

"I don't know, Red," he said when I phoned

him on Monday evening. "I'm not sure it's such a hot idea."

"Why not?" I asked. I knew even before I started dialing that this wasn't going to be easy. At least I had prepared myself for being called Red.

"I don't know," Richard repeated.

"I won't get in the way," I promised. "All I want to do is hang around and tape the guys rehearsing, maybe ask a few questions."

There was a long moment of silence.

"I don't know," Richard said again. I guess that statement pretty much summed up his philosophy of life.

"Give me a chance," I said. "One day. If it doesn't work out, that'll be the end of it. Fair enough?"

Richard paused again. I gritted my teeth, waiting for yet another *I don't know*.

"I guess we can try it," he said at last, but he didn't sound very enthusiastic. "The guys are rehearsing tomorrow afternoon in my basement. Come over around one o'clock."

"I'll be there," I told him.

"And maybe afterward you and me could take in a movie or something and talk," he added slyly.

"I don't know," I said, and hung up before he could say anything else.

Somewhere on this planet there may be a less likely bunch of would-be musicians than the four boys who made up the rock band called Rocky Road. If there is, I certainly hope I never meet them. I suppose I shouldn't have been surprised. I mean, what sort of band, after all, would trust Richard Dunwoodie to manage its musical career? Anyone who counts on Richard to handle any problem more complex than getting across the street without being hit by a truck is asking for trouble.

"What exactly do you do as manager?" I asked, my camera aimed at him.

"Do?" he repeated. His bushy eyebrows lowered as he pondered the answer to my question. "What do you mean, 'do'?"

"*Do,*" I repeated. "What's the manager's job?"

"Job?" Richard acted as if I were speaking some strange language he had never heard before.

I had only been taping for a minute and a half, and I was already on the verge of smashing the camcorder over Richard's thick skull.

"Why don't you just talk about the band," I suggested, figuring I could always edit in the questions later.

"Yeah, the band." Richard slowly nodded his head, cleared his throat, and looked directly into the camera lens.

"My name is Richard Dunwoodie," he said, a little too loudly, "and I'm the manager of a fantastic new rock group called Rocky Road. I first became interested in music at the age of eleven when—"

I cut him off impatiently. "This isn't *The Richard Dunwoodie Story*," I reminded him. "Maybe you should just introduce the members of the band."

Richard gave me a cold stare and shrugged. "You're the boss," he said sarcastically. That was when I followed him into the basement and got my first look at Rocky Road.

"On drums," Richard said proudly, "Porky Wilson!"

The boy sitting behind the drum kit ac-acknowledged his name with a crash of the cymbals. With his jowly face and upturned nose, he bore a striking resemblance to the cartoon pig who shared his nickname.

"On bass guitar," said Richard, "Larry 'Fast-Fingers' Price."

The bass player just nodded his shaved head and continued tuning his instrument.

"On lead guitar, the great Jimmy Granville."

Jimmy played a searing guitar lick that made almost as much noise as a nuclear explosion. A thick mane of greasy blond hair cascaded over his shoulders, and his broad grin revealed a missing front tooth.

"And last but not least," said Richard, "our resident keyboard player and songwriting genius, Jerry Hodges."

The boy at the electric piano smiled at me and nodded pleasantly. He looked much too normal to be part of this weird group.

"This is my old girlfriend, Maggie Devine," Richard announced, "and she's going to make our first video for us."

That did it. I shut off the camera. "In the first place, I am not now nor have I ever been Richard's girlfriend," I said loudly, giving Richard a hard stare. He just grinned back at me as if my thoughts on the subject were of no great importance. "And in the second place, I'm not making a video *for* the band.

I'm making a video *about* the band, which is an entirely different sort of thing."

My statement was met with a long silence. I was expecting Richard to throw me out of his house when Jerry, the boy at the electric piano, spoke up.

"Would you like to hear a tune?" he asked.

I looked at him with gratitude and nodded my head. "That would be nice," I said, turning the camcorder back on.

"Let's try 'Coldhearted Blues,' " he said to the group. Then he counted out the beat and Rocky Road began to play.

Well, it wasn't the best music I ever heard, but it wasn't the worst, either. The guitar was still much too loud, the bass was slightly out of tune, the drummer missed a beat every now and then, and I could hardly hear the piano at all. Still, Jerry Hodges had a nice voice, and the overall effect wasn't all that terrible.

"Well," Richard said when the number was over. "What do you think?"

I paused a moment, both to collect my thoughts and soak in the beautiful silence that followed the guitarist's final, explosive strum.

"Not bad," I said, my own voice sounding

strange in my still-ringing ears. "Maybe a little loud . . ."

"That's what I told them," Jimmy said as he retuned his guitar. "I can hardly hear myself over the bass and drums."

"Actually," I said, "I thought the guitar amp could stand to be tuned down a little."

A look of disgust passed over the guitarist's face. "Girls," he muttered, shaking his mane of curly blond hair.

"Any other brilliant observations?" Richard asked irritably.

I shrugged. "If you really want to know—"

"Why don't we do another song?" Jerry Hodges interjected. The other members of the band were glaring at me as if to let me know that they weren't exactly eager to hear what I thought about their music.

" 'Wild for Love'?" Jimmy Granville suggested. Jerry nodded his head and counted down the beat. A catchy bass riff started the tune, and Rocky Road was off again.

"Better?" Jerry asked when the song was over.

I smiled and nodded my head. For a neutral observer, I had already said way too much.

The rest of the afternoon passed fairly painlessly. Although I would eventually have to edit my tape down to ten minutes or less, I had decided to shoot as much as I could in order to have plenty of material to choose from. But after taping for almost four hours, I still didn't feel as if I had ten really interesting minutes for my contest entry.

As I was getting ready to leave, Richard mentioned that the band would be auditioning singers in a couple of days and to my surprise he invited me back to watch the auditions. I thanked him, thinking that a really good singer might elevate Rocky Road from a bunch of third-rate musicians to an almost second-rate band. Then I said goodbye to the guys and went home to view my day's work on the VCR.

I came back two days later to find Richard sitting on the doorstep.

"Go home," he said, scowling at me.

I put my camcorder down on the stoop. "I thought you were auditioning singers today."

"That's right. And you're not invited."

"But you said—"

"Never mind what I said," he interrupted. "Your invitation has been canceled."

"Was it Jimmy Granville? Just because I said he played a little loud—"

"It has nothing to do with Jimmy," he growled. "It has to do with you."

"What about me?"

"As if you didn't know! Why don't you just go home and leave me alone?"

"Listen, Richard," I said, my face reddening with anger, "I don't have the slightest idea what you're talking about, and I'm not going anywhere until I find out."

Still scowling, Richard looked at me, took a deep breath, and said, "I ran into Melanie Warner at the mall yesterday."

"So?"

"So she told me all about you and Barry Carter."

"What about me and Barry Carter?"

"You really should be an actress," Richard said. "I can't tell if you're playing dumb or if you really are."

"What did she say, Richard?" I demanded.

"Nothing much," he said. "Just that you and Barry Carter were falling all over each other at your birthday party the other

65

night—the party I wasn't invited to, I might add."

I sighed. "In the first place," I said, "Rose Sue was in charge of the invitations." That was true, of course, and Rose Sue knew perfectly well that I wouldn't have wanted Richard at the party. "As far as Barry Carter is concerned—"

"Forget it, Red," said Richard. "It's really none of my business."

"You're right. It's not. But—"

"Look," Richard snapped. "I don't want to talk about it, okay?" Then his eyes narrowed. "You want to keep taping the band, don't you?"

"Sure I do."

"It can be arranged," he said. "Let's make a deal."

"What kind of deal? What's the catch?" I asked suspiciously.

"No catch," said Richard. "All you have to do is go out with me on Saturday night."

I shook my head. "Forget it!"

"What's the matter?" Richard leered at me. "Admit it, Red. You've been madly in love with me ever since the sixth grade."

"Richard," I said, "the only person who's

been madly in love with you since the sixth grade is you."

I guess he thought I was joking, because he reached out and grabbed my hand. "Stop playing hard to get," he said. "I saw the way you were looking at me at rehearsal the other day. You're nuts about me, I can tell."

Pulling my hand away, I leaped to my feet. "No deal, Richard, no way!" Then I headed for home.

Without Richard's cooperation, I didn't know how I was going to get my contest entry completed. It was too late to abandon the Rocky Road project and start on something new. In desperation, I phoned Griff Palmer.

"So what are you going to do now?" he asked when I had explained the situation.

"I don't know," I admitted. "That's why I called you. You've been making films for a long time. What do you do when you run into something like this?"

"I've never run into this exact problem before," he said with a chuckle, "but I did have some difficulties back in film school, and I learned that the thing about making documentaries is that you never know exactly how things are going to work out in advance. You just have to play the cards you're dealt."

"Meaning?"

"Meaning, you have to make the best of a given situation. This Dunwoodie kid doesn't want to let you do any more taping unless you go out with him, right?"

"Right."

"And you don't want to go out with him, right?"

"Right!" I said fervently.

"So make it part of your story. This is a clear case of sexual harassment. Confront the kid with your camera on and the tape rolling."

"But that's not the story I wanted to tell," I protested. "My video's about the making of a rock band, not about Richard and me."

"It is now, Maggie. Your pal Richard just changed the rules on you in the middle of the game."

"But that's not fair!" I insisted.

"Welcome to the real world," Griff said. "And good luck."

"What are you doing here?" Richard asked when I rang his doorbell the next morning. He didn't look exactly thrilled to see me.

"Let's talk," I said.

"What's to talk about?" He was staring at the camcorder on my shoulder. "Hey, is that thing on?"

"I'd like to get back to work," I said, ignoring his second question. If he didn't know what the blinking red light on the camera meant, I certainly wasn't about to tell him.

"What do you mean, work?"

"My video project. You said I could shoot Rocky Road, and I still want to do it."

"I changed my mind," Richard muttered. "Anyway, the band's not practicing here today."

"Then what's that music I hear coming from your basement?" I asked.

"All right. So they're here. So what?"

"So you told me I could tape them, and then you suddenly changed your mind. I want to know why."

"I told you why," said Richard. He paused a moment, frowning at the camera. "The guys don't want you hanging around."

"That's not what you said before," I pointed out.

"That's what I'm saying now."

"You said I could continue shooting if I went out with you on Saturday."

Richard hesitated, and I could almost see the gears slowly spinning in his head.

"I might have said that," he reluctantly admitted.

"Did you say it or didn't you?"

"All right. I said it. So what?"

"Did you mean it?" I asked.

"Sure I meant it," he said with a suspicious look in his close-set eyes. "Are you going to take me up on it?"

I pretended to consider the proposition. "Maybe," I said. "Say it again, but this time say it sweetly."

Richard smiled. Moving closer to me, he murmured, "Go out with me Saturday, Red, and you can tape Rocky Road all you want."

"Richard," I replied, "I wouldn't go out with you if you were the last boy on earth!"

Then I recorded the look of surprise on his goofy face, turned off the camcorder, and raced down the steps. It might not have been the videotape I had set out to make, but I had the feeling it was going to be pretty interesting just the same.

Chapter Six

"It's cinema verité," said Griff when I called him up to describe my confrontation with Richard.

"Cinema *who*?" I asked.

"Verité," said Griff. "It's French for "truth." Cinema verité is a kind of documentary in which the filmmaker just aims the camera and films whatever happens. It's a good way to get a natural effect."

"I don't know," I said. "I mean, whoever heard of a movie where the person behind the camera talks back to the performers?"

"Believe me, it's been done."

"Sometimes it seems as if everything has

been done," I sighed. "It's sure not easy being original."

"Don't worry, Maggie. By the time we're finished editing this thing, you're going to have one terrific little videotape to enter in that contest."

"But what's it going to be about?" I wondered out loud.

"We'll find out as we go along," Griff told me.

I spent most of the next morning wondering what I was going to do for the rest of the summer. I had planned to spend at least another week shooting Rocky Road, but it was obvious that Richard wasn't ever going to let me near the band again.

"What about Barry Carter?" Rose Sue said when she described my current dilemma.

"What about him?" I asked. Actually, the thought of Barry Carter had been simmering on the back burner of my mind ever since my birthday party. When I considered the boys I knew, it occurred to me that the bright ones weren't always that great-looking, and the great-looking ones often weren't very bright. Not only was Barry Carter both cute and intelligent, he seemed to be a really nice person besides.

Of course, I hardly knew the guy. We had only talked for a few minutes at the party. Still, I think two people know when they're making some kind of connection.

I'm not talking about love at first sight. What I'm talking about is the kind of comfortable feeling you get when you meet somebody for the first time, and you know right away that the two of you could be really close friends. It's like you've known the person all your life, even though you only met five minutes earlier. It's a nice kind of feeling, and it's the kind of feeling I had when I met Barry Carter at my birthday party. But did he feel the same way about me?

"Why don't you give him a call and see what he's up to these days?" Rose Sue suggested.

"You know I hate doing things like that," I said. "But I'll think about it."

Rose Sue made a sort of clicking noise with her tongue and shook her head. "That's the trouble with you, Maggie. You think too much."

"What's wrong with that?"

"There's a time to think," said Rose Sue, "and a time to act. Life is too short to sit around waiting for things to happen."

I knew deep down that she was right. I did have a tendency to sit around and watch the parade pass by instead of jumping up and joining in.

"All right," I said. "Maybe I'll call him sometime this week."

A big grin spread across Rose Sue's face. "How about today?" she asked.

"Why do I have the funny feeling you just happen to have his telephone number with you?" I sighed as she dug a crumpled piece of paper out of the back pocket of her jeans.

I called Barry that afternoon. After some preliminary chitchat about how warm the weather had been that week, he again invited me to go with him to the archaeological dig he was videotaping. This time I didn't hesitate to accept.

I met Barry in front of my house early the next morning, and we set out for Snake Creek in his father's car. Snake Creek is on the far edge of Stony Hollow Canyon, near the state's southern border. The drive took a little over an hour, but the time passed very quickly as Barry and I listened to the radio and talked about some of our favorite movies. It wasn't exactly exciting, but it was probably one of the most pleasant hours I've ever spent in a car.

The western bank of the creek was buzzing with activity. About a dozen young men and women, mostly wearing T-shirts and shorts, were bustling around with shovels, spades, and hoes. A man with a pickax leaned against a bulldozer and studied a map while a woman with a camera around her neck carefully sifted through the contents of a small red wheelbarrow.

"There's Professor Hoyt," Barry said as we stepped out of the car. A tall, middle-aged man with a closely cropped beard and wearing a khaki shirt unbuttoned to the waist greeted us and shook Barry's hand warmly. "This is my friend Maggie Devine," said Barry. "I hope you don't mind if she watches you at work."

"Not at all," said the professor, offering me his hand. His strong fingers, callused palms, and thick wrists told me that Professor Hoyt was not the kind of professor who spent a lot of time sitting behind his desk grading papers.

"Professor Hoyt is in charge of the dig," said Barry, carefully unloading his video camera from the trunk of the car.

"It must be awfully expensive to pay for all these people and equipment," I said as I observed the hubbub all around me.

"Fortunately the state picks up most of the bills," said the professor. "Anyway, the people you see here today are volunteers."

"Anthropology students from the university," Barry added, peering at us through the eyepiece of his camcorder.

"Sort of like extra credit," said the professor with a laugh. "I find that my students learn more about the way people used to live around here from a week in the field than they do in a whole semester of classroom work."

"It's hard to imagine that *anyone* used to live here," I said, looking out at the desolate landscape.

"But they did. Of course, we can only guess what went on in their minds, but we already know a fair amount about their everyday lives. In fact . . ."

Before he could continue he was approached by a shirtless young man carrying a small spade.

"Excuse me, Professor," he said, ignoring Barry and me. "Could you come take a look at what we just found in Section Four?"

"Of course," said Professor Hoyt. He excused himself and followed the young man down the incline.

"This is really interesting," I said to Barry when we were alone.

"I know," he said. "I'm glad I could share it with you."

I looked at him and smiled. "Me, too," I said. There was a long moment of silence. Neither of us seemed to be quite sure what to say next.

"I guess I better get down there," Barry said finally, shifting the camera on his shoulder. "If they found something really important in Section Four, I ought to capture it. Want to come along?"

I nodded eagerly. "Sure. Lead the way."

We spent a couple of fascinating hours at the site before saying good-bye to Professor Hoyt and his crew and climbing back into the car.

"Great people, aren't they?" Barry said as we drove off.

"Sure are," I agreed. I was really impressed by the dedication of Professor Hoyt and his students. It was clear that these people were totally devoted to learning as much as possible about the origins of a vanished civilization.

"You don't see that kind of dedication every day," Barry said, as if he were reading my thoughts. "That's what my video is going to be about."

"What do you mean?" I asked. "I thought your video was about archaeology."

"It is," he said, "but it's also about dedication. I figure any good story needs a theme, whether it's a book or a movie or a ten-minute documentary. My story's going to be about a group of people who love their work. I picked archaeologists because that's something I'm interested in, but I could have used fire fighters or nurses or . . ."

"Rock musicians?" I suggested.

"What's *your* video going to be about?" Barry asked. "Besides a rock band, I mean."

"Good question," I said. "It's changed a lot. I guess it's turning into the story of this argument I had with the guy who's managing the group."

"What kind of argument?"

"It's not important," I said. I didn't feel like telling him about Richard Dunwoodie's never-ending quest to convince me that I was his girlfriend.

We rode along in silence for a while before Barry spoke again. "You like music?"

"Of course," I said, surprised by the question. "Doesn't everyone?"

"Not really," said Barry. "Everybody knows the current hits, but not everybody's interested in serious music."

"You mean Bach and Beethoven and stuff like that?"

"Not necessarily classical," said Barry. "Any kind of music can be serious if the musicians aren't in it just to sell a couple of million albums. It doesn't matter if it's rock 'n' roll or folk or whatever. Personally, I'd rather listen to good jazz than just about anything else in the world."

"I'm afraid I don't know much about jazz," I said. "My mother has a lot of jazz albums that she bought when she was in college, but she hardly ever plays them anymore. I don't even know the names of the artists."

"That's too bad," said Barry. "I think you'd

really like the music if you gave it a try." He glanced over at me. "There's a good combo playing at Club Jazz downtown this weekend. If you're not doing anything Saturday night, maybe we could go together."

I held my breath for a few seconds and then slowly released it. Listening to records at Barry's house or mine was one thing. Going with him to Club Jazz was a whole other kettle of fish. I really hadn't been dating all that long, and so far my dates had involved going to parties, school dances, or movies with boys my parents knew. I'd never gone out with a boy my folks had never even met. All they knew about Barry was that he was a friend from school and I was spending the day with him at Snake Creek.

And then there was Melanie Warner. I couldn't forget the way she'd behaved at my birthday party. It was hard to imagine a guy like Barry being serious about a girl like Melanie, but if they had some kind of relationship going, I didn't want to be the one to break it up. Still, if they were really a couple, why would Barry be asking me out on a date? I could only assume that Melanie's claim on him was about as meaningful as

Richard Dunwoodie's claim on me. I decided that I really wanted to go out with Barry, and if Melanie didn't like it, that was her problem.

"Maggie?" Richard said, interrupting my thoughts. "What's the matter? If you're busy Saturday night—"

"No, I'm not," I told him quickly. "It's a date!"

...in pu...
...her...
...in the...
...this boy...
...I understand...
...You like the boy...

Chapter Seven

"Tell me all about jazz," I said to my mother the next day. I knew she thought I listened to too much rock 'n' roll, and I figured she'd be delighted if I showed some interest in another kind of music. I planned to explain about Barry Carter later and then tell her about the date I had accepted for Saturday night.

"What brought this on all of a sudden?" Mom asked.

"I met this boy . . ." I began.

"I understand," she said.

"You do?"

She smiled at me. "Sure. You like the boy.

The boy likes jazz. You figure if you like what he likes, maybe he'll like you."

"Something like that," I agreed.

"I'm no expert on jazz," she told me, "but I can play a few records for you and tell you what I know about the music. I'm afraid it really doesn't amount to much. Mostly I just like to listen."

"That's okay," I said. One of the nice things about my mom is that she never pretends to know more about a subject than she really does.

I followed Mom into the living room. She pulled out a couple of old record albums from the rack beneath the stereo and blew some dust off the cabinet. Hardly any of us play records anymore since we got a CD player.

I spent the next hour listening to some of the most amazing music I'd ever heard in my life. By the time Mom finished telling me a little bit about each of the performers, I understood why Barry got that dreamy look in his eyes when he talked about jazz.

"You don't hear much jazz on the radio anymore," Mom said, "but it's definitely a living art form. As a matter of fact, there's even a club downtown where young jazz musicians perform every night."

"I know," I said. "As a matter of fact, I wanted to talk to you about that."

"Would you like to go sometime?" Mom asked enthusiastically. "Your dad and I would be glad—"

"Actually," I interrupted, "somebody has already asked me to go. It's the boy I went to Snake Creek with yesterday. His name is Barry Carter. I met him at my birthday party at Rose Sue's house."

"I see," said Mom, but I didn't think she really did.

Just then Dad walked in the door. "See what?"

"Maggie was telling me about a boy she met recently."

"He's a really nice guy," I said, aware that I was talking a little too fast. "Barry Carter. He's on the track team at school, and he's planning to go to Fieldstone to study anthropology."

Mom and Dad exchanged one of their looks. "Were you planning to go out with this boy?" Dad asked as he eased himself into his favorite chair.

"I'd like to," I said cautiously. "He asked me for a date Saturday night."

"Well," Dad said, "I don't see any reason why you shouldn't—"

"He wants to take her to Club Jazz," Mom cut in.

"The jazz club?" said Dad. "Don't they serve liquor there?"

"I don't know," I admitted.

Dad frowned. "That's kind of a rough neighborhood. I'm not sure I want you going down there at night."

"But I'll be with Barry," I told him.

"Who is this Barry anyway?" asked Dad. "Have I met him?"

"Not yet," I said. "But I'm sure you'll like him when you do."

Mom and Dad exchanged another long look. I've been observing my parents long enough to know exactly what those looks mean. Dad's meant *No way,* and Mom's meant *Let's meet the boy before we decide.* Fortunately it was Mom who won.

"Tell you what," Dad said. "Invite Barry over for dinner on Saturday. We'll decide about the jazz club after we meet him. I suggest you pick out a movie for Saturday night, just in case."

I started to protest, to point out how unreasonable they were being about the whole thing. Then my mother shot me a warning glance and I knew this was the best deal I was likely to get. I nodded my head in agreement and went off to call Barry and tell him the news.

Barry arrived promptly at five-thirty on Saturday. He looked terrific in his blue oxford shirt, chino pants, and navy blazer. Everything about him was neat, clean, and wrinkle-free, and I had a hunch that he had made a special effort to make a good impression on my parents. Fortunately, it seemed to be working.

"How do you do?" said my father as he shook Barry's hand.

"Nice to meet you, Mr. Devine," Barry replied. "I've been reading your column for years. I haven't always shared your opinions, but I've never failed to be impressed by your arguments."

That made my father smile. "I'm flattered," he said. "I'm afraid most young people today never even glance at the editorial page."

Barry nodded. "I guess that's true. I know plenty of kids who never read anything except the sports pages, but personally, I think the editorials are the most interesting part of the paper. I mean, you can get the basic news on TV, but you have to read the columnists to know what's really going on behind the headlines."

It was clear from the look on my father's face that Barry was saying all the right things.

Fifteen minutes later we were all seated around the dinner table, and Mom was serving my favorite casserole—bulgur-tahini with sauteed hijiki and zucchini bread.

"This food is delicious," said Barry after swallowing a mouthful. "It's amazing what you can do with simple ingredients like barley and tahini."

We all stared at him in astonishment.

"Actually," said Mom, "it's not barley. It's bulgur."

"Sorry," Barry said. "I haven't eaten this kind of food since I stopped working in the health food restaurant downtown."

"You worked at the Whole Grain Café?" Mom asked, sounding very pleased.

"Just as a busboy one summer." Barry tasted the hijiki and nodded appreciatively. "Nori?" he asked.

"Hijiki," said Mom.

"Seaweed," Dad interpreted. He's never been too crazy about sea vegetables.

"It's really good," said Barry. "What kind of oil did you sauté it in?"

"Peanut," answered Mom with a smile.

"I thought so," Barry said. "You just can't get this kind of flavor with regular vegetable oil."

"Do you cook?" asked Dad.

Barry shrugged. "Nothing like this. I just fool around with a couple of simple dishes. My dad does most of the cooking at home." Turning to Mom, he added, "I'd like to give him the recipe for this casserole, if you don't mind. I've been trying to get him interested in natural foods for years."

"I'd be delighted," said Mom. It had been a long time since a dinner guest had asked for one of her recipes—maybe never, come to think of it.

Mom was serving dessert—plain old vanilla ice cream—when Dad began his interrogation. "Maggie tells us you're interested in jazz."

"Yes, sir," said Barry enthusiastically. "Are you?"

"Not really," admitted my father. "Maggie's mother is the jazz fan in this family."

"Mom played some really cool records for me," I said. "Charlie Parker, Sarah Vaughan . . ."

"Sarah Vaughan's the greatest! Did you ever hear that album she made with Clifford Brown on trumpet?" he asked Mom.

She smiled and nodded, and I knew that Barry had won her over completely. Now it was all up to Dad.

"I understand you want to take Maggie to Club Jazz tonight," he said.

Barry nodded. "Yes, sir. Is that all right?"

"Frankly, I'm not sure. The club's in kind of a rough part of town, isn't it?"

"It's not nearly as bad as it used to be," Barry told him, "especially since the Planning Commission started restoring the neighborhood last year. I've been down there lots of times, and I've never had any problems. Anyway, there's a well-lit parking lot right behind the club. We wouldn't even have to step out on the street."

"I see." Dad's first objection had been overruled. "But don't they serve liquor?"

"Not at the early show on Saturdays," said Barry. "The club has been trying to get young people interested in jazz, so they don't open the bar until after the special seven o'clock performance. The whole thing was my uncle Dave's idea."

Mom looked puzzled. "Your uncle Dave?"

"David Porter. He's one of the owners of the club."

"I've met Dave Porter," Dad said. "I interviewed him for a column I wrote a while ago. A fine man, your uncle."

"Yes, sir," Barry agreed. "He's the one who taught me about jazz. I was looking forward to introducing Maggie to him tonight."

I could tell Dad liked Barry a lot, but I still wasn't sure whether or not he was going to let me go to Club Jazz with him.

There was a long silence while we all ate our ice cream. Then Dad glanced at his watch and looked up at Barry and me, saying, "You kids better get moving if you're going to make that early show."

The evening got off to a terrific start. Barry's uncle Dave was a great guy, and he made sure we had a table right up front near the bandstand. It was really fun to be in a sophisticated place like Club Jazz, listening to wonderful music with Barry Carter at my side. The trio playing that evening included an electric guitar, a stand-up bass, and a flute. They might not have been in the same league as the people on Mom's records, but they had a swinging, mellow sound that made me feel good.

We stayed at the club until nine o'clock, listening and talking while we drank soda and nibbled on cheese and crackers. Then we said good night to Uncle Dave and climbed back into Barry's car. Neither of us spoke for a while—the sound of sweet jazz was still flowing through our minds. It would have been a perfect evening if I had only kept my mouth shut.

"That was really nice," I said, innocently enough.

"Music for the mind," said Barry.

"What do you mean?"

"I always think of rock as music for the body and jazz as music for the mind. You can dance to rock 'n' roll, but it doesn't give you a whole lot to think about."

"That's not necessarily true," I said. I

thought of some of the clever lyrics Jerry Hodges had written for Rocky Road. "Rock music can be intellectually satisfying, too."

"Maybe," Barry said after an almost perceptible pause. He obviously didn't agree, but he didn't want to argue about it either, and that was fine with me.

To keep the conversation going, I said, "What do you think of movie music?"

"Movie music?"

"You know—the background music written especially for movies, like 'Tara's Theme' from *Gone With the Wind*. That's a very special kind of music that most people never think about much."

"I know I never have," said Barry. "I guess I've never really taken movies all that seriously as an art form."

I frowned. "What *do* you take seriously?" I asked. "Besides jazz, I mean."

"Anthropology," Barry said instantly. "The study of humankind."

"Oh, yeah—anthropology. It's pretty important, I guess, but I'm more interested in humans than in humankind," I said.

There was a long lull in the conversation, and I was beginning to feel more than a little uncomfortable. That's when I opened my mouth and stuck my foot in right up to the ankle.

"How's your friend Melanie?" I asked for no good reason.

Barry glanced at me briefly and shrugged. "I don't know," he said. "I haven't seen her for a while."

"Did you two break up?"

"I don't think 'breaking up' is exactly the right term," Barry replied rather coolly.

"Then you're still going together?" I persisted, prodding him like you keep on poking at a sore tooth with your tongue. I knew it was pushy, but I couldn't help it. I wanted to have some idea of where I stood with this boy.

"I'd rather not talk about it, if it's all the same to you," he replied.

"No problem," I lied. "There's probably not a whole lot to talk about anyway."

"What's that supposed to mean?" Barry asked.

I could feel the emotional temperature in the car plunge to absolute zero. But did I have the good sense to shut up? Oh, no.

"I just mean there's probably not much

anybody could say about Melanie Warner. She's not exactly a deep sort of person."

"I don't know about that," Barry said. "Besides, I'd take someone who's shallow over someone like your friend Griff Palmer any day."

"And what's wrong with Griff?" I asked stiffly.

Barry groaned. "Give me a break. I only met the guy once, but it's pretty obvious that he's a sleazeball, and a conceited one at that."

"*Sleazeball?*" I squawked. "I'll have you know that Griff's a very special person!"

"If you like the type."

"As a matter of fact, I do," I said.

"Then all I can say is you have very strange taste in guys," Barry muttered.

"Apparently I do," I said, glaring angrily at him.

Neither of us spoke for the rest of the ride home.

When Barry pulled up in front of my house, I quickly said good night and scrambled out of the car. Then I went directly to my room and cried myself into a deep and dreamless sleep.

Chapter Eight

I was just as miserable when I woke up as I had been when I went to bed. And what really bothered me was that I had no idea what Barry and I were fighting about in the first place.

"No idea?" said Rose Sue skeptically later that day. We were sitting in my backyard and I had just told her about how my dream date had turned into a nightmare. "You must have been arguing about *something*."

"No, really," I insisted. "We were just talking on the way home, and somehow one thing led to another . . ."

"What were you talking about?"

"Nothing. Just talking. You know how it is."

"I guess I don't," said Rose Sue. "When I talk to somebody, I usually have some idea what we're talking about."

"Well," I said, "we were just talking about the usual stuff, I guess. Music. People we know . . ."

"Name one," Rose Sue ordered. The girl should be a lawyer.

"Melanie Warner," I said. The name came out of my mouth sounding like a curse word.

"Aha! I think I'm starting to get the picture," said Rose Sue. "You asked Barry if he and Melanie were an item, right?"

"Of course not," I said huffily. "You don't ask a guy something like that."

"You do if you want to know."

"Maybe I *don't* want to know," I snapped. "Maybe I'm not in the least bit interested in Barry Carter or the girls he goes out with!"

"So, is he?"

"Is he what?"

"Going out with her."

"How should I know? This may come as a surprise to you, Rose Sue, but *some* people know how to mind their own business."

"Meaning?" Rose Sue gave me a hard look, and there was an icy edge to her voice.

"Nothing," I said, immediately regretting my remark.

"Name another," she demanded after a brief pause.

"Another what?"

"Another person you talked to Barry about last night."

I looked at my friend and sighed. "Griff," I said.

"You talked about Griff? To Barry?"

"Sure. What's wrong with that?"

"You must be kidding," said Rose Sue. "You saw the way they acted together at the party. I thought for sure somebody was going to throw a punch. Or maybe even a punch *bowl*."

"I suppose Barry did act kind of immaturely, now that you mention it." I said.

She shook her head. "Don't put words in my mouth, Maggie. I never said it was Barry's fault."

"You think *Griff* was the troublemaker?" I exclaimed incredulously. "Griff happens to be a perfect gentleman. Anyway, I thought you liked him. You were the one who told me to call him in the first place."

"That was before I met him," said Rose Sue. "I don't know what it is, Maggie. There's just something about that guy I don't quite trust. I don't know how to describe it . . ."

"Is 'sleazeball' the word you're looking for?" I asked grimly.

Rose Sue looked at me and raised one eyebrow. "Is that the word Barry used last night?"

"I don't remember," I said, though I remembered perfectly well.

"Sure you do," said Rose Sue.

I glared at her. "So now you're calling me a liar?"

"I don't want to fight with you, Maggie," Rose Sue said with a sigh. "I'm just trying to help."

My shoulders slumped. "I know," I said. It was impossible to stay angry at her after all we'd been through together. "I just feel like being alone right now, if you don't mind."

"Are you sure? If you want to talk . . ."

"I'll call you later," I promised. "Don't worry about me. I'll be fine, honest. The date didn't work out, that's all. I'll live."

"I know you will." Rose Sue smiled. "Call me, okay?"

"Right," I said. I managed to hold back my tears until Rose Sue was out of sight.

I've always prided myself on being the kind of person who refuses to mope around all day feeling sorry for herself when things don't work out exactly the way they're supposed to. So my date with Barry had been a disaster, and it was mostly my fault. Well, a person's supposed to learn from her mistakes and move on, and after I stopped crying, I decided that was what I was going to do. Barry Carter wasn't the only fish in the sea. There was a much bigger fish out there by the name of Griff Palmer, and I was determined to land him.

I know what you're thinking. You're thinking that Griff Palmer was totally wrong for me, that I was a silly sixteen-year-old with a schoolgirl crush on a good-looking older man with whom I had nothing more in common than an interest in making movies. That there was no way Griff could ever be romantically interested in me.

Tell me something I don't already know.

But I didn't know it then. I just hoped I wouldn't make a total fool of myself when

I met with Griff for the final edit of my videotape.

It took me a long time to prepare for that meeting. Usually I don't pay much attention to clothes, and I never wear makeup, but for this special occasion I knew I had to change my image. I wanted to dazzle Griff with my elegance and maturity, and that wasn't going to be easy. But it would be worth the effort when Griff's beautiful eyes gazed at me in astonishment as he whispered, "Maggie, I never really looked at you before. You're lovely! I adore you!" Then he'd sweep me into his arms and press his lips to mine, just like in the movies.

So I dressed with special care in an Indian print sundress instead of my usual jeans or shorts, and spent what seemed like hours trying to tame my rebellious red curls, without much success. It took even longer to get the hang of applying blusher, lip gloss, and all the rest of that stuff, but I finally decided that I looked at least a whole year older— maybe even a year and a half. And then I hurried out of the house so I wouldn't be late for my appointment with Griff.

He was staying in a luxurious suite at the

most expensive hotel in town. When he opened the door and ushered me in, I discovered that he had converted the living room into an editing room, complete with three monitors, a fancy video camera, and a lot of expensive-looking equipment that I couldn't even begin to identify.

"Do we really need all this stuff?" I asked.

"It can't hurt," Griff said with a boyish grin. "I need all these gadgets in my work, so we might as well take advantage of them for your project."

I was a little disappointed that he hadn't said anything about the transformation in me. *But maybe he doesn't want to mention it just yet,* I thought. *He probably wants to get our business out of the way first.*

Trying to sound mature and knowledgeable, I said, "This equipment must have cost a fortune."

"It's just leased," he told me. "I'll write it off as a business expense. Don't worry your pretty head about it, Maggie. That's what my father pays his accountants and tax lawyers for."

Pretty. He called me pretty! Inwardly, I was thrilled. "So what do we do first?" I asked. I noticed my videocassette lying on a coffee table in front of the sofa.

"First we check out the raw footage," Griff said briskly.

He went over to a sleek black machine and pushed a couple of buttons on the front panel. Some red and green lights came on. Then he turned on the monitors. A number appeared in the upper right-hand corner of each monitor for a moment, then disappeared. Griff slipped my tape into one of the machines and pressed another button, and I saw my father's face appear on two of the screens. He sang and did a little dance step while the camera zoomed in for a close-up of his face.

"That was when I was learning how to use the camera," I said, embarrassed. "Do you think we can skip this part?" It's hard to pretend to be sophisticated while the guy you have a crush on is watching your father perform an off-key version of "Me and My Shadow."

"If you insist," said Griff, although he seemed to be enjoying the show. He pressed another button, and I noticed that my father looked even sillier doing his song-and-dance routine in fast-forward.

"That's it," I exclaimed when I recognized Richard Dunwoodie's basement. Griff turned up the volume and we watched Richard introduce the members of the band.

Griff shook his head. "Strange-looking bunch of kids," he muttered as Rocky Road went into its first number.

I realized as I watched that there had been a great many choices to be made while I was taping, and that I had made them at the time without thinking about it much. There were times when it had seemed right to show the whole band, and other times when I had zoomed in for a close-up of the keyboard player or the guitarist's hands.

"You must have really liked that keyboard player," Griff said, grinning as the camera returned to Jerry Hodges's face. I glanced at Griff, wondering if he was just a little jealous. I had to admit he was right. I had kept coming back to the band member I liked best, whether or not it was appropriate to what was going on in the music. I obviously had a lot to learn about shooting a documentary.

We viewed the rest of the tape without speaking while Griff made notes on a pad of paper he was holding. I couldn't help smiling as I watched my final confrontation with Richard. It seemed like a dumb thing to videotape at the time, but now I realized that the scene was among the best few minutes on the tape.

When it was over, Griff stopped the tape and rewound it. "It's rough," he said, glancing at his notes, "but it's got potential. Let's watch again and talk about it as we go along."

"Again?" I said. "Can't we start editing now?"

"Not yet," said Griff. "Do you want to do this fast, or do you want to do it right?"

"Of course I want to do it right," I said quickly. It was dawning on me that this procedure was a lot more complicated than I had counted on.

"Good. Then let's get started." Griff pressed a button, and the tape began to play again. When Richard began introducing the band, Griff made a note on his pad and pressed another button. The scene appeared on all three monitors.

"I think you'll want to use this," he said, "but I don't think it belongs at the beginning. I suggest starting off with a piece of that final confrontation between you and the dopey-looking kid—what's his name?"

"You mean Richard?"

"Yeah." Griff checked the counter on one of the machines and made another note on his pad.

"But shouldn't that come at the end?" I asked. "I mean, that's the way it happened in real life."

Griff sighed and shook his head. "This isn't real life," he said. "This is *art.*"

"I know," I said, "but—"

"Listen, Maggie," he interrupted. "It's your film. If you want to do it the way it happened in what you so quaintly call 'real life,' that's the way you should do it. I'm just trying to give you the benefit of my experience."

"I know that," I said apologetically, "and I really appreciate it. I don't know anything about stuff like this. Let's do it your way."

Griff grinned at me and pressed a few more buttons. "Good girl," he said warmly, and I felt my face turning pink with pleasure.

Now the middle screen was blank and different parts of my tape were playing on the other two screens. Griff was looking at the digital counters and taking more notes.

"This part has to go," he said, nodding at the first monitor. On the screen, Jerry Hodges was talking about how he loved rock 'n' roll and how he'd rather play keyboard than do anything else in the world.

"I kind of like that part," I murmured.

Griff stared at me. "Are you serious? That kid's cornier than Kansas. This is a story about confrontation, remember?"

"Maybe it's not," I said slowly. I thought of what Barry had said about his project. "Maybe it's about people who love what they're doing."

Griff patted my hand. "Believe me, Maggie, the judges will see plenty of heartwarming videos about people who love what they're doing. What we're trying to create here is something entirely different."

"Different isn't always better," I objected. "Anyway, this is supposed to be my project, isn't it? I mean, shouldn't I be the one to decide what it's about?"

"Excuse me for trying to help." Griff stopped the tape and offered me his notepad. "Maybe you'd like to finish this by yourself."

"Oh, no," I cried. "All I meant was . . ."

"All you meant was that you don't want me taking over," Griff said. After a pause, he added, "And you're right."

I blinked. "I am?"

"Absolutely." Griff tossed his notepad down on the couch and grinned. "I'm sorry, Maggie. I guess when you've been making movies all your life, you tend to want to do things your own way. And having Les Gryphon for a father doesn't make it any easier to admit you're wrong."

"It's okay," I said softly. "I appreciate your taking the time to help me when you're so busy and all. I really do."

"Do you?" said Griff. "That means a lot to me." He reached out and took my hand. I felt as if a jolt of electricity had just shot up my arm and down my spine.

"You're a terrific kid, Maggie," he said, his hand holding mine tightly. "I liked you the moment I saw you. And the more I get to know you, the better I like you."

"I like you, too," I said. My voice sounded strange, as if it were coming from someone else's body. I was sitting next to Griff on the couch, and in spite of the air-conditioning, I could feel my palms beginning to sweat. I hoped he didn't notice.

I looked into Griff's beautiful blue eyes and swallowed hard. I tried to speak, but I seemed to be having trouble breathing. This was the moment I'd been dreaming of ever since the day I had met Griff. Hadn't I schemed to be alone with him, hoping he would take me in his arms and kiss me? So why did everything suddenly feel so terribly wrong now that it looked as if my dream was about to come true?

Leaping to my feet, I pulled my damp hand out of his grasp. "I have to go home now," I mumbled as I headed for the door.

Griff followed me. "Wait a minute," he said, grabbing my wrist.

I froze, panic-stricken. "*No!* Really, I can't stay. I forgot about—about a very important appointment. A dentist appointment," I babbled.

"Take it easy, Maggie," Griff said gently. "Nobody's going to hurt you. I guess I owe you an apology."

"Apology?" I echoed in a voice that was hardly more than a squeak.

"That's right." He let go of my wrist. "I

think you must have misread the signals somewhere along the line." Smiling, he continued, "It was obvious all along that you were interested in me as something more than a filmmaker, and that's perfectly understandable." (I could hear Barry's voice in my head, saying *conceited*.) "But since I'm so much older than you, I should have made it clear that romance never entered my mind. You're like the kid sister I never had, Maggie. I'm sorry if you're hurt or disappointed, but that's just the way it is."

I went limp with relief. "I *did* want you to kiss me when I came here today," I confessed, "but I guess I forgot something very important."

"What's that?" Griff asked.

"I *am* still just a kid," I told him. "As much as I'd like to be sophisticated and glamorous and all grown up, I'm not. I guess I forget the difference between my fantasies and reality sometimes." I was sure my face must be as red as my hair. Edging toward the door, I added, "Thanks so much for all you've done for me, Griff. I'll go now . . ."

But Griff blocked my way. "You're not

going anywhere," he said sternly, and suddenly I didn't feel relieved anymore. Then he grinned. "We have a tape to edit, remember? Or have you decided not to enter that contest after all?"

Chapter Nine

For the next three hours, Griff gave me a crash course in the basics of editing video-tape. By the time I left the hotel late that afternoon, I had a tape that was almost ready to be entered in the contest, and I was confident that I could do the rest of the editing on my own.

When Griff and I said good-bye, he gave me a brotherly kiss on the cheek. It wasn't romantic at all, but it was awfully nice. I felt a little sad—Griff would be leaving for California the next day, and I knew I would probably never see him again.

I also knew that it was time to get my life

back on track, and the first thing I wanted to do was make amends with Barry Carter. But making up with Barry wasn't going to be easy. I'd acted like a total jerk on our date, and I couldn't blame him if he never spoke to me again.

"What am I going to do?" I asked Rose Sue. "Barry's the one I really care about, I know that now."

"Yeah—now that Griff Palmer's out of the picture," Rose Sue said.

I cringed because that was probably the way it would seem to Barry, too, but it wasn't true. "Maybe I was dazzled by Griff for a while, but deep down I always knew that Barry was the guy for me," I told her. "So how do I convince *him* of that?"

After a moment's thought, Rose Sue said, "Well, obviously Barry's not going to make the first move, so I guess it's up to you. Why don't you just pick up the phone . . ."

". . . And call him." I sighed. I'd seen enough movies about this sort of thing to know how it's done, so after Rose Sue went home, I swallowed my pride and dialed Barry's number.

"Hi," I said when he answered the phone.

"I just wanted to thank you for the lovely evening."

"Who is this?" he asked.

My heart sank faster than a bowling ball in a swimming pool. "Maggie," I said.

"Maggie," he repeated with no detectable expression in his voice.

"Maggie Devine," I said, in case he had recently spent a lovely evening with some other Maggie. "I just wanted to tell you—"

"That you had a good time," he interrupted. "Is that all?"

"Well, not exactly," I said. "I mean, I realize things got a little weird toward the end, but . . ."

"Listen," Barry said, "I'd rather not talk about it, if you don't mind. I think it would be a lot better for both of us if we just accept the fact that we made a mistake and leave it at that."

"Maybe it wasn't a mistake," I said. "Maybe—"

"I've given it a lot of thought," said Barry. "If it's all the same to you, I'd just as soon call it quits right now and save both of us a lot of grief."

"But I was kind of hoping—"

"Good-bye, Maggie." He hung up the phone before I could say another word.

I felt even worse after that phone call than I had after our date. Even when I was crying myself to sleep that night, I guess I assumed that things would get straightened out between us. Wasn't that the way it always happened in the movies? Now it seemed that Barry was out of my life forever, just when I realized how much he meant to me. I'd made a mess of things, all right. When Barry was interested in me, all I could think about was Griff Palmer. Then, when I finally understood that Griff and I had no future together, Barry didn't want to have anything to do with me. I had made all the wrong moves every step of the way.

Well, there was nothing I could do about it now. As my mom always says, you just have to take one day at a time, and my goal for that day was to put the finishing touches on my videotape and submit it to the judges before the deadline. Griff had explained how to edit a tape using a regular television and two VCRs hooked together. The end product wouldn't be nearly as slick and seamless as it would be using Griff's fancy equipment, but I could do the rest of the job on my own. I borrowed our neighbor's VCR, got Rose Sue to help me set everything up, and then we sat down to watch my tape.

"It's not exactly what I expected," Rose Sue said when it was over.

"It's not exactly what I expected, either," I confessed. The tape Griff and I had produced was less about the making of a rock 'n' roll band than about a person (me) who couldn't seem to get along with any of the people she was trying to make a videotape about. If cinema verité means "truth film," that's what I'd ended up with. There was more truth in this video than I cared to admit to.

"I kind of like it though," said Rose Sue after a moment's reflection. "It's so honest."

"Maybe a little *too* honest," I said, as I rewound the tape. "Even though I'm never on camera, I feel like I'm exposing myself to the world."

"That's what art's supposed to be about, isn't it? The artist making a personal statement?"

I slowly nodded my head. Rose Sue was right, of course. What good was a film or a videotape if it didn't say something about the person who was creating it? Griff Palmer understood that, and he had helped me make a video that was as much about me as it was about the people I was taping.

"It's still a little too long," I said as I replayed the tape on one machine and began copying it on the other. "I'm going to have to cut about a minute and a half to meet the contest requirements." I glanced at the pad on which I had been jotting notes. "I think the guitar solo will have to go . . ."

I finished editing my tape on the day of the contest deadline. I watched it one last time with mixed emotions. It's hard to be objective about something you've been working on the way I'd been working on that video. I thought it was pretty good, but I also felt there were a lot of things I could have done to make it better if I had had a little more time and a lot more experience.

I brought the tape over to the university that afternoon and dropped it off at the theater department office. Then I caught the next bus to the mall. I was standing in front of Shoe Land checking out a pair of red sandals in the window and trying not to think about Barry Carter when Barry himself walked out of the store.

"How're you doing?" he said when he saw me.

My heart was pounding so hard I could hardly speak. "Pretty good," I finally replied. "You?"

"Not bad." Barry held up a blue plastic bag with the white Shoe Land logo on it. "New running shoes," he said.

I smiled as if he had just said something terribly clever.

"I'm looking for sandals," I said, gesturing vaguely toward the store window.

In a way, it was almost funny. Here we were, two people who had almost had a really terrific relationship going, standing around in the mall and talking about shoes!

"So," I said at last. "How have you been?"

"Fine," said Barry. "But I think we already discussed that."

"Maybe we should talk about something else," I suggested.

He frowned. "That's how we got into trouble last time."

"Maybe we could try again," I said hopefully.

Barry paused just a second, and a faint smile touched his lips. "Pick a topic."

"How about the video contest?"

"That seems pretty safe. Did you get your entry in?"

"Just before I came here," I said.

"Wasn't today the deadline?"

I nodded. "Last-Minute Maggie. That's me."

Barry smiled, and this time he showed some teeth. "Why don't we sit down?" he said, waving his blue-and-white bag toward an empty bench in the middle of the mall. "Unless, of course, you'd rather stand here and stare at sandals."

"I think I could tear myself away," I said. I wished I could throw my arms around him and give him a kiss. Instead, I followed him to the bench. We both sat down, my knee just an inch away from his.

"So," I said, my heart still beating much too fast.

"I think we were talking about the video contest," Barry said.

"Right." It wasn't what I wanted to talk about, but it was a million times better than not talking to him at all. "When did you get your entry in?"

"A few days ago. I'm afraid it's not all that good, though. I think I shot a lot of interesting stuff, but trying to squeeze it all into a ten-minute documentary was pretty tough. Editing is hard work."

"I know," I said. "If it hadn't been for Griff—"

I stopped in midsentence when I saw the look on Barry's face.

"So your friend Griff helped, did he?"

I nodded my head. I desperately wanted to explain about Griff and me, but somehow I couldn't find the words to make Barry understand

We sat in silence for what seemed like an hour. I was searching frantically for some other topic when a familiar voice spoke from behind the bench.

"Now isn't this a cozy scene?" It was Melanie Warner.

"What are you doing here?" I asked. I knew it was a ridiculous question even as the words came out of my mouth.

Melanie walked around the bench and stood facing us. "Shopping," she said. "That's what most people do at the mall. A better question is, what are *you* two doing here? You're obviously *not* shopping."

"We happened to run into each other in front of the shoe store," I said.

"I'll bet." Melanie gave me a withering look and then turned to Barry. "I haven't heard from you in a while," she said. "I guess you've been busy with other things."

Barry glanced at me for just a second and then shrugged. "I guess," he said.

Melanie stood in front of us looking vaguely uneasy. When neither Barry nor I said anything else, she asked, "Isn't anybody going to invite me to sit down?"

It was a very small bench. Melanie waited for Barry or me to make room for her, but neither of us moved.

"Actually, I don't have time to sit," said Melanie when it became clear that we weren't going to budge. "I've got a million things to do." She kissed the tips of her fingers and touched them to Barry's cheek. "Don't do anything I wouldn't do," she said, then spun on her heel and walked away.

"No problem," muttered Barry when she was out of earshot.

After a moment, he stood up. "I really should be going, too," he said. He looked down at me. "It was nice talking to you."

"It was nice talking to you, too," I said, although we had hardly begun. If Melanie Warner hadn't shown up when she did, I was positive something magical would have happened. Instead, Barry was about to walk out of my life for the second time, and there wasn't a thing I could do about it.

"I'll be seeing you," he said.

Will you? I wondered sadly as he turned around and disappeared into the crowd.

The names of the video contest winners were announced two weeks later. I hadn't really expected to win anything, and I didn't. But honorable mention in the documentary division went to Barry Carter for his videotape entitled "Ruins."

"Call him," Rose Sue urged when I showed her the article in the paper.

"I can't do that," I sighed. "He probably doesn't want to hear from me."

"Why not? I thought you two patched things up at the mall."

"Well, at least we spoke to each other. What does it mean when a boy says he'll be seeing you?"

"I imagine it means he'll be seeing you," Rose Sue said reasonably.

I made a face. "As in 'don't call me, I'll call you'?"

"Not necessarily. Maybe it means he's waiting for you to make the next move."

"But I made the *last* move," I reminded her. "A lot of good that did!"

Rose Sue shrugged. "Suit yourself. But if I were you, I'd give him a ring."

So I called Barry that afternoon and offered my congratulations.

"Thanks," he said. He sounded pleased. "I was really surprised when I heard the news. I mean, it was only an honorable mention, but . . ."

"Don't be so modest," I said. "It must have been a great video to win anything at all. I read that the girl who won first place in the documentary division is a film major at the university. That's pretty stiff competition."

"I suppose. Anyway, it was nice of you to call."

"What are friends for?" I said. There was a long pause. I hoped Barry was giving some serious thought to my question.

"Friends," he said softly. "Are we friends, Maggie?"

"I hope so. Just because we had a few bad moments there . . ."

"Let's not go into all that again," Barry said. "There are some things we're probably never going to agree about. I guess we'll just have to get used to it."

"I guess so," I said. I wasn't at all sure where this conversation was leading, but at least it was a conversation.

"That's no reason we can't go on being friends, is it?"

"Of course not!"

Barry cleared his throat. "Yes?" I said hopefully.

"What?"

"I thought you were going to say something."

"Not really," said Barry. "I was just clearing my throat."

"I see. Well . . ."

"Yes?" said Barry.

"What?"

"I thought you were going to say something else."

"Not really," I replied, although there were a hundred things I wanted to say: things about feelings and communication and friendship and romance. Things about forgetting the past and starting over. Things about

123

Barry and me and how we could be much more than friends if we only tried.

"I guess I'll be seeing you," said Barry before I could say anything at all.

My heart sank. "I guess so," I said. It sounded to me like a major step backward. Now he only *guessed* he'd be seeing me.

We both hung up, and I suddenly longed for summer vacation to be over.

Chapter Ten

The remaining days of summer passed slowly and uneventfully. I spent a lot of time hanging out with Rose Sue at the mall, shopping for fall clothes, though I would rather have stayed home and watched old movies on TV. It was a lot easier not to think about Barry when I was caught up in a good movie.

Another thing that happened was that Richard Dunwoodie and I came to an understanding of some sort after he talked me into letting him see my finished video. Much to my surprise, he loved it. Apparently he didn't even realize that he came off as an obnoxious, sexist clod. It didn't seem to bother him

125

at all. If that egomaniac realized the story was going to focus on him, he probably would have let me tape as much as I wanted. But he finally understood that I'm never going to go out with him, and he assured me that we could still be friends. It wasn't exactly the most thrilling moment of my life, but it was definitely an improvement. Now if only he'd just quit calling me Red. . . .

Losing the video contest in no way discouraged me from thinking about getting started on a new project. I still found the idea of becoming a filmmaker very exciting. I knew now that making a documentary was no piece of cake, but telling true stories on film is a wonderful thing to do. There are so many fascinating things going on in the world. All a person needs to make a documentary is an interesting subject, a fresh viewpoint, and a loaded video camera.

Dad had bought me a secondhand camcorder. Now all I needed was the subject and the viewpoint.

"What about you and Barry?" Rose Sue suggested. It was a question she had managed to work into almost every conversation for weeks. I had the feeling that she kept dragging me to the mall in the hope that I'd run into Barry again.

"I don't think the world is waiting for a documentary about my relationship with Barry Carter," I said sourly. "As a matter of fact, there *is* no relationship."

"If you could make a video about Richard Dunwoodie . . ."

"That was different. Anyway, there's really nothing to say about Barry and me. We're friends. Period."

"Friends who almost fell in love," said Rose Sue. "That's a movie *I'd* go to see."

"I never said anything about love," I replied, a little too sharply. I wondered if I was blushing.

"You didn't have to. We've known each other for a long time, Maggie. You're in love, all right. I recognize the signs."

"What signs?"

"For example, the way you never talk about Barry."

"Let me see if I have this straight," I said. "You can tell that I'm in love with Barry Carter, because I never talk about him?"

Rose Sue nodded. "Right. It's not so much what you don't say as the way you don't say it."

"I think you've finally flipped," I said with a groan. "Even if you were right, even if I were in love with Barry, what would you suggest I do about it? It's not as if I can just call him up and tell him how I feel."

"Why not? I would."

"I know you would, Rose Sue, but that's not my style."

"No, it's not," she agreed. "Your style is to sit around and wait for something to happen."

"That's not true," I protested. "I made the last two calls, remember? It's Barry's turn now. If he wants to get together with me, he's going to have to make the next move."

Rolling her eyes, Rose Sue said, "You're a stubborn girl, Maggie Devine. If you weren't my best friend, I don't think I'd put up with your nonsense for one minute!"

"Oh yes, you would," I said. "You'd stick around for my mother's cooking."

It was definitely time to change the subject—all this talk about love was starting to depress me.

Labor Day came and went, and the first day of school finally arrived. As Rose Sue and I started up the steps, I saw Barry and a couple of his friends. I waved and said hello. He said hello back and kept right on going. I noticed he was wearing new running shoes, probably the ones he had bought that day in the mall. If he had missed me at all since our last meeting, he sure wasn't showing it.

Somehow the beginning of the school year didn't seem nearly as interesting and exciting as it usually did. I hardly saw Barry at all, and when I did catch a glimpse of him, he either didn't see me or pretended he didn't. By the end of the first week, I was feeling pretty discouraged about romance in general, and Barry and me in particular. To take my mind off my misery, I decided to bury myself in my schoolwork.

Strangely enough, it was creative writing class that turned everything around. I had written a story about a girl who falls in love with a boy and then messes everything up by being jealous of his old girlfriend. It wasn't the most original idea in the world, but it came straight from the heart. Mr. Crenshaw, the writing teacher, passed out copies of my story to everyone in the class.

"All right, people," he said after everyone

had read my work. "What do we think of Miss Devine's story?"

No one said a word.

"Anyone?" Mr. Crenshaw prodded. "Did you like it? Did you dislike it? Did it tell you something you didn't know before?"

Linda Jenkins raised her hand. "To tell you the truth," she said, "I thought it was kind of—well, boring."

"Boring?" echoed Mr. Crenshaw. "In what way?"

Linda glanced sheepishly at me. I could see she was embarrassed. Criticizing your classmates' work is the hardest part of creative writing class.

"Well," she said at last, "nothing really happens in this story. Everybody talks a lot, but nobody *does* anything."

"I agree," said William Pratt. "The girl in the story feels sorry for herself, but she doesn't do anything to make things better."

"Exactly," Linda said. "It's not very interesting to read about someone who feels sorry for herself because she fouled up. I mean, there's no *action*. Sometimes you have to make things happen."

Mr. Crenshaw said something, and then

someone else chimed in, but I didn't hear another word in class that day. Suddenly, I realized how foolish I had been. At that moment, I understood a million things that I should have understood from the start. I only hoped it wasn't too late for Barry and me.

That night I called Barry and invited him to go to the movies with me.

"It's kind of a world premiere," I told him. "The latest Gryphon masterpiece of horror, *Nights of Terror II*."

"A horror flick?" Barry sounded surprised. "I thought you hated those."

"I do," I said. "But I happen to be in this one."

He laughed. "No kidding! This is the film they were shooting out at the canyon?"

"Right. It's opening at the nabes on Wednesday."

"The nabes?"

"Neighborhood theaters," I explained. "The really classy films usually open at a few select theaters in the big cities before they're released to theaters around the country. Horror movies open at about a million local theaters all at once, play for a few weeks, and then show up on cable TV a few months later."

"You really know a lot about the movie business." Barry sounded impressed.

"I'm learning," I said. There was a long pause before I spoke again. "So?"

"So what?"

"Will you go with me?"

After another long pause, Barry said, "I don't know, Maggie. We've tried this dating thing before, and it didn't work out. Maybe it would be better if we just go on being friends."

"That's fine with me," I said promptly. "Can't a couple of friends go see a movie together?"

"Of course they can," said Barry. "It's just that . . ."

"Listen," I said. "I'm not going to twist your arm. If you don't want to come with me to see my acting debut, I'll ask somebody else. I just thought we were friends, that's all."

"We *are* friends," Barry said, "and I'd like to keep it that way. I just don't want anybody getting hurt because of false expectations."

"Okay," I agreed. "No expectations allowed. Whatever happens, happens."

"And whatever doesn't happen, *doesn't* happen. Right?"

"Right."

There was a brief silence, and I could swear I felt Barry's smile over the telephone.

"What do you wear to a world premiere, anyway?" he asked.

Barry and I met in front of the theater that Wednesday at half past six. I kept telling myself that this wasn't a date. It was just two friends going to a movie together. No demands. No expectations. I paid for my ticket and Barry paid for his, but Barry insisted on buying popcorn and soda for us both.

I don't have much to say about *Nights of Terror II*. If you've seen one of those kinds of movies, you've pretty much seen them all. Griff had been right about the monster—even though you know it's just an actor in a lot of weird makeup, you still almost jump out of your seat every time the monster's spooky face fills the screen. My own appearance lasted about six seconds—at least I'm pretty sure it was me. There was a shot of a red-haired girl from the back as she scrambled down the side of the canyon, yelling her head off.

"Was that you?" Barry whispered as my moment of glory quickly passed.

"I think so," I whispered back. "It happened kind of fast."

"Very impressive," said Barry. "I think I see an Academy Award in your future—'Best Supporting Screamer.'"

"Funny," I said. It really *was* kind of funny when you thought about it. I had been so excited about being in the movies, and the whole thing amounted to a few seconds in a film that nobody but a bunch of hard-core horror fans was ever going to see.

Still I had met Griff Palmer because of the movie, and it had been Griff who suggested that I enter the video contest. Entering the contest was the one thing Barry and I had had in common when we met, and it was the contest that ultimately brought us closer together. In fact, if it hadn't been for my brief shot at being a movie star, I wouldn't have been sitting next to Barry in the Triplex at that very moment.

"Do you want to stay for the rest of this thing?" he asked just as I arrived at that rather startling conclusion.

"Not really," I said. I'd seen the part of the

film I had come to see. Now what I needed to do was straighten out my relationship with Barry, and I certainly couldn't do that while watching some monster with bulging eyes and dripping fangs turn a bunch of screaming teenagers into shish kebab.

"So," I said as we stepped out onto the street.

Barry grinned at me. "Let's not start that again," he said.

I returned the smile, and we walked along in silence for a while. It was one of those warm September evenings that feels more like summer than fall, but soon the leaves would be changing color and dropping from the trees. Suddenly I felt as if time were passing much too quickly.

Not sure how to begin, I blurted, "Have you seen Melanie lately?"

I don't know why I asked such a stupid question. For a moment, I almost believed I had only thought it. Unfortunately, the words had actually come out of my mouth.

"No," said Barry quietly. "Have you?"

"I'm sorry," I mumbled. "I don't know why I asked that. It's absolutely none of my business."

"It's all right," Barry said. "Friends should be able to say whatever's on their minds. As far as Melanie and I are concerned—"

"You don't have to tell me if you don't want to," I interrupted.

"I think it's time we cleared the air," Barry said. "Melanie and I went out for a while last year, but our relationship ended a long time ago. It's just taking her a long time to accept it, that's all." He hesitated. "If I had known I was going to meet someone special like you, I never would have let Melanie tag along when Rose Sue invited me to your birthday party."

I could hardly believe my ears. Barry thought I was special! "The last time we talked about Melanie, I wound up crying myself to sleep," I confessed shyly.

"Did you really?" We stopped walking, and Barry took hold of my hand. Our fingers locked, and I had to swallow hard in order to speak. "Are friends supposed to do this?" I asked, my voice sounding strange in my ears.

Barry looked deep into my eyes. "Is that all we are?"

I slowly shook my head. But there were

136

still some things I wanted to say. "About Griff . . ." I began, but Barry stopped me by gently placing a finger on my lips.

"It doesn't matter," he said. "We've both said and done things we regretted later. What I'm starting to understand is that the past doesn't really matter."

"But it does," I insisted. "The past is what makes us who we are today. We can't just pretend none of it ever happened. Besides, I really want to explain about Griff."

"I don't need to hear it," Barry said. "If whatever happened between you and Griff helped make you the person you are today, then I'm glad. I've never known anyone like you before, Maggie. I wouldn't want you to be any different than exactly the way you are."

Suddenly I heard my mother's voice in the back of my mind. *Living and loving,* she said. *That's what it's all about. Work you care about and people to love.*

As Barry and I stood hand in hand, my mind raced into fast forward. I could see myself in a film studio. MAGIC PRODUCTIONS it says on the door. Beneath the watchful eye of their proud father, a couple of beautiful children are playing on the set while their adoring parents are hard at work planning their next film project. The mother glances at the father and smiles. They understand each other, these two, without saying a single word. They've learned a lot, these two, and someday, when the children are old enough to ask, they'll explain it all just as simply and clearly as my mother once explained it to me.

Then slowly the vision faded, and I was back on the street corner, gazing into Barry Carter's dark eyes. Everything seemed incredibly clear and uncomplicated.

"Is this the part where we kiss and live happily ever after?" I asked on that beautiful fall evening when I was sixteen and in love for the very first time with a boy who loved me back.

"Let's find out," said Barry as he gently pulled me into his arms.

And so we did.

As she leaned to obs[...]
forward, obscuring his body from her view – whereat
she impatiently shrugged the garment from her shoulders, whose white perfection, set against the dark of
the night and only slightly yellowed by the torchlight,
now showed in brilliant contrast to the ruddier gold of
his own. Her breasts were perfectly formed, their
enticing curves shaped by an attentive gravity, which
pulled them gently from her body as if envious to
possess them, and her posteriors – seen to greater
advantage by those fortunate gentlemen sitting to the
leftward of the stage – resembled nothing so much as
a ripe peach, the delightful flesh of which any full-
blooded gentleman would wish gently to nibble . . .

Eros in High Places

Adventures of a Lady and Gentleman of Leisure

Anonymous

HEADLINE

First published in 1991
by HEADLINE BOOK PUBLISHING PLC

10 9 8 7 6 5 4 3 2 1

ISBN 0 7472 3622 4

Typeset in 10/12½ pt Times
by Colset Private Limited, Singapore

Printed and bound by
Collins Manufacturing, Glasgow

HEADLINE BOOK PUBLISHING PLC
Headline House
79 Great Titchfield Street
London W1P 7FN

**For the convenience of the reader
we here record a note of
IMPORTANT PERSONS APPEARING IN
THE NARRATIVE
in the order of their appearance**

Andrew Archer Esq., our hero.
Sir Franklin Franklyn Esq., of Alcovary, Herts.
Lady Margaret Franklyn, his wife.
Tabby, a maid.
James, a footman.
Mrs Samuel Treglown.
Betty, her maid.
Mrs Sophia Nelham, our heroine.
The Viscount Chichley, a friend.
M. Emile Foutarque, of the French Embassy.
H.M. King William IV.
M. le Duc de Laval, H.E. the French Ambassador.
Jacques, M. Foutarque's footman.
Mally, a rude servant.
A number of French gentlemen.
A congress of actors.
John Rice, one of them.
Anthony Treweers, a butler.
Dolly and Jane, two lady wrestlers.
Squire Dick Treleaven.
Lady Holland.
Tollersly, her senior footman.
Mrs Teazle, a lady.

Betsy Pascoe, an ancient.

Jem, her Great-Uncle.

The D*v*l.

Mrs Treleaven.

Hermes, Apollo, Zeus and Pan, four actors.

Chimaera, Dryope, Metis and Selene, four actresses.

The Rt Hon. the Earl of Stow.

Glaws, a fishergirl.

The Rev. Ebenezer Polscoe.

Flannery Fitzchrome, his lordship's racing manager.

Lady Opimion, a fool.

Six jockeys.

Six professional ladies.

Bess and Nell, two strumpets.

Betsy, a Negress.

Samuel Treglown Esq., M.P.

Maurice le Semblant.

Two French plotters.

Mrs Blowser, a Madame.

Miss Xanthe Holden, a lady.

George Float, a Negro.

Mrs FitzNott, a society lady.

Chapter One

The Adventures of Andy

At the end of my last volume of memoirs, published under the title *Eros in the Far East*, the constant reader left my friend Mrs Sophia Nelham and I in that haven of relative civilisation, Singapore, where we were intent for some weeks upon relaxing after a series of adventures which had somewhat enervated us – not surprisingly, since they had included our being captured by pirates and barely escaping execution, together with other hazards which I need not recapitulate (the aforesaid account still being in print, and available from the London firm of Headline, its publishers, upon payment of an insignificant sum).

We returned to England, and to our respective houses – Sophie (as I was privileged to call her) to her elegant domicile in Chiswick; I to the large house whose windows overlooked Regent's Park, and which I found to have been maintained in every degree as I would have wished by the small band of servants I had left there.

I had spent only three nights in my own bed, however, before the post brought a letter from my old friend (and Sophie's half-brother) Sir Franklin Franklyn, Bart., of Alcovary, in the county of Hertfordshire. I had of course sent him a message apprising him of my safe return to England and promising to regale him with the narrative of my adventures at an early date, and he wrote now to press me to propose myself to him on the earliest possible occasion – not merely because he was eager to hear my story, but because he had a favour to ask of me.

I lost no time in packing a small trunk and setting forth, and in a matter of two days' journey – with a single night's residence at the Chequers Inn at Fowlmere (a favourite hostelry, upon the same route, of the late Secretary Sam Pepys) – rode once more at dusk up that well-remembered drive of elms, to be met at the front door by my friend Frank and his wife, the delightful Lady Margaret, whose embrace was rather more than sisterly, despite the presence of her servants. (I do not say 'of her husband' for there was no combative jealousy between Frank and I; we had shared too many amorous adventures for that to be the case, and indeed, though we did not speak of it, my carnal knowledge of his Lady had by several years preceded his own!).

'My dear boy,' said he, 'come in and take a glass of wine and some food!' and swept me into the familiar and comfortable drawing-room, where we ate and drank well, a delicious fricassee of wood-pigeon being prefaced by some trout and followed by a couple of fowl.

I had some difficulty in giving due consideration to the meal amid the continual fire of questions which my host and hostess pressed upon me, and the rest of the evening proved too little time for me to detail all my adventures together with those of Sophie, who had not yet had the opportunity to convey them in person.

But what, I asked finally, was the favour my friend wished to ask of me?

Frank glanced at the clock, which now showed a quarter of one.

'Time enough for that tomorrow,' he said. 'Perhaps you will wish to sleep late?'

No, I replied; I was quite recovered from the fatigue of the journey. Eight o'clock would do for me.

'Eight it shall be,' said Frank, 'with a cup of chocolate, to which I remember you are addicted at that hour. We will see – shan't we, my dear?' he said to Lady Franklyn, with what looked like a wink, 'that it is promptly served.'

I fell into a sleep as soon as my head touched the pillow, and it seemed indeed but a few moments later that I was awakened from a dream by the sound of the bedroom door opening, and through lazily opened eyes saw the figure of a maidservant enter the still darkened room and set a tray down on the bedside table.

She then walked to the windows, and turned back the shutters. As she did so, the sun shone directly into the room – for the windows faced towards the east – and the thin gauze of her dress was turned almost transparent, revealing the silhouette of a charming, buxom figure. It was unmistakably English, if I may say so: that is, charmingly solid with generous curves of bosom and hip that contrasted with my memories of the sometimes too slim sinuosity of the eastern ladies to whose company I had recently been more accustomed.

The girl turned from the window, and strode to the bed – where to my amazement she leaned over me, and immediately planted a smacking kiss upon my lips, with the words: 'Surely you ha'n't forgot your old friend at Rawby Hall?' – and slipping her hand beneath the bed-clothes laid hold upon my riding-muscle (which I must admit was akimbo, as seems invariably the case when I am aroused suddenly from a dream).

My aversion to the gentle touch of a female's hand in
that quarter is not so great that I hastened on this occasion to disengage it; nevertheless, I was a little put about
by the familiarity of the servant's action, and must have
showed it. 'Well, I believe you ha' forgot, hoity-toity!'
she said, removing her hand of her own volition, and
beginning to pour the chocolate.

'A thousand apologies, my dear – but you do have the
advantage of me,' I said, 'no doubt because the light is
behind you.'

'Think of the laundry-room at Rawby Hall!' she said,
and at that moment turned half away, so that the light
shone upon her face. 'Twas that of Tabby, who had been
one of my fellow-servants only five years before, when I
had been for a brief time footman at the house of Lady
Franklyn's father (she then being Lady Margaret
Rawby, one of two sisters whose beauty and cultivated
manners were equalled by the lasciviousness of their
appetites).

'My dear Tabby!' I cried; whereupon she put down the
chocolate cup, whisked her gown over her head, and in
less time than it takes to tell had stretched herself along
my own unclothed body, which was no less sensible of her
country charms than it had been of those many others
which had delighted me since we last lay together, which,
if I remembered, had been in an attic room at Rawby a
night or so before I left.

'That's more my boy!' said she with a familiarity
before which our present distinction of rank became as
nothing; and turning to throw herself upon her back,
clasped me with arms and legs in a grasp so delightedly
enthusiastic as to raise my spirits (by the close cons-
anguinity of our naked bodies) while at the same time

making it impossible (at the same time) for me to set about relieving them.

In a short time, however, by placing my hands upon her hips, I was able to contrive such a space between our bellies as enabled me to present the tip of my instrument to its proper entrance, into which it slipped with what seemed like an uninterrupted familiarity.

The reader will not wish me to detail the pleasures which followed, save to say that the intervening years had done nothing to diminish her charms – her breasts were as round and firm, her bum as fleshy and bounding, her loins as eager, as they had been years before. Removing at last her heels from my shoulders, where she had placed them in order to offer the fairest target to my advances, she ran her hands over my shoulders, which were liberally greased with perspiration (the day was already warm, and promised to be warmer), and wriggling from beneath me sat upon the edge of the bed and completed her pouring of my morning chocolate.

'My dear Tabby!' I exclaimed (the pleasure of love now to be followed by the pleasure of conversation). 'How came you here? What of Rawby Hall, and what of – what the devil was his name?'

'Tom,' she said, 'you mean Tom.'

It had been on account of the jealousy of her *beau*, one of my fellow-footmen, that I had left Rawby, his having taken a poor view of our coupling for the convenience of an elderly gentleman – the grandfather of the house – who wished to draw us in *coitus* for the purpose of illustrating a naughty book. And indeed I must confess that the pleasures concomitant with the nature of the postures we were forced to adopt were even greater than those of the guineas that Beau Rust was happy to pay us for our services.

'Tom's downstairs,' she said.

'I had thought he might have married you.'

'Not Tom,' she replied; 'or rather not me. 'Tis not that he's not asked often enough, but I've taught him in the years that I'm not for the snaring. As for how we come here – the Lady Elizabeth being commonly in London, life became tedious enough at Rawby, so, the Lady Margaret coming on a visit with Sir Franklin, I asked the favour of transferring to his establishment, which was soon enough granted. Tom followed, for where I go, he goes, though not by my special encouragement.'

'But do you not . . . ?'

'Surely,' she said; ' 'twould be out of conscience cruel to refuse him – but you know he was never the most accomplished rider in the stable, and Sir Franklin keeps an open house to visitors, some of whom are pleased to be entertained by a good countrywoman, by contrast to some namby-pamby town slut.'

Handing me my chocolate, she replaced her free hand upon my now declined instrument, which despite its recent activity swelled somewhat beneath it, at which she grinned.

'The years have not decreased your powers,' she said.

'Nor yours,' I replied, bending to plant a kiss upon one pert nipple, about which a ring of chocolate from my lips now darkened still further the shady circle which encompassed it.

We talked further as I drank; during which conversation I gathered that her favours were not denied to the master of the house. Frank having been ever a lusty youth, and now married for some years, it was no surprise to me that so enthusiastic a young woman as Tabby had found it possible to penetrate his defences; and said so.

' 'Tis not,' she said, 'that he does not love Lady Margaret; but a nightly diet even of caviare must grow somewhat tedious; and my lady understands it. In permitting my master a free rein, she feels herself at liberty to gather new garlands where she may – though being of somewhat effete tastes, the visitors she welcomes to her bed are not such as would stoke my own fires. But are we to spend the rest of the morning in mere talk?'

Taking my empty cup, she placed it upon the table, and bending over lifted my pliant tool upon the palm of her hand and took it between her lips as though it were a favourite fruit (which may not have been so far from the truth). However, though charmed by the gesture, and unable to resist a final squeeze of those delightfully full, pendant breasts, I denied her another bout, making the excuse that I had a business to discuss with Sir Franklin (which was nothing but the truth).

Tabby insisted however upon filling the large bath tub in the corner of the room and sponging my body with cool water (most reviving after our recent efforts), then drying me thoroughly with a soft towel and assisting me to dress – only then resuming her single garment. With a bob which was more humorous than deferential she left the room whereupon I made my way down the salon.

'Andy, my boy!' said Frank, who was sitting at a table upon which a map was spread. 'The sounds I heard as I passed your room half an hour ago suggest that I was right in assuming that you would be happy to be reunited with an old friend.'

My reply was simply to slap him upon the back, whereat he laughed more, and winked.

'A game one, Tabby,' he said; 'and not only game, but discreet. Mum's the word, old boy!' From which I

inferred that he believed his wife not to know of his
adventures with young Tabby; whereas I knew different.
However, it was not for me to interfere between husband
and wife.

He motioned me to a seat.

'Now, to business,' he said.

'You will not be aware – no more was I – that Sir
Fitzroy Franklyn, who held this place a century ago,
purchased at the same time another property in east
Cornwall, near the famous port of Fowey. Upon a closer
acquaintance, however, he for some reason disliked it,
and visited it but the once, whereafter he let it out upon a
long lease – a lease so prolonged that 'twas forgot, the
income merely disappearing into our coffers. Two
months ago I received notification that, the last of the
line of tenants having died, his lawyers discovered that
the place properly belonged to me! Now you know I have
become domestic, and hate any disturbance, but I had
steeled myself to the necessity of visiting the property
when I heard of your return – and, knowing your predilection for continual motion, it instantly occurred to
me that you were just the fellow to go down and inspect
the place – to find out, you know, what condition 'tis in,
whether 'tis agreeable – in short, the whole aspect.'

I instantly concurred. I had indeed had no notion of
what to do with myself during the coming months, and
knowing well enough my hatred of idleness, had begun to
wonder what task I could set myself to banish boredom.

'I shall go at once,' I said. 'You can let me have a
horse?'

'A horse!' Frank said; 'nay, a coach! But stay for at
least the weekend – we haven't heard nearly enough
about your adventures. And by the way' – he winked

again – 'Tabby is of course at your disposal; her pleasure at my announcing your arrival suggests her willingness to entertain you and, as you well know, what's mine is yours.'

We spent half an hour over the map – which was of Cornwall and showed Vycken Hall appearing to be set in a valley at the end of a road leading nowhere else – and in looking over some deeds to the place, which revealed little except that it must at the very least be three hundred years old.

The weekend passed pleasantly enough. Tabby, however, though she brought my morning chocolate, and was friendly enough, made no attempt to renew the familiarities with which she had greeted me; and for my part I was tactful enough not to attempt them, for having seen Tom's sullen visage in the distance while walking in the grounds (he made no attempt to renew acquaintance) I assumed that my presence was the subject of altercation between him and the object of his passion – and while I knew Tabby to be a young woman of strong natural affection coupled with a will of her own, I had no wish to make trouble between them.

I was not however entirely without female entertainment for the remainder of my stay at Rawby Hall, for having spent Sunday evening in pleasant conversation with my host and hostess, and bade them good night, I had retired to my room and was about to climb into my naked bed when there came a knock upon my chamber door. Thrusting on my shirt, I opened it – to reveal Lady Margaret, herself in charming *dishabille*.

I had been offered proof, during the evening, of the warmth of her regard for me, for she had made a point of sitting upon the floor at my feet, and even of leaning back between my legs, so that her head rested just at the bifurcation of my thighs, my manhood signalling by its swelling my appreciation of her presence, and the nearness of her lips to my most apprehensive limb. Frank in the meantime sat smiling amicably, being nothing if not complaisant at the friendship between his wife and myself.

It was now clear from the panting of that bosom which she pressed against mine, that Lady Margaret was eager for a consummation; indeed, even before the door was shut, her hands had slid down the length of my back and, raising the hem of my shirt, clasped the globes of my buttocks the better to press our bodies together at the point at which such contact most readily raises both desire and confident expectation.

Thrusting the door shut with one foot, I carried madame to the bed, where, laying her upon the sheets, I opened the leaves of the book in order more closely to examine the pages, where indeed I found inscribed just that picture I recalled: viz., breasts generous, but not to excess, their pouting expressive of desire, and the beating of the heart beneath them clearly to be seen under the flesh, itself so tender and white as to reflect the golden light of the candle almost as from the surface of a burnished vellum. Then, about the shoulders, one errant lock lying high upon the bosom, were swathes of lustrous copper hair, which the lady had now grown much longer than formerly, and which formed almost a pillow upon which not only her head but my own might be cushioned. That other, smaller cushion which disguised the entrance of her cave of delights was similarly lustrous, and so tempting that (first gently removing the small white hand which lay upon it) I planted a kiss there.

I could not but fear, despite these beauties, that marriage had somewhat dulled the edge of the lady's appetite; for while at our previous meetings she had been if anything over-ready to grasp at pleasures, now she lay lethargic, almost as though disinclined for combat – though her eyes were large and deep, and seemed to draw me towards her – which invitation I was only too happy to accept, first lifting my shirt over my head, seeming to hear a quick in-drawing of breath at the concomitant revelation; and indeed before I had entirely removed the garment I felt that touch between my thighs which could only be that of a lover's lips, and which reminded me of the excitement with which this very lady, when I was but a child, had introduced me to those sophisticated pleasures with which the gentry amused themselves, but which until that moment had been unknown to me, who had been familiar only with the rougher amours of the fields, or at best the servants' hall.

'Twas now I who was confined to inaction, for Lady Margaret, once having that morsel between her lips for which she had always shown an inordinate affection, had half-raised herself from the bed and crouched in an attitude most becoming (though what attitude of the naked female body is not?) – for as I looked down, her thick hair lay along her back, parting only at the waist to reveal the lower traces of a backbone delicately marked, ending only where the globes of a full and charming bottom hung (as it were) like a peach upon the bough.

Bending forward, I could but part the hair further to stroke that long, white back and those panting sides; for the rest, I could only concentrate on reserving some of my emotion for what might be to come – for I was like to burst with the pleasure of her attentions, her lips being ever adept at the provocation of pleasure. With the palm of one hand she supported my cods, a single finger playing softly upon that small disc of flesh which lay beneath them, inherent (as she knew all too well) with the utmost sensitivity. The other hand supported, between two fingers, my delighted riding-muscle, now engorged almost to pain; for not merely contented to suck upon it as an infant sucks at the breast, she drew from time to time her lips from it in order that her small, pointed tongue might play about it, now running its length to the foot, now mounting again to the head, then flirting about the dome barely maintaining the contact; then once more embracing the whole pillar, the lips drawn apart with a seeming reluctance, so that their plump fullness allowed a smooth resistance to its entry.

At last, with a gasp, I took her head between my hand and almost with violence thrust it away.

'You must allow me, my Lady,' I said, 'to pay you a similar compliment before the pleasure of your company positively kills me!'

With apparent reluctance, yet with a smile, she raised herself upon her knees, and, transferring her hands to my shoulders, pressed a kiss first upon one pap, and then upon my lips. I gathered her up in my arms and laying her upon her back prepared to graze upon her as a grateful stallion upon the most luscious meadow.

My memory served me well as to the pleasures which most delighted her, for while every woman's body resembles the same instrument, each demands different skills from the accomplished player. My teasing of her nipples with my teeth brought forth a remembered paroxysm of pleasure, as did the running of my tongue about the little whorls of her ear; thus I progressed down the length of her body. The sucking of her toes had also the remembered effect, for after but a moment, seizing me by that apparatus which fell most readily to hand, she began to draw me back into a position which . . .

But now we both distinctly heard a cry of pleasure which had been emitted by neither of us. I caught my Lady's eye, at which a mischievous glint came into it; and putting a finger to her lips, she stood upon the bed, catching me by the hand and raising me to a similar posture. Then, turning, she drew aside a tapestry which hung above the bed head and revealed there two small holes in the wainscot, to one of which she applied her eye.

Upon my doing the same to the other, I found the next bedroom revealed to me, which was that of her husband, my friend Frank (Lady Margaret's own being beyond it again, along the same corridor). Frank's bed lay just below us, and upon it I saw – not altogether without surprise – my friend lying at length, with our mutual mistress Miss Tabby mounted upon it, and trotting at a brisk pace, the rise and fall of which was giving my friend that pleasure which had called forth the cry that had attracted our attention.

As we watched, the pace became hotter and my friend's face more and more contorted with the joy of it, until, just as Tabby herself let out that mew of bliss with which I was not unfamiliar, he lifted her body and threw her aside just at the moment when there burst from him an eruption which sent a generous fountain of the liquor of life to a height of perhaps eighteen inches before it fell back upon his belly.

My Lady was as moved by the sight as I, for, clinging to me, she drew me back upon the bed, throwing out her thighs so that I fell between them as neatly as a ball within its cup; and our own trotting match held its course for only a brief period before we, like the happy couple next door, reached the apogee of pleasure and lay in each other's arms in a fulfilled relapse.

It would have been wise – and certainly common to those practised in deceit – for us immediately to have parted; but as it was, we both fell into slumber, and when I awoke, some hours later, it was to find myself lying beside not one figure but two. Frank had entered the room unheard by me and now lay at my side, his wife cradled happily in his arms, showing, most generous of fellows as he was, not the least infelicity in sharing her with his friend.

I fell asleep again; and was awakened only by the entrance of Tabby with my chocolate, upon which I thought I descried some irritation in her at the occupation of my bed also by her master and mistress, it being more than possible that, knowing that I was departing that morning, she had counted upon a farewell buff. However, having drawn the curtains, she merely asked whether she should bring more chocolate, and having received a lazy affirmative from the Lady Margaret, withdrew somewhat sulkily, leaving we three to greet each other without embarrassment – having on more than one occasion lain between the same pair of sheets, though generally accompanied by Sophie, whose absence we remarked upon, wondering why we had received no news of her. Frank, who had looked somewhat nervously at Tabby, as though expecting some reference to the cavorting of the previous night, was quick to embrace his wife, which she returned in the friendliest manner, so that out of tact, and seeing that he was ready to prove that Tabby had not exhausted him beyond a fresh demonstration of his powers, I roused myself from the bed and made my toilet behind the screen in the corner of the room. Between the cracks in that useful structure I saw that my two friends were indeed pledging their matrimonial affection in the approved fashion.

By nine o'clock I was in my borrowed equipage, comfortable enough in sufficient space for two or even three travellers; my luggage piled upon the roof, and the two spirited horses directed by James, a young chap of about my own years, whom I seemed to recognise (and who indeed turned out to have been a footman at Rawby at the same time as myself. I recalled, when I considered it, the difficulty he had in cramming himself into the tight breeches supplied him on the occasion of the great Waterloo Ball there, his member being, if I remembered aright, of inordinate size).

Our journey on that first day was to Oxford, into whose High Street we rattled in the cool of the early evening, the setting sun gilding the tops of the honey-coloured buildings. We put up at the Mitre Hotel, a decent inn whose landlady at first assured me that there was no space, but then impressed by that readiness with coin which I generally assume in order to secure proper service, led me to a handsome set of rooms on the first floor, and upon my insistence allotted James a bed in the long room which, above the stables, served for her own servants.

I slept well, and after an excellent breakfast we were upon the road early the following morning, for Chippenham. The landlady of the Mitre having provided us with a hamper which comprised beef pasties, cold meats of other sorts, and fruit, we pressed on without pause. We had passed through Wooton Bassett by mid-afternoon, and, in sun remarkably warm for late spring, were making to Tockenham Wick when through the window, which I had fully opened in order to take the air, I thought I heard a woman's cry.

I called out to James to stop; and on his pulling up, we both heard an appeal for help issue from the woods upon our right. I took my pistol – robbers being by no means unknown upon this road – and James a stout cudgel and we descended and made our way upon a recently trodden path between bramble and briar towards the spot from which the sound issued. The cries now grew more distinct, and seemed to issue from two throats; and, breaking into a small clearing, we found indeed two females firmly tied to two small saplings which, though weak enough to be broken perhaps by the strength of a man, were sufficient to keep them in thrall.

They were clearly mistress and maid, for one was dressed in servant's clothing, while the other was wearing a gown of some elegance, though sadly bedraggled, and indeed torn so that it hung from her waist leaving the whole top of her body bare except for the ropes which crossed it – a circumstance which even in her cruel circumstances drew a blush to her cheeks as I came sufficiently close to release her, upon which she immediately gathered her clothing together and held it to conceal those handsome globes upon the surface of which livid marks had been left by the entrapping ropes.

Though distressed, she was by no means in an extreme of terror – more of anger – and indeed rebuked her maid, whose sobbing and crying had mounted to an apogee as we came into sight, and who was now in a state of advanced hysteria. The lady's calmness was such that she immediately advised me that the robbers who had tricked them from their coach were long gone.

' 'Twas a coach I hired at Oxford, sir,' she said; 'but the driver was clearly villainous, for he stopped nearby complaining that one of the horses was lame – which I believe was not the truth; and our having stopped gave his friends the opportunity to attack, to tie us here, and to make off with the coach and its contents.'

'You were not . . . otherwise incommoded?'

'Thank you for your inquiry, sir, but no. The state to which my clothing is reduced was the result of my struggling rather than of any attempt upon my virtue. Oh, do be quiet, Betty!' she said to her still hysterical maid, who, stifling her sobs, now leaned upon James's arm with a degree of confidence that seemed suspiciously admiring.

Of course, I offered the lady the convenience of my coach as far as Chippenham, where she could at least enquire about her lost coach and belongings. But what were we to do about her clothing? For it was in no state for entry to a town. I had plenty of clean trappings for myself, but, needless to say, no female clothes. Instructing James to get down a trunk, I reached from it breeches and shirt which I was pleased to offer her.

On her returning to the coach from the bushes where she attired herself, I was pleased to hand her into the coach – for she made a handsome figure, though by no means boyish, for her breasts, though no more obtrusive than was pleasant, were delightfully full, and pressed against the linen of my shirt with an insistence which revealed her womanhood in a positively provoking manner. My breeches were also at stretch across her hips – the manner in which she filled them excusing (if

excuse were needed) the lack of manhood which fashion
at that time insisted should be shown at that place where
in earlier days a codpiece would have announced it.

With the lady sitting opposite me, and the now quiet
Betty upon the box with James, we resumed our journey, and I was able to inquire more of the lady's
circumstance.

Her name, she said, was Constance Treglown, and she
was returning to Cornwall from the north country, where
she had been upon a visit with her sister, who had married
a squire in Northumberland. She was somewhat taciturn
of nature, and would say little else, except that her
husband was the Member of Parliament for a Cornish
town – her shortness in the acknowledgement of which
led me to believe that there was little love lost between
them.

I asked no more, since she seemed unwilling to volun-
teer more.

Noting the discomfort with which from time to time
she lifted the front of my shirt from her bosom, I reached
for the flask of cool water with which I had supplied
myself, dampened a handkerchief and offered it to her –
which, taking, she applied to her breasts, soothing (as I
guessed) the troublesome irritation of the flesh provoked
by her bonds. Though she used a most ladylike delicacy
of motion, she could not but betray a glimpse of those
globes of which I had had too short a view upon our
meeting, and though as a matter of course I averted my
eyes I could not but hope for an opportunity of a closer
inspection. Given some hours, during our drive, to talk
to and look at her, I concluded that indeed I might have
had a far less attractive travelling companion. She was, I
believed, my elder by a few years – but of a handsome

appearance which could almost have been called noble, the carriage of her head and body being poised and graceful, her speech distinctive and metropolitan with little trace of a country accent, and her manner to me perfectly assured.

By the time we reached Chippenham we were on such terms that I had no hesitation in offering her the convenience of my coach into Cornwall – for her home was upon the coast to the west of Fowey, and would be easy to reach from the road upon which I was set. Her reporting the theft of her carriage to the local magistrate met merely with assurance that 'twas a common occurrence, and that she need not expect to meet with her belongings again – which caused her only a slight impatience for, she said, she had carried nothing valuable in it apart from a few jewels; the chief inconvenience being the loss of her clothing, which however she was able to some degree to correct through sending for a local sempstress, who was able by morning to produce a gown perfectly decent though of merely rural fashion. I must confess that I regretted the return of my own clothing, for despite her most evident femininity she made a charming figure in breeches.

Setting off, then, we were most comfortable. Betty showed as little dismay as her mistress at their new mode of travel, and settled upon the box with James in perfect equanimity, if not indeed with a trifle more enthusiasm than might have been expected of a young woman forced to such familiarity with a stranger. When I came to consider, the familiarity with which they greeted each other may not have been unconnected with the fact that their sleeping quarters had been in the same area of the small inn where we had rested, and it may be that they were already greater friends than a mere twelve hours' company would have led one to expect.

Passing through Bath with only a glimpse of its delights, we entered at the end of the day into Bristol, where we stepped into the Cross Keys and engaged rooms, and after a pause for the necessary refreshment of our persons enjoyed an excellent meal of fresh fish and good boiled mutton in Mrs Treglown's private room, in the corner of which stood a large four-poster. The meal was served by a woman who clearly, by her winks to me behind the lady's back, inferred that the meal was a mere prologue to seduction, and that the juxtaposition of dining table and bed was no mere accident – and indeed might have been a convenience afforded by the landlord to any who seemed likely to make use of it. As the evening went on my appreciation of the circumstances grew keener. My companion was extremely attractive and, as our familiarity grew, gave some reason to suppose that she might entertain an advance.

I saw no ready opportunity in our conversation to suggest it, however, and when, as ten o'clock struck out, she rose and, extending her hand, supposed that we should retire, since it would be necessary to make an early start on the following morning, I merely pressed that hand with affection and planted a kiss upon its slim fingers, at which she showed only pleasure.

I was confident that her gratitude for my aid would extend to the mutual enjoyment of a more inspiriting pleasure than that of mere aural conversation, and in my own room performed my toilet with all that care suggested by the probability of intimate caresses, even summoning James to bring hot water from downstairs, which he did with an ill grace, appearing with an unbuttoned shirt and unbraced breeches – which led me to suppose that he himself had been engaged a moment previously in just such an amorous dalliance as that I was shortly to enjoy.

Having donned a clean shirt, it was with a quivering apprehension of delights to come that I stepped out of my room and slipped along the passage to Mrs Treglown's, and merely tapped upon the surface of the door with my fingertips. I found it unlocked, and slipped through it – to find the lady abed, a candle lit upon the bedside table. I stepped forward, my always ready weapon already beginning to show a happy anticipation of the pleasure which awaited it.

But instead of throwing back the sheets to welcome me, she sat up, clutching the counterpane to her breast, and with an air of surprise.

'Why, Mr Archer!' she said, with an air of surprise. 'Is there some danger that you should approach a lady unannounced, in her bedchamber?'

This, as can be imagined, stopped me in my tracks.

'Why, madam . . .' I stammered.

'Your room is, I believe, somewhat along the passage?'

She smiled in a manner which I could have believed inviting – had she not at the same time maintained a firm grip upon the bedclothes, which showed no more than those alabaster shoulders, bare to the rise of her breasts, merely suggesting other delights which were clearly not upon offer.

'I beg your pardon, ma'am,' I said, bowing with what dignity I could command. 'I was under a misapprehension which I trust you will forgive.'

I then made my exit, my tail between my legs – or, indeed, 'twould have been between my legs had its size permitted the gesture, for my rejection had reduced it to a shrunken state in which no posture other than of utter dejection was possible.

It can be imagined that I spent a sleepless night; so much so indeed that upon the following morning I was capable only of greeting the lady somewhat sheepishly and seeing to the loading of the luggage, after which I fell into a sound sleep which even the ill condition of the road towards Devonshire could not disturb.

Chapter Two

Sophie's Story

While never averse to travel, it is always with considerable pleasure that I return to London, that most inspiriting of cities; and to my home, a small but handsome building standing within its own grounds at Chiswick, which I had been able to acquire as the result of wise investments made upon the advice of a number of gentlemen friends – including my brother Sir Franklin Franklyn, and the Viscount Chichley, a nobleman to whom and to whose wife I had been of some little service in reconciling a difference between them.

I cannot say that I stirred much from the house or grounds for a week or so after my return from my recent adventures in the Far East – even neglecting to send to Frank at his house in Hertfordshire, for I was sure that my erstwhile companion Andrew Archer would have done so; and to be plain, I was exhausted both as to mind and body.

However, I am nothing if not resilient, and in ten days or so began to feel once more capable of, and indeed eager for, society – so that I greeted with pleasure my footman's announcement, at ten one fine morning, of a visitor.

Chichley strode into the room looking not a year older than when I saw him last: though he was now in his mid-twenties, his complexion was still that of a young girl, and while his body was certainly more solidly built than when I had first encountered him, under somewhat embarrassing circumstances (recounted in those of my memoirs incorporated in a volume entitled *Eros in Town*, and published some time since), a greater assurance of manner advertised that he was now a man of perfect self-possession.

'My dear Sophie!' he exclaimed, using that diminutive form of my name by which my intimates always address me; and after sweeping a low and formal bow, descended to the more enjoyable familiarity of planting a smacking kiss upon my lips, while his right hand fell, by what accident I cannot say, upon the upper reaches of a breast decorated rather than concealed by the morning-gown which it was my habit to wear at breakfast.

'I have just heard of your return,' he said, 'your man having met my own (who, you know, is his cousin) at the coffee-house yesterday.' He stood back, the better to observe me. 'Clearly your journey has been intriguing, for you look if anything more interesting than ever!'

I bowed my head; he had ever been a charming companion, able to say – and perform – just those things which delight a woman when discharged by a personable young man.

'You must tell me all your adventures,' he continued.

'Certainly!' I concurred; 'but I was about to dress and ride into town. Come into my dressing-room and talk, while I make my *toilette*.'

It may surprise the reader to find me inviting a young man to observe my *toilette*; but my familiarity with Chichley was such that he took the suggestion for what it was – the evidence of friendship; and taking my hand as

I arose, handed me into the neighbour room with the greatest ease and lack of awkwardness. There, I sat him in a chair, and while I applied those cosmetics which polite society now represents as decent, told him something of myself; then retired behind a screen to divest myself of the *peignoir* before donning my gown.

I cannot say that I was much surprised, on looking up, to see Chichley leaning with one arm upon the screen, while he inspected my person – devoid now of the encumbrance of vesture.

'You have not, I see, been able altogether to resist the compliments of the sun,' he said – and indeed, unfashionable though it is in London, I had grown somewhat fond of the foreign habit of sun bathing, or exposing my body to the comfortable rays of the planet Sol, and my skin was therefore rather browner than is normally the case with ladies of fashion. This, Chichley clearly was stirred by, and stepping forward pressed his lips to my shoulder, his hand meanwhile once more stealing to a breast, which, now unencumbered by clothing, it was able to caress with all that tender and apprehensive sensitivity of which he had been master from the first, and which was now supported by the experience of his years of manhood and an education in the courts of love in which I, myself, had been one of the tutors.

I must confess that, having for the past several months been exclusively in the company either of natives of eastern countries whose bodies were naturally darker than those of Europeans, or of men of European birth whose skins had been tinted by the fierce sun of the tropics, the sight of Chichley's body as it now emerged white as a wand from the clothing which, in his eagerness, he dropped to the floor, was as interesting to me as my

darker flesh was to him; though I reflected as he took me
in his arms that that limb which now knocked insistently
at my belly was indistinguishable from that of any other
male instrument except in those details of size and shape
which naturally differentiate lover from lover.

I could not but recall, also, as, gently displacing a
thigh, he presented himself at that portal which was now
ready and happy to receive him, that my earlier encoun-
ters with him had been relatively brief: as a mere boy, he
had been no more capable of prolonging the act than any
other of his age and inexperience; and when, scarcely
older, he had on his wedding night been disappointed
by the coldness of pride and come to me for solace,
his loving had been remarkable more for a kind of
melancholy passion than for either adeptness or
persistence.

I now found, however, that all had altered – no doubt
as a result of that domestic happiness to which I had
contributed (in the unlikely event of the reader not
having perused my previous volumes, Chapter Sixteen of
that entitled *Eros in Town* recalls the circumstances under
which Lord and Lady Chichley were reconciled as the
result of a lascivious trick). That he was strong and vigorous as ever was evidenced by his now lifting me from the
floor, being careful to maintain the connection between
our bodies, striding into the next room, and depositing
me once more upon my bed! But once reclining, rather
than that boyish force which he had previously used, the
gentle and languishing sway (as 'twere) of his body now
moved his prick – stern and adamant – between my
lower lips with a sensation all the more stirring for its
tender and leisurely motion; and continued with unrelent-
ing softness to delight me until my bosom rose and fell

with the apprehension of immediate release – when with an equal tenderness he withdrew, lying quietly at my side, merely pressing soft kisses upon my neck and shoulder until my passion had almost subsided; whereupon I raised myself and looked with a quizzical eye upon him.

He raised an eyebrow; whereat I felt myself blush (an unusual occurrence, it must be admitted) and to disguise my confusion, bent to plant a kiss of my own upon that part of his body which he had allowed to languish slightly, though it had diminished in inflexibility rather than either in breadth or length; and as I took it between my lips, I felt the tissues once more harden – the more so as I began to draw upon its length with a regular motion, encouraged by the gentle touch of a hand upon the back of my neck.

It was now my turn to bring my friend almost to the splutter; when, encouraged and warmed by pleasure, I turned my body so that he could return the compliment, feeling in a moment his tongue exploring that part but recently evacuated by the limb I was now kissing; first running this around my outer lips, he then – as I felt – parted them with his fingers so that he could reach that bud which, in women, imitates in sensitivity and even somewhat in contour the most interesting part of man; and tickling its responsive tip, soon brought me once more near my summit – while at the same time, warned by the tightening of his cods in the palm of my hand and the involuntary upward motion of his loins, I drew away, and as my own body clenched with the delight of amorous explosion, withdrew my lips just in time to see a positive gusher of liquid issue from the tiny aperture which marked the summit of the steeple.

It now being mid-morning, I rang for coffee – forgetting that Charles, the footman, had been engaged during my absence by my housekeeper, and was not used (as my household had formerly been) to my habit of occasionally entertaining gentlemen in my bedchamber: to facing with equanimity the sight of a naked couple charmingly embedded, and indeed sometimes even engaged in the lists of love. However, the man's face – which was not unhandsome – showed only the slightest tremor of emotion upon discovering myself cleansing with a handkerchief the belly and thighs of a gentleman whose contented aspect no less than the bedewed state of an only half-subdued staff betrayed a very recent happiness; and upon his return with the coffee, he set down the tray without the least sign of perturbation.

'So, Chichley,' I said, when he had withdrawn, 'tell me the story of your life. Lady Chichley, I trust, is well?'

'Very well,' he replied; 'Frances indeed sends you her kindest wishes, and hopes to see you soon. She is engaged this morning with her hairdresser . . .'

'That fact relieving you of any suspicions that she may be enjoying a similar activity to us,' I remarked – it being in general the case that hairdressers are madge culls whose interest in women is restricted solely to the hair of their heads.

'The contrary is true,' said Chichley, with a smile; 'for this gentleman is more than usually attentive – indeed so much so that Frances has had to insist that the conversation which as a matter of course takes place between them does so before her hair is dressed, lest the excellence of the one exercise should be negated by the impetuosity of the other.'

My expression must have betrayed my surprise, for he

went on: 'My indifference to the connection arises not from any lack of concern for our union; it is merely that your introducing her (as you will remember) to the knowledge of the pleasure to be found in a variety of lovers has resulted in her having much more the appetite of a man than of a woman; so that while we celebrate our happiness with regular and satisfactory union, she feels the need of a regular change of diet; and has informed me that if she is to recognise my own desire for occasional dalliance outside the marital bed, it must be in return for my compliance in a similar exchange of attentions between her and other gentlemen – which of course I am happy to agree to!'

If I was surprised by these words, it was only at finding that Frances Chichley, originally so tender, apprehensive and modest a woman, now took the same view of the matter as myself; and silently applauding her good sense, I accepted with sanguinity – after we had each enjoyed a cup of coffee – her husband's entirely successful demonstration of the recovery of his spirits.

We lunched at home, and Chichley enlarged to me the death of the late King and the accession of the new, which had taken place during my absence from the country. King William IV was proving, he said, an amiable monarch, though at first the more dignified courtiers had found him intolerable, raised to the throne as he was from a position of obscurity and neglect, of living in miserable poverty, surrounded by a numerous progeny of bastards.

If nobody regretted the passing of the late King, nobody expected much of his successor; yet King Billy had begun well, showing himself entirely lacking in false pride – and on being given the instrument with which to sign the declaration of his monarchy, merely remarked in his usual tone, 'This is a damned bad pen you have given me' – which so startled the Clerk to the Privy Council that upon beginning to swear in the members of that body, he did so in the name of 'King George IV – William, I mean,' to the great diversion of all present.

The late King's funeral was, it seems, a merry affair. In the Abbey the new King was of course chief mourner, but instead of remaining decently behind the body, darted about shaking hands cordially with his friends, waving to others, and chatting to anyone who came near. But if this behaviour seemed to some to be indecent, the man's good nature, simplicity and affability to all about him were also striking; he has rather the manners of a country gentleman than of a great monarch, while Queen Adelaide is by no means delighted at her elevation, and lives as quietly as possible at Bushy House, about a mile from Hampton Court.

Chichley promised that he would introduce me at court upon the first possible occasion, for it seems that nobility is not, there, a prerequisite for attendance, His Majesty being more interested in companions who are lively and agreeable than in those whose presence is secured by right of aristocratic succession.

We lunched in *dishabille* (I always kept at home a robe in which my gentlemen friends could attire themselves should they wish to do so, rather than resume that clothing discarded for reasons of informal conversation). Then, gossip for the time over, we retired once more to the bedroom, where we found that my new footman had carefully laid out the clothing which Chichley had in haste thrown upon the floor (that young man showed distinct promise). My friend dressed, while I completed my toilet and donned that dress which I had meant to put on some hours earlier; and we set off for town in his carriage, he dropping me – as I wished to call upon my dressmaker – at Bond Street (near the place, as he reminded me, where we had first met).

Having fulfilled my errand (having been absent for some months from the country, it was now necessary that I should order some new gowns in the latest fashion), I was walking down the Burlington Arcade towards Piccadilly when I became conscious that a gentleman was walking not far behind me and at precisely my pace.

This was perhaps not a great surprise, for the rooms behind or above the shops in the Arcade were still at that time devoted largely to the entertainment of gentlemen by ladies whose virtue could be discounted at the cost of a few shillings; and indeed some women of fashion would not have been seen there. I however cared nothing for such apprehension, preferring to walk where I liked at whatever time pleased me.

However, I did not care to be followed indefinitely by some fellow who had a false understanding of my character – for when I paused to look into a window, so he paused; when I resumed, so did he. Turning the corner into Piccadilly, towards Lord Burlington's House, I therefore suddenly stopped and, dropping a glove, made to pick it up; whereon my shadow, abruptly rounding the corner, almost walked into me, and halting in some confusion, removed his hat and bowed.

I must confess that I was not unimpressed by his appearance, which was gentlemanlike, though he was clearly foreign, being dressed in a style which was not entirely English – and indeed his words of apology for almost knocking into me were in an accent that I recognised as the French. He was dark-haired, dark-eyed, and somewhat swarthy as to complexion; his face, a little angular, was handsome enough, and the smile which played upon his lips immediately intrigued me by its decidedly sardonic air.

I made my curtsy, and accepted his apologies with a smile; and when, bending once more to take up my glove, I was forestalled by his swiftly recovering it, I accepted it with a smile perhaps as sardonic as his own – for I was convinced that he knew that I knew that he was aware that I had recognised that he had been following me, and had contrived the exchange.

'Perhaps, *madame*,' he said, 'I may be permitted to accompany you, if you are walking down to St James's?'

I bowed, and on his falling into step, enquired whether he had been long in London, receiving the answer that he had been in town for only a month, attached to the household of the Duc de Laval, Ambassador of France to the Court of St James.

I was able to exchange courtesies with him about the difference between London and Paris society, for though I had never visited the French capital both Andy and Frank had done so, and indeed Lady Margaret Franklyn, the latter's wife, had spent some time there with her sister; so that in conversation I had gleaned much information about the somewhat loose society of the place.

On our reaching St James's, M. Emile Foutarque (for such was his name) made his bow, and hoped that we might meet again. London society, I remarked, was sufficiently small that that hope might indeed be realised; whereat he bowed again, and looked as though he wished to say considerably more – but retired.

My thoughts returned to M. Foutarque from time to

time during the next two days, for while he had not that light-hearted gaiety and charm which most attracts me in the other sex, I must admit that his person had a volatile fascination for which I could scarcely account. His manner was strictly polite, yet casual almost to insult; he seemed the kind of man under no circumstances to be trusted with the person of a lady. I had almost felt that he might at any moment have seized me, and, throwing me into the nearest doorway, have ravished me in the full view of society! – something which would in all events have been unusual, if possibly with embarrassing results for my reputation, if not his own. It was an uncomfortable, but by no means uninteresting, apprehension.

However, I had fittings at my dressmaker's, appointments at my hairdresser's (not the same hairdresser, I may say, as Frances Chichley, and much more interested in the hovering presence of my footman Charles than in any part of me other than my hair), and other matters to occupy my time – for Chichley had sent to say he would present me at court at the end of the week.

This was an evening court, and took place at St James's Palace, in the presence not only of the King but of the Queen, who is very ugly, with a horrid complexion, but has good manners, and played her part well enough (though she spoke as though she was acting, and wished the green curtain to drop). His Majesty was amiable, and on my being presented said, 'Happy, very happy,' taking my hand with great affability.

Returning to my place with Chichley, who should I see standing opposite me across the room – at the side of a plump, saturnine elderly man with powdered hair, who I took (rightly, as it turned out) for the French ambassador – but my friend M. Foutarque. He bowed slightly to me, and I nodded to him; whereat Chichley looked a little startled, and said: 'Do you know Foutarque?' – and on my replying that I had met him, looked as though he would say something more, but refrained.

We sat in conversation for a while, and took some wine; when at ten o'clock His Majesty rose and said, 'Now, ladies and gentlemen, I wish you a good night. I will not detain you any longer from your amusements, and shall go to my own, which is to go to bed; so come along, my Queen.'

There was some amusement at this frankness, though it was but normal behaviour in our new monarch; but the party indeed broke up. When I had been handed my cloak and was waiting for Chichley in the outer hall of the palace, M. Foutarque approached me and asked if he might present me to the Ambassador, which took place. We exchanged a few phrases – the Duc spoke little English – then excused ourselves, whereupon Foutarque offered me the convenience of his carriage, the Ambassador leaving in the company of other diplomatic colleagues.

Chichley was now standing by, and had clearly expected to escort me; but on my glancing at him gave, somewhat to my surprise, an almost indistinguishable nod, and immediately retired. I therefore acceded to Foutarque's invitation, whereupon he offered me his arm and escorted me to the door of the palace; when after a while a carriage drew up and a footman descended to open the door and hand me in, the carriage then setting off at a rattling pace to the north.

On our turning into Regent Street, I drew to M. Foutarque's attention the fact that my house was in fact in quite another direction; whereupon he immediately apologised.

'I beg your pardon, *madame*,' he remarked; 'but I had assumed, the hour being early, that you would be happy to take a glass of wine with me at the Embassy.'

While M. Foutarque was not of such impressive parts that I would otherwise have thrown myself (as it were) into his arms, I was pleased at the opportunity of being entertained at the French Embassy, for a more or less cool relationship existed between our two countries, and the French Ambassador, perhaps especially because he spoke our language but poorly, held open house but rarely. So I chose to ignore my new acquaintance's somewhat over-ready assumption of my willingness to be kidnapped, and assented.

I did not, however, see much of the formal parts of the building; for though we entered through the main doors of the impressive building, I was hurried up the main staircase, a footman holding lights which only briefly illuminated a gilt balustrade and picture-frames, to a first floor; then up a narrower staircase to a second, where at last we entered a small but elegant panelled sitting-room, an open door suggesting a further room beyond.

Dismissing the footman with some words in the French language, which alas I comprehend but haltingly, M. Foutarque lifted my wrap from about my shoulders, pulled forward a chair and poured me a glass of claret; then, taking one himself, sat opposite me in another chair, and for a time the conversation circled about the subject of the British weather and the possibility of a warm summer, which indeed seemed in prospect, the evening even now being warm and unoppressive.

After a while, the gentleman remarked upon not

having seen me in society before, though he had been in England for some months; whereupon I informed him that I had been travelling in the East, which interested him, and provoked many questions as to the society of the nations I had visited. These questions eventually settled upon social behaviour, and, questioned about such matters as the marriage customs of certain tribes, I found myself describing a ceremony I had observed in Fiji, and necessarily going into certain details which might have been considered indelicate by a less uninhibited narrator.

M. Foutarque was now showing considerable curiosity; and with permission loosened his *cravate*, as the French call a neckerchief, and even undid the topmost button of his shirt; while when I came to the most intimate details of the ceremony (a full description of which can be found in my volume *Eros in the Far East*), he leaned forward with an intense gaze.

On my finishing, he stood, revealing by the swelling clearly to be seen in his breeches that his masculine sensibilities had responded to my story as appreciatively as his intelligence, and was now at attention in the hope of my perhaps continuing. He refilled my glass, and his own, then once more sitting at my side inquired whether my travels had enabled me to, er, examine the disparity in dimensions which were said to distinguish the citizens of the eastern countries from those of the west.

'Forgive me if I am indelicate, *madame*,' he said, 'but there is some suggestion that I might be appointed to those parts, and . . .'

'Think nothing of it, sir,' I responded (for his eager interest had given point to my descriptions, and I warmed to them).

'I have always heard,' he continued, 'that the, er, masculine appendages of the Eastern men are less impressive as to proportion than those darker African races; that, in short, while the latter are remarkably well provided for as to the magnitude of their generative organs, their Eastern brothers are relatively diminutive. Of course,' he added, 'I do not suppose that personal experience will have confirmed this; but it is possible that you may have some anecdotal evidence.'

I was able to assure him that personal experience could indeed confirm what he had heard; for I had once in my employ, when I ran a house of pleasure for ladies in West London, a young black man whose prick – though he assured me it was by no means so superior as to its dimensions to that of any other man of colour – was of a size which would certainly impress any white person. The instruments of those Eastern men whose acquaintance I had been privileged to make were (I confirmed) of a lesser bulk – but M. Foutarque would perhaps be familiar with the female opinion of the male organ, that it was the employment of it which was most important, rather than the dimensions.

'You interest me strongly, *madame*,' said the Frenchman. 'I have myself a trifle which I might perhaps offer by way of comparison,' and, standing, he swiftly unloosed his breeches and without further ado there sprung from its confinement a stout white caduceus which was certainly as lengthy as any with which I had become acquainted in Europe, though as to its breadth there was perhaps something wanted, for though it terminated in a bulb whose circumference was generous, the supporting column was somewhat slender.

Presuming that he offered congress, and finding him

not unpleasant – if perhaps a little precipitate in assuming my interest – I also rose to my feet, and stepping forward embraced him, taking his prick in my hand to discover that while it was certainly slim it was also as rigid as was concomitant with the circumstances.

To my surprise, however, he stepped back, and with a slight bow turned to pull at a silk bell-rope just behind him; then, in somewhat undignified posture – having to support his unloosed breeches with one hand – indicated the open door at the end of the room, through which we passed to a fine panelled bedroom, the main item of furniture in which was a comfortably proportioned couch towards which he bowed. Without more ado, I disrobed and laid myself down, while he too divested himself of his clothing – but refrained from approaching, which I found somewhat puzzling.

After a moment, to my greater astonishment, the door opened and the footman who had previously attended us entered the room.

I could not imagine what service M. Foutarque could require; perhaps some brandy, I thought, or even coffee – if he had indulged too freely in alcohol during the evening. But this was not the case, for addressing the man in his own language, he had scarcely completed two brief sentences when the lad bowed, removed his wig, then his coat, then his waistcoat, then his breeches – and in no time at all was standing naked before us, his tool, while by no means extended, showing some apprehension that an equally naked lady was upon a nearby bed.

Foutarque now turned to me.

'You will forgive me, *madame*, but for reasons which will not interest you, I am at present entirely unable to oblige you; but in order not to leave a lady in a state of dissatisfaction, may I offer young Jacques, who I believe is capable of fully gratifying any desire you may express.'

Of course it was open to me to take offence and to leave. However, the *monsieur* was a highly placed official in his country's service; I felt in the position of one who must offer such hospitality as would reflect well on my king and country; and must anyway confess that, lacking a regular cohabitant, and not having had the pleasure of male copulatory attention since my passage with Chichley almost a week ago, I was by now ready for a romp.

Moreover, now I looked, young Jacques, who had presented a *chic* figure in uniform, was quite as handsome out of it. Though young, he was clearly a man in all essentials, and every moment showing more evidently the signs of physical maturity. Though as slim as the wand-like youths of the East, he was entirely European, not merely as to the whiteness of his body, but as to the hair which grew upon it – which the Eastern men lack, their arms, legs and breasts being as bald as eggs. Upon Jacques' chest lay a mat of black hair, his forearms and thighs also bearing a pleasant fuzz, and from the deep dint of his navel a line of black, springy filament led down to a positive grove from which his manhood rose rampant as a young oak.

He was clearly aware of what was required from him, for without any of that embarrassment which an Englishman might have shown in similar circumstances, he stepped forward and kneeling upon the bed between my legs (which I had unconsciously thrown open to his inspection) placed a hand on each side of my body and lowered himself so that he could place his lips upon mine, whereupon I felt his tongue, sharp and lively as a young fish, playing upon my teeth and the inside of my lips with all that inventive assiduity which a Frenchman can command (the men of that race being, as to osculation, by far the most ingenious).

I will admit to my pleasure being heightened by once more feeling beneath my hands (which played now over the hillocks of his lower back) that downy covering of hair which is so attractive to some women – though lack of it in certain men (I mention the Viscount Chichley as only one example of a Western male whose person was largely devoid of it) is no mark of femininity. In young Jacques it seemed to emphasise that virility which he was soon demonstrating in the most conventional manner; my palms, resting upon the rounded platform of his buttocks, feeling a rippling of muscles beneath the hair which was conveyed through every limb.

I was conscious now, as he riveted me with energetic thrusting, that M. Foutarque, kneeling at the side of the bed, his own instrument clutched in one hand, had placed his other hand upon my thigh, pressing it downward so that he could the more clearly command a view of his footman's baton as it entered and left its welcoming sheath; at the same time manipulating his own person with a vigour which matched Jacques' thrusting. On my signalling the ultimate satisfaction, which was soon enough given me, Foutarque gave his man's bottom a slap, whereat the man with a final thrust lifted himself away, the nectar of love falling upon my body as his master, with a carefully timed flick of the wrist sufficiently adept to suggest a lifetime's practice, brought himself off; so that in a strange tableau, he sat exhausted at the side of the bed while I lay equally dissipated upon it, and the footman – whose privileges did not include the right to exhaustion – rose, fetched a towel from a nearby chair, and with the most tender discretion began to wipe the perspiration from my damp but satisfied person.

M. Foutarque showed no sign of embarrassment, politely turning his back as young Jacques (who seemed also entirely devoid of any consciousness of the occasion being unusual) assisted me to dress. A less experienced woman than myself might have been abashed by the situation, but having learned that the vicissitudes of behaviour in the human male are innumerable – nay, inexhaustible – I carried the occasion off with what the Frenchies call a *sang-froid*, and declining the offer of more refreshment, permitted Jacques (having lately resumed his uniform) to summon what I suppose was one of the Ambassador's carriages, which took me off to Chiswick. I was not unamused by the evening's adventure – my anticipation of M. Foutarque's favours not having been so keen that I had been entirely offended by his appointing a deputy in the courts of love, and that deputy having been sufficiently personable to render his service pleasant enough.

Next morning, as I was still abed, Chichley was announced, and I received him together with my morning chocolate; whereupon he enquired as to my adventures the night before.

Our relationship was sufficiently candid to permit of my describing the incident in some detail, upon which he raised an elegant eyebrow to an almost comic extent.

'This might be extremely useful to His Majesty,' he said.

It was now my turn to signal surprise and incomprehension.

'This must go no further,' he said, 'but His Majesty's Government has for some time been looking for a means of discovering the real attitude and intention of M. le Duc de Laval; and anyone who could contrive a friendship with M. Foutarque would certainly have *entrée* to the Ambassador. It may also be the case that (though our French friends are to an extent shameless in matters of love) Foutarque would not especially wish his somewhat individual approach to amour to be advertised at large to the rest of the diplomatic *corps*.'

But what was this? I asked. Was Chichley now a diplomat?

'A patriot, merely,' he said; 'and this is a sensitive time. With a new King on the throne, it is important that this country secures an advantage in matters of foreign policy. But I must not bore you – it is merely . . .'

I interrupted my friend to assure him that the fact that I was of the female gender was no index of an ignorance of politics, and that I was as great a patriot as he, and would be glad to be of service.

'Then be so good,' he said, 'as to accede to any request M. Foutarque might make – short of course of your own security, and indeed of safety and decency, for we would not wish—'

I held up a hand.

'As to safety,' I said, 'you will know that I am not unaccustomed to inconvenience and even danger; and as to decency . . .'

He smiled, and said that I need say no more. He then proceeded to question me closely about so much of the Embassy as I had seen – which was not a deal; and then as to M. Foutarque – everything he had said and done, and his personal appearance (which I was certainly able to describe in some detail) and behaviour. As to the latter, I could only say that it had been impeccably polite, and that even when entirely devoid of clothing and in a state of excitement, his manners had remained those of the *salon* rather than the bed-chamber.

Eventually, Chichley took his leave, and without any familiarity other than a kiss; remarking as he left that should I, through the *monsieur*, be able to achieve the acquaintance of the Ambassador, this would no doubt be useful; a thought not especially inspiriting, since the latter gentleman, though dignified, was of greater corpulence than rendered him obviously attractive. However, I had more than enough to think about as I rose, made my *toilette*, and considered my future life as an unofficial secret agent of His Majesty!

Chapter Three

The Adventures of Andy

A beautifully warm morning saw the enigmatic Mrs Treglown and I once more upon the road, this time for Exeter, having paid my bill of six shilling for the night's accommodation for my servant and myself, and four shilling for supper. The journey passed without incident until between Cullumpton and Exeter the road became very bad, and one of the horses fell as we came down a steep hill into Bradninch. Mrs Treglown was very alarmed and clutched my arm with an intimacy which in other circumstances would have been most promising; but though she was at all times friendly, and did not once refer to the *contretemps* of the evening before, neither was there any sign of her regarding me as anything other than a casual acquaintance – which I found dispiriting, for the more I enjoyed her company the more I warmed to her person.

The horses being unable to bear up the carriage, we were, after the accident, obliged to walk up another hill, which in the heat wearied Mrs Treglown somewhat, who was forced to lean upon me, again not entirely to my displeasure despite the fact that the exertion brought me out in a positive muck of sweat.

We reached the London Inn at Exeter at about half past six, where my first act must be to lave my body, which was already beginning to stink from the exertions of the day. The London Inn must have been used to welcoming travellers in just such a state, for the room to which I was conducted already contained a metal bath full of warm water, into which I plunged after a brief pause for the removal of my soiled clothes.

In a very short while, the water was as dirty as my body had formerly been, and not for the first time I wondered why there had not been invented some scheme which would enable one to bathe in running water, so that there would no longer be a necessity to recline in a stagnant pool. However, I had no sooner thought it, than a knock came upon the door, and, covering the bath with a towel, I called upon the visitor to open – who was revealed as a plump, cheerful Devonshire girl who bore in her arms an immense pitcher. She explained that this contained warm, clean water with which I might freshen my body before leaving the bath; and before I could enquire how this was done, she had set the pitcher down, whisked the towel from the bath, drawn up a chair at its side, and invited me to stand. I did so, whereupon she mounted the chair and poured the water slowly over my body.

It had an invigorating and exhilarating effect, and a brisk towelling was all that was now required to recover me entirely from the effects of the long journey; but on my asking the maid to pass me the towel, she rather brought it, and, placing it about my shoulders, began to buff the skin with a delightful motion. Having dried my back to the waist, she turned her attention to my bosom, then my arms, finally inviting me to step out upon the towels which were spread at the side of the bath for that purpose – and on my doing so, bent to wipe the water briskly from the cheeks of my arse, then my thighs and legs.

I am ashamed to say – but no! shame did not enter into the matter; rather, 'twas entirely natural – that after spending a dry day in close company with a beautiful but unresponsive woman my sensual apprehensions were heightened, and the touch of female hands roused me. However, I blushed somewhat at the readiness of my riding-muscle, which was now at an angle of forty-five degrees and, as she leaned forward to reach behind me, was doing its best to nestle into the cleft between her generous young breasts, the touch of which did nothing to diminish either its dimensions or its eagerness. The young lady however was no whit abashed either by the sight nor, evidently, the touch – for, while rubbing my cods gently with the towel, she took a corner of it and wiped the remaining beads of water from the device which stood so proudly above them.

She then sat back upon her heels, and examining the phenomenon quite frankly, said in the broadest of accents, 'Why, zur, 'tes a braave set o' gingambobs! Would 'ee care for a jock?'

I cannot pretend to have understood her words, but the implication was clear, for releasing the strings of her bodice, she took my cock in her hands and laid it between her breasts, when an irresistible warmth spread instantly through my limbs, and, raising her to her feet, I drew her gown over her shoulders, when its falling to the ground revealed her quite stark. I attempted to draw her to the bed, but she resisted (later, I gathered that it was a house rule that only guests should copulate between the sheets), and, gripping me by the shoulders, took me with her to the floor, where fortunately clean – though damp – towels were still spread, and there I was in a moment engulfed and at work.

It must be admitted that Mally was not the most sophisticated of lovers, her command of the amorous art being restricted to congress of the simplest form; but I was not at that moment in search of poise or discrimination, and what she lacked in this she made up for in enthusiasm – for I was forced to place my hand over her mouth in order that her yowls of pleasure should not bring in the landlord or alarm the other guests; and the seismic bound with which her apogee was reached positively dislodged me from my seat, whereupon she seized my piece with her hard hands and brought me off with a spirited and cheerful dexterity.

The dear girl rose from her recumbent position to don her clothes – or, rather, her single garment – and, positively running from the room, fetched more warm water to sponge down my body for a second time, a task she did with no less assiduity and conscientiousness than formerly, though without the same effect.

I pressed four shilling into her hand, which delighted her (I had somewhat the impression that her services might have been taken as an element of the night's entertainment, and that she was surprised that I should have been inclined to hand her an extra tip). Then, dressing myself, I took tea with Mrs Treglown, and we walked out for a while before bed time. My passage with the girl had the effect of somewhat dampening down the fire which had previously been fanned by the company of the lady, and I was able to enjoy rather her conversation, which was witty and elegant, and to take a pleasure in her appearance and deportment unaffected, for the moment, by her more corporeal beauties.

On retiring to my chamber, I undressed and put out the lamp – but walking to the window to open it against the still warmth of the night, saw across the inn yard, on to which my room looked, the figures of James, my man, and Betty, Mrs Treglown's maid, in an embrace whose passion was no doubt excused by the fact that both were bare as the day they were born. That they had been friendly, I had known; and the fact that, as they sat side by side upon the box of the carriage, they had kept their knees covered by a rug despite even the heat of midday, had suggested some familiarity; however, here was proof of a friendship which owed as much to aphrodisia as to concord.

Indeed, if further proof was needed as to the extent of their ardour, it was now offered, for as Betty drew away so her lover's grinder could be seen in all its splendour, and though he was merely a servant, it must be admitted that as to both length and circumference, his weapon was of conspicuous dimensions. I had vaguely remembered him complaining, when we were together at Rawby Hall, of the difficulty of cramming himself into the doeskin breeches of his livery; and I was now reminded why – the miracle being that such an instrument could be disguised by the loosest unmentionables.

Miss Betty did not, however, show herself in the least discomfited – which surely demonstrated that they had been intimate before; for any woman setting eyes for the first time on so grandiose a weapon might be expected to faint away at the prospect of its splitting her most tender part. She immediately knelt, and, holding it with both hands, managed with an effort to take its tip between her lips – whereupon young James instantaneously doubled up in an ecstasy which proved sadly conclusive. Betty recoiled with a furious expression, while from the end of that remarkable cylinder dripped the discharge which had done his business.

It was impossible not to sympathise with the young woman, whose expression was of a child from whose grasp a lollipop had been seized after but one taste of its flavour! She battered at James's chest with her fists, and even (I shuddered as she did it) directed several slaps at the shrinking phenomenon which, though impressive even in its relaxed state, now hung loosely between his thighs.

Those gentlemen who are of experience would have given her at least the compensatory pleasure of other attentions; James clearly knew nothing of the art of love other than simple rogering, and now merely backed away, blushing and stammering. In a moment, pausing only to pick up her clothes from the bed, she left the room, whereupon he threw himself upon it in an attitude of such despair that I could only conclude that the sad culmination of the passage I had witnessed was not unusual; and I took myself to bed with the promise that he should be educated – for we owe it to others less fortunate to communicate to them those skills which we ourselves have mastered.

I rose the following morning at half past five, and paid my bill, which was eleven shilling only – an improvement on the ever increasing sums charged by those houses nearer the metropolis. Mrs Treglown was down but a few minutes later than myself; but complaining that her maid had not yet shown her face – which was also true of my fellow: but I could guess why.

Indeed, when the couple did appear, they wore matching expressions of disconsolate misery, and each declined to address the other, which led to some difficulty and confusion in loading the coach. When Betty had almost to be forced to mount the box beside James, rather than showing her customary eagerness to adopt that position, Mrs Treglown showed considerable curiosity; whereupon I must explain to her – something which I did with as much delicacy as possible, putting Betty's disappointment down to cursory treatment by her friend, whose impatience had rendered him less attentive than a lady had reason to expect from a lover. Whether she fully understood me, I cannot say, but she looked thoughtful during the rest of the time it took us to reach Chudleigh, where we breakfasted at the Clifford's Arms, which appears to be a good house, kept by Mr Weston, who with his wife was very civil and attentive, though the place itself has not much to recommend it.

We then passed on, the bright sun with a brisk breeze raising not only our spirits but those of our servants, who we were pleased to see now held each other's hands (when the management of the horses permitted, which was often – for the roads were not only narrow but highly fenced and therefore very safe), though their knees were no longer covered by the concealing rug (whose folds, I was now convinced, had enabled Betty manually to examine the dimensions of James's better part, thus raising hope in her which had subsequently been dashed by the precipitate nature of its firing mechanism).

We changed horses at the Golden Lion at Ashburton – a good house – and were happy to get to Ivy Bridge at two o'clock, where there was an excellent good house – the London Inn – in a retired, cool and pleasant situation. Here we dined for twelve shilling, and strolled for a while along a most romantic walk on the other side of the river above the bridge, where we sat and drank tea in the garden of a small cottage – Mrs Treglown accepting my arm on our return. We stayed at the inn until seven, when we proceeded for Plymouth, which we reached at about half after nine, and upon Mrs Treglown's recommendation – who knew the place – took up our quarters at the Fountain, Devonport, where we were very well accommodated.

Devonport is that part of the neighbourhood chiefly given over to naval matters, but is now as handsome on its own account as its elder relative, Mr Foulston having designed a splendid Town Hall which proudly overlooks Ker Street Hill, and serves a population of no less than thirty-three thousand – while Plymouth itself houses twelve thousand fewer citizens. This place is still, by Plymouthians, called Plymouth Dock – which was indeed its nomenclature until a few years ago, when the King was petitioned, and Sir Robert Peel, at that time Home Secretary, pronounced that it should be known by its present name. Its citizens are very particular in the matter, and still talk of the celebrations which marked its re-naming, celebrated by a triumphal column – again designed by the ubiquitous Foulston – which soars into the sky alongside the Town Hall and offers all who care to climb to its summit a remarkable view of the surrounding harbour and countryside.

The following day being fine, we not only mounted the monument – which provoked Mrs Treglown's generous bosom to a panting highly stimulating to the observer – but walked upon the Hoe, that splendid promenade which rises above the Sound (as the stretch of water between the harbours of Plymouth and Plymouth Dock is called), and took coffee in a small but respectable hostelry upon the Barbican, or quay, near which we were informed the earliest settlers had sent out for the New World.

Apart from these pleasures, the delights of Plymouth were soon satisfactorily inspected – and a theatre being discovered at the centre of town, the lady and I took ourselves there in the evening to a moderately satisfactory performance of Mr Farquhar's comedy of *The Beaux' Stratagem*. Mrs Treglown continued to observe the strictest rules of propriety, and, while happy to lean upon my arm and to tolerate its lying along her own while we sat in close proximity in one of the small boxes of the theatre, met the slightest familiarity, the pressure of a thigh or the insinuation of a gesture, with an innocent assurance the more titillating for its being invulnerable.

We returned to the Fountain Inn late in the evening, and the lady took herself to her room, bidding me good night with (again) a steadiness which denied any attempt upon her virtue – a virtue which I was by now suspecting of being permanently inviolable.

I sat for a while, then summoned James to bring me a night-cap to my room; which, when he appeared, I encouraged him to share – my attitude to my servants always being one of friendship, and even (should they warrant it) a certain informality. James and I having been at one time fellow-servants, a natural pleasantness was to be expected, short of absolute familiarity – which he was sufficiently well-trained to avoid.

I could not but notice that he still wore a disconsolate air, and would have been glad to offer some comfort and advice, could I but think of a way of opening the matter – which must be of some embarrassment to any man. Finally, I offered the observation that he seemed to be pleased with the company of Mrs Treglown's maid.

'Oh, she's a fine girl, sir!' he replied, energetically.

'And a giving one, I would suppose?' I answered.

He nodded, but with no special enthusiasm.

'You seem in doubt of it,' I observed.

' 'Tis not the matter of her willingness,' he said, 'but of . . .' and stuttered into a silence.

'If you will forgive me,' I said, 'while I am of your own years, more or less, I am perhaps more experienced in the way of the world, and am aware of the difficulties that may arise between a young fellow and his mistress. If I can be of any assistance . . .'

'No matter who, they could not help,' the poor young lad asserted, 'for I fear 'tis a matter for a surgeon.'

'Why, you have not the clap?' I asked (knowing full well that was not the question).

'By no means, sir,' he said, somewhat indignantly; 'no, 'tis more – more – a mechanical matter.'

'Slow to stand?' I inquired (still purposely upon the wrong track). 'Well, that is certainly a serious matter . . .'

'Not that, either,' he said, with a certain indignancy. 'Rather, being too quick to stand, I be also . . .'

'Aha!' I said – 'too quick to fall.'

The lad blushed. 'Right,' he said.

'But, my dear James, 'tis a very common problem, and one easy of cure, with the help of the lady concerned. Would your maid be willing to assist . . . ?'

'I'm sure of it,' said James; and in short he went off to seek the maid, and to persuade her to come to my room, where I could offer what advice I had in the matter. I rather wished that my sister Sophie was with us, for it had been she who had imparted to me the knowledge which I was now about to share, and while I was never shy in the company of young ladies, it would have been more proper that she should have had a private talk with

Betty than that I, not only a male but a gentleman, should open it to her.

However, there was nothing for it; and by the time James and his mistress knocked at the door, I had mustered my thoughts.

I invited them to sit, which they did – James upon one of the only two chairs in the room, with Miss Betty upon his knee, while I occupied the second chair.

'My dear,' I began, 'James has done me the honour to confide in me the difficulty which stands between you in the matter of love.'

She lowered her eyes and a delightful blush suffused her cheeks, though I could tell from her demeanour that my servant had conveyed to her the matter of which I was to speak to them.

'As I have informed him,' I continued, 'it is a question that often arises (or, rather, falls) between young lovers inexperienced in the art; the young man does not realise that for a mistress fully to enjoy the act of which we speak, the passing of considerably longer time may be necessary than that which brings him to his conclusion, and that disappointment must necessarily be the result. And even when it is made clear to him that the act must be sustained, he frequently finds it impossible to contain himself and remain at a stand for a sufficient period of time.

'I do not blush to say (for it is a common fault) that I, in my younger years, faced this same problem, but happily was offered the solution by a knowing friend, and will be happy to pass the secret on to you – though in doing so I must speak more plainly than a gentleman usually does to a female, and perhaps especially to one in your station.'

Betty blushed again, but after a while almost whispered her gratitude and her willingness to hear my explanation.

I then explained, in the simplest words at my command, that the pleasure given to the male instrument by the caresses of a willing female was so acute that in no short time a pitch of delight was achieved which must inevitably end sooner than later in the flushing forth of vital fluid, and the consequent shrinkage of the conveying cylinder.

'Now,' I continued, 'this problem necessarily becomes acute when we love. In commerce with a whore – to use frank language, Betty, for you know we are at this moment friends rather than employer and servants – it is of no moment; but with one we love, pleasure is heightened, and therefore disappointment enlarged. Something may be done by eschewing those delightful courtesies – of kissing and caressing – which normally preface the act; but we must be reluctant to reject these, while at the same time anticipation is sufficient aphrodisiac to make the eventual embrace of the male part by the equivalent female part the trigger which sets off the premature explosion.'

I saw from the cloud upon Betty's brow that my words were insufficiently clear to her, and was forced to be more explicit: 'What I mean,' I told her, 'is that toying and playing, kissing and licking, so raise the heat that the pot too quickly boils over.'

She smiled at this, though coyly hid it behind her hand. The other hand, I could not but notice, lay upon James's thigh – or rather upon the bulge within his breeches which signified just that warmth against which I was preaching!

'But you know that there are various positions which can be adopted in lovemaking.'

It was a statement rather than a question – but again I saw from the cloud upon the young girl's brow that she misunderstood me, and realised that her youth was such that in fact she had not so much as considered the matter. Happily, I had the means of illustrating my statement, and going to my luggage removed from it a portfolio of drawings copied from the works of Aretino, and showing a handsome couple in those postures which the educated lover must command. Handing these to James, I permitted him to turn the pages, which I noticed he examined with an attention quite equal to that of his mistress, and inferred that he was almost as ignorant as she in the matter of the postures of love.

In parenthesis, I should say that upon considering the matter later, I concluded that my own familiarity with these same drawings – which dated from the period when I was James's fellow-servant at Rawby – was somewhat unusual in a young person of ignoble birth; I was shown them, originally, by the grandfather of the Rawby sisters – one Beau Rust – who himself not only knew and studied them, but wished to counterfeit them, and to that end had paid myself and young Tabby to imitate them, which we had done with all the enthusiasm and energy of youth, it being our first lesson in that variation which to the educated lover lies at the very heart of the successful continuation of a connection which might otherwise swiftly be vitiated by the lethargy of boredom.

James and Betty were, by the time they reached the end of the folio, both red in cheek and somewhat flustered, and James shifted uncomfortably in his chair.

'Now,' I said, 'for the purpose of this experiment, you, Betty, must assume the position in which James lies upon his back, and you mount him – 'tis shown, I believe, in the fifth of those drawings.'

They turned the pages, and Betty giggled somewhat.

'I assure you,' I said somewhat sternly – for if the matter were to be resolved this was no matter for mirth – 'that pleasure is not diminished by the posture; indeed I am assured that for the lady, 'tis somewhat increased. At all events,' I continued, 'having assumed the position, you may enjoy your congress until that moment when James almost reaches his apogee . . .'

Another blank look interrupted me.

'Until he is about to come,' I resumed, somewhat impatiently. 'At that moment, you must raise yourself from him and grasp his instrument firmly just below its head, applying a steady pressure – almost to the point of pain. This will result in the suppression of the explosion which otherwise would be inevitable; and after a while you may resume your pleasure.

'This may be repeated several times, until either you have achieved your own satisfaction, or by some accident James's delight overflows. But in any event after a few repetitions you will find that the time which elapses between the moment of your first mounting him and the collapse of James's instrument will be lengthened, and in due course sufficiently so for you to play upon each other like a peal of bells, timing to a certainty the final chime.'

There was a short pause.

'Thank you, sir,' said Betty, though somewhat uncertainly.

'You do not trust my judgement in the matter?' I asked, perhaps upon the edge of ill-temper.

'No, no, sir,' she said hastily; ' 'tis just that for folk like we 'tis much to take in at one time. Perhaps you would allow us to borrow these papers . . . ?'

But to this I could not consent, for they were bought in Italy at no small expense, and 'twas my rule never to let them out of my possession.

Betty at this point whispered something to James, who whispered back, and then in a moment turned to me, though very uncertainly.

'Betty asks,' he stuttered, 'wh – whether you might consent to – to allow us to practise for a moment under your commanding – if 'tis not asking too much.'

I could not refuse such a request, for having offered advice 'twould have been of the utmost cruelty to decline to make it clear.

There needed no pause for readying, for the moment James's breeches were off his instrument sprang up against his belly, and indeed was so emboldened by anticipation that when he was laid upon his back and Betty, bare as a bodkin, knelt over him, 'twas almost painful to him to have it raised to the vertical. That she too was prepared for the event was beyond doubt, for, lacking no lubricant, she sank upon even that giant cock without the slightest sign of distress, its length vanishing until her bush met his own in the closest conjunction.

What would have happened had I merely loaned them the Aretino drawings I cannot think, for neither had the slightest idea of how to act. Though I have no reason to doubt that James, at least, was entirely unaccustomed to swiving, this strange (to him) posture seemed to deprive him of all instinct, while Betty contented herself with a kind of shuffling movement, rubbing her buttocks against his thighs, and at the same time bending his tool in such a way that his discomfort clearly outweighed his pleasure. This in itself might as a matter of course have had the desired effect; but that was not my intention.

There was some difficulty, too, in that Betty had never sat a horse, so my instruction to her to trot on went for nothing; and in fact it was necessary for me to climb upon the bed, stand behind her, and, placing my hands beneath her armpits, to lift and drop her several times before she got the idea, and of herself took up the proper motion. Happily, when set upon the right road, instinct is quick to learn; and within a very few moments James was incoherently attempting to convey his imminent death – at which Betty showed no sign of slowing (so keen was her own pleasure), and I had once more to take a hand, lifting her bodily from him. Seizing her hand, I placed its thumb and finger in the desired position just below the handsome bulb which stood at the end of his riding-muscle.

The pressure she exerted must have been considerable, for I could see the flesh giving way to it. The expected effect was produced, and in a short time James was inviting her to ride again – until the finishing-post was once more sighted, when the action was repeated. No less than five times he refused the final jump, until Betty, with a happy cry and an increase from trot to canter and finally to gallop brought both herself and him off in happy simultaneity, both then collapsing in a happy mass of perspiring flesh.

Their gratitude need scarcely be reported; having dressed herself, Betty went off to fetch fresh linen – my own being dampened and crinkled by their actions – while James wrung my hand again and again.

The couple then left me to myself.

I must confess that I was somewhat in pain, for the exhibition at which I had been a mere spectator (though in a manner the manager) had, I confess, roused me. Yet where was I to turn for satisfaction? I would not force myself upon Betty, even if a buttered bun (as is the common parlance for possession of a woman recently had by another) had appealed to me. Mrs Treglown was no doubt in a sleep of passionate purity; and 'twas too late now to seek out a lady of the town, though, Devonport being a naval port, there was no doubt a harbourful of such pussies to be had for a shilling.

Few men will not recognise my state, nor fail to follow me when I speak of the interminable fantasies and memories which pressed themselves upon my sleepless brain – most particularly, I must confess, of the house which my friend and I had managed in Brook Street, London (an adventure retailed in my volume *Eros in Town*); being then some years younger, I had not – at least, so it now seemed – been aware of the privilege of living day in and day out in a house populated by some of the most beautiful young women in the city, each for much of the day clad in the most appealing *dishabille*, and any one of whom would have regarded it as no less an honour than a duty to have permitted me the most egregious intimacy, or to have given me, upon my request, every pleasure at their command.

What would I not have given to be for half an hour returned to that harem, to repair to the bed of Sally or Xanthe, Cissie or Rose, or the charming Ginevra, and to enjoy their practised caresses? Then there came to plague me the most vivid memories of other women – the delicious girls of Italy, of Egypt, of Ceylon, of Siam . . .

But in short, I was condemned to my lonely bed,

relieved only towards dawn by the dream of a Circassian maid whose attentions brought me to involuntary ecstasy.

Next morning, we set out for Cornwall – for it was agreed that Mrs Treglown should travel with me as far as the town of Liskeard, where we would go our separate ways. We crossed the river Tamar into that county upon a ferry rowed by eight strong men; and on the further shore our luggage was placed in a carriage commissioned for the purpose – Frank's equipage having been stabled at Plymouth Dock until I should need it for a return to London, for it would have been expensive and super-erogatory to ship it across the wide river.

As we drove into Cornwall it was to the sound of the merry voices of James and Betty, singing as they sat upon the box.

Mrs Treglown in a while observed that they were more cheerful than had been their wont of late, and asked whether I knew why?

I said that I believed that their high spirits were the result of the resolution of a problem.

She was silent for a while, and then asked if I meant that their affair had progressed to the point at which James had been permitted the ultimate favour?

It was, I remarked, a little more than that.

In what way, she asked?

Whether it will be considered the conduct of a gentle-man or no, I must confess that I enlightened her. Truth to tell, I was by now thoroughly tired of her touch-me-not flouncing. If she was determined to permit a gentleman no familiarity, why had she consented to travel in a closed carriage with him for several days? Was my action in rescuing her from an uncomfortable – nay, perhaps fatal – circumstance to go entirely unrewarded?

At all events, goaded by her goodness, I described in full detail the predicament our servants had faced, my advice in the matter, and the culminating passage which had resulted in their mutual enjoyment of each other, and the consequent lifting of their spirits.

It took no great powers of observation to remark that her own spirits were lifted by my narrative. Her breath now came short, her breasts rose and fell more quickly, her fingers toyed with her fan. Nor could I believe that she did not remark my distress – distress I say, for my arousal was such that my trousers, fashionably tightly cut, now painfully constricted that part of my anatomy analogous to the instrument with which Betty had so admirably coped, in James.

I could not resist it – I threw myself upon her, my hand slipping into her bodice, there to find a springy, delicious dome the tip of which was an adamant knot which almost scratched my palm, so ardently erect was it! There could be no doubt: the lady was as ready for the combat as I! Indeed, her lips parted to meet my own, her tongue as ready as mine to embrace.

Yet what was this? Once more, after but a moment, she withdrew her lips, seized my wrist and wrenched my hand from her breast. For a moment she panted, then drawing herself up:

'Mr Archer,' she said, 'I beg you, desist. Cognisant as I am of all your kindness, apprehensive of your generosity, proud to be the object of your passion – I cannot be yours. A gentleman such as I know you to be will be unwilling to take advantage of a female who cannot permit those familiarities which . . .' (her eyelids drooped to hide eyes in which, I could swear, passion still burned) '. . . would lead to a result desired only by the senses, and which would be, I assure you, tragic for both.'

I could do nothing but withdraw – though to pretend that I did so with good grace would be to put myself forward as an angel; and at that moment 'twas the Devil who would have had the upper hand, had I given him the opportunity.

We rode on in silence – I am ashamed to say, sullen silence – until, not long after midday, we drew into the main square of Liskeard.

There, Mrs Treglown descended, and had to walk but a few yards to a carriage which awaited her (summoned by a fast messenger sent the previous day from Plymouth Dock). She made her curtsy to me; I bowed to her. I was in no doubt that her feelings towards me were warm; but could not comprehend her refusal to be kind. Our parting was regrettably cold – which could not be said for that of Betty and James, whose embrace was long, and sufficiently hot to provoke encouraging cries from the yokels standing nearby.

I descended and took lunch at Webb's Hotel, while Mrs Treglown's carriage rattled down the street and down the county. I realised that I had not the slightest notion where she lived.

Finally – and after, I must confess, several glasses of claret – I shook my head, and turned my thoughts to the estate to which I must now make my way.

Chapter Four

Sophie's Story

It was not long before I heard again from the interesting M. Foutarque.

A message was brought me one morning, written upon writing-paper bearing the seal of the French Embassy, and requesting an interview later that day. I sent back by the footman (none other than the ready Jacques, who met my eye with a frankness illustrated by a smile at once friendly yet devoid of pertness) a note requesting the Frenchman to call upon me after luncheon.

He greeted me with the greatest politeness, accepting coffee rather than wine, complimenting me upon the decoration of my rooms, and not giving by the slightest hint of discourtesy any intimation of undue familiarity.

After a while, he came to the point, which was that his Ambassador wished to give an entertainment for a party of visiting representatives of his Government who (though M. Foutarque did not put it in so many words) it would be to his advantage to impress. The gentlemen concerned were young – as were many members of the Ultra-royalist party now in the ascendant in France – and it was the Ambassador's understanding that female company would be welcome to them. He – M. Foutarque, that is – had been commissioned to look about the town in quest of young persons of my sex who might be secured for some entertainment; but had been disappointed, the company most readily available being invariably of a low order, and not such as would give an impression of amiability.

I gathered that the gentlemen in question had little experience of intrigues of an amorous nature, and M. Foutarque readily admitted his own inexperience in the matter – King Louis XVIII being, as he explained, a cold and distant monarch not given to pleasure, who had collected about himself a court and ministers whose members shared his lack of interest in the earthier matters of life, which indeed had in general been condemned since the late Revolution.

However (the Frenchman said, coming at last to the point), some of the younger politicians of the age took a more vigorously amorous view of things, and the Ambassador had been given to understand (under the secrecy of his diplomatic boxes) that an entertainment of an erotic nature would be welcome to the visitors. So what was needed was someone to organise the same.

'You will correct me, *madame*, if I am mistaken, but I am given to understand that in time past you presided over a house of entertainment in Chiswick.'

I admitted it; but pointed out that it had been a house in which gentlemen were kept for the entertainment of ladies, rather than the other way about.

'So I understood,' said Foutarque; 'yet I cannot but believe that the experience must have brought you a considerable knowledge of the way in which such matters are best set about; and it is my commission on behalf of the Ambassador to invite you to arrange an evening's entertainment of a – a – of such a nature as you will understand. I need not say that any fee you may think proper will be paid to the participating ladies, and to yourself; while as an earnest of his goodwill the Duc asks you to accept this gift' – whereupon he whipped out from his back pocket a small leather pouch, and from it drew the most magnificent emerald ring, which he set upon the small table at my side.

Preventing myself – if with some effort – from diving straightway upon it, I inclined my head and said that it would give me great pleasure to serve the Ambassador, for the mutual friendship of our nations, and enquired the number of gentlemen to be entertained – which was to be a round dozen – and the date by which the entertainment must be ready – which was within the week, and gave me little time for my arrangements. I then rose immediately, assured M. Foutarque that the matter was in good hands, bade him farewell, and straightway sat down to write some letters.

My experience at Chiswick was of little use to me – but what perhaps the Frenchman had not known was that my half-brother Frank and his friend Andy had at that same time furnished and equipped perhaps the finest house of pleasure for gentlemen in town – and being of a methodical nature, I had kept about me a list of some of the ladies who had worked there, many of whom indeed I counted as friends. Though they were somewhat dispersed, there were some upon whom I believed I could count if not for their personal intervention, at least for advice. Sending out the letters upon that same day, I did not rest, but set about other matters not entirely unconnected with the coming event, which involved the bespeaking of a large room in Covent Garden and its furnishing, at one end, with a low stage; the decoration of that stage with various cloths and properties; and the provision of certain comforts for the body of the room itself.

Upon the day in question, mid-evening saw me fully prepared to receive the guests, who in time appeared, escorted by M. Foutarque and replete from a good dinner at the Embassy at which wine had evidently flowed freely – not too freely, I trusted, to have deprived the gentlemen of their sense of corporeal pleasure, for I did not wish my efforts to go unwasted.

I soon concluded that I need have no concern, however, for the gentlemen were young and lusty, and, though I understood that no hint of the kind of entertainment in store had been dropped, upon their first sight of the room I had prepared their eyes brightened, and they exchanged a number of comments in their native tongue which I understood as being expressive of proper anticipation.

The room indeed had an air of seduction. The gentlemen who had decorated the Brook Street apartments of my half-brother had hung it in velvets and silks which disguised otherwise bare, cracked walls (the room, though indeed used in general for the purpose for which I intended it, was usually contracted to the poorer sort of person, and lacked the conditions of luxury). At one end of the room stood the stage, covered with a green cloth and hung about with curtains which I had obtained from the Theatre Royal in Drury Lane, suggestive of a woodland glade. Here also were soft stuffed cushions representing little mounds or grassy banks, obtained from the same source.

The body of the hall contained twelve small gilt chairs set out in rows; but around the walls and elsewhere in the room were comfortable sophas or *chaises-longues*, together with more large cushions spread for comfort as much as decoration; and the whole lit by candles, the brightest light being at the front of the stage, where a row of candles was set out before reflecting mirrors, as used now in the best theatres – the rest of the apartment being lit merely to a soft glow.

The gentlemen were greeted with a glass of champagne, borne upon a tray by a young black boy – the son of a gentleman who had been one of the most popular stallions of my Chiswick stable; and in a buzz of interest settled themselves upon the chairs and waited with what seemed keen anticipation – answered almost immediately by the soft sounds of a guitar behind the scenes, and the appearance upon the stage of six maidens apparelled like Grecian nymphs, who disposed themselves in a pleasant group for the approbation of the audience.

I am the first to admit that my knowledge of the fashion of clothing worn by nymphs is not great, and was in this case based merely on the appearance of those classical statues upon view in the great Museum in Russell Street. I had obtained from a shop in the Burlington Arcade a length of the finest material, so thin as to resemble something spun by spiders rather than by the hands of man. This had been cut into half a dozen lengths – which allowed only a relatively skimpy portion for each girl, the material being sufficiently costly to inhibit my spending more upon it (despite M. Foutarque's assurance that all my expenses would be met). Both by its nature and skimpiness it revealed as much as it concealed; and where it concealed, did so most imperfectly.

I had been fortunate in my friends, who, though they were all now permanently retired from the profession which had first brought them into contact with me, had

been from their nature unable entirely to separate themselves from the society in which they had formerly been
employed, and were thus able to recommend a number
of handsome young ladies whose charms were as diverse
as their faces and figures: here a chubby cherub whose
youthful figure was full, her breasts positively inviting
the support of a gentleman's palm; there another whose
torso might almost be that of a boy, were it not that her
movements were clearly informed by a feminine grace;
here a tall and willowy girl whose thighs seemed prolonged almost to an infinite extent; there one who could
only be called plump, yet whose appeal was in direct
proportion to the plentiful, rosy flesh which hung upon
her frame.

There was a ripple of applause from the interested
audience as the ladies took their places – when almost
immediately, with a discordant note upon the guitar, an
equal number of satyrs leaped rather than strode upon
the stage. The reception given to them was one as much
of surprise as approbation – for they seemed almost
inhuman, much of their bodies covered with thick animal hair, and their male members each entirely ready
for amorous conquest, so that both in their appearance
and readiness they provoked as much astonishment as
envy.

As to the latter, I should explain that, until a moment
before the girls entered upon the stage, they had been
employed – on my instructions – in provoking their
partners, by various means, into the proper state of
excitation, the angles of appreciative rigidity diminish-
ing by only a degree or so before they presented themselves to the public view; and now, each making for his
partner, the prospect before them was sufficiently

inspiriting to maintain them in the state of arousal in which they were first seen.

Their general appearance had been achieved without difficulty. The manager of costumes at the Lane had supplied to me a large quantity of human hair, generally used for the provision of beards for those actors incapable of growing their own, and a bulk of horse-hair used for other purposes. After explaining the nature of the entertainment I had devised, I encouraged my players, first removing their clothing, to daub their bodies with a quantity of gum which I had obtained from the same source.

They at first showed considerable reluctance – but one of them, himself an actor, was able to assure the others that the gum could be easily dissolved by the application of a certain spirit (of which I also had a supply), and even demonstrated the same, whereupon they surrendered, and in no short time were using the gum to apply the hair to their own and each other's bodies, covering their legs, buttocks and lower chests with hair – so that in a brief time they bore the closest resemblance to satyrs that could be wished for. My own task was merely to provide the finishing touches, ensuring that their appearance was sufficiently wild by applying here and there an additional tuft or curl.

The ladies, when brought together in rehearsal, were at first amused and then to a degree excited by the sight of their partners – which indeed was an interesting one, for amid the clusters of hair which covered the gentlemen's bodies there soon arose, upon their closer proximity with the nymphs, an element which, while recognisably as human as it was male, was by its relative nudity even more striking than was usually the case.

Indeed, so amorous did the couples become (upon my pairing them off) that I had some difficulty in restraining their enthusiasm to the proper degree, resulting in mere excitation rather than any actual accomplishment.

Once upon the stage, however, there was no further need for restraint – and indeed that would have been inappropriate. The largest of the satyrs was a man normally engaged in delivering coals, and therefore equipped with an enviable strength (he was also, incidentally, so sufficiently hirsute that it had been almost unnecessary to decorate him with additional material!). Chosen by me for the central role of my tableau, he now seized upon a nymph and raised her into the air by the simple expedient of placing his hands beneath her buttocks. As the others formed an admiring group about the couple, she threw her legs about his waist, and he was able, simply by drawing her body towards him, to insert his powerful instrument into the sheath most appropriate for its receipt, aided by the youngest nymph, who appeared a mere child (though in fact older than she was ready to admit), who ensured that the target was properly reached by the careful manipulation of the coalman's remarkable member. Upon his fully accomplishing of his aim, there was more applause from the audience as he began by the motion of his powerful arms to move his mistress in such a way as to give them both satisfaction.

The other couples now disposed themselves in various ways about the stage. One satyr turned his maiden – the plumpest in view – so that while she bent double, holding on to the lowest branch of a tree (actually, of a chair covered with a green cloth) he was able to enter her from the rear – affording the audience an excellent view of the proceeding. Another laid himself down upon a tussock while his friend bestrode him; a fourth, over-eager for the fray, merely threw himself upon his partner in the most conventional of poses, their eagerness – her loins reaching upwards to meet his on the descend with a positive and vigorous *slap*! – compensating for the mundane nature of their action; while a fifth addressed his attentions to an aperture which, while proximate to the proper one, is more rarely used for the purpose, his friend giving a short cry of surprise which in no time turned to an expression of pleasure as the unusual friction was joined by that afforded by the application of her lover's forefinger to the most eager part of her body. The final couple took up a position right at the front of the platform, so that the candle-light burnished their skins almost to gold; here, the nymph lay upon her back and persuaded her satyr to kneel above her in such a manner that while he could pleasure her with his agile tongue, she at the same time was able to take his member between her lips while simultaneously toying with his cods in a suggestive and pleasant manner – so pleasant, indeed, that in a very short time his excitement was too great to bear, and his pleasure reached its apogee as he spent liberally upon her breasts.

At this, a young Frenchman sitting in the front row – and therefore only a short distance from them – could no longer contain himself, and, pausing only to remove his breeches, gave the red-faced satyr a push which sent him sprawling, and took his place (though in a more usual pose). In no time he was at the game, his coat-tails swinging over his bare rump as he lunged appreciatively.

I now gave a signal, and a further six young ladies, all clad – or rather unclad – for just such an evening's entertainment as was now under way, entered the room;

and in less time that I can relate, each of the French gentlemen was in Britain – or in a Briton; and my satyrs disconsolately made their way from the stage, their partners now otherwise employed.

Pausing only to see that matters were as I would wish them, I took myself to the neighbouring room, where most of the gentlemen were already removing the hair from their bodies, and moved among them with purses of guineas, which were most appreciatively received – even by the couple who, too moved by their recent experience to remain unsatisfied, lay together in a corner, pausing only momentarily in their activities to take their purses with mumbled thanks (their mothers evidently having failed to instruct them not to speak with their mouths full).

In a short while most of the gentlemen had taken themselves off; I realised then that I had still one purse with me. Searching for its owner, I walked upon the side of the stage, and saw a satyr concealing himself behind a curtain and watching with attention the scene before him (which indeed was one which, while I hesitate to describe it for fear of offending the sensibilities of my readers, was of a perfectly amorous nature).

Walking forward, I tapped him upon his shoulder, whereat he started and looked up, proving to be the most youthful of the group, a mere boy of perhaps seventeen years who was engaged by the company at Drury Lane for small parts – an activity for which he now seemed to me to be but imperfectly suited, for on his turning he revealed a part which was far from small, and indeed so distended that it must surely be positively painful to him.

I must confess that it is ever my sorrow to see hunger unsatisfied – especially in those of tender years; and stretching out my hand raised the unwilling satyr to his feet, attempting with my other hand to conceal that part of his anatomy that even two hands could scarcely have disguised. By laying my hand upon the limb in question, I at once signalled that I was not offended at its impudence, while at the same time conveying the hope that its hunger might shortly be assuaged. The satyr, young in years but clearly quick in apprehension, accompanied me without argument to the now deserted dressing-room, where, laying myself down upon a pile of spare cushions, I drew him after me, and in a moment was able to satisfy myself that the boy was as able as he was willing.

The truth was that he was the satyr who had over-speedily reached his climax, and started the party which still progressed next door; but this, it seems, must have been due to his inexperience, for the more conventional congress which now took place was quite sufficiently prolonged to satisfy me, his at first excited and febrile thrusting soon quieting itself to a sort of swinging gait which by simple perseverance raised me not once but twice to my apogee; whereat, satisfied, I brought him off by the simple expedient of twisting some of the hair which decorated his rump and tearing it away by sheer force, the sudden pain of which did his business.

On his raising himself, we found that the muck of sweat which had perforce accompanied his efforts – the heat of the candles having greatly raised the temperature of the apartment – had loosened the hair which had decorated his thighs, lower belly and chest, much of which now adhered to my body; something which caused us considerable amusement. The superfluous decoration however was easily removed by the simple application of a wet cloth, while I was forced to assist the boy by using spirit to remove the hair from his back, revealing a body as devoid of hair as a girl's, a pair of deliciously round and hard posteriors rousing my spirits so that only his exhaustion precluded a renewal of our recent enjoyment. His instrument, while enlarging itself under the pleasure of my touch, stopped short of complete rigidity, even under the attention of my lips; whereat the boy apologised prettily, admitting in the end that on that morning he had twice enjoyed a maid at his lodging house – and that the fourth encounter of the day had 'finished him'.

Needless to say, I sympathised, carefully taking a note of his name before he left, professing his eagerness to serve in any future entertainment of the same nature, for (said he) being paid to perform an action he so enjoyed was positively gilding the gingerbread.

It was past three in the morning before I was able to persuade my French guests to leave, for while several of them had by midnight fallen into a sleep comprised equally of drunkenness and corporeal satisfaction, three or four seemed insatiable, and each partnered several girls before they declared themselves contented. I could not but feel that M. Foutarque should be satisfied, as I saw the last of the girls from the now disordered room and locked the door upon a state of chaos which it would be a matter for others to clear up.

To be short about it, M. Foutarque was as good as his word – as was indeed M. le Duc de Laval, for, apart from providing the purses of gold for my performers, on the day following the entertainment he had another purse delivered at my house, which upon examination contained some fifty pounds – a payment which seemed distinguished by profligacy – so the exercise was quite as satisfactory (in a financial sense) as might have been hoped.

The week after this interesting escapade, I was invited by Chichley to make use of his box at Drury Lane – he and his wife being absent in the country – on the occasion of Mrs Sloman's performance of Juliet; whereupon, on the Nurse entering the stage accompanied by her servant Peter, I thought his appearance to be somewhat familiar to me – and on his speaking was assured that it was none other than John Rice, the young man whose attentions I had enjoyed during the closing hours of my entertainment. I found myself surprisingly pleased to see him again, and after the performance – during which he distinguished himself as much as was possible given the diminutive nature of the part – went around to the stage door-keeper's box and on slipping him a shilling gained entrance to the back of the stage and made my way, on direction, to the lad's dressing-room.

I am not sure that I could satisfactorily explain my motive in so doing – except that I had taken to the boy, which in itself is surely a sufficient motive for a lady of spirit? As I was some years his elder, it would perhaps provide the opportunity for me to help him in his theatrical career.

On reaching the dressing-room door, I knocked and immediately threw it open, revealing a number of gentlemen in, or partly in, or partly out of, their small-clothes – who nevertheless, being used to close proximity with actresses, who are as little given to the taking of offence as to undue modesty, took little notice of me, and continued their dressing and undressing.

I must remark, in parenthesis, that I have some sympathy with the late Dr Samuel Johnson, who, upon introduction to the pleasures of the theatre dressing-rooms, remarked at length to his friend Mr Boswell that he would go no more behind the scenes, lest the bosoms of the actresses arouse his amorous propensities. There is indeed a peculiar attraction about the scene, attributable perhaps to the glamour of the performances in which the actors have lately been engaged – and partly, no doubt, to the fact that for the most part their companionship is to be easily purchased by any interested party. It has been the custom for certain members of the aristocracy to introduce their male progeny to the art of love through the convenient services of actresses, who even in youth have through the moral laxity of their profession gained experience in the matter valuable to schoolboys adept at the conjugation of Latin verbs, but not in conjunction of a more corporeal nature.

The sight which met my eyes, then, was a delightful one; and when from among the cluster of male bodies my friend came forward immediately, though dressed only in his shirt (which offered entrancing confirmation of my recollection of a pair of lower limbs remarkable both for muscularity and shapeliness), and greeted me with a kiss upon the lips which I much confess to finding sweet, I was the more pleased.

'So my note reached you, Mrs Nelham!' he remarked; 'I trust it gave no offence?' – a remark which reduced me to a puzzled silence. Seeing my expression, he himself was confused, and when I informed him that no such communication had reached me, his expression changed to one of embarrassment. However, when encouraged he confessed that he had been so taken with my company (I report his words without the intention to boast) that he wished to ensure a further meeting, and had therefore invited me to accompany him to a stage entertainment on this very evening!

The coincidence was too convenient not to be meaningful, and I accepted with pleasure – at which he immediately donned his breeches, and prepared to set forth. On my inquiring the nature of the entertainment, he blushed somewhat, and said that 'twas one of which he had had no personal experience, but which, judging from the occasion on which we had met, was something in which I would be interested – that is, of a libidinous nature (though he expressed it by the statement that ' 'tis a cock-raising occasion', which was clear enough; and I did not embarrass him by pointing out that such entertainments were not the usual thing for me, outside of a business engagement).

We walked from Covent Garden to a house in the district of Soho, where, on his knocking on a street-door and exchanging a word, we were admitted to what seemed a private house, and escorted to a room on the first floor where a table was set for supper – and indeed shortly a very decent meal was served, with sufficient beer and wine.

The company was a mixed one, the other ladies present being of a somewhat lower social class than was usual with me – though agreeable enough; and at any event my own experience was such as had brought me into contact with women of every condition, all of whom I took as I found – usually discovering most of them to be good-natured enough, if unprovoked.

The feast having come to an end, we sat for a while over our wine, and John was good enough to pay me the compliment of saluting me several times with his lips, first upon the cheek, then upon the shoulder – my gown being cut low enough to permit not only this, but a further kiss upon the upper part of my breast. He was by now somewhat warm, as I discovered when, entirely by accident, my hand fell upon his upper thigh, discovering as it travelled inadvertently upwards a tumid pipette which signified the arousal of his spirits. My unconsciously pressing the same with my palm resulted in his slipping his hand, no doubt idly, under my skirts, where he soon found what he sought.

I cannot say what would next have occurred, had there not been a sudden stirring at the end of the room – when there entered a guitarist whom I recognised as the young man I had myself engaged (London is a small city) accompanied by a fellow with a tambour or small drum; and on their striking up a dance, a couple dressed in the manner of the Italian *commedia del' arte* as Columbine and Pantaloon, entered the room, leaped upon the table and began a spirited dance.

It soon became clear that their elaborate costumes were in fact ingeniously constructed, and fastened not by the usual employment of needle and thread, but by some other means which enabled the dancers to escape from them without effort – for upon Columbine reaching out, she in a second detached Pantaloon's collar; then he her *fichu*; then she one of his sleeves – then he one of hers; until, dancing the whole while, they were both reduced to nothing but a scarf about the loins, almost entirely revealing two bodies handsome enough to give as much pleasure to the eye as the most elaborately designed costume.

The rhythm of the dance now slowed, and in a languorous weaving motion they moved about each other upon the table above us, their hands gliding over each other's persons, over shoulders, under arms; one moment his hand would brush the engorged nipples of her breast, the next the back of hers would glance across his belly, whence a line of dark hairs descended into his groin, where the distinct shape of an upright staff revealed that his enjoyment of the engagement was as keen as that of any of the onlookers.

Many of the latter (though not my companion, whose youth was necessarily accompanied still by some shyness) had by now climbed or been helped out of their clothes, and were paying the dancers, without embarrassment, that peculiar form of compliment always aroused by the demonstration of beauty in action.

Finally, the dancers having performed every libidinous action which could be conceived, each at the same time, upon a peculiarly bitter chord upon the guitar, reached out and divested the other of the last covering – the lady revealing a quim entirely devoid of hair: a mouth entrancingly marked by lips of the palest pink, between which a slash of darker flesh marked the enviable entrance. Her partner, a man of uncertain years, but clearly in the greatest vigour, wore a muff which must have been carefully trimmed, for there were no random curls, but a closely cropped crown which enhanced by emphasis the base of a staff the angle of whose standing bespoke ample strength for its purpose – which was shortly accomplished, the lady merely dropping backwards so that, like an acrobat in an old picture, she supported herself upon her hands and feet, like a table, her body parallel to the ground.

Her companion now stepped forward between her open thighs, and, dropping to his knees, in a moment speared her – whereupon she threw back her head, her

fine black hair falling to the very table's top, and emitted
a positive yowl of pleasure, like nothing so much as that
of a cat being pleasured upon a neighbouring roof-top.

Though, as my constant readers will know, I do not
proclaim myself a *voyeur*, I must confess that this handsome couple, engaged in the act in such close proximity,
conveyed the pleasure of it to me so keenly that I almost
felt I was experiencing it: my seated position permitted
me to look up between the lady's legs, where with the
utmost clarity I saw her partner's member working,
piston-like, at its duty, the light of the candles (almost
dangerously close-by) gleaming upon its shaft, now
lubricated by the natural serum of love – while the
unthatched lips of her pleasure-cave seemed to embrace
it almost with the motions of a mouth, for I could swear
that I saw them tighten about it as it withdrew, to close
again as it re-entered.

Suddenly I was brought back to reality, for – quite
unconsciously, I assure you – my hand had under the
excitement of the moment found its way inside John's
breeches (whether unloosed by him or by myself, I cannot say) and my fingers had closed around his apprehensive part – which now, to my horror, I felt give a bound
which seemed to signal the immediate downflow of those
liquids whose release must deprive a lady of all further
pleasure.

I whipped my hand away as from a flame – and at the
same time with my other hand removed his own from
between my thighs, where by an incessant movement it
had, I confess, been giving me some pleasure.

The poor boy looked hurt, but by my smile I was able
to comfort him by the assurance of better things to
come – while at the same moment, above us, another cry

from the lady signalled the culmination of the act; for, withdrawing, her partner laid upon her belly the tribute of his pleasure; whereupon a strange noise echoed around the room, a kind of soft drumming which at first confused me, until looking about I discovered that the gentlemen present were applauding the performers by knocking their distended members upon the table-top!

Some of them, the moment the table had been cleared, disappeared beneath it with their partners; others made their way slyly from the room – no doubt to other private rooms available in the house.

John looked at me somewhat confused, not knowing, I think, what to say or do. I however rose, and resting my hand upon his bade him button himself.

'I have a more comfortable place than this,' I said, and motioned him to accompany me.

The journey to Chiswick was all too long, especially as I had to spend much of the time (much against my will) dissuading my companion from those over-warm familiarities which I feared might lead to the dissipation of his energies before our arrival. Once at my house, however, my bedroom provided us with more luxury than would have been available in any common knocking shop. John's face was a picture as he saw the extent of my comfort. I am sure that he had not realised the state in which I lived; but his amazement did not last long, for in a moment he had thrown off his clothes and was bouncing upon the sheets of my bed, and clearly inviting me to join him.

However, he had not washed himself since leaving the stage of the theatre, and if there is one thing upon which I insist (if it is convenient) it is the cleanliness of my partners in the act; in the ecstasy of love we need not repine should we be led to intimate caresses the pleasure of which would be inhibited by the presence of grease and grime. (I speak, of course, for those of us for whom the rank sweat of an enseamed bed, as Shakespeare's effete Hamlet put it, does not contribute to sensual excitement.) My servants' last duty every night is to place several containers of hot water in my bedroom, in case I should have company. In the winter these are kept warm by the propinquity of a large fire; in summer, however, as it now was, the waters are of just such a pleasant warmth as to be refreshing.

John was at first doubtful of the whole matter; but on my persuading him to enter the water, I was able to show him that the very act of being sponged by an attentive lover can contribute much to the anticipation of pleasures to come; and it was indeed my own delight to ensure that the most intimate crevices of his slender body were so clean that, should I wish to kiss any part of it, nothing but sweetness would await me.

Taking the idea, he was now pleased to attend to me in turn, taking special care of my breasts, which he clearly admired – for on our retiring at last to bed, it was to these that he paid particular tribute, kissing and mumbling the nipples, softly nipping them with his teeth, taking them between his fingers almost with the curiosity of a squirrel examining a nut; and finally, kneeling astride me, tickling them by the application of his very member itself, drawing back the skin at its tip so that its bland domed end could gently buffet them. This gave me such painful pleasure that the distension could no longer be born, and, taking his staff in my hands, I wrapped my breasts about it, simply in order to prevent for a moment the tickling.

His expression at this was one of the most egregious pleasure; and in a moment he began that motion which was wasted in such a pose. I threw up my legs, and with a heave of my body I positively pinned his neck between my calves; and seizing his small buttocks forced him not unwillingly to serve me as Adam first served Eve; our joint apprehension being such that only a very few motions of his body brought us off – whereat we collapsed and in a moment fell asleep in each other's arms.

Twice that night I was roused again: the first time by his instrument growing within me, for he had not withdrawn it, and in its shrunken state it had not fallen away (our close propinquity being such); and the second time when I awoke to find him lying behind me, a thigh thrust between my own, and his member again showing signs of affection which it was my duty to return, which I soon did by the simple expedient of reaching between my thighs and persuading it once more into its proper place, whereupon, half-asleep, he reached around to seize my breasts, pressed his face into my neck, and began a rocking motion which by its very quietness aroused feelings of such tenderness that I almost sobbed with the pleasure.

I next awoke when Charles brought my breakfast tray – retiring to return with a second cup, having with his sharp eye discerned the tousled black head of my companion almost concealed beneath the bed-clothes. John, waking at this, looked confused; but, upon seeing that Charles was not disconcerted, sat up, thrust his arm about me, and gave me a smacking kiss while at the same time reaching for a piece of bread.

Though he made a pretence of ease, I could see that he scarcely knew how to address me; whereat it was my duty to place him at his ease – and in brief, to offer him the hospitality of my house for a while. This may, but need not, surprise the reader: the truth is that I had been for some time now deprived of constant male companionship – something of which I am always keenly apprehensive; this young man interested me, and apart from the pleasure of his company – which I admit I found considerable – it seemed to me that I could be useful to him in educating him in the manners of the better sort of person, which would be of help in his career (for it is to the advantage of acting folk that they can counterfeit the behaviour of gentlemen).

Though my house was somewhat distant from the theatre, its comfort and – who can say? – perhaps the pleasure of my company persuaded him to accept my invitation, and fetching his belongings (which were not so numerous that they could not be encompassed within a couple of parcels) he moved into one of the servants' rooms – to him luxurious by its space, and convenient to us both by its being separated from my own only by a corridor and a staircase, neither of which proved obstacles to his progress to my bed on frequent occasions, even after the most exhausting of theatrical performances; none of which precluded the performance of a part more universal even than that of the drama's most notable hero.

Chapter Five

The Adventures of Andy

It was clear from the moment I was driven through the park gates at Vycken that my friend had inherited a very fine estate indeed.

Passing through the town of Lostwithiel, now insignificant but once the capital of the country, we had mounted one hill, descended another, then made off to the south and entered a series of narrow lanes winding through deep, heavily wooded clefts in the Cornish hills, eventually coming to a small keeper's house where two tall granite columns surmounted by mossy balls held a pair of handsome wrought-iron gates. The hills then drew aside, as if in deference to the visitor, and a broad valley stretched before me, its floor a broad parkland, trees giving heavy shade to cattle, which stood in groups that seemed carefully arranged to give the landscape point and drama.

At length there came into view the house itself – its façade of that granite from which so many buildings of the county are constructed. Consisting of a single-storeyed central building with two wings, one at each end, it had a symmetry exceedingly graceful to the eye, and seen at its best as the pathway swung about before it, to pass through a gate-house (from the window of which an ancient retainer hung, waving a hand and shortly afterwards retiring to ring, with a fine clangour, a bell which hung above the gateway).

From the gate-house, a splendid avenue of beeches and sycamores led to a second gate, through the east wing of the house itself, where was a cobbled forecourt where we stopped before the main door, which opening now disgorged at least twenty servants who by the time I had descended had formed into double ranks through which I passed, nodding from left to right like a monarch, but without at that time being able to take note of any individual faces.

I was greeted with a low but informal bow by the housekeeper – the steward – the butler – I know not what to call him – Mr Antony Treweers, who as it was to turn out had reigned over the place for the past thirty years, since the owner himself had virtually retired from life to reside solely in his bed-chamber, a poor room at the back of the house. His mania was for complete quiet, to which end he had thick blankets hung in many layers about his room on all sides, covering even the windows, his life being lived entirely by candle-light. The candles catching light to some of the hangings, he had been smothered one night in his sleep, and the burning down of the entire building only avoided by the lucky accident of a maid, rising early, sniffing smoke as she passed down the corridor outside his room.

It was at five in the afternoon that I arrived, but on walking into the hall – set just inside the main door, and proving a nicely proportioned long chamber panelled in some dark wood – I found nevertheless a table groaning under an immense quantity of food which, after a short pause to refresh myself and answer the necessities of nature, I was glad to sit down to.

The Cornish notion of hospitality depends largely upon food, which one finds always offered in great profusion, even by the poorest family living in the utmost poverty: when potato cakes or even seaweed pie will be placed before one, and one must eat it with enthusiasm if one is not to offend.

On this occasion I had in fact a healthy hunger, and was able to do some justice to the table – despite the fact that the banquet seemed to me to be strangely composed, for rather than coming in courses, as we in London eat it, the food was all set on the table at once. Here was fresh-boiled buttock of beef with onions; squab pie (layers of apple, bacon, onions and mutton, all piled upon a young squab or pigeon); leek and pork pie – into which thick cream had been poured; goose and parsnip on one dish; giblet pie (the neck, liver and other entrails of a goose, flavoured with raisins, sugar and apples); and at the centre of the table a chief delicacy of the county, known as starry-gazy pie: that is, a pie of pilchards baked with the fish lying in it, their heads projecting through the crust and their eyes goggling at the ceiling!

My enjoyment of the latter dish, to which my attention was drawn with great ceremony, was somewhat dampened when I discovered upon my plate a fish's backbone of extraordinary hardness. The woman who had served me immediately said 'Let me see, my dear!' and seized the plate, rooted about upon it, and then exclaimed: 'Why, that edn' no fish bone at all. That's our Johnny's hair comb, what he lost two days ago – careless little emp!'

This would have put some people off their meat – and I might have been among them, had not the food been so rich and delicious, and the servants so eager and willing to please – Mr Treweers among them, who stood at my side throughout, seeing that a large tankard before me was kept full of first-rate cider, prepared upon the estate, for which it is justly famous. I might have been less inclined to consume so much as I did had I known at that time that the drink's excellence was owed in no small degree (so the master of the cider press later informed me) to the practice common at Vycken, as elsewhere in Cornwall, of always putting a toad into the cask, the cider being purified by passing again and again through the creature's body. Indeed, no cider in this county is considered up to the mark unless it has a toad to 'work' it, some toads living for over twenty years in this fermenting work (when the cask is empty the creature is tipped out through the bung-hole, and the people standing by exclaim: 'Mind the toad, mind the toad, save 'un for the next brewing!').

Mr Treweers, encouraging me to try this dish and that, finally so pressed upon me large helpings of excellent blackberry pie that I could scarcely stand when, it being almost eight o'clock, I rose and made my way unsteadily to the chamber prepared for me. I only dizzily noticed that this was a fine, great room over the main hall, with a window stretching from floor to ceiling through which I had an expansive view over the park even from my bed, before, thrusting off my clothes and falling upon rather than into the vast four-posted bed, I instantly fell into a deep sleep from which I awoke to see the sun slanting over the park as he rose, and to hear a dawn chorus which, truth to tell, sounded extremely clamorous to a brain still somewhat under the effect of the cider – a drink which, while inspiriting to a degree, is not kind to the heads of those unaccustomed to it.

I staggered from the bed to the window, squinting at the sun; and only upon hearing laughter from below the window realised that I was standing in the full view of a quartet of maidservants, who now stood quite frankly goggling at the sight of their new master displaying himself entirely uncovered, and in that state in which gentlemen frequently awake after a night's debauch – *id est*, piss-proud. It being too late for concealment, I gravely inclined my head and raised a hand in greeting, merely clutching at the window curtain and raising it, as though absently, to cover that area of my anatomy which is normally concealed from public view. The maids dropped me a curtsy and passed on, their heads together, and their laughter continuing, though somewhat stifled.

I now rang, whereupon two girls – not, I was somewhat relieved to see, from the group which had made up my audience – carried in hot water and poured it into a bath concealed behind a screen, then offering to take from me the sheet which I had wrapped about myself; whereupon I made my ablutions aided by them in the matter of washing my back. Cornish maids, it seems, grow up in so close propinquity with their brothers (most families being crowded into small households) that the sight of a naked man is no great matter to them; moreover many of them are used to helping to cleanse their menfolk upon their return from working at sea, or in the fields, or in the tin mines. The result of this is that their attentions are severely practical rather than arousingly amorous, and one of them seizing my private parts and wringing them as she might a dish cloth gave me considerable anxiety as to whether she might render me incapable of paying a tribute to any notable beauties of the country who might fall in my way.

On my breakfasting, Mr Treweers waited upon me to ask whether it would be my pleasure to be driven over the estate; and, its promising to be a fine day, I commissioned the kitchen to provide a hamper of cold meats, and we set out.

The estate was, as I had thought, a comprehensive one, the land near the house (given over to a park) maintaining cattle, while further away towards the sea (of which an occasional glimpse could be caught, the sun sparkling on the waves) it became common farm land. At the extreme southern end of the estate, my friend's land marched with that of another estate, which was that, I was told, of Sam Treglown. The name came upon me strangely; Mrs Treglown had given me no sign that Vycken (a name which I had clearly pronounced to her several times) was next her husband's estate!

We ate our lunch upon a grassy knoll near a headland called Gribbin, commanding a fine view eastwards to that arm of the land concealing the harbour at Plymouth, while beyond could dimly be seen in this remarkably clear weather a cape which Treweers claimed was Prawle Point, protecting Dartmouth and Lyme Bay; to our west lay the small bay of St Austell, the Dodman Point, and beyond it again in the far distance the Lizard, west of which only the Mount's Bay separated us from the Land's End and that vast Atlantic ocean which stands between us and the Americas.

Our lunch consisted of a pasty, or wrapping of pastry placed about meat, potato and turnip, then baked in the oven – making a pie convenient to be carried; the same invented in order to provide a package of food for the tin miners, who carry it with them for their luncheon – it being an axiom with them that the best pasty is one which can be dropped from the mouth of a mine shaft, and which upon reaching the bottom of the mine remains intact (indeed the pastry is sometimes of considerable toughness, though the contents delicious). Some Vycken cider completed the meal, under the influence of which I fell after a while asleep – to be wakened only by a number of voices; and, on propping myself on an elbow, saw a procession of men making their way along a pathway near me.

I looked about for Treweers, who had however vanished; so getting up I followed the passers-by and in a mere hundred yards found myself upon the brink of a round, grassy hollow, a natural amphitheatre, where I saw Treweers sitting on the ground a little way away. On my joining him, he explained that this was to be a Cornish wrestling – an almost weekly occurrence upon a Saturday (which this was). I was tempted to believe that he had led me this way especially in order to attend the wrestling, and was further persuaded to the opinion by his exchanging compliments with a number of other gentlemen in the crowd.

This Cornish wrestling was a curious affair from the start, and was to become more curious. The number of young men who took part were clad in a sort of baggy trousers cut off at the knee and a loose coat of cloth, and seemed intent upon destroying each other with as much celerity as was consistent with the entertainment of the crowd. Only the use of their teeth seemed to be prohibited, for otherwise they caught each other not only by the clothing, but by the hair or any other part of the body, at the same time delivering kicks of considerable violence, directed at any vulnerable area which presented itself – meanwhile urged on by the spectators with cries not only in the vernacular but in the ancient Cornish language. A great deal of money changed hands, being betted upon the fighters – and in particular upon one Ned, a fine young giant of a fellow whose limbs were like young trees and who succeeded in disposing of every rival, emerging as the clear winner.

There was then a pause, during which there seemed an air of expectancy among the crowd. After a while a stout fellow stood upon the centre of the ring where combat took place and announced the final bout, which would be – he explained – between Dolly, of Par, and Jane, of New Quay – the latter champion of her *towen* or district, and newly come to the east of the county in search of new honours. He then asked who would buy? – at which there was a clamour of voices each contending with the other.

On my inquiring of Treweers what was going on, he informed me that though 'twas frowned upon by authority, unofficial meetings such as this one often culminated with a match between two women wrestlers; and that to raise money for them spectators were invited to 'buy'. The man who offered the largest sum attached to the eventual winner became entitled to a proportion of the whole sum promised to both; while the winner took an equal share.

This seemed a reasonable proposition; and in this case I was much taken by the smaller of the two contenders who strode upon the grassy sward. One – Dolly – was indeed an Amazon, broad as she was tall, with a swart, ugly face full of malevolence – and for her there was a great rivalry of bidders. However, it was the other, Jane, who caught my attention, having a lively little monkey-face from which a pair of black eyes twinkled merrily, and whose body seemed to me, though less powerful, to be no less sturdy and capable of quicker movement than the other. I therefore bid for Jane, and after only a little opposition won. Her being from a distant place (New Quay lying upon the northern coast of the county, to which few eastern men travelled) no one knew anything of her; and her frame being so much the smaller, it was not considered likely that she could prevail.

The manager of the affair having taken charge of the papers upon which we wrote our bets, there was now a hush among the crowd, the two women stepping forward and eyeing each other with some caution, each standing with her hands upon her hips. Their clothing was the same as the men's – that is, baggy trousers and loose coats of coarse cloth, the latter cut sufficiently loosely to afford an opponent the opportunity of clutching at it in order to be able to swing the other about – the aim of the combat being (as I should have said) for one to to deposit the other upon the grass, both shoulders upon the ground, for the space of a count of three. At this point there is a general shout of *Hal*!, and a point is awarded, two points being counted a complete victory.

Now, with a movement quicker than might have seemed possible for a woman of her size, Dolly stepped forward and caught the other by the front of the jacket, sweeping her sideways and across a raised leg so that she fell to the floor. In the fall she twisted herself free of her opponent's hands, and, contracting herself almost into a ball, rolled over and in the same movement regained her feet, to cries of approbation from the crowd. Jane then danced in, and, raising her foot almost to the level of her shoulders, delivered a smart blow with the sole of it to the side of the other woman's head, which sent her stag-

gering. She followed by catching her by one arm, swinging her about, and, grasping the collar of her jacket,
pulled it down over her shoulders so that it trapped her
arms. Parting her own arms widely, she brought them
together so that the insides of her forearms clapped the
other's head as in a vice, and she fell dizzily to the
ground – at which Jane leaped upon her, turning her so
that her shoulders touched the greensward. A count followed, a round of applause (somewhat mild, the victor
being a 'foreigner' – from a distant place in the county)
signifying the first point.

Dolly, as she rose, looked extremely displeased – as
well she might – and adjusted her coat with a business-
like air. (I should say that Jane's rearrangement of it had
disclosed what I had suspected – that beneath their coats
the women wore no other covering, a pair of white, pen-
dulous breasts having been revealed by the slighter woman's skilful disposition of her rival).

The pair now positioned themselves for a new skir-
mish, Dolly this time waiting for Jane to make the first
move – which in a moment she did by moving forward,
ducking beneath the slow, protective movement of
Dolly's arms, and throwing her own about the body of
her rival. The grip was obviously a tenacious hug, for the
stouter of the ladies soon grew red in the face in her
attempt to break free – whereat, taking advantage of
one great effort, Jane loosed her opponent, and with a
skilful motion (too speedy for the eye to discover precisely how it was accomplished) swung Dolly about, and
gripped her from behind, her arms beneath the larger
woman's armpits, and her hands placed behind her
neck – a position obviously painful, for poor Dolly
groaned audibly at the pressure put upon her, her head

sunk towards her breast. But then, in a moment, she freed herself by the simple expedient of throwing her own arms above her head, and throwing herself downwards, thus slipping from Jane's grasp.

There was a ripple of applause at this ruse; but now Dolly rolled away, and in one movement was upon her feet and had grasped the hem of Jane's garment. She threw her to the ground, hurling herself upon her opponent and seeking to pin her. Grasped in each other's arms, the two women rolled upon the grass, gripping each other as best they might, their coats flying open to reveal their sweating bodies – Dolly's white (though grubby), Jane's as brown as a nut, presumably from working unclothed in the open air. That this was a sight most stimulating to the eyes of gentlemen need not be said – for to the concern of speculating on the eventual winner was added the interest of observing the unclothed bodies of two females in continual and exciting movement.

The noise was by now indescribable – catcalls opposed to enthusiastic applause, shouts of encouragement to the one woman combating cries of enheartenment to the other. Not that either seemed to pay attention either to supporters or denigrators, each being entirely fixed upon triumphing over the other.

I had for a moment turned from the main spectacle to look upon my fellows – arms raised in imprecation or approval, mouths wide open the better to give vent to noise; and in short each man entirely taken up in the combat before him, and its consequence. But in the moment when my attention had been diverted from the fight, it had taken a fresh turn, Dolly having once more gained a hold upon her opponent's coat, and, twisting it about, trapping one of Jane's arms in its folds – which gave her a sufficient advantage to be able for a moment to throw the other off-balance. A quick kick to the belly deprived her of breath, and enabled Dolly easily to throw her to the ground and hurl herself across her upper body, rendering it possible for the referee – a little, squat fellow with a squint – to make the necessary count; upon which Dolly rose with a smile of triumph, and, treading upon her still winded opponent's neck with her foot as she did so, raised her arms in a gesture of victory.

There was now a pause, while two old women came forward with water and bathed the combatants' faces and necks; when the referee exclaimed 'Time!', and both women rose to their feet, Jane, with a gesture which spoke defiance, immediately threw off her jacket and stood for a moment bathed in sunlight – the very picture of some warrior from the great age of heroic Greece or Rome, when women stood by their men in readiness for battle.

After a short and sharp intake of breath through the entire crowd of spectators, there fell a moment's complete silence, even those who most ferociously supported the popular local heroine being impressed by the splendid picture made by her rival, shoulders thrown back, proud breasts, brown as the rest of her body, seeming as though carved from teak, and beneath the surface of a skin whose smoothness showed no sign of wrinkle or looseness muscles which moved like metal springs. No opponent, man or woman, could surely face such a figure without some feeling of doubt, if not of positive fear? The next moment the surmise was confirmed, for with a vigorous leap Jane rose some feet from the ground, at the same time throwing both feet out in a kick which connected with the head of the unfortunate Dolly, sending her sprawling while the leaper dextrously regained her own feet, and threw herself after the other. As she pounced, Dolly, regaining her scattered senses, moved swiftly away – yet Jane had grasped the hem of her trousers, and clutched with such a recalcitrant grip that, despite any feelings of reluctance the other may have felt, she was forced to squirm out of them, whereat with a cry of disgust Jane threw them into the crowd!

Dolly now stood, clad only in her coat – beneath the skirts of which a large and heavy-cheeked bum disclosed itself – again ready for the attack; but once more Jane was too quick for her, and this time with a movement which again was almost quicker than the eye could follow, precipitated herself at the other woman's feet, at the same time curling her body so that it was half behind the other's legs, and threw her backwards – half-rising at the same time to lift Dolly's lower limbs so that her ankles were pressed one upon each side of her neck, her shoulders firmly to the ground, and displaying to those opposite a view of the larger woman's posterior parts which was as full as it was unappealing – at least to me, though not (from the roar of the crowd) to many of the rougher sort of spectators, some of whom from the descriptive nature of their comments may have had a closer acquaintance with the generously displayed anatomy of the loser than a mere transitory glimpse could afford.

The referee – who, being a local man, was partial to the local champion – counted as slowly as he could; but was not able to deny the smaller woman's triumph – whereat she rose and with a splendid show of disdain threw her defeated rival's legs to the ground and raised her arms once more in triumph.

There was now a great bustle as the few people who had bet upon the winner surrounded the referee to collect their gains; after which he stepped to me and handed me a purse which, from its weight, comprised a considerable sum – consisting, as I have said, of a proportion of all the bets placed upon both winner and loser. Dolly, meanwhile, was surrounded by a clutch of local men intent upon comforting her, while the winner stood alone (except for her attendant crone) – whereupon I stepped up to her, and with a bow presented her with the purse.

She looked astonished, such generosity (as I guessed) being far from common in those parts, at the same time, with a diffidence that touched me, reaching for her coat and holding it to conceal her still naked body. I bowed again, and turning looked for Treweers, who however had vanished from sight – gone, I guessed, with some cronies to comfort himself with cider (for I doubted that he had supported anyone from outside his own district, being, as one or two remarks of his had shown, intensely patriotic not merely of his county but even of his parish).

I began slowly to make my way along the path back to the place at which our horse had been tethered. After a moment I felt a touch upon my arm, and turning found Jane, still looking reserved and not in the least the picture of assurance which she had appeared when ready to give battle. On my raising an eyebrow and asking whether I could be of assistance, she merely smiled and tugged again at my sleeve, turning me off the path and through a gap in the hedge into a thicket, where a small clearing was paved by soft grass; and there, without further ado, she removed the jacket which alone covered her upper body, and, throwing herself upon me almost with the same enthusiasm with which she had attacked poor Dolly, bore me to the ground, where she kissed me with a violence which was as appetising as it was eager, at the same time wriggling her body accommodatingly against mine so that I was forced to open my legs, for my own comfort, whereupon she slipped between them. Forcing her thighs beneath my own, she began with eager fingers to unloose the ties of my shirt and then the catch of my belt.

It would be a fiction were I to say that I was not stirred by this turn of events; for the recent spectacle had been one which few men could have witnessed wholly without arousal; while a closer inspection of my captor's body confirmed that it was one which must surely appeal to every masculine emotion, her breasts being sufficiently full to be entirely feminine, yet without the merest touch of that slackness which comes with greater maturity, the nipples, brown as berries, neat and peaked, her flesh firm, with so little fat that at her sides the bones of the ribs could clearly be seen, and upon her shoulders and upper arms muscles which, moving beneath the skin, felt (when I placed my hands upon them, as now I did) like little lithe animals.

She paused now in her unbuckling, as I slid my palms down from her shoulders, resting for a moment to caress those delightful breasts (which now rose and fell more swiftly, it seemed, than they had done at any moment of her recent combat) and feel the beating of her heart; then descending to her waist, where, as they slid beneath the cloth of her trousers, I could feel again how firm and unencumbered with surplus flesh her body was.

My attempt to unveil her further was disallowed, how-ever, by the fact that she was squatting between my thighs – and indeed that fact prevented her, once she had undone both shirt and belt, from disencumbering me of my clothing; whereat what I could only describe as a grin passed over her face, and, raising herself to her knees, she caught at the legs of my own trousers, and shuffling backwards drew them off – releasing from its discomfort a part of me that had been increasingly con-fined since the engorgement provoked by her presence.

It was the work of but a moment to wriggle from my shirt, to kneel, throw my arms about her and to press my face to that delightful bosom – at which I discerned that it was indeed firmer than any other in my experience, and supported by muscles which were clearly the result of considerable exercise. The nipples seemed to be almost as hard as finger-nails – so much so that I could not resist taking one between my teeth and nipping at it, whereat only a little chuckle of laughter came from Jane's lips, whereas other women would have expressed discomfort or positive pain.

I could not, meanwhile, prevent my hands from slid-ing up her thighs beneath the wide bottoms of her trou-sers (which, the reader will recall, reached only below the knee) and taking in my palms the tempting curves of her bottom, my fingers straying into the cleft between them – whereat, with a simple tension of her muscles, she exerted such pressure that it was almost impossible to remove them – and again that charming chuckle of laughter was heard.

But now she bent to draw off her trousers, and as she straightened I found within inches of my eyes a quim whose shape and proportions seemed to me then – and even in memory – to represent the ideal: the mound was marked and emphasised by a covering of black hair which was caught up into curls which stood around about it as though carefully disposed, decorating the portals like the proscenium of a theatre, embellishment without concealment. The portals themselves were of a deep red darkened almost to purple, giving way almost immediately to a lighter shade that became – as I parted them with fingers which now trembled not a little – the faintest and most delicate pink, while at their top there stood that miniature facsimile of the male instrument which is present in all women, but rarely is so perfect in verisimilitude as here, even to the tiny head to which I now paid tribute by the tip of my tongue – at which Jane, leaning, gripped my shoulders with such a hold as was positively painful.

But she was unwilling to spend any more time in preliminaries: simply sinking to the ground, she rolled backwards, drawing me with her by the simple expedient of gripping my upper arms with an entirely unbreakable hold, and, throwing her legs apart and transferring her hands now to my waist, without any more delay lifted me into that position most favourable for congress – whereupon, not unwillingly, I entered her.

It would be fruitless to advise every young man at some time in his life to lie with a female wrestler, for outside Cornwall I have yet to discover any; but the experience was one which I would recommend to anyone who can command it. That control, dexterity and forcefulness which Jane had displayed in her recent combat was equally disposed in her present activity – and she seemed intent on such display, adopting figures and poses which no woman without a similar nimbleness could have achieved. Moreover, that control over her muscles which she must have cultivated for her craft extended throughout her body – I mean that those parts which in most women are either uncontrolled or (in some whores) only a little commanded, were by her entirely subdued and regulated. Not only by their movement was she able to caress my instrument in a manner I had never before experienced, positively stroking and squeezing it without any movement upon my part, but upon my showing a sign of death before she herself was ready to concede the game, by a sudden contraction of those same muscles she gripped my cock with such a painful constraint (seeming to enclose it with an iron ring) that in a moment I had recovered my equanimity and was able to continue until she was ready – whereupon, dextrously twisting her legs beneath her, she raised herself upon them and her arms, so that I was able, curling my toes and gripping the grass as well as I might, to assault her with all the force at my command. She met thrust with thrust as powerfully as I could give them, until we both cried out at almost the same moment and fell to the ground in a positive excess of pleasure.

I must confess that the nature of the fight, while entirely pleasurable during its progress, left me sore and bruised; though I did not express myself in that sense to Jane, merely dressing myself and taking my leave of her with every expression of pleasure and gratitude – which she received merely by grinning and holding aloft the purse of money I had given her; this leaving me with mixed feelings, for it was clear that her actions had been performed out of gratitude rather than any particular admiration for my person. However, the experience had been one which I would not upon any account have missed.

On our reaching the pathway, I found Treweers leaning against a post and talking to the old crone who was my companion's friend. I wondered whether he had looked for, and even found me (for in the excessive enjoyment of the time I would not have noticed the attention of an audience of hundreds). Certainly his expression left me in no doubt that he was aware of the entertainment in which I had been occupied; nor did this worry me, nor prevent me from once more taking leave of Jane with considerable affection, though this was returned only by a cheery wave as the couple made off, and we returned to the trap, which then was driven back to Vycken. There, as I drove into the courtyard, I saw a carriage drawn up.

'Ah,' said Treweers, ' 'tis Squire Treleaven come to pay you his attentions.'

One of my duties being to make it clear to my neighbours that the estate would now be managed on a more sociable basis than hitherto, I hurried into the hall to make myself pleasant to the Squire, whose estate was some miles to the east, towards Restormel. He was a plump, nay corpulent, figure, dressed in clothing of a previous age – and his acquaintance with the present day indeed was embroidered with the manners of the past, evidenced in the flowery manner of his address.

'My very dear Sir,' he said, 'a pleasure indeed! 'Tis too many years since Vycken was alive, and I cannot properly express the pleasure with which the county has heard of your presence! I have been dispatched here, indeed, by some of the gentlemen of the area in the hope that you might be persuaded to attend a supper party on Monday night, at which you will meet some of your neighbours – both gentlemen and ladies, I may say, so your good wife—'

'Alas, Squire, I am unmarried.'

'Indeed – I was not aware. Indeed, I had understood . . .'

'But have no aversion to the sex,' I hastily added (which indeed was nothing other than the truth).

Staying only to take a glass of cider, the Squire departed; and Treweers then was able to inform me that he was an influential figure in the county who had only just resigned – his heart being expressed as weakly – from the position of Member of Parliament for the town of Lostwithiel. A Tory, of course, through both tradition and sentiment, Cornwall being a stronghold of interest in landowning and merchantry rather than of the dissenters, industrialists and reformers of the Whig Party.

I spent Sunday in quiet, attending service in the small church which stood just behind the house, and which was in considerable disrepair; there was a sermon whose length was well balanced by its tedium and during which I slept like a babe in the high-walled pew which happily concealed me from the public view; and in the afternoon walked about the grounds and dozed in the sun.

Monday was spent going through the accounts with Treweers, and in writing a long letter to Frank in which I explained as best I could upon relatively little knowledge the state of the house and grounds – which as to beauty and relative attractiveness I could not fault.

On my enquiring the nature of the supper party, Treweers explained that it would be as grand as local custom allowed – which left me in the quandary of not having brought any good clothes (it not having occurred to me that I would be required to attend any social occasions). The late tenant of the estate had left a trunk full of clothes, however, from which I dug out a suit which must have been made no more recently than the 1790s, Treweers nevertheless expressing himself confident that not only would I pass in the crowd, but would be singled out as perfectly well clad. So, on Monday evening, in a coat with tails of extravagant length, boots rather than shoes, an extremely short waistcoat, a collar which towered above the back of my neck, and a neckcloth so voluminous that it rose over my chin and bade fair to conceal my very mouth, I set out for the Squire's house, which stood upon the banks of the River Fowey, some miles upstream from that town.

Squire Treleaven's house was what had once been a large farmhouse, but was now something more pretentious, a wing having been opened out from the original building, and what had once perhaps been the kitchen contrived now into a large hall.

It was a warm evening, and the heat of a room crowded with people was added to by the smallness of the windows and by the multifarious candles lit to provide a reasonable light, which soon enough fell upon a society running with sweat engendered by the closeness of the atmosphere and the confinement of their clothes – which were as elderly as those I wore, and thicker and therefore hotter than would have been the case had more recent fashions found their way into the county. The women were better off than the men, being dressed still in the *robes en chemises* which had been the fashion thirty years earlier. These, consisting as they did of high-waisted muslin, cambric or calico garments, were so transparent that they almost exposed the women's bodies to the air, and were so thin that they were almost invisible – and would have had a delicious effect had not the bodies they clothed been on this occasion matronly and stout.

The society consisted of the gentry of the neighbourhood, and was (as the reader may understand) very different from that of London. The ladies, for instance, were older, it seeming to be the case that younger women were prohibited from gatherings of this sort. In fact I later discovered that they absented themselves by choice – and could not blame them, for there was nothing to attract them except the food and drink; whereas left to their own devices they enjoyed themselves in their own way, which was often in rustic matters frequently not unconnected with sensual pleasure.

So here, as I looked about me, were their seniors: couples whose average age must have been the middle forties, but who often appeared older, sated as they were by rich food and drink. The latter here consisted more of red wine than cider, though the latter was available and was drunk in plenty by the ladies (in particular). The food was of a coarse nature, much like the feast I had enjoyed upon my arrival at Vycken Hall – but added was a great quantity of fowl, viz. duck, goose and chicken, swimming in grease which soon transferred itself to the chops of Squire, Parson and accompanying gentry.

All I could do was give myself over to the spirit of the occasion, which the application of a bottle of claret to my stomach soon made more palatable; plied on one side with food by Mrs Treleaven, I could only nod from time to time in her direction while my attention must be given to Squire and Parson, the latter the very picture of a clergyman of the hunting and drinking sort, and the two of whom were hot upon the Tory cause (though admitting reluctantly to the service performed by those

Whigs whose cooperation had resulted in the defeat of
the hated Wellington and his administration). Lord Grey
being sent for to form a Whig administration had set
these local Tories into a sweat of fear and hatred, the
mere rumour of the Reform Bill making them fear for
their property and even, ludicrously, their lives! As they
grew more heated, so they applied liquor to cool themselves – which in turn heated them once again. Forced to
drink glass for glass, I soon found myself as heated as
they, dilating at length about the good old days of Can-
ning and his Ministry, of Castlereagh's neutrality and its
effect upon Britain abroad, of Catholic emancipation,
constitutional reform and the economic and social injus-
tices of the country.

The heat grew greater, the candles guttered and
leaped; I was dimly conscious that Mrs Treleaven had
left and her place been taken by a large dog of strangely
mixed parentage who had leaped upon her seat and was
guzzling the scraps left upon her plate; the wine continued to flow into my glass, and I tore at my neckcloth
and opened my collar to let the air at my body – yet there
was no coolness in it. I felt a certain dizziness overtake
me, and gradually slipped towards an oblivion.

I regained partial consciousness as I found myself
lifted from my seat and apparently conveyed to another
room. There, deposited on a sopha, I lost consciousness
again – but was at the same time aware of a bustle and
noise about me – and woke once more to hear Squire
Treleaven in the midst of what I took to be a political
speech. I forced myself to listen, made myself shift in the
place and half sit up – at which a round of applause was
heard – and from a great distance I heard the tail-end of
the Squire's speech.

'Therefore, my friends,' he said, 'with the approbation of Parson Polware, and I hope that of all present, it is with the greatest confidence that I ask you to celebrate by acclamation the proposition that our candidate in the forthcoming by-election should be our new friend Sir Franklin Franklyn, of Alcovary and Vycken Hall, in the counties of Hertfordshire and Cornwall!'

I staggered to my feet to a cry of 'Hear! Hear!' – then, looking about me, saw nothing but a sea of faces and lifted glasses as the company tossed down their wine in a toast – and I realised that not only had they mistaken me for my friend, but that under that impression I was now the official Tory candidate for the parliamentary constituency of Lostwithiel!

Chapter Six

Sophie's Story

It was perhaps not astonishing that Chichley should, in the course of time – indeed, within a week of the most recent events I have described – procure for me an invitation to that most glittering of all London salons, Lady Holland's circle at Holland House, where the most intelligent Whig politicians mingled with the most aristocratic and literary men of London.

Perhaps the company was not as distinguished as it had once been – Lord Byron no longer limped up the steps to the grand entrance of that fine house erected soon after Shakespeare's day, with its sparkling oriel windows, its Dutch gables, its square towers, and its private park (where the Parliamentary Army had set up its chief camp in the days of the Civil War). But a remarkable number of gentlemen still attended regularly at the House for conversation and other pleasures – this had always been a society chiefly for gentlemen, since the more fastidious ladies could not overlook the fact that Lord Holland had married his wife Elizabeth only two days after her first husband, Sir Godfrey Webster, Bart., had divorced her, naming the noble lord as correspondent.

The lady had had a remarkable career. Despite the criticism to which her liaison with Lord Holland had exposed her, she had nevertheless upon repairing to his house in Kensington – to which it was already the habit of a brilliant circle of wits, statesmen, men of letters and others of distinction to repair – soon established herself altogether in control of it, and that despite natural qualities which were by no means admirable – for, polite, cold and haughty to all those she met in social intercourse, she was most offensive to any to whom she took a dislike.

Even those men of letters whose distinction marked them out for respect were belittled by her – Lord Byron himself felt the sharp edge of her tongue at a time when he was perhaps the most famous man in the country, while to Samuel Rogers she once said: 'Your poetry is bad enough, so pray be sparing of your prose.' 'Poets inclined to a plethora of vanity,' Moore once remarked to me, 'would find a dose of Lady Holland now and then very good for their complaint.'

However, Lady H. was nothing if not amiable to me – though by the time I met her she was in her sixties, when perhaps age had mellowed her. Lord Holland, I knew less of – except of course that he was one of the great luminaries of the Whigs, and estimated to command high office on their return to power. His statue, by Watts, had just been placed in the grounds of Holland House when I first entered it – and indeed that very act brought one face to face with him in effigy if not in fact, through the place set aside in the entrance hall for not only a bust by Nollekens but a portrait by Fabre, both of which are imposing. I met him but three or four times, when he impressed me as the most amiable of men – and known as a refuge to the helpless and the oppressed.

I was naturally diffident during my first two or three

visits to the house, and was noticed by Lady H. only, as it seemed to me, in the most perfunctory manner; so it was to my surprise that on my third or fourth visit I was sent for by her to the library, a handsome room at the western extremity of the house, where I found her half-lying upon a *chaise-longue*, the place where she had left off reading in a handsomely bound volume marked by one languid finger.

'My dear Mrs Nelham,' she said, politely gesturing towards a chair, upon which I carefully sat (the furniture being for the most part foreign and therefore delicate), 'I wonder if I might ask of you a favour? My senior footman, Tollersly, has unfortunately been taken ill of a bad leg, and is confined to his room. He is a man of considerable talents, but these do not include literacy, and I fear that he is extremely bored at his confinement, being usually a person of considerable activity. Would it be asking too much of you to pay him a brief visit, and to read from some improving work? I have picked a volume from my library which perhaps might be of an improving nature' – with which she passed me the volume at her hand.

What could I do but acquiesce? The lady had kindly received me at her house when others less liberal in their nature had failed to do so (on account of adventures which they considered indelicate, and which I have already related in my previous writings, a list of which may be found opposite the title page of the present volume).

Lady H. rang her bell, and, a maidservant appearing, instructed that I should be taken to Tollersly's room. Making my obeisance, I followed the girl from the library, and by a circuitous route through innumerable and warren-like passages to a back staircase, then up it and through a dormitory (by the small-clothes strewn about it and a single tousled head upon a pillow, one shared by a number of the male servants) to a door upon which she knocked, and on receiving the command to do so, admitted me.

The room was somewhat better than might have been expected to be occupied by a servant, its windows looking over the park behind Holland House, towards the rose-garden, the adjacent ice-house and the orangery. Near the window, which was open so that the sultry air of summer could waft into the sick-room, a bed was drawn up, and upon it lay the gentleman in question. By Lady H.'s words, 'my senior footman', I had expected an older man than the one I saw, who in fact was perhaps in his middle twenties. Nor did I expect him to appear half-naked, for he seemed to be clad only in a sheet thrown across the lower half of his body, from the bottom of which a foot dressed in bandages protruded. His visage was a strong one, without any sign of that weakness which marks the subservient employee; dark brown eyes were surmounted by eyebrows which in a man of superior rank I would have said were neatly plucked, while above a firm chin marked by the dint of a dimple was set a mouth whose sternness seemed set off by the suggestion of a somewhat satirical smile.

As for the rest: his shoulders were broad and well-formed, his skin white as a girl's, so that the paps which decorated a broad breast seemed by contrast purple rather than pink, and were decorated by a spring or two of hair no less black than that which curled upon his brow and fell almost to his shoulders – devoid of any hint of powder (for Lady H. was among the first ladies in

London to refrain from insisting on her footmen powdering or wearing wigs).

Clearly the man had no idea who I was; but when I introduced myself as a guest sent him by his employer with the duty of reading to him, he showed what seemed to me a proper embarrassment, attempting to lift himself sufficiently to make a little bow; an expression of pain passing over his brow, caused no doubt by his injured limb.

I waved him down; and, having drawn up a chair, opened my book: it was a treatise on Gnosticism, with special reference to the Gospel of St Thomas, which the author translated in full. I had read no more than two pages, when glancing up from my page I caught Tollersly in mid-yawn – a fact which would have distressed me more were I not by now in the same state of boredom. Meeting my eye, he I believe recognised the fact; and, whether purposely or not I cannot say, in moving himself to a more comfortable position betrayed the corner of a book protruding from beneath the sheet.

'What, Mr Tollersly!' I remarked – 'You are a reader, after all?'

'Somewhat slow, ma'am,' he replied; ' 'tis a volume a friend brought in the hope that the pictures might amuse me; the matter, however, is in a foreign tongue, and I cannot go forward with it.'

I leaned forward to take up the volume, but with a blush he seized it. ' 'Tis not a work for your eyes, ma'am!'

Which as a matter of course made me the more eager to recover it; which I did without difficulty – and found in my hands a finely illustrated edition of *Monsieur Nicolas, or the Human Heart Laid Bare* – the memoirs of M. Restif de la Bretonne – illustrated (as I could see at even a cursory glance) with the most delightful drawings, the artist not shrinking from portraying the personages concerned in the most intimate attitudes of love.

'I am sorry, Mr Tollersly,' I said, 'that your lack of knowledge of the French language has prevented you from enjoying the narrative . . .'

' 'Twould have been much the same were it in English,' he said morosely; 'for I never attended school – nor have I regretted it until the present moment. The story, I take it, is . . .'

'Of a French gentleman,' I said, 'more honest in telling the story of his life than many gentlemen are prepared to be.'

'You know it, then?'

'I saw it first some years ago, when in Paris; but in no less than seventeen volumes. This appears to be a compilation in which the editor has concentrated on those areas of la Bretonne's life which . . .' I paused.

'You are familiar with the French tongue, ma'am?' And on my nodding, 'Perhaps you could English some of it for me?'

I opened the book almost at random; its pages fell apart at that point when la Bretonne, a vigorous young man of nineteen or so, was sitting alone in his attick in Paris, with a new book which he had just acquired. I began to read: ' ''A great libertine, Molet – whom I have already mentioned, and who was a fellow lodger of mine at Bonne Sellier's – had come to see me one Sunday morning when I was still in bed, and had brought me a copy of that most lascivious of books, *Le Portier des Chartreux*, which I had once glimpsed at La Mace's. Filled with a lively curiosity, I took it eagerly and started

reading in bed. I forgot everything – even my mistress,
Zephire. After a score of pages, I was on fire. Manon
Lavergne, a relative of Bonne Sellier, came on behalf of
my former landlady to bring my linen and Loiseau's,
which Bonne continued to wash for us. I knew what
Manon's morals were like. Throwing back the bed-
clothes and revealing myself ready for combat, I threw
myself upon her and with one action rent her few clothes
from her body. Nothing loath, she met me with equal
passion (ever ready for the game), and we played the
beast with two backs in a paroxysm of energy which
provoked screams of pleasure on her part and cries of
delight on mine.

'   "Gathering together her rended clothing, and taking
with a happy grin the gold *livre* which I handed her as
compensation for the damage I had done (which was no
greater than many other men had done before me), she
left me, and I resumed my reading. Half an hour later
there appeared Cecile Decoussy, my sister Margot's
companion, who came on her behalf to ask why she no
longer saw anything of me. Without any regard for this
young blonde's position (she was about to be married) or
for the atrocious way in which I was bringing shame
upon my sister in the person of her friend, I put so much
fury into my attack that, alarmed as much as surprised,
she thought that I had gone mad. I returned to my bane-
ful reading.

'   "About three-quarters of an hour later, Thérèse
Courbisson arrived, laughing and bantering. 'Where is
he, that lazy scamp? Still in bed!' And she came over to
tickle me. I was waiting for her. I seized her almost in the
air, like a feather, and with only one hand I pulled her
under me. 'Oh! After what you've just done to Manon?

A fine man you are!' But she was caught before she could finish, and as she was very partial to physical pleasure, she did nothing more but help me. At last she tore herself from my arms because she heard my landlord coming upstairs. She went out, leaving the door open. I finished my book.

' "The bed had warmed me up; the three pleasures I had enjoyed were just a spur to my senses: I got up with the intention of going to fetch Zephire, of bringing her to my room, and of abandoning myself with her to my erotic frenzy. At that moment someone scratched at my door, which I had only pushed to. I started, thinking it was Zephire. 'Who is it?' I cried; 'come in.' 'Seraphine,' said a voice which I thought I recognised. I trembled, thinking it was Seraphine Destroches who had come to scold me for my conduct with her companion Decoussy. 'Who is it?' I repeated. 'Seraphine Jolon.' The only person I had ever known by that name was the housekeeper of a painter who was our neighbour in the Rue de Poulies, and I had whispered sweet nothings to her once or twice; but then Largeville had turned up, and Jeannette Demailly, and I had left the house. Reassured, I opened the door. It was she.

' " 'I have come,' the pretty girl said to me, 'on behalf of Mademoiselle Fagard, now Madame Jolon, my sister-in-law, who begs you to introduce me and recommend me to Mademoiselle Delaporte, who thinks highly of you and can render me a great service.'

' " 'Immediately,' I said; 'sit down, pretty neighbour.' She was charming. As she turned round, she showed me a perfect figure, her charming little bottom jutting under a thin dress, and a tiny waist showing off her hips to perfection. I seized her, and pushed her back

on the bed. She tried to defend herself. That was adding
fuel to the fire. I did not even take time to shut the door. I
finished, I began again.

' " 'I . . . did . . . not . . . tell . . . you . . .' she cried,
in time to my thrusting, 'that . . . my . . . sister . . .
Jolon . . . was waiting for me!' – the last few words
culminating in a squeak of pleasure.

The thought spurred me on. I was like a madman,
when the door opened. It was Agathe Fagard.

' " 'Help! Help!' cried Seraphine. Lifting myself
from the bed I left her uncovered, jumped up, kicked the
door to, threw the lovely brunette on to my bed beside
the other, and submitted her to a fifth triumph no less
vigorous than the first, carried away as I was by the force
of my imagination. Agathe Fagard had not yet recovered
from her surprise when I blushed at my frenzy and apologised to the two sisters-in-law.

' " 'He has to be seen to be believed!' was all that
Seraphine said – the two girls not being entirely
displeased at the compliment I had paid them. Such is the
effect of erotic literature." '

As I put the book down, I could see that Mr Tollersly's
interest in it had been keen, from the light in his eyes no
less than from the movement of his hand beneath the
sheet, which I surmised was meant to conceal the upris-
ing of his spirits in a form he thought might offend
me – though I was conscious that my own bosom was
rising and falling faster than usual – a phenomenon
concomitant with the blush that suffused my cheeks – a
blush less of offended modesty than of a pleasant warming from the scenes M. la Bretonne had described.

In leaning forward to replace the book at Mr Tollersly's side, my fingers inexplicably became tangled in

the edge of the sheet, and on my removing my hand the sheet came with it – revealing (without my intending it in the least) that his hand was indeed engaged in attempting to subdue (by pressing it down against his belly) an engine of such proportions that one might be pardoned for supposing it capable of just such feats as those M. la Bretonne had spoken of.

The gentleman in question coloured, and now joined a second hand to the first, though both were incapable of completely hiding the instrument whose engorgement caused him such embarrassment.

'My dear Mr Tollersly,' I exclaimed, 'please do not give way to any feelings of mortification. In the first place, I am a married lady' (true, though my husband had died many years before) 'and not unacquainted with a gentleman's physiognomy; and second, it is but natural that a man should show some acknowledgement of so warming a tale as that we have just heard.'

His answer to this was immediate, and consisted of his removing both hands, thus showing his device in all its proudness – and an attractive assemblage of flesh it was, the sun as it shone through the open window giving the bronze hair at its base an almost golden glow and setting off the dark column which rose through and above it.

To allow such an implement to waste its vigour was unthinkable, and – since in warm weather I have always maintained the custom of eschewing the relatively modern fashion of wearing drawers – it was the work of but a moment to mount the bed and, throwing a leg across his body, to join our bodies in that manner hallowed by years of custom.

I can conceive that Mr Tollersly, when in full command of all his limbs, must be a man of considerable

vigour; and even now, while suffering from considerable
pain in his foot (the cause of which, I gathered later, was
gout from making too free with Lady Holland's strawberry beds), he was incapable of remaining completely
still, his thighs and shoulders combining to lift his middle
body to meet my own, the rolling of his eyes at the same
time showing the pleasure his action, and the reaction to
it of my own person, gave.

Preoccupied with my own delight, it was not until our
pleasure was some way advanced that, glancing out of
the window at my side, I saw Lady H. standing on the
gravel below; dressed in a day-gown and bonnet, she had
clearly been taking the air, and pausing was now presented with the view of a lady (myself) whose upper person, displayed at a window, was moving with a regular
motion as though she sat upon a vigorously propelled
rocking horse.

I doubt not that she realised what we were at; but
merely nodded in a friendly manner – to which it was
impossible for me to reply in any rational manner, my
emotions at that moment being at their keenest; so that
all I could do was to wave at her with one hand – the other
being pressed upon Mr Tollersly's belly in an attempt to
relieve myself from the pleasurable but over-keen thrusting which otherwise threatened to split me open!

Such an improbable fate was of course not to be mine;
and at all events Mr Tollersly had reached the apogee of
his ecstasy at almost the same moment as myself (as I
could apprehend from the scalding fountain which
erupted within me). We lay – or rather, he lay and I
sat – supine for a moment or two while we recovered our
breath; after which I lifted myself from him and (he
moving obligingly to one side on his couch) laid myself at

his side, when he gave me a most friendly kiss upon the cheek, and thanked me for my attentions.

'Nay, Mr Tollersly; the thanks must be at least partly upon my side,' I replied; after which no words were exchanged for several minutes – when (whether or not prompted to it by recollections of M. la Bretonne's accomplishments) I felt his hand slide within my dress to caress a breast.

'Mrs . . . er . . .' (I supplied the name.) 'Mrs Nelham, might I crave the boon of setting eyes on your very person?'

It was a simple enough request, and simply enough answered by my removing the small amount of clothing necessary upon so delightfully warm a day. I noticed that Mr Tollersly was more ready in his movements than he had previously been, and wondered whether our recent bout had not been an efficacious treatment of his gouty foot; for, half-lifting himself upon his couch with no more than the merest wince of pain, he inspected me with the utmost keenness; and I could not but notice that his principal part, which had subsided to a mere squab, began to lengthen and thicken appreciably as his eyes grazed upon my body; a novelty which was accelerated as, in order that he should have a more thorough view of those pleasures he had enjoyed, I placed one foot upon the couch, thus by turning out my thigh and opening my most intimate parts first to his appreciative eyes, and then – as he raised himself still further – to the touch first of inquisitive fingers and then to the complementary touch of his lips as he planted a kiss which was meant (by the keen action of his tongue) no doubt to rouse in me those emotions recently spent, but, as I must admit, now once more mounting.

By now his engine was once more engorged – and, my palm told me, if not of such iron firmness as previously, of quite sufficient sturdiness to perform its most necessary function. I again approached; but Mr Tollersly, regardless of the pangs of his foot, now turned me with dextrous hands so that I fell upon the bed, whereupon in an instance he lay between my legs, and I felt his cock nuzzling my quim with affectionate enthusiasm.

It did not nuzzle for long: so unctuous were we both with our previous pleasure that no sooner had the shaft parted the lips of the grotto than it slid between them with almost too much ease – and it was now that the ingratiating footman revealed an uncommon side to his nature: uncommon I call it, because men of his station are for the most part over-eager to complete the act of love – no sooner in than out, no sooner up than down (as I may put it). The present gentleman, however, displayed a leisure which – whether the product of previous passages with ladies of a superior station, I can of course not say – was excessively pleasant; his motion was gentle and slow, his hips sufficiently limber to be able to withdraw his dibble almost completely from me, while at the same time the rest of his body – from upper belly to breast, from upper thighs to calves – remained fully in contact with my own. Yet again, from time to time he would lift himself upon his elbows and knees, so that the only thing that joined us was that column of flesh which all the time continued its movements with a regular and probing rhythm, arrested only at one moment by the joining together of bronze and black hair, and at another by our mutual reluctance that we should, at that point, be separated.

We climbed the hill, this time, at so laggard a pace that

it was by almost unnoticeable degrees that mild pleasure gave way to keener gratification, that to a yet sharper delight, and finally to that supreme delectation in the moment of which my limbs seemed to melt away entirely under the weight of the gentleman's body; while entirely eschewing that almost painful thrusting which too often accompanies the final throes, he accepted the culmination of the bout with a mere shuddering – the almost bulging of his eyes and the tightening of his palms upon my shoulders, however, offering indication that he was not unmoved.

Gentlemanlike, he soon relieved me of his weight, and we lay once more at each other's sides, imperceptibly drifting into sleep; from which I awakened, who knows how long later, my head upon his breast, a cheek tickled by that insignificant sprig of hair which sprung from below his left pap. My foreshortened view took in, below this, a flat belly below which the instrument of my pleasure lay contracted to the size of a thumb: and once more I wondered at the contrast which so often makes it impossible to estimate to what size the male member (when relaxed) may grow, or (when engorged) diminish.

In this case, I was in no doubt of its efficiency when in action; yet marvelled at its small size in its present state, and carefully raising myself (so as not to disturb the sleeping footman) bent to examine it – and was incapable of not smiling at the sight, for as it lay raised upon the mounds of the attendant cods (lifted as they were upon the platform of his closed thighs) it reminded me of the coarse name of *prick*, so often given it; for indeed, the skin at its head now wrinkled and lax and gathered to a point, it was of such a shape that the name was not entirely ill-judged.

Moistening a finger at my lips, I gently stroked the unconscious rod – more from affection than in expectation, for even a man ten or fifteen years younger than Mr Tollersly would be barely ready for another pass. Yet after a moment there was already a change, a slight swelling; then an acceleration, and at last a positive celebration of my touch (which must now be rather that of an entire palm than a single digit) in the complete extension of the appendage – which seemed compact and inflexible as formerly – though without waking its possessor it would be impossible to ascertain the extent of its rigidity.

I glanced at his face: there was no sign of apprehension there – he still slept firmly; and the naughty proposition came into my mind, whether 'twould be possible to excite him to the limit without waking. This is something which, I am told, occurs to young gentlemen with great readiness in their salad days; less perhaps to older men. In this case . . . I could not resist the trial.

Gently as possible, I placed a finger and thumb at the tip of his member, and with the greatest care dragged the skin downwards, revealing the pink head, bald and glistening, its single eye winking (as it seemed) conspiratorially at me from twin lids. I feared the subject of my experiment might wake as I latched the skin below the ridge – but found the instrument not yet so inflexible as to require a positive force to achieve the effect. He slumbered on – or seemed to. I raised my head for a moment and regarded him; no, the eyes were firmly shut, no hint of expression upon the somnambulant features. Lowering my head once more, and drawing my tongue over my lips, I slid them, as gently as possible, over his member.

The emotions attendant upon this action, as always, brought on a ready salivation; with the result that it was possible almost entirely without friction to convey to the surface of the pillar – whether to the column itself or to its head – the impression of a tender caress; that piece of flesh being so apprehensive that, while I would scarcely have believed it possible to produce such an effect with so little effort, I felt it harden between my lips until at last it could have been made of a warm marble – and it seemed to me that the blood within it moved rhythmically in time with my own motions, the pulse quickening and (as it were) solidifying until the hand which I had now placed upon his cods felt that tightening and lifting which was the invariable signal of a coming spasm. I lifted my head just in time, for with another tightening of his balls in my palm, there oozed (rather than leaped) from the proper aperture an unmistakable sign of ultimate satisfaction – while at the same time, with a start, my subject awoke, and gave vent to a 'Damn me!' redolent at the same time of surprise, embarrassment and – regret.

My own laughter had the result that he, too, soon recovered his equilibrium and smiled, the trick played upon him being (as he confessed) new to him – and one he would not have thought possible. Yet, he said, it seemed a pity that by my action I had deprived myself of some pleasure – my reply that the experiment had been worth the deprivation not seeming to satisfy him. But at all events, it seemed unlikely that he could recover himself yet again, this being beyond most men I had ever met; and after a further twenty minutes' dozing, I raised myself and prepared to dress, Mr Tollersly lazily smiling at me from his pillow.

As I lifted my dress from the floor where it lay, however, there was the sound of an altercation from below.
Cautious not to show too much of my naked self, I
climbed over the gentleman's frame and leaned my
elbows upon the window-sill to watch the fun as two
maids fled from another whom they had been teasing,
and who was now pursuing them through the shrubbery.
What was my surprise when I felt a pair of hands upon
my shoulders, and the pressure against my back of Mr
Tollersly's lower parts, which, though its most notable
feature not yet extended to a useful degree, was none the
less far from completely limp!

It appeared that, like many men, he was attached to
the sight of a woman's posterior, and on my presenting
him with a close view of that part of my person, he was
now confident of being able to pay it proper tribute; his
vigour being accompanied – unlike our last passage –
by a kind of fierceness, his hands now descending to
grasp my breasts, his teeth nipping the base of my neck,
and his belly rubbing against the cheeks of my arse with
an insistence speedily made more pressing by his
member's rousing itself further, unbelievably, to what
appeared to be full vigour.

Complimented by this, I reached back to grasp it and
(though it bucked between my fingers with what seemed
a life of its own) introduce it between my nether lips,
whereupon, with a grunt of satisfaction, Mr Tollersly
transferred his hands from my bubbies to my shoulders,
raised himself, and thrust vigorously at me – so that
gripping the window-sill with my hands, it was all I could
do to prevent myself being hurled, naked and sweating as
I was, on to the gravel below (where Mr Holt, the elderly
butler, was at this moment walking with the house-

keeper, Mrs Hacker, no doubt discussing some matter of household importance).

Bringing me fairly speedily to a conclusion, Mr Tollersly was (as might be expected) less quick to satisfy himself, his bucking continuing for rather longer than I found comfortable (my unprotected bosom pressed as it was against the wooden window frame). However, at last, with an expression as much of triumph as of satisfaction, he gave one final shove, and withdrew himself to his bed, where he lay panting (as well he might) from his efforts while I took the liberty of using the pan of cold water which stood in the corner of the room to refresh my person before taking my leave – yet not until I had complimented him.

'Yet M. Bretonne did better!' was his comment.

Frequency, I was bound to point out, was not the *sine qua non* in such matters; moreover I suspected la Bretonne of exaggeration (for no man I have experienced has completed so many bouts within so short a time – even in the early and most vigorous years of manhood). I am not sure Mr Tollersly believed me; but that he had passed an enjoyable afternoon I was in no doubt – nor did I draw attention to the fact that as I left he was not only standing but moving merrily about, on the foot injury which had formerly confined him to his bed.

Downstairs, tea was being served in the white drawing-room to Lady Holland and the Hon. Mrs Teazle, a pleasant, plump lady to whom I had previously been introduced.

'And how did you leave Tollersly?' enquired my lady.

I replied that he was much recovered.

'I make no doubt of it,' said she – but with a face

apparently devoid of irony. 'He profited, I trust, from your reading? My sight of you suggested that you found it surprisingly inspiriting.'

'What book was this?' enquired Mrs Teazle. I passed it to her.

'Why, this would recover any gentleman – or lady either,' she said, turning the leaves.

'It is a work highly recommended to me,' said her ladyship, 'by the Bishop of Durham.'

'I am almost alarmed at the liberal views of our senior clergy,' said Mrs Teazle.

'Yet they must be allowed to judge in matters of which we would as laymen be incapable of holding an informed view,' said Lady Holland.

'That is as may be,' said Mrs Teazle, closing the book with a snap, and handing it back to me – whereat with a start, I saw that I had handed her M. la Bretonne's memoirs, brought by mistake from Mr Tollersly's room. I hastily covered it with my palms, and asked my Lady whether, since I had found it so interesting, I might take it home with me for further study – permission for which was readily given; yet I cannot think that Mrs Teazle thought any the better of me for my application than of Lady Holland for her acquiescence – the latter's position in society being such, however, that none of her guests would have dreamed of questioning, much less criticising, it.

However, her disapproval was not complete; for within a week I received a message asking me to call upon her at her house in Upper Brook Street. There I found her in considerable luxury, surrounded by the most beautiful pictures and objects – her wealth being that of her husband Wellesley Teazle, Esq., who had made a fortune through the manufacture of fashionable footwear.

Mrs Teazle was somewhat slow in making it clear what she required of me. 'First,' she said, 'pray take advantage of me cellar' – and pointed to a table laden with bottles of wine and spirits.

I helped myself to a cup of wine, and asked whether I should pour her some.

'Ah, my physician forbids it, alas!' she said, but repairing to another side-table, poured herself a large tumbler of water, which she threw down in a single draught, then pouring herself another. When she began once more to address me, I could not but notice that her words were somewhat slurred; and on her approaching and sitting at my side, an overpowering odour of gin made it quite clear that she was a toper in no small way of business. And indeed during my visit she drank two more large tumblers of the liquid – enough to set most men I know beneath the nearest available table – yet her gait was sober enough, and she remained in control of her senses, though her words became less and less intelligible as our conversation continued.

In the end, however, and with many haws and hums, I understood that she wished to give an entertainment for her husband upon his fiftieth birthday – for him and a number of cronies from his club, whose interests, she readily confessed, were more amorous than artistic, or even gustatory. A feast however was to begin the evening, after which she wished some tableaux to be performed in the garden – which she then showed me: a handsome, small, terraced place, on to which large windows gave from the rear of the building.

'You will forgive me, ma'am,' she said, 'if I shay that

your reprush . . . reprutle . . . reputation has gone before you, and that I am given to supposh you convershant with the kind of entertainment of which . . .'

I let her go no further, but nodded gravely.

'There will be some expense, ma'am,' I said.

'You mean you have already some idea?'

I nodded: indeed, the sight of the four handsome statues of young gods surrounding the fountain at the centre of the garden had given me some idea. Would it be possible, I said, for me to rearrange the garden as I wished? That would be no difficulty, she replied. And as for money – that would be entirely a matter for me; such expenses as would be incurred should be paid, and as for myself, would a fee of one hundred guineas be . . . ?

It was a magnificent sum indeed; and on those conditions I had no hesitation in closing upon the matter, and left the lady leaning heavily upon a table and singing quietly to herself a chorus from *The Beggar's Opera*.

Chapter Seven

The Adventures of Andy

My emotions as I woke upon the morning after my nomination as Member of Parliament for that area of the county of Cornwall in which I found myself can readily be imagined; the tribute had been great, nor would I have repined, except that the compliment had been paid to another man, my friend and brother Sir Franklin Franklyn, the proper owner of the estate over which I was only temporarily presiding.

I should of course have made the error public upon its first being made; but once having failed to correct it, through my over-indulgence of the excellent local cider, which had followed several bottles of claret, my embarrassment, together with the friendliness of the local people, had seemed to make it impossible. That sooner or later – and, by preference, sooner rather than later – the correction must be made, went without saying; but the accomplishment of the task was clearly not going to be altogether pleasant.

The thought of all this dizzied me, and I rose from my bed to find myself dizzied in another way, my head spinning from the remaining fumes of alcohol; hanging on to the bed's end, I rang for a maid, who came with a pail of water, and kindly bathed my head before helping me to immerse myself in an almost cold bath, which restored me to some sort of equilibrium. The recovery was aided by breakfast – I found that as usual to force some food down upon my rebellious stomach was the quickest way of recovering a feeling of health, and a plate of bacon, broiled egg and mushroom followed by a steak of beef and accompanied by a pint of ale went far to recover me to full health.

I then decided upon a walk in order to complete the treatment, and set out across the estate, where here and there small cottages stood in which resided the estate workers, some of whom came of families which had lived there for as long as memory could relate. Stoutly built with walls of clay, their roofs thatched, they were pleasant places enough, and the men and women who inhabited them exchanged greetings in the friendliest way – if with accents so rough that it was impossible for me, more often than not, to tell their meaning.

I walked for two hours, until, almost at midday, and at a spot some miles from the house, I came upon Treweers, sitting on the ground with an extremely old woman whom I had seen about the place. Between them was a leather bottle, from which I was offered a drink – and which turned out to contain an anonymous liquor of such roughness and strength that it knocked my head almost back into its pre-dawn muddle, and I sat down to recover myself.

The old woman was introduced to me as Betsy Pascoe, who, Treweers later told me, was a hundred and seventeen years old – something which I might dispute were it not the case that many Cornish men and women, pickled by long exposure to alcohol and bad weather, indeed live to an extraordinary age. At all events, from the depths of a vastly wrinkled face, the happy crone conversed for some time; and upon my asking her age declined to give it, stating only that she hoped e'er long to be in Beelzebub's bosom.

'Surely,' said Treweers, 'you mean in Abraham's bosom?'

'Abraham or Beelzebub,' replied Mrs Pascoe, 'I been fifty years a widder-woman, and zo long as 'tes some man's bosom, 'tes no matter whose.'

I could not but laugh at this; it reflected well the attitude of the local people to religion – which was that it was by no means as potent as legend. Even the activities of the Nonconformist preachers have had little effect on the natural beliefs of the Cornish, which extend in the direction of superstition of every kind: ghosts and pixies, or piskies as they are known, haunted places and tormented animals of all descriptions. The presence of the Devil is strong in some places, and the belief of the people in his activities tenacious – this resulting in all kinds of pagan ceremonies intended to placate him or his officers. Mrs Pascoe was full of stories to this effect, and nothing I could say would shake her conviction – which was based, as she said, on a wealth of evidence, and on one story in particular, which she retailed with great vigour.

My pen falters in any attempt to render the dialect in which she spoke, its being so obfuscated with intrusive vowels of a strange and foreign nature – only in the interior of Ireland have I heard the English language so maltreated; so I render into a more readily comprehensible narrative the following anecdote:

'My great-uncle Jem,' said Mrs Pascoe, 'went one warm late Tuesday in the summer of 'forty-three to hear John Wesley preach over to Zennor. 'Twas a great occasion, as with all that man's meetings, and ended in an uproar of triumph and song. My great-uncle recognised a number of friends and neighbours in the crush, and among them a young woman of New Mill, his own village, who had been recently married; she was a handsome creature, and Jem was glad to see her there, for she had had a somewhat flighty reputation, and he was in no doubt that she was in need of saving, for he doubted whether her husband – a weak-bodied young man she had married more for his possessing two mules, a horse and seven acres of land than for any better reason – was capable of exercising the authority to keep her in order.

'Jem had to confess, he said later, that she was a veritable beauty, her mob-cap hanging about her neck and releasing a tidal wave of black hair which hung down almost to her waist, and the modesty of her dress was a little belied by its lightness, and the way it revealed a rosy bosom heaving with emotion as she joined in the final hymn. However, said Jem, 'twas a good thing to see her there, evidently intent on storing up weapons against the Devil and all his wiles.

'Jem, like most of the crowd, had only Shanks's pony as conveyance, and set out on his way back home to New Mill with a crowd of others, which gradually diminished as one after another of his companions turned off upon their own way until he was left alone on the moor. He came, after a while, to Chysauster, where the ancient people of the country had dug a pit in which, it was said, they had worshipped the Devil. Jem, as usual, was keeping well clear of that place, especially since the daylight was beginning to fade; when suddenly the hair on the back of his neck rose, for he heard a terrible row coming from the Devil's Pit – the sound of a woman moaning and sobbing. Cautious by nature, he fell to the ground and wriggled like the serpent upon his belly [these Cornish are full of Biblical phrases] 'til he could see into the hollow – where to his amazement he saw his neighbour's wife, her dress thrown upon the grass and now without so much as a stitch upon her body, lying upon the turf and groaning in what could have been pleasure or pain.

'Great-uncle Jem looked about, warily, wondering whether perhaps there was some lover who for the moment had left the girl friend, perhaps to answer a call of nature. But no such thing. And then, with a chill, he realised that there was an unseen presence in the little hollow, for the young woman threw herself upon her back in just such a position as to receive a man, and thrust her secret parts upwards, holding out her arms – yet at the same time seeming fearful of the weight which might be laid upon her.

'It was at that moment, said Great-uncle Jem, that he realised that the unseen man was the Devil – and that it was his duty to rescue the fair distressed. His grandfather, the seventh son of a seventh son, had been an adept conjurer, and in many a conversation had told him of the wiles of the Devil, and what must be done to defeat him, and, given courage by the words of Mr Wesley, he threw off his clothes and descended into the hollow. Standing above the girl, whose bosom rose and fell with a panting desire to be at one with her invisible Tormenter, so under his sway was she, he recited in the Cornish language a rhyme best calculated to send the horned one scampering home – and hurriedly, so as to prevent him reassuming his place, laid his own body on top of the girl's and – his pistol having cocked itself without prompting – took the Tormentor's place.

'Jem always remarked that should he have had any doubt of the Devil's presence, that action would confirm it, for, he said, no other young woman (and he was a young man not without experience) had ever bucked so violently, clawed so vehemently, received him with such heated embraces, as she! 'Twas hot as hell, he said; and having completed the act which would exorcise the unwelcome Visitor, he made to withdraw, upon which the girl laid hold of his arse and so wrapped her legs about him that retreat was impossible – for, she said, her scut itched so that more of the same treatment was required if the Devil was not to be drawn back by its warmth!

'It was, Jem said, some three hours before he was able to soothe the poor, tormented creature. But gradually, as dusk fell and the stars began to punctuate the night, she felt able to resume her clothing – as he did – and the couple walked back to New Mill, where he delivered her to her husband. Jem was ready to explain the circumstances which had detained them, but the young wife desired his silence, for, she said, it was known that the Devil attacked only the most beautiful women, and she would not wish to disconcert her female friends by a seeming boast.

'Sadly, as we can all testify, the Devil is not easily put off when he finds attractive metal, and for some years, often as much as three times a month, he would take advantage of the absence of his victim's husband to visit her. Fortunately, the smell of brimstone always preceded him, and upon smelling the faintest whiff of it, she would send a neighbour's child over to the field where

Jem was working, with the message that her copper needed stoking – which was the code they adopted, not wishing to frighten the good people of the village. Jem would then drop his task of the moment, and by a deep lane make his way to a place where, scaling a wall, he could drop down into her backyard and enter the house through the bedroom window, where he would find the victim already bereft of her clothes, since no time was to be lost if he was to be in position before the Devil's arrival.

'For some years Jem continued in this good work,' Mrs Pascoe explained; 'but doubtless through his efforts, the visitations miraculously ceased just at the time he himself got married – to a beautiful but jealous maid from Gulval; though after they had taken their own farm near Penzance, I hear that the lady concerned appealed to another neighbour to help her in the same manner, so Beelzebub may have been more tenacious than Jem supposed.

'Well, 'twas a strange story,' the old woman concluded; 'but there's no surprise in it, for where the husband is a weak thing, the Devil will try to enter, and we poor women must take what means we can to keep him out.'

Having delivered herself of the story, Mrs Pascoe fell asleep under the hedge, and Treweers and I walked back to the house talking of other things – he asking me if I would care to come, in three days' time, to see the ceremony of the Bodmin Riding, which always took place on the Sunday nearest the seventh of July. Enquiring its nature, I was pleased to note that it might give me the opportunity of returning the hospitality I had been offered, and made arrangements for the erection of a great tent and the provision of considerable quantities of our own cider, and sent out invitations to the local gentry, being specially careful to include all my friends of the previous evening.

I should explain about the Bodmin Riding: it is a custom which began in time immemorial – certainly long before the memory of the parents of the oldest man in the place – and it is said to commemorate the return to the town of the body of St Petroc, the patron saint of the parish, whose relics were stolen in the twelfth century and taken to the Abbey of St Méen in Brittany. An appeal was made to King Henry II, who sent a concourse of soldiers to St Méen and ordered the people there to give back the body, which they did, and it was returned and joyfully reinterred in the Church named after the saint.

The ceremony is not however now notably a religious one, but consists largely of the local people enjoying themselves in whatever manner most appeals to them – some of these traditional and some involuntary. I took myself off to Bodmin on the night before the Riding Day, and established myself at the best local inn, where every room was occupied, some by more than one person. Most of the people were wealthy farmers and their wives, some from as far away as St Ives in the one direction and Boscastle in the other, all looking forward to the the gaiety of the morrow, and most indulging in considerable drinking in preparation, or as it might be by way of practice.

Enormous quantities of beer are brewed in the preceding October, and kept until the day of the Feast, when in the early morning barrels of it are paraded around the town – so that I was awakened at six o'clock by a

tremendous bawling below my window, and on looking
out saw five young men of the town, each bearing a
barrel so large that he could barely carry it, and
accompanied by a band of fifes and drums and other
instruments playing what I was told was the Riding
Tune, halting before each house and, with a blow upon
the drum, crying: 'To the people of this house, a prosper-
ous morning, long life, health, and a Merry Riding!' –
when the master of the house was supposed to descend,
taste the riding-ale from a cup filled from one of the
barrels, and toss into a basket a piece of silver later to be
spent by the bearers.

There was then a motley procession to the Church, the
men and women of the town being mounted upon any
beast of burden they could find – from fine hunters to
mean donkeys or mules – and after a blessing from the
priest, the people made their way to the edge of the moor
above the town, where the fun began, consisting of racing, the ringing of hand bells, cudgel-playing for a silver
cup, jingling-matches, foot races, bobbing for apples
and of course wrestling – a prize of ten sovereigns being
offered for the best man, and five shillings for every
standard – that is, every man who succeeded in throwing
two opponents during the contest, or threw one and
stood for a certain time with another. This was altogether a more violent matter than the wrestling match
which I have already described, the men fighting almost
with desperation for the prize, which in some cases repre-
sented their only chance of making a considerable sum in
money.

I cannot say that I found this an enjoyable spectacle,
for it degenerated into a fight not only with bare fists,
but with metal buckles, metal-tipped shoes, and even

staves; so that the contestants were frequently one mess of blood before the bout was half over. The ladies, however, particularly of the lower sort, were much addicted to the sport, the shouts and screams of encouragement from the maidservants, dairymaids and so forth spurring their favourites on, the sight of blood seeming to be an aphrodisiac of sorts, as their flushed faces and heaving bosoms testified. The winners, moreover (as I learned), could have their choice among their admirers, retiring to a nearby copse to satisfy both their own raised appetites (for physical action of the one sort engendered the other) and those of the maids for whom to have their bodies smeared with the blood of their victorious lovers was a tribute of which they boasted to their friends. Even the losers, provided their defeat had been courageously sustained, were rewarded in a similar way, having to be content however with those ladies rejected by the victorious few.

Those ladies and gentlemen to whom I had sent invitations gathered in a large tent or marquee which I had sent for to Truro, and which was fitted up in luxurious fashion, with tables properly clad with linen, with decent glasses and wine to be drunk from them, and an excellent feast of delicacies the preparation of which I had supervised in my own – or rather Frank's – kitchen, and with some homelier local food – viz. pasties and pies both of fish and of meat, with potatoes and turnips cooked with them. It soon became apparent that both the ladies and the gentlemen felt that upon this occasion they should partake of the local Riders' ale, whereupon I sent out for a barrel.

This was announced by a drum and a fife which came before it, whereupon there appeared in the entrance of the tent a well set-up young lad of sixteen or seventeen years, upon whose naked shoulders the barrel sat, and who as he walked down between the tables I was astonished to see assaulted by the ladies, who reached out to clutch at his thighs or what lay between them in an attempt to make him drop the barrel, which however (he being presumably prepared for this treatment) he did not do, and on reaching the end of the tent set it down and received much applause for his pains.

The speed with which the ale was disposed of was considerable, the lad remaining and himself taking more than one jug of it (this also being the custom). In the midst of the jollity, I announced that if the gentlemen would accompany me, I had arranged some entertainment for them, and led them to a second tent erected behind the first. There I bade them to make a circle, and that having been done gave a signal whereat into the midst of them came Dolly and Jane, who I had commissioned for the day. (They had proved, I may say, confidantes and friends, their apparent enmity being carefully rehearsed for any occasion of a battle!)

They immediately began to wrestle, and in no time had divested each other of their upper clothing, revealing to the audience (who were as pleased with the sight as I had formerly been) one body perhaps somewhat overblown, yet still in excellent condition, and one whose lithe torso and fine, firmly delineated breasts, whose back, slender yet rippling with muscles, were particularly pleasing. The weather being warm and the atmosphere further heated by the airlessness of the tent and the enthusiasm of the audience, the girls' bodies were soon running with perspiration, the sight of which, as it laved their limbs, added an irresistible glamour to the sight.

But this was not the sum of the entertainment I had

devised. After a certain time, it was clearly Dolly who was in the ascendant – which caused some consternation, as Jane, the more handsome of the two, as is invariably (unjustly) the case, was favourite. Dolly succeeded in throwing her opponent to the ground, and, sitting upon her belly, began belabouring her about the head. At this point there sprang from the audience a fine upstanding young fellow, clearly from his loose linen breeches also a wrestler, who, throwing off his shirt, hurled himself at the pair, and seizing Dolly by the shoulders toppled her from her seat. But now a second fellow, another wrestler, well matched to the first, came forth and took Dolly's part, attacking the first.

There now followed a general *mêlée*, during which it gradually became clear that the participants found a greater interest in amorous engagement than the more antagonistic sort. This was first suggested when, one of the young men being pinned to the ground by the other, Dolly turned to Jane and nodded, whereupon the former thrust her hand into the waistband of the pinned man's breeches, and found there (by her expression) a muscle as impressive as those which worked in his shoulders as he endeavoured to throw his rival off.

However, Miss Dolly's exploration had its effect, for a somewhat stupid expression of satisfaction spreading over his face, he soon gave up his endeavours, and lay without struggling beneath the body of his enemy. The latter found this puzzling enough for a moment – but only a moment, for now Miss Jane, not to be outdone, laid herself along his back, and, by rubbing her breasts against it, while at the same time reaching down to run her fingers through the fine growth of hair which decorated his chest, conveyed to him the fact that the ground of the battle had shifted.

In no time, the two men (not surprisingly, for so they had been instructed) released each other and turned their attention to the girls, drawing their breeches from them in order the better to admire them (which, by turning them about and about to explore each plane, also displayed them to the now entirely engrossed audience). Not to be outdone, the girls knelt before their swains, and loosing the cords which tied their nether clothes, drew off the breeches – not without difficulty, a serious obstruction to this course being their distended staffs, which even before the tribute of a kiss (now paid by the girls) had swelled to such a proportion as was not disappointingly at variance with the rest of their splendidly substantial frames.

There now followed a match scarcely less inspiriting than the serious display of wrestling which at the same time was taking place not far away – and which I had had some difficulty in persuading the two men to withdraw from, my argument being clinched only after the payment of a sum greater than the prize money they could have expected to win. The fitness of the couples contributed to their – and the audience's – enjoyment, for it enabled them to assume attitudes which only those fully in command of their limbs could enjoy: viz. Jane standing upon her hands while her lover, holding her legs as he would those of a wheelbarrow, eased his pego gently in and out of its natural home, each movement being accompanied by an equivalent swaying of the hips of the other gentleman, whose instrument was caressed by her lips; while at the same time Dolly, not to be outdone, hung by her bent legs about the latter's neck, her outstretched arms enabling her hands to reach the shoulders of the first man – which resulted in her quim being in such close proximity to the second's lips (do I make myself clear? – the tableau was an interesting one, but difficult to describe) that his tongue was easily able to explore it, giving Dolly such pleasure as was expressed in little yelps of joy.

By nature, such a tableau could be sustained, even by such athletes, only for moments; but its accomplishment was greeted by delirious applause just before it collapsed, and the four participants dissolving in laughter laid themselves out more conventionally, two by two, and to the continued applause of the gentleman viewers, satisfied themselves to the full in a posture more relaxed but none the less pleasure-giving.

I was glad to see that several gentlemen threw a coin or two on to the grass next the panting quartet; but before the audience could begin to disperse, I took my opportunity.

'Gentlemen,' I said, 'it seems that you have enjoyed the little spectacle which I have presented to you' – at which more cheers were heard, together with cries of 'Sir Franklin for Westminster!' 'I have, however,' I continued, 'to make an admission to you. I am not what you think I am.'

There fell an enquiring silence at this.

'I am not Sir Franklin Franklyn,' I continued; 'yet no impostor – having been commissioned by him to come among you and familiarise myself with the area. The mistake was mine in not making myself clear from the first; and for that, I apologise. I am Andrew Archer, Esquire, a gentleman of London. Yet should you wish to continue in desiring me to represent you at Westminster, I shall be pleased to do so.'

The silence which again followed my announcement did not last for long: rather, there was a call for three cheers for Mr Archer! – followed by enthusiastic huzzas. Only one man showed signs of impatience – this being Squire Treleaven, who I suppose discomfited by the fact that he had been the first to make the error of taking me for my friend, scowled and stalked from the tent. The rest seemed extremely pleased, from the applause; after which most of them, rather than turning to accompany me back to the tent where their wives and no doubt their mistresses had been left, slipped out by a side entrance, perhaps to go in search of some means of satisfying those spirits raised by the performance.

Myself, however, did return to the other place – expecting perhaps to face some dissatisfaction from the ladies, left to their own devices; but finding that far from this being the case, they had made their own fun – for I now discovered the beer-carrier spread upon a table while a young lady bestrode him, thoroughly enjoying a ride to the pleasure of which from his expression he was not entirely indifferent. The other ladies were gathered around, those who could not positively approach the couple cheering their representative on, while those nearer were unrestrained in their tormenting of the young man by pinching his nipples, scratching his flesh lightly with their nails, fondling his cods – one of them upon her knees sucking the toes of one foot, while another stood in a kind of trance while he sucked upon the thumb which she had inserted in his mouth.

The stamina of the young steed was remarkable, for he had clearly been successful so far in resisting a final ecstasy – as could be seen by the renitency of his riding-muscle as it appeared and disappeared between the caressing nether lips of his rider. However, sadly I was the destroyer of the scene, for my entrance distracted him from whatever concentration enabled him to deal with the situation, and, his eyes meeting my own, with an incoherent cry he evidently gave up his soul, at the same time however wrenching his hands from those ladies who were caressing them, to reach for the breasts of the young lady whose thighs bestrid him and squeeze them with sufficient force to bring her to an equivalent culmination, so that it was with an air of repleteness rather than disappointment that she dismounted, revealing his proud tool only a little less adamant than it had formerly been.

This was indeed so much the case that, hoping for a quick recovery, the ladies once more fell upon him, devising ever more inspiriting caresses in an attempt to raise once more his spirits – the likelihood being that they would succeed; but I turned my attention away, for at this point my eyes had fallen upon none other than Mrs Treleaven, whose eye, meeting my own, showed by the largeness of its pupil and the frankness of its gaze that she had enjoyed the spectacle to which she had just been treated – though at the back of the crowd, and so deprived of the possibility of engaging physically with the actors.

I gave her a bow. She was, as I have perhaps intimated, no longer young – perhaps of as many as forty years; but a handsome woman, her frame, though large, being by no means flaccid, and her carriage sufficiently upright to be that of a woman half her age.

She stepped towards me and gave me her hand –

pressing my own, and to my surprise lifting it to her bosom, which I found to be unsupported by any artificial means and, concealed only by a light cambric material, yielding yet firm to the touch. Even had I seen no advantage in getting her goodwill, I would not have found her unattractive; as it was, it immediately occurred to me (and I say it without shame) that it would be no bad thing to make myself pleasant with her.

'Perhaps, Sir Franklin, you would see me to my carriage?' she said. 'My husband is nowhere to be seen, and the heat has somewhat overcome me!' This with a flushed face and a panting bosom which may indeed have been the result of the heated atmosphere of the tent – though I imagined that the recent scene had perhaps contributed to it.

Taking my arm, she guided me to where, in a small stockade next the ground in which the Riding was held, a number of carriages were placed, and led me to the largest, which, though not of the proportions which would have commended it to London society, was nevertheless sufficiently capacious.

'Perhaps you would sit with me for a while?' said Mrs Treleaven; and in order to assist her into the carriage I must confess to placing my palm beneath her haunches, in closer juxtaposition to the ultimate seat of emotion than would normally be polite. That she received this without complaint gave me little surprise; nor was I amazed when, upon my mounting behind her, I found that she had already loosened the neck of her dress so that her bosom was almost completely exposed.

'You will pardon me, Sir Franklin,' she said; 'the heat is so oppressive . . .'

'Madam,' I exclaimed, 'the only protest I might make is

that the proximity of so beautiful a lady is likely to inflame my passion to the extent that I might take advantage—'

'Let the flames rise!' she said immediately; 'oh, let them rise!' – and pausing only to draw the blinds of the carriage, threw herself upon her knees before me and immediately reached for my breeches buttons, fumbling in such haste that her fingers were quite incapable of performing the task upon which she was set.

Happily, I had had no congress for some days, and on releasing my person from beneath my clothing, found the touch of her enquiring hands quite sufficient to result in an extension complimentary to the lady, whose patent admiration, and the ingenuity of whose caresses, resulted soon enough in a turgescence sufficiently impressive.

The dimensions of the carriage were somewhat confining; yet divested of the rest of our clothing, we found it possible to assume an attitude satisfactory to the lady – this consisting of her turning her back to me and resting her folded arms upon the seat opposite, so that I could guide my staff between her thighs in order to reach heaven. The ample proportions of her person were no hindrance to my enjoyment: I had quite forgot, indeed, the pleasure to be got from embracing a well-covered female, which has the effect of romping among a pile of cushions. In this case, too, the lady's appetite proved aphrodisiac, for the enjoyment she received was expressed in a controlled hysteria – so much so that after a while she was entirely unable to maintain the attitude she had adopted, and suddenly standing threw me off, turned about, and bestriding me placed her hands beneath my arse and lifted me bodily until, my cheeks resting upon the edge of the seat, she was able at her own pace to work away, my face buried in the ample convexities of her by no means unattractive bosom, and only the unusual attitude in which I found myself enabling me to keep my countenance until, her teeth nipping her lips to prevent herself crying out, she finally ceased her movements and let me fall with a thump to the floor.

It was at that moment that there was the rattle of a stick upon the door of the carriage, and a cry of 'Flora, m'dear – are you there?'

It was Squire Treleaven!

The lady showed considerable quickness. Pulling aside the blind only a little, she called out in a weak voice:

'My dear, I am a little fatigued by the heat, and taking a little rest. I will join you for dinner at the Punchbowl.'

After but a single enquiry as to whether he could fetch a glass of ale or some other comfort, the Squire left – to my considerable relief, for had he discovered that in addition to deceiving him as to my identity I had now swived his wife under his very nose (so to speak), my reputation would have become as nothing to him.

His lady had now recovered sufficiently to reach for me once more; but unsurprisingly my tool had shrunken under the effect of the Squire's appearance, and for a moment declined to rise (despite the fact that I had not participated in the consummation which the lady had experienced).

Expressing, however, no dismay, she sank to her knees and administered such attentions with her lips as the most experienced whore would be hard put to it to contrive; whereat I recovered soon enough, and was able not only to satisfy her once more, but to pay her – without any difficulty whatsoever – the compliment of a discharge sufficiently generous to confirm my admiration; indeed, her adeptness, willingness and pleasure in the game were such as to overbalance entirely the disadvantage of her years.

I had, I must confess, meant to take advantage of the opportunity to explain myself to her – in the sense, I mean, of excusing the embarrassment over my identity. Yet it was impossible to do as we both lay in that delightful lethargy which invariably follows satisfactory congress, and after a decent interval I merely assumed my clothes (having some difficulty in sorting them from the tangle of garments now scattered upon the floor of the carriage) and made my *adieux*.

That evening, I made my way to the Punchbowl Inn, where a number of gentlemen with their ladies were dining with the Squire, and screwing my courage up entered the room fairly late in the evening, when I judged that good food and drink might have lifted the heart even of the most serious Whig among them.

To my relief, I was greeted by a round of applause, as the provider of the afternoon's entertainment; and even Squire Treleaven seemed to look on me kindly, and making room waved me to a chair at his side, then rising to address the company.

'Gentlemen!' he said, 'Due entirely to an over-speedy act on my own part, I introduced this young man to you as Sir Franklin Franklyn, of Vycken Hall. It appears that this is not the case . . .' A murmur ran about the room. The Squire lifted his hand: 'But it is no matter!' he said. 'Mr Andrew Archer is a person of the utmost probity, intelligent and personable' (here I caught Mrs Treleaven's eye, and was in no doubt that she had commended me to him) 'and subject to your agreement' (he looked around the table, in the entirely confident expectation that no one would dare to cross him) 'I have no hesitation in suggesting that he should none the less be our candidate for the coming contest.'

Mrs Treleaven immediately applauded, and after the slightest hesitation was followed by most of the company – the gentlemen perhaps in part because they were in the midst of a congenial evening, and in part because they had enjoyed the afternoon's entertainment – the ladies less wholeheartedly, though led by the Squire's wife. It may be, I thought, that I should have to ingratiate myself further with the weaker sex if my position was to be entirely assured. As it was, however, I took more than a single glass of wine with the company, and sat until the candles guttered and the faint hints of dawn showed themselves beyond the blinds.

Chapter Eight

Sophie's Story

Organising the party at Mrs Teazle's was no great problem for me, since by now I had at my command a considerable knowledge of those circles in the city which could provide me with the *dramatis personae* for almost any amorous performance which the inventive mind of man – or woman – could envisage. It is also the fact that I actually enjoy the process of putting such matters in train, which in this case involved merely a visit to certain theatres in the town, both to the green-rooms where always could be found personable ladies and gentlemen happy to engage in employment outside the walls of the playhouse, and the rooms where the scene-makers could be relied upon to help with the construction of scenes or, as on the occasion of which I speak, the provision of certain paints to be applied to the skin, were it wished to give it a resemblance to the darker skins of other climes – or indeed of no known clime!

It was with some confidence that, having made my arrangements, I arrived at Mrs Teazle's house in Upper Brook Street at eleven o'clock in the morning of the day in question, just after Mr Teazle's departure for his Club; there I spent the day making my preparations, with the help of a gang of men whose first task was to remove the garden statues from their plinths, and who then helped in the decoration of the garden by hanging bands and swathes of flowers and greenery, and building *torchères* for torches which would illuminate the place.

Promptly at nine o'clock, Mr Teazle and nine of his friends arrived from their Club, where they had already spent the day celebrating the anniversary of the gentleman's birth – though not, I hoped, to such an extent that the coming pleasantries would be entirely lost upon them.

They sat down to dinner, somewhat surprised, I believe, at the absence of female company; for having heard by devious means that an entertainment was being organised, they had assumed, quite understandably, that it would include, besides meat and drink, those conveniences which permit gentlemen to satisfy other appetites.

However, the dinner I had ordered was sufficiently delicious, and the wines sufficiently excellent, to keep them in a good mood: the soup, a delicious *bisque d'écrevisses* was followed by turbot in lobster sauce; pheasant, green-goose and turkey preceded *fondue*, cabinet-pudding, orange jelly and *meringue glacés*, each with its wine; and by the time the port was circulating – a pint bottle to each man, of course – there was a general feeling of *bonhomie*. It was at this stage that, upon a signal from myself, the candles in the dining-room were extinguished and footmen drew back the curtains which had until that moment obscured the view of the garden – which was now revealed, lit by flaming torches.

At first, Mr Teazle must have thought that some Midas had been at work and turned his four garden statues upon their plinths to gold: there, in fact, stood four young gentlemen selected for their likeness to the marble effigies which I had had carefully removed and stored, to be replaced by human flesh.

Upon the first plinth was Hermes, holding his lyre – a splendid gentleman of perhaps twenty-five, slim of waist and narrow of hips, but fully developed and in the prime of young manhood; next him was a fellow of perhaps thirty and five, of a heavier build, his broad chest (normally decorated with a thick bush of black hair, which had for this occasion been shaved) expressive of the power and majesty of Apollo.

Opposite this pair stood a sturdy man fully of Mr Teazle's own age, yet preserved by action and energy – he was a professional fighter who had only recently given up the game, and whose face expressed all the burly forthrightness of Zeus; and next him the goatish figure of Pan, his horns rising out of his curly hair, his legs covered in hair, a stumpy tail perkily protruding above the cleft of his buttocks.

These gentlemen had had their bodies all gilded, even to their hair (which was painted and stiffened by the application of spirit gum, so that it looked, both upon head and body, as though 'twere made of gold thread), and were standing so still that, as I said, they seemed at first to be made of metal itself. There was some admiration from the audience, who none the less seemed to wonder what such an exhibition could have to do with them, who were not known expressly for their love of art, and were certainly not of that disposition best to be pleased by an exhibition of unclothed persons of their own sex!

But now upon the scene came four ladies, each dressed in flowing robes in the Greek fashion, sufficiently loose to reveal, as they walked, glimpses of thigh and breast – first, Chimaera, bearing her jug of wine, then

Dryope, the shepherdess, with her crook; then strode in Metis, the Titaness – a commanding figure whose burly shoulders were scarcely veiled by her flowing black hair; and finally Selene, that innocent young girl at whom Pan set his sights.

Hidden musicians now struck up an enticing air by the French musician Jean François Lesueur, and the show began. As the others held a pose at the back of the garden, before the fountain, whose drops were turned to liquid gold by the light of the torches, Chimaera approached the plinth upon which Hermes stood, and, lifting her jug to her shoulder, smiled as though inviting him to drink. I believe that some of the gentlemen in the audience believed the statues really to be of gilded stone, for there was a slight gasp as the young god came to life, moved his golden limbs, and descending from his plinth took from her the jug and drained it. The magic liquor immediately had its effect, for his legs weakened beneath him, and he swayed – whereupon the girl lifted one of his arms about her shoulders in order to support him – but was unable to hold such a weight, and the god slumped to the ground, where he lay apparently unconscious!

She stood aghast, the reduction of so promising a gentleman from vivid life to seeming death being the opposite of what she desired. Kneeling beside him, she laid her cheek against his, to discover whether he still breathed, or no; then, confirmed in her hopes at least of that, laid her hands upon his breast, which gently rose and fell beneath their palms. As she leaned to observe him, her robe fell forward over his body, obscuring it from her view – whereat she impatiently shrugged it from her shoulders, whose white perfection, set against the dark of the night and only slightly yellowed by the torchlight, now showed in brilliant contrast to the ruddier gold of his own. Her breasts were perfectly formed, their enticing curves shaped by an attentive gravity, which pulled them gently from her body as if envious to possess them, and her posterior – seen to greater advantage by those fortunate gentlemen sitting rather to the leftward of the scene – resembled nothing so much as a ripe peach, the delightful flesh of which any full-blooded gentleman would wish gently to nibble.

Now, freed from the encumbrance of clothing, Chimaera fell more minutely to examining and admiring the limbs of the fallen god, which she did with growing pleasure as her palms grazed the planes of his breast, belly and hips, then after only a moment's hesitation at what might seem behaviour improper between human and god, played for a moment among the gold curls where lay his manhood. But – alas, poor Chimaera! – what disappointment was here? – for rather than turning under her caresses from twig to tree, from acorn to oak, his shrunken piece remained so small as almost to be hidden from sight.

I must confess to admiring the powers of young Robin Phibb, whom I had found in the company of players at His Majesty's Theatre; for despite her lifting his squab part upon her palm and stroking it in the most insinuating manner with her fingers, he managed to contain himself – by, he told me afterwards, attempting to recall the entire part of Helicanus in *Pericles, Prince of Tyre*, a part of which he was memorising in preparation for a coming production of that neglected work of the great Bard.

However, such reticence scarcely contributed to the gaiety of the evening, and in accordance with our rehearsal of the scene, after a while – though his body remained still, his face expressionless and his limbs relaxed – he nevertheless showed signs of life, when the beautiful Chimaera now laid upon his reluctant firing piece a tender, exploring tongue, first gently withdrawing the skin, which disclosed beneath its gold rim an almost strawberry pink flesh, then testing it with just the hope of pleasure summer fruit would give; whereupon almost in an instant he permitted the blood to flow, and a ramrod of quite sufficient dimensions established itself between her lips – at which she started almost with fear, yet not such apprehension as prevented her being at the same time delighted.

Since the still unconscious god showed no sign of movement other than between belly and thigh, rolling upon her back the impatient maid pulled his body upon her own, opening both arms and thighs to embrace him. Yet even so poignant an invitation was ignored by Hermes, who still lay insensible, his head lolling upon her shoulder; and while a hand had fallen upon one delicious breast, it made not the slightest gesture of taking advantage of the prize within its palm. There was a stirring in the audience, and some comments to the effect that were certain humans to take his place, such reticence would be instantly banished.

But now, again disappointed, the furious Chimaera sat up, Hermes' body falling to one side – the most remarkable feature of it still extant and (to judge by her expression as she handled it) capable of performing the task demanded of men by women – yet without waking motive, inactive.

Once more taking command, and rolling Hermes upon his back, Chimaera brought things to a more satisfactory head by the simple device of mounting upon his body as upon a bareback horse, and rising upon her knees momentarily, in order to present the ramrod to the barrel, then sank upon it and with every sign of gratification began to trot – with a mounting enthusiasm which communicated its warmth to the onlooking gentlemen, who watched with keen interest as the rosy skin of a human youth began to appear upon each of still sleeping Hermes' sides, where the gilt with which his skin had been painted now transferred itself to the inside of Chimaera's thighs; and soon, indeed, the length of his swiving tool returned by exhilarating friction to the normally flushed hue of a handsomely distended prick.

To his credit, young Mr Phibb maintained until the last a pretence of unconsciousness, not the slightest flicker of apprehension appearing upon his features even when (no doubt apprehensive of the tension of his muscles) Chimaera after a final wriggle of her lower person rose, releasing from its socket the delightful wand just in time to prove by the exuberance of a suddenly released fountain that she had brought the sleeping god beyond the borders of ultimate pleasure.

The pair for a moment held the pose; then, as the onlookers broke into applause, rose to their feet and took their bow – something which no doubt broke the illusion; but it would have been unkind, even in the warmth of summer, to have them remain upon the cold flagstones during the rest of the entertainment, which followed without pause, the frozen group behind them broken by the figures of Apollo and Dryope, who moved forward, the god revealing as he strode into the full torchlight that his own torch was already burning with desire – a view of the previous combatants having been sufficient to set light to it.

In order that there should not be a climax of pleasure too soon in the evening, I had ensured that these two should present no unusual aspect: taking Dryope's crook in his hand, Apollo therefore drew her immediately towards him, and taking her by the waist lifted her upon the edge of the fountain, where, raising the skirt of her dress, he parted her thighs, and standing between them began that work which – from her silent shriek of pleasure (for my actors were strictly enjoined to make no sound which would dispel the charm of the performance) – gave her no small joy. Lifting her arms, she lost no time in tearing her single garment from her, and clutching Apollo's head directed his lips to those rosy nipples which shone upon her full breasts.

Apollo and Dryope completed their coupling in a few minutes; for I did not wish the interval of conventionality to be too long. I had anticipated, and warned them, that they would not receive the acclamation accorded their predecessors, and so having given a final thrust of his arse, Apollo placed his muse's arms about his neck, and, lifting her with his hands below her buttocks, walked from the scene – as it turned out, without either himself having reached an apogee, or giving his lady that pleasure – they being a professional couple whose participation was solely for the profit involved, while my other pairs showed an enthusiasm for the game which was the equal of, or even surpassed, their desire for monetary consideration.

This was certainly true of Zeus and Metis, who now took the stage. I have said that Zeus was a gentleman of considerable parts; but if his limbs were sturdy and his frame massive, he was matched by his companion, to whom I had been directed at a circus on the heath behind the village of Hampstead, where I found her earning coppers by the lifting of weights and the bending of iron bars.

Now, striding towards the centre of the garden, she loosed her upper clothing so that it fell about her waist, and with both hands raised a bar she had brought with her above her head and bent it with a steady motion until it was doubled. The extraordinary aspect of the performance was in the appearance of her torso, which, her arms being raised, could have been that of a well-developed man; her breasts were no larger than those rounded muscles upon the chest of a burly fellow, while cords stood out in her arms and across her shoulders which would have been the envy of many a seaman!

Indeed, the whisper ran about that she was a man – which notion however was dispelled upon Zeus stepping forward, for, immediately eager for the fray, she threw her clothing altogether aside, revealing between two thighs with the dimensions of tree-trunks a fleece of thick black hair barely concealing lips already pouting with desire as their owner's eyes fell upon the protuberance which sprouted from the equivalent area of the body of her would-be lover. His sturdy appliance seemed knotted and banded with muscles of its own, resembling ribs, giving it such an appearance as would justify some men's description of it – a weapon indeed!

I must here remark that upon my putting to her the scheme of entertainment which I had devised, Mary Morgan (for this was the giantess's name, she being of Welsh descent) had been delighted to acquiesce, for, because of her size and somewhat masculine appearance, it was (she confided) but rarely that she could entice a lover to satisfy appetites which were as keenly resident within her large frame as in that of the prettiest girl. Moreover, her passions matched her size, and lovers of conventional powers found themselves confounded, for in her frenzy she frequently did them some injury, such as the dislocation of an arm or even (on one sad occasion) a neck.

In this case, however, Metis was well-matched with Zeus: and the clashing of the two titans was like the coming together of two great jungle beasts – a bubbling sound of anticipatory pleasure boiled low in their throats as their bodies met – which itself took place with a peculiar sound, a sort of dull thud. Neither appeared to wish to give way, and for a moment they appeared like wrestlers embracing each other, arms upon each other's shoulders; then – I am convinced through desire rather than lack of strength – the titaness fell backwards upon the flagstones with sufficient force (it seemed to me) almost to break them, and threw up her legs to reveal a cavern of such dimensions that only a such a fellow as Zeus could hope satisfactorily to fill it; which, on the instant, he did, her under-thighs meeting his breast and belly with a sounding *smack!*

The appetites of this pair were as strong as their bodies; by contrast to their predecessors they engaged for a considerable period of time, the size and muscularity of their bodies giving at every turn new cause for interested attention; now he would be in the ascendant (as at first, ploughing to admiration), now she, as when with a sudden effort she grasped her lover about the hips and lifted him bodily from her, then raising him until, supporting him thus, she was able to nuzzle that massive instrument which at every moment seemed to grow more considerable, and could scarcely have been outdone in size or combativeness by those of the most prized bull of a show! Whereafter he, not to be outdone, stood, legs apart, took her by the hips and lifted her high in the air, then lowering her until he was able to return the compliment by planting an enthusiastic kiss upon that cavity which, a moment later, returning her to the ground, he again plugged with proper flesh.

I must confess that the show was as remarkable for acrobatics as for amorous play, and regarding the audience believe that they shared my own feeling in the matter, for their look was rather admiring than enthusiastic; something which however was swiftly repaired when, upon Zeus and Metis retiring (to the nearby garden shed where, ignoring Apollo, who was busy cleansing his body of gilt, and Dryope, who was engaged in sewing a skirt, they continued an enthusiastic amorous contest, their zestful enthusiasm not yet having been quenched), there now entered upon the scene the goat-like Pan, startling the virtuous Selene, who had clearly never before seen such a remarkable creature.

At first, he appeared to her with his lower person hidden behind the wall of the fountain and his hair ruffled to conceal his little horns; so that all she saw was a handsome youth, at whose presence only her shyness mitigated against welcome; though her eyes widened at his appearing, from a lack of clothing upon the upper part of his body, to be entirely naked. Upon his moving closer, she was immediately relieved, clearly believing his legs to be clad in some sort of hairy breeches, and permitted him to take her hand, and even to kiss it – whereupon, smoothing his hair with a hand, she found to her surprise those protuberances which upon closer examination revealed themselves as horns.

This clearly astonished her – yet she did not withdraw, no doubt because by now his tiny tongue was insinuating itself between her fingers, and his lips in turn sucking upon them. Transferring those lips to the back of her hand, then her wrist, and finally travelling the length of her slim white arms, he reached at length (by way of one shoulder, revealed by the fall of her tunic) her own lips, tickled the corners of her mouth, and even exchanged greetings with her own tongue, which could be seen pinkly to greet his.

But it was a different matter when, encouraged by her lack either of fear or anger, and eager to be at her, he took her hand and placed it between his thighs – for there she felt, as her expression denoted, something she had not expected: a hard yet warm prong of flesh which from its throbbing boded her no good.

She rose as though to flee: but he was too quick for her, and clutching caught the edge of her tunic, which immediately fell from her (a process encouraged by our unpicking the seams of it almost entirely before the commencement of the programme), revealing a body white as a wand, and of quite remarkable beauty, poised between the purity of girlhood and the ripeness of womanhood – she was in fact one of the most beautiful girls upon whom I had had the pleasure of setting eyes (who was, under the name of Mrs Hunbert, to become one of the admired actresses of the age, excelling in the parts of Perdita, Hermione and Ophelia). She was a person of great probity, and had only been persuaded to participate in my entertainment by the fact that she was violently in love with the young person who was impersonating Pan, and who had formerly ignored her.

I must now reveal that the actor playing the part of Pan was none other than my young friend John Rice, who but a few weeks previously had by his appearance as a satyr rehearsed for his present, more prominent – but equally hirsute – characterisation. It may be thought remarkable that I had consented to his wish to participate in the entertainment – expressed as soon as he had heard of its going forward; but my constant readers will know how devoid I am of that most wasteful of emotions, jealousy; and revenged myself somewhat upon him (if revenge is not too strong a word for what amounted merely to a prank) by appointing him a partner who I knew had for some time experienced the unrequited love of which I have spoken!

If he had previously not so much as looked at the lady, he was now – as who would not be? – struck by the loveliness of her body, its slim waist hung with generous hips below which lay thighs firm yet enticing; slight shoulders supporting arms which seemed boneless as they curved about him – and a bosom the whiteness of which was decorated by two little marks like ripe berries: and, from the tender manner in which he set them to his lips, as sweet.

For a moment, Pan forgot himself, and seemed about to treat his nymph with an unwonted tenderness; but then remembered his part, and throwing her to the flagstones – while she pretended horror and distress – knelt upon her shoulders, so that above her stood at attention an instrument so fierce-looking, being decorated with hair which had been stuck upon it with no small difficulty, that it aggravated her terror to an hysteria that only I, from my intimate knowledge, knew to be feigned.

The struggle that ensued was convincing enough to

suggest a rape; and I, knowing the secret history of the pair, realised that the passions of Pan (or rather, of my friend John) were indeed roused by the surprising generosity with which the lady not only offered him those delights of her body to which ignorance had previously rendered him indifferent, but put herself about to contribute to their coupling such inspiriting caresses that one might wonder how they came into the head of a young person who had but recently left the comfort of a Leicestershire parsonage for the more interesting but less cloistered life of the stage. I was once more impressed by the speed with which actors and actresses can command a part, speed of study clearly being one of Mrs Hunbert's many virtues.

However, to return to my narrative, the audience now saw Selene, delighted at her proximity to the person she so admired, rouse him yet further by the little bites which she inflicted upon his limbs, thus exciting him to new displays of coarseness. With an expressive display of acted repugnance, it was at first with reluctance that she shrank from the ill-manners with which he brandished his private part before her, forcing her to caress it; but gradually she seemed to find this more interesting than repellent, then curiosity encouraged her to kneel before him and inspect further such an odd device, entirely new to a maid, stroking the hair which covered its surface, and, withdrawing the skin at its end, greeting with astonished pleasure the bald head which seemed to admire her with its single eye!

After an interval, his similar attention to her own parts – informed by experience (as much the amorous experience of the actor as of the god!) – led inevitably to coupling sufficiently spirited in its vigour and exciting in its postures not only to delight the lady but to to excite the audience; and a storm of applause went out on the still night air as the torches guttered to darkness just as the embracing god and his mortal mistress with a final embrace satisfied each other.

Allowing no time for the gentlemen's emotions to cool, I entered the room from behind the screen where I had been concealed, and announced that if they would follow me to a neighbouring room, they would find the material with which to satiate any appetite raised by the spectacle. Yet there was one condition: the ladies, who were of the finest society, had asked me to spare their blushes by insisting on a paucity of lighting, and permitting them to wear masks.

The gentlemen were in no mood to argue; and followed me to a room equipped with several *banquettes* and cushions, where an equal number of ladies waited, their unclothed forms only dimly to be seen in the light shed by two candles, and upon whose bodies the amorous gentlemen fell like thunderbolts, having paused only to remove their clothing (or in some cases, merely that part of their clothing which would have hindered them from carnal connection).

The following saturnalia was satisfactory to all parties; yet I must confess it was with some anxiety that, upon the last of the couples ceasing their writhing, I entered together with three footmen bearing candelabra – whereupon the ladies, in a light now sufficient to be revelatory, removed their masks and revealed themselves as . . . the wives of the male guests!

After an initial amazement and embarrassment – some of the gentlemen having paid to their partners such amorous attention as had previously been reserved only

for their mistresses – the gentlemen took the prank in
good part – even those who, through some misalign-
ment, had been the partners of each other's wives; and so
delighted were the latter that the reticence with which
they usually embraced their husbands gave way to
unusual enthusiasm, and a recoupling was commenced –
at which I retired, making my way to the shed where
my actors were now resuming their day clothing, and
disbursing those fees promised.

Returning to my house, my only regret – to be frank
with readers sufficiently familiar with my previous
adventures not to take offence at the confession – was
that I had myself been unable to take part in the tableaux,
for I was convinced that my own person was not so sufficiently advanced in years as not to be attractive to the
discerning gentleman. Moreover, my senses had no more
been dormant under the stimulation of the exhibition
than those of my audience, and I was increasingly
conscious that they required satisfaction.

My house was dark, the servants having permission to
retire at their own time when I was from home (since
there was no knowing at what time I might return). I
disrobed in my bedroom, yet was confident that the arms
of Morpheus were entirely unready to welcome me –
and so, slipping on a *robe de chambre*, set out down the
corridor and through the door beyond which lay the
servants' quarters, and in particular the room appointed
to John Rice, who I believed, despite his adventures
of the evening, might welcome me – indeed, who had
better welcome me, in view of my hospitality to him, to
say nothing of my equanimity in watching his attentions
to another female!

None of the servants' rooms were capable of being

locked, it not being the custom in those days to allow them that privacy which a more civilised society now permits; and the door to John's room was no exception, so on my softly turning the handle, it freely opened, and in the dim light shed by a waning moon I saw upon the bed his charming person, lying face down, the moonlight falling over his body and giving it the appearance of polished marble (though a marble here and there smirched with gold, and here and there marked by small patches of hair, which he had been unable altogether to remove).

Taking two steps forward, I stood above him, and in a moment laid my fingers gently upon that most sensitive spot just above the bifurcation of the buttocks, the slightest grazing of which raises the spirits of the most lethargic of men; and indeed, upon my merely scratching the surface of the skin with a fingernail, he stirred, and turning stretched up his arms still in half-sleep and clutching me about the waist buried his head in my lap, and murmured the name of Melody, by which name Mrs Hunbert wished to be known (her given name, Joy, being considered insufficiently euphonious for an actress). Though not resentful, this was not a sound welcome to my ears, and I could not resist the rebuke of giving a gentle twist to those twin spheres which are sensitive to such attacks, whereupon he woke completely, and had the grace to blush.

Any fears that his powers might have been exhausted by his attentions to Mrs Hunbert were within a short time dispelled. I will not detail the engagement itself further than to say that with vigour balanced by tenderness, rudeness mitigated by admiration, gentleness stiffened by determination, he entirely fulfilled – as he was always capable of – those expectations I had of him. Lying in his arms after we had both experienced the final peak of pleasure, I could not but enquire whether in the matter of such amusements as that in which he had taken part, affection could ever accompany so public a display, or whether mechanical contrivance alone produced the effect? I believe he knew by my expression what I meant, and I was rewarded by the reply (though hesitatingly expressed) that I should not be amazed that a vigorous young man should be attracted to youth and beauty – though on completing the sentence it was immediately softened by his assurance that years had by no means diminished the effect of my own charms, 'else', he said, 'how could I have raised my spirits after already twice this evening paid tribute to Venus?'

I could not but enquire, 'Twice?' – whereupon he admitted that he and Mrs Hunbert (who, I should say, is not nor ever has been married, but takes the appellation of 'Mistress' for the sake of respectability), having left the garden, had been encouraged to repeat their amorous engagement by the emotion engendered by her assisting him to remove the false hair from his loins (which I considered was taking a liberty with a young person of the opposite sex to whom she had only recently been introduced).

However, all in all I must admit that I approved the engagement; for though the young man was pleasant enough, and I was happy to continue to give him shelter, it went without saying that our connection was not such as could lead to permanence; and upon the time coming when I must ask him to leave the house, it was best he should have some companion to afford him upon a regular basis those pleasures to which I was still, for the moment, happy to contribute.

So, having given him a final embrace, and assured myself by manual examination that he was for the time incapable of renewed excitation (a circumstance for which he offered shamefaced apologies), I returned to my own bed, and fell into a satisfied and deep sleep as dawn began to rise.

Mrs Teazle was prompt in the payment of my considerable expenses, adding to them a generous fee. But the matter did not end there, for within the week a footman called upon me, asking me to attend upon the Earl of Stow, the leader of that society whose chief interest is in the breeding and racing of horses. Calling upon him at his mansion in Park Lane, I was forced to wait until a clatter of hooves in the courtyard announced his return from riding in the Park, and looking out of the window I saw a personable young man of perhaps thirty and five throwing over the back of his mount a leg of elegant proportions, and leaping to the ground with a nimbleness and athletic grace which immediately marked him as energetic and vigorous.

Upon his entering the room, this impression was confirmed – and though he apologised for his state, having been (he explained) trying out a new mount, the masculine odour of perspiration, no less than that humidity which caused his shirt (open to show the pillar of a strong and graceful neck) to adhere to a chest whose manly firmness was beyond question, was far from distressing.

His Lordship explained that, as was usual with him, he had organised a party for the Newmarket race meeting, a week hence; and that he was eager to place before his guests some entertainment for the Sunday upon which no racing, of course, took place. Such entertainment, he said, should take place in the open air – 'but will not be

public' (he hastily assured me) 'for my estate is guarded
by spinneys, and cannot be seen by passers-by.'

'From that remark, my Lord—'

'Call me Stow,' the gentleman generously remarked.

'—I infer that the kind of entertainment you wish—'

'—Might not be too far removed in tone from that
which I understand you recently provided for Billy
Teazle, who was full of praise for it at the
Club.'

I bowed. 'I shall be delighted,' I said – and enquired
whether he had anything specific in mind?

No, he remarked; though should it in some way
include an allusion to the art of horsemanship – or
horsewomanship, he added with a smile – that would
not be untoward.

We discussed the matter for a while, for there were
arrangements of which I had to be sure – such as the
provision of hospitality for the ladies and gentlemen who
should provide the entertainment; the disbursement of
expenses—

'And your fee?' enquired Stow.

'I am happy to leave that in your hands,' I replied –
for I was wealthy enough to ignore the matter, having
been drawn into the work merely by accident and inclination, and not relying upon it for the provision of bread
and wine.

Stow was good enough to offer me lunch, and having
bathed himself (an exercise with which I would have been
happy to assist, had I been invited, for he was an
extremely attractive gentleman) we sat down to a cold
collation accompanied by an Austrian wine, which we
took alone, off splendid silver and from equally magnificent glasses, at one end of a long table in a sumptuous

dining-room in which a hundred people could easily have been served.

During the meal he regaled me with tales of his recent tour in the Orient, which was taken for the purposes of sport, and during which (he told me with some pride) he had killed twelve brace of elephants, twelve couple of rhinoceroses, thirty-two couple of buffaloes, three camels, seven brace of ostriches, a crocodile, one hundred and thirty-seven brace of humming-birds, three boa-constrictors and two pair of rattlesnakes – upon which I expressed some surprise that any wild creatures of any sort remained upon that continent. And indeed, it seems to me curious that gentlemen should take such pleasure in the execution of their fellow-creatures. However, 'twas none of my business, and I cannot say that it detracted more than a very little from the attractions of my new friend, upon whose behalf I was shortly once more enquiring for specific talent among my friends of the theatre.

Chapter Nine

The Adventures of Andy

My passage with Mrs Treleaven, more interesting, perhaps, than positively inspiriting, seemed likely to be the last episode of erotic interest for some time, as I now found myself plunged into politicking – something of which I had no experience and in which (to be frank) I had previously had little interest.

The burning topic of the time was on the one side the popularity of Billy the King, and on the other popular dislike of the Tory Government – yet at the same time by no means a majority of people were in favour of the Whigs, most of whom were high-living artistocrats, fonder of claret and free love than of water and work.

And so I found myself a Radical, for despite Squire Treleaven (who had it not been for tradition would have been an Ultra-Tory High Churchman, but who from the accident of his birth, was a Whig Nonconformist!) this seemed the easiest way of ingratiating myself with the voters of the district. It was by no means a hardship to me, for I had much sympathy with the newly founded and growing trades unions, formed to save men from the hours of monotonous toil which made them little more than slaves.

There were no machines to break in east Cornwall, where farming and fishing were the chief occupations of

the natives – yet even here people had heard of Robert
Owen and what he called British Socialism, and I was
astonished to find, in the hand of an artisan I encountered at the weekly cattle market in Liskeard, Lieuten-
ant Hodgskin's pamphlet *Labour Defended against the
Claims of Capital*, which, published some years previously, bore all the signs of repeated reading.

The whole county was full of election fever (I should
explain that at that time the death of the Sovereign auto-
matically dissolved the Parliament), and this persisted
for some time, the polls opening in July to remain open
for three weeks, during which activity was great not only
in the making of speeches but the buying of drinks for
voters, and even – on the part of my Tory opponent –
the transfer of leases of houses, the provision of suits of
clothing, small-arms, mittens and fur tippets for the
ladies, and even swaddling clothes for infants.

All this I scorned (apart from any other consideration,
Squire Treleaven and his cronies showed no signs of con-
tributing funds to the election campaign, and I was certainly not inclined to squander my own funds upon it).
Incidentally, I had of course sent word to Alcovary and
my friend Frank of the circumstances of my standing for
Parliament, and assuring him that should I obtain a seat
in the Parliament, it would as a matter of course be
resigned to him should he at any time require it; to which
he had returned a message of congratulation and encouragement, good friend that he was.

If nothing else, my travelling about the county on this
occasion taught me much about a part of the of world
which I had previously been entirely in ignorance. The
county is particularly marked for the splendour of its
churches and the poverty of its houses, for apart from a

very few (such as the one in which I was privileged to reside) the homes of the Cornish are small and mean. They are built of cob or clay, sometimes faced with local stone or slate if such is available, generally whitewashed upon the outside, and with their roofs thatched.

They look, I must admit, extremely pretty, fitting in well with the landscape, solid and foursquare, and weathered by the winds which commonly lash both coasts and inland hills. They straggle across the countryside, often isolated and lonely – for you will find them almost anywhere: tucked in odd corners by the roadside, on rocky ledges above the fishing coves, or amid the burrows and debris of the tin mines which provide (apart from fishing and farming) a chief income for the people.

They are built by the people themselves, often without the help of professional 'builders'; even the window frames are often made by the inhabitants, with such results in the terms of crookedness and small holes admitting the winds as I need not describe. Many of the cottages were built in great haste, for it was believed that any one who built a house in one night could claim the freehold of it for ever after – a belief much contested by landlords, and now beginning to be disclaimed.

Where cottages did cluster together in small groups, they made for strange villages indeed, higgledy-piggledy places with streets which so twisted and turned (and indeed so narrow) that they scarcely deserved the name: often have I ridden along streets so narrow that, by merely stretching out my arms upon each side, I could touch the buildings which faced each other. The windows of the upper rooms, which sometimes thrust out beyond the ground floor, are almost in juxtaposition, which must make for extreme ease of passage should there be extramarital concupiscence among the natives of the places.

As to the people, they are much as people anywhere else in the country, yet particularly given, as it seemed to me, to an interest in medical matters, and extremely ready to pass on even to a stranger the intimate details of their medical history. At a place called Trevarian, I was detained for an hour while two gentlemen hot in the Whig interest, and who I could not afford to offend by an over-precipitate retreat, told me of their discovery of Dr Lamb's medicines, a cure-all newly brought from Bristol, and efficacious in the curing of all manner of indigestion, bilious and liver complaints, difficulty of breathing, delicate constitutions – and above all, worms.

One man claimed that John Code, the manager of Screed Moor Clay Works, in the parish of St Austell, after taking a course of Lamb's medicine, passed a tape-worm seven feet long, with upwards of 200 joints, the symptoms of which had been pain and giddiness in the head, pain in the back and side, weakness between the stomach and the bowels, tightness across the chest, et cetera, et cetera.

No soon had I digested (so to say) that story, than I had to hear of Walter Nancarrow, miner of Mount Charles, near St Austell, who, after taking a course of the medicine, passed a tapeworm three yards long and with upwards of 400 joints – and was offered a sight of the worm, should I wish it; however I declined, and got myself off cheaply by purchasing a bottle of the medicine for three shillings – it being revealed that the gentle-men concerned were agents of the said Dr Lamb. The medicine I disposed of in a hedge directly I had turned the corner from their house.

After two weeks of riding from place to place speaking and shaking the hands of my future constituents (as I hoped) I began to fear for the health of any future pretender to Parliamentary membership, should common suffrage ever come in. Should every man have the vote, how would it be possible to survive such a campaign as would be necessary to secure election when I was exhausted almost to death even in the present circumstances – to say nothing of having to know, or pretend to know, about such matters as Mr Peel's betrayal of Protestantism, the disenfranchism of Gatton and Old Sarum, the sedition trials – and, when talking to the ladies, which perforce I must (since many of them clearly dominated their husbands to the extent to being capable of persuading them to vote for an entirely ignorant and unsuitable fellow, should he catch their eye), to discuss the present King's predilection for the actress Mrs Jordan, their *ménage* at Bushy Park, his proposal to a West Indian heiress of vast wealth but doubtful sanity, and the strange relationship of the Duchess of Gloucester to her cousin, commonly known as Silly Billy?

It will be supposed that I was more than ready for a little relaxation, and found it in the small town of Looe, which lies upon the coast about halfway between Fowey and the headland which protects the infinitely greater port of Plymouth.

Looe seems almost two places, two towns lying on opposite sides of the river from which they take their names – of East Looe and West Looe; and which, I guess, was itself named from its situation, for it runs between high hills, and the valley through which it meanders is indeed low – a word the Cornish pronounce as *looe*.

West Looe is the older place, but also the poorer; East Looe is of more recent origin, and seems a likely enough place – yet its houses seem literally to be built upon sand, for their walls are often askew and seem about to tumble. However it has lasted for some centuries, and has been of sufficient importance to be garrisoned, for the town towards the sea is faced with a garretted wall.

Thanks to Treweers – who had now become my election agent as well as my butler – I was given shelter at the Vicarage, a fine, humble house near the ancient church, and with a view over the bustling harbour which almost every tide filled with a plethora of fishing boats, some tiny, some substantial – for fishing was the heart and soul of the place.

The Vicar, the Rev. Polscoe – a local man – was a rough and ready soul, who kept a good cellar and an excellent table, rode to hounds whenever he could, and twice or thrice a week could be found, cassock about his waist, paddling in the mud looking for worms with which to bait his hooks (for he loved freshwater fish, and the river above the town was an excellent home to them).

Among the entertainment he proposed for me was to spend a day upon a fishing boat; this, he said, would endear me to the local people, and would also prove of value in recreating me, for nothing (as he said) was so calming and pleasant as a day spent upon the Channel in good, sunny weather.

I was happy to accept, and thus found myself sailing out of Looe harbour at five o'clock in the morning, on board the *George of Looe*, a hearty vessel with a crew of five men – the captain being a grizzled man of perhaps some sixty summers, his two sons of forty and five, and three grandsons, two somewhat older than myself, and one a beardless youth of perhaps eighteen years. Hoisting our brown sails, we made out into the channel until we were perhaps six or seven miles from the coast, then began to throw out our nets, and after an hour were at leisure, only having to maintain our station while the fish entered the nets.

The fishermen thereupon produced a small barrel of cider and packets of food, which we consumed sitting upon the deck in a warm breeze, with the sun beating down not so fiercely as to be oppressive, but merely pleasant in the extreme. I began to think that the life of a fisherman was not altogether to be despised (though reminding myself that it were entirely another matter in winter, when the storms in the Channel can be irresistibly fierce, resulting in much bereavement by drowning and shipwreck).

However, for the time everything was placid and recuperative, and after a while the warmth was so considerable that I followed the example of the other men (except for the youngest) and removed my shirt – they having done so long since, upon leaving port – the Cornish being a modest race, it was not considered polite to be shirtless upon land unless participating in a sport, which was considered a proper excuse.

It was, I supposed, such modesty (often accentuated in youth) that persuaded the younger man to retain his shirt, which was buttoned to the neck; yet he was not subjected to such scorn or rough humour as might have been expected from his brothers – who presumably were used to this nicety. They were a good-looking family, I reflected – rather against the grain of the local people, whose frames tended to the squat and thick, whereas these were more like the people of the eastern part of England, with long bodies, well-proportioned, though their shoulders and arms were broad and muscular from the efforts of their work (they were each to be seen upon the quays heaving baskets of fish about which would take two men of London to lift!). They seemed indeed to be of a different strain altogether, whether from their descending from another race (as, for instance, those Spaniards wrecked upon these shores at the time of the Armada, many of whom it is believed are amalgamated into the Cornish race) or from inbreeding, for as the saying is, incest flourishes where the roads are bad, and the roads of this part of England are notorious for becoming impassable in winter.

The younger brother seemed however to be slighter than the others, and I asked whether he had not been so long a fisherman as they had – receiving no reply from him, and merely a shake of the head from his brothers, which tempted me to believe that perhaps he was deficient in intelligence (as is often the case when families too closely intermarry, and went somewhat to encourage me to believe my former theory).

I was somewhat disappointed to observe that by midday the nets were drawn in so full of fish that the decision was made to return to port, thus cutting short what I had hoped would be a full day of relaxation, and which I had begun thoroughly to enjoy. Seeing my rather downcast visage, the old man asked whether I would care to prolong my outing somewhat, and look over St George's Island, which lies only about half a mile from the shore to the west of Looe. They needed, it seems, to replenish their supply of samphire, or *Herbe de St Pierre*, which they use for pickling. It grows commonly upon cliffs – and indeed there had been several accidents resulting in the death of those poor people who had attempted to gather it from the precipitate cliffs of east Cornwall; but it grew upon St George's Island in considerable proliferation, and Glaws was to be set ashore there, with the small coracle which was towed behind the fishing boat, to gather the herb and bring it back to Looe on the evening tide.

I agreed with pleasure, but was slightly confused at the name of 'Glaws' – but upon my asking, the skipper indicated the younger son, explaining that it was the name commonly given to her since upon her first walking she had fallen into a mess of *glaws*, this being the Cornish name for a cow-pat.

My confusion was now doubled at hearing the young man being referred to as a female; which however explained her slim figure and her retaining her shirt – and also her modesty or demeanour, rather different from the freer manners of her brothers.

On our reaching the neighbourhood of the small island, she leaped with great dexterity into the little coracle or dinghy, watching with what seemed ill-concealed scorn as I climbed more carefully into it; and then, seizing the single oar and using it thrust out behind, sped us with remarkable precipitation towards the beach, where on our landing she hauled the boat upon the sand with a greater strength than I would have given her credit for, and without a second glance at me set off around the coast, leaving me to explore as I might.

The island must be one of the smallest about the coast of England, for it is barely a half mile in circumference, rising to a low hill at the centre, and with beaches about most of its shore, though here and there there are rocks. Around the strand sea-birds breed in great numbers; they rose in great clouds as I moved about, though many declined to take notice of human intervention, so that I almost fell over them – as was true also of the conies, which played positively about my feet. Between the island and the low shoreline to the west of the town of Looe itself, is a stretch of water which is perhaps a quarter of a mile only in breadth, and now shone bright blue under the sun. It turned to a deeper blue, almost to purple, as it met the deeper water towards the south, where upon the horizon stands a lighthouse marking the famous Eddystone Rocks, upon which many a handsome vessel has foundered.

I mounted to the top of the hill, whence there was nothing to be seen – or, rather, whence nothing was to be seen except the now mild and delightful coast (turned in the storms of winter to a positive death-trap, but now most mild and agreeable). Below me, a disturbance among the sea-birds, to the south, showed me where Glaws (I knew no more elegant name to give her) was at work; and it was thence, after a while, that I strolled, eventually finding myself upon the edge of a little cliff – if a rise of but seven or eight feet can be dignified by the name – along the bottom of which she was making her way, and in a moment came to the top of, in order to reach clumps of samphire which clung to the face of the rise, and just below its rim.

For what reason she so relentlessly ignored me, I could not tell; I had not been in any way scornful of her – indeed, I had scarcely addressed a single word to her; or rather only the cursory greeting I had addressed also to her brothers. I watched her beneath lowered eyelids as she came near the place where I lay; and must admit to myself that my knowledge of her sex added an attraction which had been lacking when I had been under a misapprehension about it. She had gone so far, in acknowledgement of the sun's heat, as to undo a button or two at the neck of her shirt – but this showed, as closely as I could examine it without revealing my interest – no notably swelling bosom; however, as she presented me with a rear view of herself, on kneeling to reach over the edge of the cliff, I could not but believe that even had I not been told of her sex I would have guessed it, for her arse had that swelling roundness, almost heart-shaped, which could not for a moment be mistaken for that of a boy.

After a while, she retired with a bundle of the herb to a spot some fifty yards away, where she stuffed it into an already bulging sack, which she began hauling towards me – for the coracle lay upon the strand upon the other side of the place where I lay. With a pretence of awakening, I leaped to my feet and immediately offered to take the sack from her, which at first she refused, and then with something of an ill grace gave it over to me; whereupon I placed it upon the ground and suggested that we might take our ease for a while before the effort of rowing back to the town.

' 'Tes not so much effort,' she said, 'ef 'tis done day by day.'

Nevertheless, she did sit down, and after a moment or two seemed to withdraw her hostility somewhat – to the extent of replying, if somewhat tersely, to my enquiry about her way of life. This proved to be not so bad: the profit of the families of the place mainly accrues, as I had supposed, from the weekly markets and from industrious fishing from boats of a middle size – and I learned from her that her family's craft, the *George*, was but the latest of many of similar name, the first having taken part centuries since in a furious fight with a French man-of-war.

I could not but remark that her eyes seemed to play a great deal upon my body, which was still unclothed above the waist, and on our becoming more familiar and less constrained in our conversation, asked her why. To my amusement, a blush spread over her face – and she admitted that she had believed all gentlefolk to have white skins, whereas mine was as brown as that of her brothers!

This was not always the case, I told her, though many *beaux* who liked to think themselves men of fashion carefully preserved their bodies from the sun. On the contrary, I had from the time I was a boy enjoyed the sun, and took it whenever I had the opportunity – and took care at the same time to say something of my childhood, which, as my constant readers will know, was as far removed from gentility as her own. This she was eager to discuss; and revealed that her ambition was to 'become a lady' – which as far as I gathered meant marrying a farmer and keeping her own farmhouse; for, as it turned out, she heartily despised the fisherman's life as merely providing sufficient sustenance to keep body and soul together.

To that end, she explained, while many of her sex who worked upon the boats threw off their shirts as freely as the menfolk, she had always been careful to keep her body white as milk, for it was known that only those women who engaged in physical labour were brown of skin – and in proof, turned her back, unbuttoned her shirt entirely, and, slipping it from her shoulders, displayed a back which was indeed as white as that of any Bond Street lady.

It was perhaps natural in me to desire a view of her bosom, and taking her gently by the arm I endeavoured to turn her towards me; but she was reluctant to do so, and on my persuading her – with an insistence mild enough not to frighten her – to turn, kept her arms crossed upon her breast. It was only by taking her wrists and, with a smile, quietly drawing her arms down, that I saw before me a breast that might indeed have been that of a boy. Her breasts were little more rounded than saucers – though delightfully marked by twin nipples of the most beguiling pink, whose erect state contradicted that modesty with which she still struggled to release her arms – a struggle of such mildness as to convince me that she was by no means averse to revealing herself to me, if, from her look, fearful that she was insufficiently attractive.

'They'm too small, bain't they?' she said, finally, looking down herself at her breast.

My answer was to lean forward and plant a kiss upon each bosom in turn – at which, as though a spring had been released, she threw her arms about me and hugged me with a strength fired by eagerness. I was not averse to this, and, taking her head between my hands, pressed a kiss upon her lips – which betrayed her innocence by remaining adamantly closed; yet upon my first attempt to force my tongue between them, they not only opened to me, but soon began a most delectable sucking upon my lower lip.

That she knew to an extent what she was about was plain, for without more ado she plunged one hand into

my lap and began to seek for my riding-muscle, which
from its prominence was by now easily to be found. But
although she was clearly no maid, it was equally the case
that her experience of the art of love had been brutish
and short, for her wriggling her body against me indicated that she was free from any supposition that the act
might be prefaced by tenderness.

Since there were some hours still of light and warmth,
and since we were in that most enviable position of being
upon an island devoid of any inhabitants but ourselves
(and those conies whose own amorous habits are a lesson
in enthusiasm and frequency) I determined to give her a
lesson in the art; first persuading her to let me go, and to
recline upon the grass, where in a moment I loosened the
rope which secured her breeches (no more elegant than
those of her brothers) and drew them down, accompanying this disrobing by disposing a series of kisses
upon the body thus revealed – the little dint of her navel,
the prominent hips, the soft skin between thigh and
belly, the thighs themselves, then the knees – keeping
until last that most tender spot of all, guarded by a perfect, jet-black triangle, so perfectly formed that it was
difficult to believe that it was not manicured.

Somewhat to my relief, her whole body was clean and
sweet-smelling – from the heat of summer persuading
her, as is the case with some (but by no means all) of the
local inhabitants, to bathe night and morning in the sea,
and then, to avert the evil effect of salt upon the skin, to
wash in the clear water that springs in plenty from the
Cornish earth both in running streams and wells.

It was, then, with equal delight and admiration that I
continued for a while to caress her; and after a few gestures of surprise and protest, she soon became aware of

the delights of a more gradual approach to love than she had hitherto been afforded, and ceased plucking at my breeches with her hands, merely reclining and allowing my lips to graze upon what indeed was a perfectly white and soft skin.

Though my perfect appetite is for a body more rounded and ample than hers, I must confess that through the charm of the open air, the novelty of her slender frame, and her own delighted approbation, my passion was much aroused, and – as is invariably the case – communicated itself to her, for as I leaned my cheek upon one breast while teasing the other with my tongue, I could hear her heart knocking within her bosom as though 'twould in a moment break out and leap away upon the hill to join the conies who gambolled there, almost within arm's reach.

My own impatience now roused, I stood and loosed my own trousers, and permitted the sun to shine upon that machinery which was more than ready for an engagement. However, rather than continuing to recline in such a position as would have invited immediate congress, the girl immediately raised herself upon her knees, and with a shyness which was infinitely more exciting than the most gross actions of a practised whore, began to examine my appliance with the most minute attention.

I must here, and in parenthesis, reveal that I later brought up with Mr Polscoe the subject of country copulation – he being a gentleman of the broadest temperament, and (as is usually the case) knowledgeable of the most intimate habits of his parishioners.

'Ah,' he said, 'young Glaws. She was, I fear, introduced to carnal pleasures at an early age. Most families here live in two or at most three rooms, and that family is

no exception. The old man has his bed in an outbuilding;
his two sons and their wives have their beds in one of the
two upstairs rooms of their cottage, and the three cousins share a pile of bedding in the second room, where nets
and crab-pots must also be stored. The close confinement of three young people must lead to an early sharing
of every form of experience, every bodily habit being of
necessity performed within the sight and hearing of the
others.'

But, I enquired, was not incest a sin?

Doubtless, the reverend gentleman opined, that was
the case, where circumstances allowed the enforcement
of the strictest rules of morality.

'But it has always been my own view,' he continued,
'that where there is no evil result, animal behaviour in
humans frees rather than confines the spirit; and' (he
remarked, to my surprise and without the slightest hesitation) 'there are to my certain knowledge four respectable men of this town, regular church-goers and one of
them a Warden, whose fathers are also their uncles, and
whose brothers are also their cousins. And none of them
the worse for it.'

But was this an open secret, I enquired?

'It is not commonly spoken of,' the clergyman replied;
'and you would not find it easy to extract a confession.
But there are few families where occurrences of this
nature are not known. The sadness is that such acts,
being performed at night and in haste, do not educate
these classes in those enjoyments which are the prerogative of the more educated classes. Another glass of
claret, Mr Archer?'

My surprise at Mr Polscoe's openness was somewhat
mitigated when, before the end of my stay, on rising in

the night to make water, I heard from his neighbouring bedroom the unmistakable noises of congress, and noted next morning the late rising of Mrs Instance, the plump and pleasant housekeeper whose room was in a further wing of the Vicarage.

But to return to the island: it was with an interest sharpened by ignorance that Glaws used the bright sunlight to make a detailed survey of an area of the male body with which she had, as I now suppose, been familiar only in haste and darkness. At first she looked, only; then with an irresistible impulse laid a finger upon the tip of my cock, pressing it downwards as though to test its resilience, and at the same time looking up at me as though to enquire whether the familiarity were to be permitted. On receiving a smiling asset, she became bolder, and with the fingers of both hands assessed the thickness, circumference and length of the instrument, measured the angle of its erection, gauged the extent of its firmness, investigated the spheroids depending from its base, verified the elasticity of the pouch which contained them – and in short, so provoked and stimulated me by her touch that I was ready to burst, and had to draw away.

That this disappointed her, I could see; but, sinking to my knees, I pressed upon her shoulders with my hands, returning her to the turf, and drawing the length of my body along hers, began to pay my compliments to that area of her body similar in position, though not in landscape, to that from which I had distracted her attention.

The supposition had clearly never occurred to her that a man could have any interest in that part of her, other than to split it with his weapon; and my moistening my finger and with it caressing the most sensitive part of it, brought from her a feverish shivering which shook her whole frame; while when I followed by caressing the length of the aperture with my tongue, then flicking with its tip at that same apprehensive nodule, she let out a shriek so loud that the sea-birds rose from all over the island in a black cloud, swirling in a circle above us and casting a shadow over our bodies.

She was clearly unable to bear such pleasure longer; and myself excited almost beyond bounds, I drew myself once more upon her, and sheathed my sword in its proper scabbard, another cry and an ecstatic bounding of her loins bringing about my surrender before I could even begin those motions which normally signify congress.

My own rapture was extreme, with that almost bitter joy which marks an ecstasy too keen to be prolonged; and from her almost fainting, her upturned eyes showing white beneath their lids, from her gripping my arse with her fingers, from her fixing her teeth almost painfully in my shoulder, from her throwing her legs about my waist as though they clutched a refractory horse, I could infer that Glaws experienced the same pleasure.

Such indeed was that pleasure, on her part, that, while I would have been happy to doze in the warmth, she before long pushed me from her, upon my back, and began caressing me; an action which at first, so soon after congress, was merely irritating (though I bore it with equanimity, feeling it proper to allow her the experience), but soon once more became inspiriting, as, with my example before her, she went about to discover whether oral stimulation of the male parts could impart such pleasure as I had allowed her. The immediate recovery of my spirits, signalled in the almost instant

tumescence of a limb which a moment earlier had been
entirely debilitated, delighted her; and that she had an
instinct for the game was soon demonstrated – for,
while paying quite sufficient attention to the primary
source of pleasure, she showed invention in performing
such pleasurable tricks as sucking upon my fingers and
toes, taking my nipples between her small teeth and giving them apprehensive nips, thrusting her tongue into the
whorls of my ears, and suchlike. Finally she returned to
the centre of such gratification, and taking its most
prominent part between her lips, played upon it with
such delicacy that she soon reduced me to just such a
fever as, previously, I had provoked in herself; whereon,
my exhalation of breath, and a moaning I could not
control, persuaded her to relinquish her comfort and
once more welcome me between those slim thighs. My
having so recently given forth my soul enabled me,
despite the extremity of my pleasure, to make those
movements lacking from our first encounter; movements which she met with a lively thrusting of her own
narrow but strong loins; our joint enjoyment reaching a
culmination almost at the same moment.

We did, then, lie in each other's arms for an hour;
until, the sun beginning to sink, it began to grow chilly,
whereupon we resumed our clothes, and without a word
descended to the beach and climbed into the coracle,
which with the same skilful movements of the single oar,
she propelled towards port.

Her brother – or perhaps a cousin – met us upon the
quay, so that any elaborate farewell was impossible; nor
I think did she expect it, for it must have seemed to her
that I was so far above her in station as to make any
further conversation impossible; perhaps she even

believed that I merely amused myself with her – and truth to tell, that was the fact; though I flatter myself that I had been something of an education to her. I made a point of leaving a purse with Mr Polscoe with instructions that he find a way of enriching her by a gift, perhaps on the occasion of her marriage, for I now heard that there was an understanding between her and a young fisherman from Killigarth (who will, I trust, be pleasantly surprised upon his wedding night – for it is my experience that once an elaborate appetite has been awakened in a young woman, it is by no means the case she forgets how to satisfy it).

That the Rev. Polscoe guessed what had been between us, I make no doubt; but he made no mention of it, being as friendlily disposed upon my leaving Looe as he was upon my coming there, and contenting himself with the statement that his own vote was certainly mine, for he admired one who was at once free in his manners and considerate to those with whom he engaged (which indeed has ever been my ambition).

Chapter Ten

Sophie's Story

The Earl of Stow had kindly invited me to come to Catterby, his mansion near Newmarket, as soon before the commencement of the races as was necessary for the preparation of my entertainment for his guests. I travelled there a full four days before the occasion, partly for the purpose he proposed, and partly (I must confess) in order to allow myself time to become familiar with any of his guests whom it might later profit me to know. (The calculation may offend; yet even such a fortune as I had accumulated – which was not insignificant – might in time be spent, and ingratiation with the wealthy and fashionable was a form of insurance I was minded to provide for myself.)

Catterby is set between the village of Cheveley and the town of Newmarket, in a part of East Anglia with which I was not familiar, it being some fifty mile or so from the city of Cambridge, where I had spent some time in the company of my late husband, the egregious astrologer Mr Nelham (my unfortunate marriage to whom I have detailed in a volume entitled *Eros in the Country*, which must be regarded as necessary reading by those to whom my adventures have proved sufficiently amusing).

The house was first built in the time of Queen Elizabeth, but modernised by the Earl to the extent of

almost excessive comfort, for he was a man not only of
wealth but of taste. It is approached from the east by a
bridge over a tributary of the River Kennett, and along a
splendid avenue of lime trees, when through a gateway
with four small, square towers one enters an open piazza
or walk around which the main rooms of the house lie on
the north and south side, with upon the west side is a ter-
race of slight elevation before the dining hall, beyond
which is an inner court completely enclosed by ranges of
rooms.

The great architect Sir John Vanbrugh, engaged by an
ancestor of the Earl's, had in 1721 enlarged and enliv-
ened the great hall, making a fine stone arcade of two
tiers with three arches in each, from which two flights of
stairs with gilt iron balustrades were constructed to lead
to an upper room where it was the Earl's habit to entertain his guests before dinner, and where innumerable
portraits illustrated members of his family, painted by
the most fashionable artists of the times.

Stow having made it clear that his household was mine
to command, and that every facility must be allowed me,
introduced me to his secretary, Mr Fitzchrome – his
country secretary, I should perhaps say, who resides at
Catterby and looks after his lordship's interests
there – including his stable, which upon my first morning I was taken to see. My interest in horse-flesh is not so
keen as might be, yet even I could remark that his
lordship's horses were handsome enough – some fifteen
or eighteen splendid animals, cared for in the most
luxurious conditions; more comfortable in their
stables, where clean straw was provided every morning,
and warm oats on cold mornings, than a great portion
of humanity (though Stow, I must confess, made his

own people comfortable enough).

Flannery Fitzchrome was a young gentleman of Irish extraction, of perhaps twenty and five years, whose duties included the running of Stow's stable, the ordering of which was the envy of the county (as he assured me). He was one of those young gentlemen whose eye immediately declared an interest in any attractive woman in his vicinity, and without the least familiarity conveyed that interest in an unmistakable manner. Being by no means averse to admiration, I got on with him from the first quite splendidly, and he was quick to answer my many queries about the running of the house and the stables. He had clearly been told the purpose of my visit, and without impertinence made it perfectly clear that he would be happy to give me every assistance.

The first request I made of him was that I might be introduced to his lordship's jockeys. Those unfamiliar with the customs of the running of an ambitious stable may not be aware of the scale upon which such things are done in the country. Indeed, it was with some slight surprise that I learned that Stow kept no less than six young gentlemen whose sole purpose was to exercise his stable and to ride his mounts at the Newmarket races, and occasionally elsewhere.

At the time when I made the request, it was impossible to fulfil it; it was late afternoon, and the entire crew was engaged upon taking the horses out of their stables in order to exercise them. The most I could do was to watch them pass by, remarking that they seemed extraordinary small gentlemen – which Fitzchrome confirmed, this being, as he said, a prerequisite, for the smaller the rider the swifter the mount. However, they were, he told me, young men who were physically exceedingly fit, having as much daily exercise as their mounts; and if I would present myself in a hour, I could confirm this for myself.

I thanked him, and for the intervening period of time amused myself by walking about the gardens, which had been laid out some seventy years previously by that excellent landscape artist Mr Lancelot Brown, and where there were several elegant buildings designed by Mr Robert Adam – two temples, a Palladian bridge, an obelisk and the Elephant Gateway, with a great stone elephant and two enormous decorative vases.

Beyond the Ionic Temple lay a beautiful Elysian Garden – a tree-lined glade bisected by a little river, which enters from the south by a rustic cascade, and runs northwards beneath the Palladian Bridge. Upon each side of the river – which here is of no great girth – run two lawns; and it immediately struck me that this was the ideal place for my entertainment, performers upon one side of the stream, audience upon the other!

An hour passed swiftly enough, and on my returning to the stables (which lie behind the house and some way from it) I was met by Mr Fitzchrome, who led me to the place where his lordship's jockeys lived. This was a long building built originally to house the servants (who now however lived in a wing of the main building). One of the Earl's ancestors, at the time of the Commonwealth, had (I was told) been much engaged in plotting to restore the Monarchy, and had become much concerned that his servants were spying upon him. He had therefore insisted that they live in one room, at the end of which was a place in which he or some trusted fellow could conceal themselves to overhear any conversation which might betray illicit purposes. This was no longer used, but (said Mr Fitzchrome) it would provide a place from

which I could observe without being observed, 'for', he
remarked, 'I must assume that you have in mind their
participation in your entertainment?'

I could only admire his quickness, for this was indeed
my purpose. So I found myself in a small, cupboard-like
closet, completely dark, with an aperture in its wall
through which I looked down the length of a room in
which were six beds, with between them a cupboard and
a low table with a washing bowl, and little else. Mr
Fitzchrome excusing himself – and indeed there was
room only for a single person – I settled down with an
eye to the aperture, and in a moment into the room
tumbled the six jockeys, who immediately – heated by
their equine exercise – began throwing off their clothes
and sponging themselves down.

I will not bore the reader with an exquisite description
of the scene; let it merely be said that Mr Fitzchrome had
been entirely in the right when he said that the lack of
inches among these young gentlemen did not indicate
any disproportion or stunting of growth elsewhere;
indeed their arms and shoulders (through holding back
and encouraging their mounts) and their thighs and buttocks (through the necessity to grip them) were developed to perfection; and I need look no further for
male participants in my pageant – should they agree,
which would no doubt be secured either by bribery, by
their wish to remain in his lordship's employ, or – upon
the nature of the occasion being explained – by simple
lust.

Mr Fitzchrome was lounging against the stable wall as
I descended the staircase from my perch, and on my
asking readily agreed to introduce me to the jockeys. He
instantly led me to their room, pausing only to ascertain

(through a gentlemanly instinct which I appreciated) that they were properly clad before I entered, when I found them garbed chiefly in towels hastily taken up and girt about their loins.

'Boys!' Mr Fitzchrome said. 'Here is Mrs Nelham, a friend of the guv'nor's.'

In the respectful silence which followed, I introduced myself as someone engaged to set out an entertainment for his lordship's guests; and from the looks exchanged by the lads, saw that they were in little doubt as to the sort of entertainment of which I spoke – from which I divined that similar scenes had previously been observed at Catterby to what I now proposed.

I had in mind, I said, a pageant which would involve them and their mounts; and should they agree to participate, could assure them of five guineas each.

'This is somewhat dependent,' I said, 'upon your not being entirely averse to female company, for I must not conceal from you the fact that your skill in riding will not, on this occasion, be confined to horse-flesh.'

The boys exchanged glances which at once assured me that they would have no objection to what I suggested; and having announced that a rehearsal would be held the day before the entertainment, I left them all a-chatter and walked back to the house with Mr Fitzchrome. He was somewhat aghast at my proposal, not having had previous notice of it. He said it was usual that the lads should have no other preoccupation before the racing than riding and winning; and he ventured whether the kind of activity I had in mind might not drain the energy which would be needed to participate properly in the winning of races.

I assured him that my experience in these matters was

such that the activity I envisaged was nothing less than animating and uplifting to the spirits of young men, and that it would surprise me if it did anything other than encourage the winning spirit among them; and that in any case, Stow had given me a *carte blanche* in the matter – at which he somewhat grumblingly assented to my proposition.

Having commissioned the other participants in the pageant before removing to Catterby, I was now free for a day or so to enjoy my visit; and although I was not unused to luxury, was able once more to observe with how much ease and pleasure the enjoyment of large funds endows life.

My own apartment was comfortable enough, possessing its own side-room for dressing and bathing – hot water being continually available through the interest of a series of servants, two of whom – one male and one female – seemed to have orders to devote themselves entirely to my service. But it was enjoyment of the house itself which gave me my chief pleasure; apart from the grounds, in which it was always a delight to stroll.

It was in the saloon that I chiefly spent those hours of the day which coolness or the occasional shower rendered inappropriate for outdoor activities. This was a fine room which had been fitted out in 1785 by Sir Pothcoat Stow, an ancestor of the present Earl – the date appears over the west door, where his coat of arms and the impaled coats of his two wives are painted. The ceiling of this room is divided into compartments, the divisions marked by pendants and strapwork and the panels filled with decorative figures consisting of ships, mermaids, whales, scabbards and fabulous sea-monsters. Through the interest of these, the saloon is called, by his lordship, the Fish Room; and I was wont to spend some time lying flat upon one of the couches in order that I might gaze upward at the ceiling and enjoy the plaster fantasies proposed by the artist.

It was here, indeed, one morning, that I was lying when a maidservant entered and, having ascertained (as she thought) that no one was present – for I was concealed by the back of the sopha on which I lay – began to dust and polish. In a moment, the door opened and in came none other than Mr Fitzchrome, who, on seeing the girl, without hesitation walked up to her and, placing a hand upon her rump, greeted her with a smacking kiss upon the back of the neck.

She was not in the least discomfited, by which I assumed that such passages were neither infrequent nor unwelcome (Mr Fitzchrome being, as I may have previously noted, a fine, upstanding young man whose attentions might be enjoyed by any apprehensive female not averse to the compliments of the opposite sex).

I was about to betray my presence by a cough, not wishing to embarrass the couple, when the gentlemen followed up his first caress by slipping a hand into the bosom of the girl's dress – at which, motivated no doubt by experience, one of her hands immediately found its way to that part of his body where the most corporeal evidence of his admiration might be expected to lie.

It had now become difficult for me to show myself, for it would be apparent to them that I had seen all; and I was forced to remain out of sight while their congress developed from a relatively innocent kiss to something less ingenuous. In less time than it takes to tell, Mr Fitzchrome's breeches were about his ankles, Miss Betty's skirts above her waist, and the gentleman enjoying the lady in the simplest posture – she leaning with her arms folded upon the back of one of Stow's handsome tapestry chairs, and presenting him with a mark which (judging from her barely stifled cries) he hit at first shot, and continued to hit with each lunge of his somewhat hirsute arse.

That the pair were used to such stolen moments seemed demonstrated by the speed with which they started, pursued and concluded the business, and the adeptness with which Mr Fitzchrome resumed his breeches, while Miss Betty, her skirts now decorously lowered, thanked him with but one quick kiss before continuing with her dusting while he strode from the room – not a single word having been exchanged between them!

I must confess now that I was in something of a tizzy, for her discovery of me must surely indicate that I had been an onlooker at their feast; however, a pretence of sleep saved us both the embarrassment. They having been careful to preserve an almost total silence, it was easy for her to believe that I had slept throughout their encounter – for though I heard a quick and anxious indrawing of her breath upon her discovering me, she finished her cleaning and left the room while I still pretended unconsciousness. On my encountering her later, in the drawing-room, only a blush gave any indication of apprehension.

In the evening, on entering the drawing-room, I found Stow sitting with a motley crew of eight or ten gentlemen, together with their wives – the latter seeming however almost invisible, for the gentlemen conversed among themselves, and with so little apprehension of the presence of their ladies that not only their business but their pleasures were discussed with entire frankness, their tones so little lowered when they spoke of their whores that their ladies cannot but have been apprehensive of the details they did not hesitate to reveal, with greater colour of language than I would have permitted myself even in the drawing-room of a close friend. Upon our retiring to the drawing-room after dinner, while the gentlemen began that carousing which would in all probability cease only with their inability to remain upright, my sensibilities were pummelled by the failure of their consorts to comment upon their shortcomings.

One, Lady Indigo Opimion (whose husband was a gross, great man of seventeen stone, most of whose weight was concentrated in the region of his belly) gave the rest of us a lecture, indeed, upon the superiority of that sex to our own:

'In the character of a noble, enlightened and truly good man,' she remarked (to whom could she have been referring? – not surely to that sot, her husband?), 'there is a power and a sublimity so nearly approaching what we believe to be the nature and capacity of angels, that no language can describe the degree of admiration and respect which the contemplation of such a character must excite.'

But surely, I observed, it was not necessary to ignore those blemishes of character which in my experience flawed the most perfect character, setting it off (indeed) by contrast with entire virtue?

'No, Mrs Nelham,' was her answer; 'to be admitted to a man's heart, to share his counsels and to be the chosen companion of his joys and sorrows! – it is difficult to say whether humility or gratitude should preponderate in the feelings of the woman thus distinguished and thus blest.'

At which I made my excuses and left, saying (which was

indeed the truth) that I felt suddenly nauseous; and as I passed the dining-room, was assaulted not only by a great wave of smoke from the execrable weed tobacco – to which Stow and his friends were much addicted – but by the sound of retching and the sight of Lord Opimion vomiting into the fireplace while his friends, oblivious, continued their carouse.

My entertainment was to take place upon the day before the opening of the Newmarket races, providing as it were a preliminary potpourri which should gratify the senses of the gentlemen before they set off to watch their mounts run – heightening the pleasure if they won, compensating the lack of it if they lost.

The day before this, I went over to Bury St Edmunds in a carriage followed by two others in which the six jockeys travelled. On my explaining what would be required of them they had shown no diffidence; but this morning had become less enthusiastic, and only the threat of Stow's displeasure, together with the promise of an additional two guineas each persuaded them into the coaches.

At Bury, the six ladies whose services I had commissioned in town had been put up for the night at the Parson's Nose Inn, and it was thence that we made our way, and were shown to a large private room which I had secured entirely for the purpose of introducing the two parties. There, while I went to greet the girls, Mr Fitzchrome persuaded his lads to remove their clothing; for the sake of an immediate informality, I had decided that the excellent luncheon I had ordered should be taken by all in a state of nature – which I have ever found the quickest way of ensuring familiarity.

I returned to the room to find the six young men

huddled together at one end of it, Mr Fitzchrome alone
lounging, entirely at ease, before the fire which, despite
the fortunate warmth of the day, I had ordered to be lit.
On my entering with the girls (clad, necessarily – for we
had traversed the public parts of the inn; yet clad but
lightly) the boys clustered even more closely together,
endeavouring with their hands to hide from view those
parts which they no doubt believed would be offensive to
the eyes of the maidens – whose eyes, however (I could
have told them) had seen a greater number of male
appendages than most men!

On my signalling the girls, both they and I removed
what covering we had and (none of us believing that our
unclad bodies would be offensive) strode towards the
middle of the room – which instantly resulted in the
young gentlemen showing some interest, to the extent
that there was an immediate and involuntary movement
away from each other, and towards us.

'Mr Fitzchrome – some ale!' I directed; at which he
took up a great flagon and began to fill the tankards set
out on a side-table, and indicated that his boys should
serve the ladies. This they did with a decreasing aware-
ness (or perhaps simply a more natural admiration) of
their nakedness, my girls continuing in their informality;
and no doubt the sight of Mr Fitzchrome and myself
equally unclad encouraged this – as I had hoped, though
I must confess that it was he who had originally suggested that two people clothed, among others who were
not, would necessarily dampen enthusiasm.

By the time each lad had consumed a pint or so of
strong ale, informality had certainly increased; and on
my suggesting that the meal should commence, it was
natural that the sexes should be spread alternately about

the table – where somewhat narrow benches ensured
that it was impossible to be entirely separate from one's
neighbour; even I being cheek by cheek (to use the
phrase) with Mr Fitzchrome upon one side, and one of
the jockeys upon the other – who found great difficulty,
as I could see, in dividing his attention equally between
me and his neighbour, fearing to offend one by undue
attention to the other.

Mr Fitzchrome had no such difficulty, and I could not
but admire his dexterity in making an excellent lunch
using his left hand alone, his right lying for some time
upon my thigh, and then making its way between it and
its fellow – which I found not unpleasant. Upon my
dropping my napkin and hastening to retrieve it, I found
my searching hand, falling into his lap, obstructed by a
prominent Something my accidental connection with
which evoked rather the indrawn breath of pleasure than
an exhalation provoked by either embarrassment or
pain.

However, I was too concerned to encourage geniality
among the company to be able to give myself over to sensation, however agreeable, and concentrated rather in
pairing the couples in my mind's eye – something which
however was no problem, for I could now see that such
coupling had been naturally achieved by the instinct of
the men and women concerned, each man gradually, as
the luncheon continued, beginning to pay more attention
to one young lady than the next, and, their spirits raised
by ale, by the end of the meal being sufficiently at ease to
intersperse the business of kissing with that of eating,
while the occasions upon which a dozen hands were all in
view above the table grew increasingly rarer.

At length the time came when a young man opposite

me actually lowered his head and applied his lips to the breast of his neighbour; at which I banged my hand upon the table, and announced that the time had come for them all to pay attention to the plan for the morrow – at which, with a somewhat comic effect, they came to themselves, reluctantly unhanded each other, and sat at attention.

My recitation of the diversion I had contrived did not take long, but certainly interested the parties most intimately concerned – not least because they by now felt a certain warmth towards each other which, had I encouraged them, would in due course have led to a natural consummation. This, however, I was determined to avoid, on this occasion, lest it take the zest from the performance tomorrow – and in any event that the jockeys should be reduced to utter lethargy before the races to come was not to be thought of, if Stow was to be satisfied by the entire outcome of the season.

So, having come to the end of my recital and the consequent instructions, and having distributed papers upon which I had roughly sketched some illustrations of the postures which I had devised and told them of, I invited the gentlemen to take leave of the ladies – a ceremony to which I had again to put a forcible end, to their regret (and indeed somewhat to my own, for, with a dexterity which ensured that his manoeuvres were not seen by the company, Mr Fitzchrome had occupied himself during my speech by investigating the extent to which he could explore that lower part of my body which was within his grasp without so distracting my attention that I broke down into stuttering and silence – which I confess almost to have done; and would with some pleasure of my own have joined in any celebration of the occasion, was not the circumstance against it).

To be short, my ladies were eventually persuaded to don their clothing, and I led them from the room, the grumbling of their male companions somewhat mitigated by the knowledge that they would meet upon the following day.

At ten next morning, Stow's lady guests were sent off in a procession of carriages to Audley End, the great house some twenty mile off, where Her Majesty the Queen was holding a reception – for King Billy had been persuaded away from his beloved billows to the unaccustomed racecourse, and his Queen to meet the local ladies of fashion at a celebration which gave her no pleasure, though it provided them with an occasion for decking themselves in their finery and behaving as though they were women of fashion (most of them however being no more distinguished than squires' wives).

Their husbands bade them farewell with equanimity – and then settled down to an early bottle before luncheon, which they took *al fresco* in just that spot I had reserved for them; they sitting upon rugs spread on the grass while the servants bore among them a cold collation of delicacies, each accompanied by its own wine. I had myself devised this feast, and with some care – for reasons of my own ensuring that they were plentifully supplied with wine. Then, at precisely half past one, there was a fanfare from hunting horns, and on to the sword at the other side of the stream came a procession of Stow's mounts, each ridden by its own jockey – as though riding to the ring before a race, but with the difference that the riders were not wearing his lordship's colours: indeed, were wearing no colours at all, each being entirely unclothed – as indeed were their mounts, which had neither saddle nor bridle. These were skilful riders who as a matter of course were able not only to preserve their balance merely by the exercise of their muscles, but to control their familiar animals without recourse to such aids as were necessary when racing.

They rode to the front of the lawn, and facing across the stream, saluted the company by raising their arms; then wheeled about and faced the thicket which backed the glade – from which, in slow and delightful procession, came my six ladies. The effect, I must admit, was an enticing one, for, clad in diaphanous clothes of white, hanging from their shoulders, they appeared like supernatural beings summoned from the shades by the horns of huntsmen. They stood for a moment; and then, as one (taking a signal from me, who was behind a bush and out of sight of the audience, but within that of the performers), dropped their concealing garments, and appeared in a state of nature. If anything they seemed yet more strange than before, partly through the unexpected sight of unclad females in such a setting (for, unlike the ladies of southern Europe or yet hotter climes, our own females are largely unaccustomed to unveiling themselves in the open air) and partly through their taking attitudes which I had taught them, and resembling those of the ancient statues of an antique age.

Both they and the riders for a moment were entirely still – then as a patter of applause broke from the gentlemen upon the opposite bank, the jockeys urged their mounts into a walk, and bore down on the nymphs, who preserved their inanimity until the final moment when, the horses reaching them, they stretched up their arms and with the help of an outstretched hand at once leaped . . . to the horses' backs, some before and some behind the gentlemen already mounted there.

The six horses now took up their stations in a semi-circle around the greensward, and one at a time came to the centre of the stage while their riders took up the attitudes I had described to them. These were sufficiently complex and precarious to amaze, no less than amuse, the onlookers – and I must confess to the reader what the audience did not know: that my six ladies had been, with some care, recruited from the same circus as had supplied the female Amazon who had performed on my behalf at Mrs Teazle's. I had, on the occasion of meeting her, attended a performance during which I had been astonished by the skills of the young Austrian riders whose task it was to show off their mounts in a series of jumps and turns, gallopings and trottings and canterings, which had proved to me an ability and tenacity in balance at least the equal of the jockeys; for which reason I remembered them on receipt of Lord Stow's commission, and secured their services at only a moderate cost, they being eager, as horsewomen, to attend the Newmarket races, which are famous upon the continent of Europe as an occasion for showing off the finest mounts and riders.

But to return to the narrative: each couple of riders, upon their mount reaching the centre of the stage, used him as a platform upon which to demonstrate a particular posture of congress – these mounting in difficulty as time went on. The first pair were content with the simplest attitude, the jockey sitting astride his mount while the young lady, facing him, was astride his thighs. In this disposition the horse was urged into a trot, the natural rise and fall this encouraged in the jockey – which will be familiar to all those who have ridden horseback – so resembling normal congress that an amused laugh rather than a sensual snigger came from the audience. This however was not shared by the performers, the motion to which they were subject being such as to give them extreme pleasure.

This was not so keenly shared by their colleagues, for the postures they adopted required more skill simply to maintain them; and indeed I wondered that the jockeys were able to maintain the extension of their most important limb, since much of their attention must necessarily be concentrated simply on remaining upon the backs of their mounts. In one case, for instance, the youngest and most daring of the men actually stood upon the broad back of his mount while his partner hung about his neck while he manipulated her lower person into such a position that, her calves clasped behind his waist and her arms about his shoulders, he was able to enter her so that they remained joined for a complete circle about the lawn.

The other four pairs were not as adventurous as this – one lady lying herself full length upon the horse's back, her companion then placing himself upon her in that most conventional of all human copulatory postures: yet so skilfully maintained during their mount's progress that they attracted much admiration. Another pair embraced each other by the simple device of the jockey mounting his partner from behind, she bending to secure her position by holding the horse's mane while he entered her from behind – the posture having the advantage that the audience was able to view the connection without obstruction. This was the case with the third couple, for the lady, with a dextrous twist of her body, stood upon her hands, bringing her intimate parts

in proximity to her partner's face – he also being standing, while her lips were able without difficulty (they
being of a height) to fix about his engorged prick. Thus,
each entertaining the other as keenly as the spectacle
entertained their audience, they rode about the ring
– alas then providing an unrehearsed incident by losing
their balance and toppling from the back of their steed,
who continued a dignified trot while they lay for a
moment, their breaths taken from them, in a tangle of
limbs; then leaped to their feet to chase the steed, the
jockey's quickly shrinking cock flapping in an undignified manner as he did so – which caused the kind of
laughter among the gentlemen of the audience with
which I have often had cause to note one male will insult
another in such a circumstance. However, the man eventually catching the horse by its mane and swinging himself back into the saddle – or rather the place where the
saddle would have lain had there been one – his companion in a moment joined him; though such was the young
man's discomfiture that no attempts on her part to bring
him back to a stand were successful, and their departure
from the scene was thus a muted one.

The final tableau was provided by the most skilful
pair, for the jockey was Stow's finest, much envied by
the other owners of the district, while his partner was the
leader of the troup of ladies. They began simply by a
round of the ring during which they exposed their handsome bodies to the audience's admiration – the jockey,
while being necessarily small and slender, having the
finest muscular shoulders and arms, cultivated to admiration by his art, while his thighs showed by their
rippling muscles the strength inherent in them, also
communicated to his buttocks, which seemed to be made

entirely of muscle. The lady was equally picturesque, her
body, while entirely feminine, also profiting from continual exercise, so that while breasts, sides, belly and arse
were all sufficiently generous to attract the admiration of
any gentleman, yet there was no trace of supererogatory
fat about them.

Having received the tribute of a round of applause, the
jockey now took up a position upon the broadest part of
his mount's back, his legs astride, while his partner
weaved her body about his as sinuously as any snake,
bringing (as it seemed) every part of her person in turn in
juxtaposition to a piece of masculine equipment, which
seemed by its resolute extension to be at least as adamant
in its muscular control as any other part of his body.

Then, standing before him, her hands resting only
lightly upon his shoulders, she raised her right foot and
caressed his lower legs, then his thighs, with prehensile
toes, before inserting the ankle between his legs, the
upper surface of her foot as it were providing a platform
upon which his cock and balls were happy to lie in demonstration of their size and proficiency, which she next
tested by falling to her knees and proving every part with
her tongue, now at the same time passing her hands
behind to test whether the muscles of his arse were
not, though however strong, susceptible to a soft
caress – which proved so much the case that (as I could
see, though the audience might not) a grimace passed
over his face indicative of a keener pleasure than he
would be able long to sustain. I was on the point of
hissing a warning when (perhaps, I know not, from some
involuntary muscular contraction) the lady became
aware of the situation, and removing her lips from that
part of his anatomy likely to succumb to his excitement

now gave her attentions to a more general insinuation, by passing her entire body between his legs, making a point of bringing first thighs, then belly, then breasts into close contact with his most intimate parts – continued control of which he maintained only at the cost of clenching his teeth upon his lower lip, where beads of blood sprang.

Now behind her friend, the lady clasped his whole body to hers, moving her hands about his breast, then below it, rather showing off his body by her gestures than further arousing it – to his relief; now with the most dextrous leap mounting upon his very shoulders, and after one round of the ring, with a somersault landing before him and astride the horse's neck – when she had only to turn, by throwing a leg over the beast's back, to fall astride himself, so that he could bury his staff within her and bring himself the relief for which by now he was so eager that he could not restrain a cry of pleasure and satisfaction – echoed by the applause of the delighted audience.

The six couples now took their bows, each in turn riding to the front of the grassy stage; but there came a general commotion, for the gentleman viewers – who had had no way of satisfying their own sensuality except by a quiet manual manipulation of their parts (which in most cases pride prevented them from) – clearly took the view that they should be permitted to slake their lust upon the visiting ladies, and to that end three of them plunged into the water and began to swim across.

However, I had made it quite clear to my Lord that our contract did not include such an engagement; and the ladies speedily effected their escape – their partners without hesitation once more lifting them upon

horseback; and by the time the swimmers had reached
the bank, and the other gentlemen had found their way
across the water by means of the nearby bridge, the glen
was deserted except for myself and Mr Fitzchrome,
whose presence restrained the ardency of the excited gentlemen; and who then announced that the carriages
awaited to take them to Newmarket, where the brothel
that is invariably set up in propinquity to the racecourse
contained females who would be able and willing to satisfy their lusts.

Though not without grumbling, they assented; and
went off, somewhat to my relief – and my admiration of
Mr Fitzchrome, whose conduct had been irreproach-
able; despite the fact that as I had seen from my vantage-
point he had not himself been unmoved by the spectacle,
and even now was moving with a care which seemed to
indicate an uncomfortable constriction below the
waist.

Seeing the direction of my gaze, he was good enough
to apologise for his state.

'My dear sir,' I said, 'what man is so incapable of
feeling as to resist being engaged by such a demonstration as we have just witnessed? Indeed, what person –
for as you will know, we women are not immune from
such emotion.'

He looked at me with an eyebrow slightly raised, and
then in silence stepped forward and, taking me in his
arms, placed an expressive kiss first upon my eyes, then
my lips. It was only when I showed by my responding
embrace that I was not impervious to his approach that
he busied his hands with releasing my clothing – and not
to tire the reader with a description of the intervening
action, which was of a conventional but no less enter-

taining description, we were in due course satisfactorily engaged, and within a short time had slaked each other's appetites. I must confess that the engagement was by no means remarkable for its ingenuity; yet performed its purpose, after which Mr Fitzchrome courteously raised me to my feet and assisted me into my clothing before resuming his own – and even began stumblingly to express his gratitude, when I stopped him by raising my hand:

'Sir,' I said, 'the day when a lady and a gentleman cannot satisfy their appetite in such a manner without one coming under an excessive obligation to the other will in my view be a sad one for civilisation.'

At which we returned to the house, pausing for a while at the jockeys' buildings in order that I should inform the ladies of the hour at which the coaches would return them to their inn, and thence, the following day, to London, and to hand them the purses in which was their fee. We found them and their friends dispersed about the room, some in attitudes merely of friendship – for whom the display had been merely a matter of technique rather than of corporeal pleasure – others more intimately engaged; I was pleased in particular to see that the couple whose misfortune had occasioned some untoward mirth were particularly lost in the digital manipulation of each other's persons, a compensation which I trusted would return the rider to such a degree of confidence as would enable him to perform with more adroitness upon his beast during the coming races.

The following day I went with his lordship to the races at Newmarket, where I had the pleasure of seeing three of his mounts – their riders clearly none the worse for their engagement of the day before – win their races.

Stow was in high good humour, and that evening handed me my expenses together with a fee far in excess of the one I had asked, and provided one of his personal carriages to take me by stages back to town – where, within a week, I was to hear from Chichley news of a most remarkable nature, concerning not myself but the entire kingdom!

Before I continue with this narrative, however, I must issue a warning, especially to my younger and more adventurous readers: serious injury could follow any attempt to counterfeit the activities which I have described, and any reader, male or female, who owns a horse and feels the inclination to attempt one of the poses with a friend, should reconsider and refrain.

Chapter Eleven

The Adventures of Andy

That I should win the election was a foregone conclusion, not only because of my superiority as a candidate – for the common sort of Cornish people found me the acme of civilisation and wit, while those who knew better were convinced that upon election I would be tractable to their wishes, and not inclined to be wild in demanding such unconscionable matters as universal suffrage.

Nevertheless, it was pleasant enough to stand upon the balcony of Webb's Hotel at Liskeard and to hear the Mayor announce that my candidature had attracted fully twice as many votes as that of my rival, the notorious and egregious Methodist Whig, Philosophy Beswarick, a thin and inconsequential little man who would in any case have been of no assistance to my Lord Grey in the administration he was now to form, and to which it was my duty to be implacably opposed.

The local Tories had as a matter of course engaged the main rooms at Webb's for a celebration of my victory, which as I have indicated was considered a certainty; and we spent some hours in a – for me – tedious round of drinking with Mr This and Mr That, supporters from the villages around (St Pinnock and Doublebois, Warleggan and Bocaddon and Penpillick) who had ensured my

election through a process of persuasion and bribery
(now I can admit it – though it amounted only to the
buying of beer and ribbons). At ten o'clock, however,
Squire Treleaven sidled up to me as I was talking to Mrs
Penplodden, the wife of the Rector of Bodmin and more
like a bishop than a laywoman.

'My dear Archer,' he said, 'may I draw you away?
– with many apologies, Mrs Penplodden. I have a
deputation anxious to meet you, come down from
Plymouth.'

Bowing to the lady, whose incipient moustache quiv-
ered with disapproval at the sudden end brought to our
discussion of the amendments necessary to the Reform
Bill, he led me off and up the staircase to the first floor.

'You deserve a little recreation, my boy,' said the
Squire; 'and I trust that you will enjoy it – at our
expense. It is the best that can be secured within a hundred miles, and comes on the recommendation of Sir
Brinsley Fordice, the Member for East Devonshire, who
is a connoisseur in such matters.'

Upon which, he threw open a door and propelled me
through it. I found myself in the chief bedroom of the
hotel – which, it being by London standards a miserable establishment, consisted merely of a plain room the
walls of which were hung with hunting prints, and the
chief furnishing of which consisted in a great, clumsy
square bed whose four posts, bearing a tattered velvet
canopy, were hung with the coloured ribbons of the Tory
Party, and upon which reclined not one but two young
ladies whose only covering was a set of the same ribbons
entwined about their limbs. They were, as I could
immediately observe, of complementary form – one
being slim and lithe, the other of a more rounded and

chubby form. Both with an equal enthusiasm rose from their semi-recumbent posture and, approaching me, threw their arms about me and congratulated me upon my victory, accompanying their kind words with kinder kisses, and an exploratory gesture towards the fastening of my clothes, which they succeeded in undoing with such ease and rapidity as suggested that the exercise was not new to them.

Since my pleasant excursion to St George's Island, I had devoted myself with considerable attention to the duty of ensuring my election, and had therefore had no greater opportunity of carnal connexion than was offered by the cursory embracing of small children and an occasional doffing of my hat to the wife of some brewer or baker whose interest it was important to secure; so that on one of the young ladies falling to her knees before me and further fortifying by her caresses a limb already sufficiently adamant for her purposes, I realised to what extent I had missed the pleasure of the company of the fair sex.

In less than no time, therefore, I was stretched out upon the bed, with Bess and Nell (as they informed me were their names) demonstrating the extent to which they fulfilled the expectations aroused in Mr Treleaven by the praises of Sir Brinsley – praises no doubt founded in experience, the ladies in question apparently being among the conveniences offered to their Member by the Tories of East Devonshire.

It was necessary however to persuade them to modify certain aspects of their behaviour, for one of their earliest actions was to turn me upon my face, when in a moment, expecting the soft touch of lips and hands upon my nether regions, I felt rather the cutting pain of a blow from what proved to be a leather belt. Presumably this was Sir Brinsley's pleasure, and had impressed itself upon the ladies as a procedure invariably welcomed by politicians in general and Members of Parliament in particular; but as I informed them, the application of a belt to my posteriors was the speediest way to ensure the abortion of our pleasures – my member indeed already shrinking at the action, as was discovered when, apologising for their mistake, the young ladies laid me once more upon my back. However, the joint application of kisses to the offending limb soon restored it to a proper state of tumefaction – indeed, to such dimensions as brought forth congratulations from the ladies, from which I gathered that, whatever the size of his majority, Sir Brinsley was not notable for the dimensions of his manhood.

While Miss Nell, the plumper of the two, contented herself with lying at my side and admiring, with tongue and fingers, each part of my body in turn, Miss Bess was more active – unable indeed, it seemed, to be still for a moment; now bending to explore with her tongue the environs of my cods, or suck them with a most delightful sensation (at the same time presenting me with the most inspiriting view of her buttocks, the full fig of her womanhood open to my admiration), now turning to nip with peremptory pleasure at my paps, to offer to my lips her small but elegantly formed bosoms, or to (as it were) stroke my whole upper body with their tips as she slid down to such a posture as offered to the slippery caresses of her lips an organ strained almost to bursting with the desire to couple.

This indeed soon mastered me, so that without pausing to choose between the ladies, I was in a moment sheathed in a kindly orifice, the relief of an almost immediate expulsion of desire being such that in my pleasure I forgot the courtesy of ensuring that the lady in question was equally in receipt of sensual gratification. Bess (who, I now saw, was the one who lay beneath me) showed no sign of disappointment, however; from which I divined – accurately, as it turned out – that she was one of those ladies who did not find such gratification necessary; nor did my temporary collapse dismay Nell, who merely reclined upon one elbow, in the position from which she had observed the conclusion of my joy, and meeting my eye merely smiled, showing no sign that she regretted that I was now in no state to gratify her.

I must confess that I now fell into a doze, the fatigue of the past few weeks joining with the lethargy of my limbs to render it necessary; and when I awoke it was not to the renewed caresses of the ladies, but to see them rather gratifying each other, for they lay top to tail, their heads between each other's thighs, enjoying those pleasures which often compensate such women for the necessity of farming their bodies out for the pleasure of men.

They made a pretty picture, however; and even the realisation that they could not have found my person as attractive as they found each other's could not prevent my spirits rising; and indeed I was considering the possibility of intervening to play some part in the scene when I heard voices outside the door, and the protests of Squire Treleaven, who seemed to be attempting to stop someone from entering.

Bess and Nell drew apart, and I, reaching out for the crumbled counterpane, succeeded in covering myself with it before the door burst open and into the room, striding past the protesting Squire, came – Mrs Samuel Treglown!

To say that I was surprised would be to fail altogether to convey my feelings: although it would be untrue to say that I had forgotten her, I had certainly done my best to reconcile myself to never encountering her again – or if that were not the case, to regard her as a citadel impossible to conquer, since her repugnance to my person appeared to be complete. Yet now, holding the door open and gesturing to the two girls to leave – which they did, still in a state of nature (which evidently intrigued the Squire to the extent of forgetting his strictures upon her entry) – the lady stood, closing the door firmly, and for a moment simply regarded me gravely.

I must confess that I felt the blood rushing to my cheeks: had I been able to choose, would I have selected the moment at which I was abed with two whores to be seen by this admired lady? Yet she made no reproach, either by gesture or attitude; and indeed walking towards the bed, sat upon the edge of it, and reaching out a hand laid it upon my thigh (which was one of those areas of my unclothed body which was not covered by the counterpane), and smiled in the kindest manner.

What was this? Here was a lady who more than once, upon my expressing my keen admiration, had repulsed me, making it quite clear that she regretted my attachment to her – yet she was now, quite unmistakably, of an opposite view – for her fingers gently moved upon my flesh, edging upwards along my thigh in a most ingratiating manner.

My jaw must have dropped, and she was unable to repress what could only be described as a giggle.

'My Archer,' she said, 'allow me to explain myself.

You will perhaps be surprised that I now come to you in such a situation as this, when on the previous occasions when you were kind enough to express your approbation of my person, I repulsed you.'

I was able only to nod, swallowing hard as her hand now fell upon that part of me whose condition proved conclusively that my admiration was not merely retrospective.

'I must tell you that on that occasion I had left London under the circumstance of having been forced – I may even say raped – by Mr Treglown, my husband. I should explain that our marriage was contracted as the result of an arrangement by our families, made when we were still children; that we have not for some years lived together in the same house; but that my husband, in a condition of drunkenness, hearing that I was in town, came to me and insisted upon a connection; then – upon my remonstrating – positively boasted that he was poxed, and had given me the disease!

'You can imagine how distraught I was at such a revelation! And with what distraction I found myself, only a day or two later, in the presence of a gentleman whose personal attraction, and clear admiration of my person, was such that it would otherwise have given me the greatest pleasure to gratify in his desires! Yet could I do so in the knowledge that I might contaminate him? And could I explain the reason to a stranger?'

I felt my riding-muscle contract under the import of her words: was I to be invited to catch the French gout?

She must – for her fingers still lay along its length – have felt the effect of her words; for she now continued:

'Fear not! – my physicians have conducted the most

full examination, and entirely clear me of any suspicion
in the matter, for signs of such a condition would, they
assure me, by now have made themselves plain. My husband, with a bestiality of behaviour such as even I would
have hesitated to believe possible, no doubt invented the
entire story in order to distress me. Can you believe that,
while it must appear unladylike, I could resist, upon
hearing his words, coming to offer you at the same time
my congratulations upon your election, and the opportunity, should you wish it, of . . .' But here it was her
turn to blush; upon which I kissed her full upon those
rosy and enticing lips – then drew back, remembering
the circumstances in which she had discovered me.

'My dear madam,' I said, 'I fear that I was occupied,
on your appearance, with . . .'

'Please,' she said, stopping my lips with another kiss,
'say nothing of it. A gentleman must have his amusements, and as long as your strength is not
exhausted – which' (with an appreciative squeeze) 'I can
tell is not the case, can I repine at others participating in
that pleasure which it is now my keenest apprehension to
enjoy?'

Rising to her feet, she unloosed the buttons of her
gown, and, letting it fall to the floor, revealed at last that
body at whose proportions it had only so far been possible for my imagination to guess. She was in every way
the fruition of my hopes: her shoulders were broad, yet
shaped with such delicacy that the least suspicion of
masculinity was at once dispelled. Her breasts were as
full as womanly nature demanded, yet were so supported
by the musculature of her frame that they stood proudly
from her body without the least suspicion of looseness,
the buds which marked the centre of each circle erect,

confirming the passion which I could see in the wide pupils of her dark eyes no less than upon her glistening lips.

Her waist was narrow, but broadening immediately to the platform of her hips, where between her thighs lay that dark triangle at the centre of which a darker cleft invited first my eyes, then my palm, and finally my lips.

It will not be supposed that I objected when she now lifted the counterpane from my body, and took her time in examining the latter, with (modesty must not prevent me from recording) many expressions of admiration, turning in time to assertions of desire; nor will the reader be amazed to learn that words only by a little preceded action – and must allow me merely to assert that neither of us was disappointed in the other during the hours that followed.

I was perhaps fortunate in that my passage with Bess and Nell had to an extent taken the edge off my passion, so that I was able to contain my emotions until I had brought the lady to not merely one but two expressions of entire satisfaction – taking, I must confess, some pleasure in bringing to her lips the shrillest and most passionate cries of pleasure. However, it will not be the reader's wish that I should detail the pleasures which followed – the strokings and scratchings, the kissings and nippings, the joinings of each part of one body with each part of the other: so that by the time the first rays of the sun fell across the square outside the hotel window, we were in an exhausted sleep, having – as it seemed – achieved within only a few hours the utmost knowledge of each other's bodies, and explored the furthest reaches of each other's desires.

It had been fixed that upon the following day I should set out for London to take my seat with the other elected

members of the Parliament at Westminster; and Mrs
Treglown insisted upon accompanying me (not that I
made objection). Squire Treleaven was not amazed to
see us together at breakfast, for, occupying the neighbouring room to ours, he had (as he told me in an aside)
been kept awake for some time by the sounds of our
enjoyment – until, driven by the demands of his own
flesh, roused to passion by the evidence of his ears, he
had sent for Bess and Nell and himself enjoyed some pale
reflection of our pleasure.

We were seen off from Webb's by a cheering and congratulatory crowd (Mrs Treglown being recognised by
the assembled throng, and being a popular lady through
her charitable work in the county). During the following
journey, broken by two charming nights at convenient
inns, we got to know each other on polite as well as on
intimate terms: my learning, among other matters, that
her name was Charlotte, though she invited me to
address her by the diminutive of 'Charlie'.

During the hours of travelling, she told me a rather
alarming thing: something of which, doubtless to my
shame, I was not aware: that should our present monarch die, his successor was – a woman! That is, the Princess Victoria, daughter of Princess Charlotte and Prince
Leopold of Saxe-Coburg, now a young girl of thirteen or
fourteen years of age and living in Kensington Palace.

You can imagine my distress at this news: that our
great country should be ruled by a female – despite my
devotion to the sex – is not to be thought of! Yet what
can be done about it? She is indisputably heir! Charlie
was much amused at my distress upon hearing this news,
being of the opinion that a Queen was by no means likely
to bring the crown to disrepute. The young girl, she tells

me, is being well educated, taught not only anatomy but alchemy, not only English literature but music, of which she is fond; she also sketches, attends the theatre, and is steadfast in attendance at church. All this set aside, it seems to me reprehensible that no male heir can be discovered.

Upon our reaching London we went straight to my house, which had been alerted by a post rider, and where (for the sake of her reputation) a separate room had been prepared for Mrs Treglown – though not so far from my own as to render my nightly attendance upon her dependent upon too arduous a journey.

She felt it incumbent upon her to seek out her husband, who was (have I said it?) Member of Parliament for an obscure northern town, where he had recently been re-elected in the Whig interest; and met with him in a chamber at Westminster while I with a horde of other members was attending upon the Speaker of the House of Commons to take my seat, a ceremony rendered somewhat perfunctory by the great number of those participating, so that I was less impressed than I had hoped. However, I was determining to make my mark by a speech early in the Parliament – even perhaps during the first twenty-four hours – when I received a message summoning me to wait upon my friend.

I found her in the most curious state of apprehension. Reaching the corridor in which was the room where her husband had appointed to meet her, she had been shown by an attendant of the House into a neighbouring chamber, where the intervening door had carelessly been left ajar; and had overheard her husband speaking in French to someone with him. Her knowledge of the French language was imperfect, but, she told me, she had heard

enough to suspect that Treglown was involved in a plot
to place a Pretender upon the throne of England on the
death of the present monarch – that such a Pretender
was to arrive in England soon, from Calais, whereupon
an insurgency would be set in motion.

I repressed my natural feeling that even an illicit King
would be better than a Queen; for, after all, even from
motives of concern at the crowning of a female monarch,
could I not reprehend a foreign plan to interfere with the
British succession?

But could it be true? Charlie was unshakeable. She
had, she said, upon overhearing the gist of the conversation, betrayed her presence by a start and a small cry,
upon which the person speaking with her husband had
instantly ceased. Upon immediately entering the room
she had seen only his back as he left, and had been
greeted in the most cursory manner by Treglown, who
did his best to discover what she had heard, which she
disguised by saying that she had that moment arrived,
and had heard only voices, not what they said. He
seemed relieved at this; and after an exchange of views
regarding his property in Cornwall (which he wished
to sell, but needed her consent) they had parted –
whereupon she had immediately sent for me.

'We must discover more,' she said; 'but by what
means?'

In what respect was he vulnerable? I asked. Was there
nothing reprehensible in his life, no incident which we
could use to blackmail him into revealing the plot (if such
there was, for it seemed to me at present to be as tenuous
a matter as a fairy tale)?

Nothing, she said.

Could she not (I hesitated to suggest it) use her female

wiles to obtain information?

No – to my relief – was her reply. He had long since forsworn her bed, his recent attack upon her person being informed more by malice than by lust. From what she had heard he contented himself with an alliance with Lady Pauncefoot, a female of imperfect morals with whom he had formed an alliance some years hence, whose attentions appeared to satisfy his requirements.

Then was he not susceptible to female beauty?

No, she replied; unless it was something extraordinary.

I considered for a moment; then after some consideration put forward an idea which, after a little persuasion, Charlie agreed might extract the information we required. I left her, and making some enquiries of some old friends, then took myself to a house in Greenwich where I renewed my acquaintance with a young lady who had been, though briefly, an employee of Frank's and mine at our house of pleasure in Brook Street. Betsy is a Negress who combines an extraordinary beauty of person with a keen intelligence and wit, and indeed within three weeks of taking up residence at our house had been enticed away by a young gentleman of rank and wealth, who had established her at his house in Hampstead, where she still lived. We had parted on good terms – it never being our wish to stand in the way of our girls improving themselves; and upon my knocking on her door, at an hour when her lover was from home, she expressed herself delighted to see me, and on my explaining the matter was pleased to help us, her devotion to her adopted country (to which she had been brought as a girl by a sea captain who had rescued her from a slave-ship sailing to the Americas) prompting her to an immediate acquiescence.

Within a day, Treglown had received a simple message

inviting him to an appointment at a house in the suburb of Chelsea, where a reward would be waiting for his attentive encouragement of 'the plan we know of'. It was signed in the name of the Duc de Laval, Ambassador of France. We took the risk that Treglown did not know his signature; and were evidently right, for at the appointed time he knocked upon the door of the house which we had taken for the occasion, and was shown by a manservant (one of my own) to a room upon the first floor.

This was a bedroom which was fitted out in the most luxurious manner (it, and the house, belonged to another lady of my acquaintance, a Mrs Jopling Rowe, who used it for the entertainment of her numerous lovers). It also had – 'twas the chief reason for using it – the convenience of a neighbouring room from which an aperture carefully contrived not only afforded an opportunity to observe, but to hear, all that went on in it.

What met Treglown's eyes as he entered, was chiefly a large bed made up with the whitest of sheets, which presented to advantage the body stretched upon it, that of Betsy, now a ripe eighteen years of age, but still with the figure of a young person three or four years her junior: that is, with the full development of a female of the most luscious description, yet entirely lacking that slackness which too often is the product of a life devoted to amorous exercise (for she had kept herself solely to the young gentleman who was her friend, he being not only kindly but possessed of considerable wealth; only her debt to me, who had been the instrument of her obtaining her present position, persuading her to make this excursion).

I now set eyes upon Treglown for the first time (for, need I say, Charlie and myself were placed with our eyes

at the spyholes). He was just such a man as I had imagined: coarse and unmannerly, and from his posture suffering from the effects of a life too much devoted to food
and drink. Indeed, so clear was it that it was to gluttony
that he was chiefly devoted, that I feared that even the
sight of Betsy would not tempt him. However, here I was
wrong – though perhaps as much through his pride that
his employers (the French) had honoured him with such
a reward, than from natural concupiscence.

At all events, no sooner had he closed the door than he
began to divest himself of his clothing, all the time keeping an eye upon the prize upon the bed: which indeed was
a sufficiently enticing one even to interest me, who only a
few hours before had held in my arms the beautiful creature who now, with her hand upon my arm, observed the
scene with an interest equal to my own. Closing the shutters, we had lit the room by candle-light, which now
gleamed upon the Negress's body, laying trails of golden
light upon the purple of her skin, and drawing as it were
an outline about her limbs, which here and there, in
shadow, darkened to complete black. As Treglown loosened the waistband of his breeches, she drew up a leg
and, leaning it slightly to one side, allowed a silver of
light to lie along the inside of her thigh, making yet more
enticing the pitch-black shadow at its top, where now she
laid a lethargic hand, as though to hide what was already
obscured by the darkness.

A tightening of Charlie's fingers bespoke her approbation of the situation. When I had explained my plan,
she had doubted whether any woman could entice her
husband to any greater interest than he had shown,
recently, in her; but in default of another plan had
agreed to this, and was now generous enough to admit

that she had been wrong – for Treglown, divesting himself of the last article of apparel, revealed a corporeal admiration of the banquet set before him; though not one such as would necessarily delight, let alone frighten, a woman.

His person, unclothed, was much as one would have expected from his appearance in polite society. Too indulgent an appetite at the table had thickened his frame, so that while his chest and shoulders were still those of a strong man (he was, I should have said, approaching the age of fifty), about his waist there hung those circles of flesh which thickened what had once no doubt been slender, while his belly was a converse vessel of mutton which swung somewhat as he moved.

His thighs, too, were thicker than they should have been, and there – as upon the lower parts of his arms – the skin had stretched to contain more blubber than a self-respecting gentleman would be happy with. The lack of hair upon his head, he could not be blamed for; neither was it his fault that the hair upon his chest and belly, and even that private hair below, was now grey and somewhat sparse. But was it a matter for congratulation that that chief advertisement of masculinity, confronted by such a delicious dish as was now set before Treglown, could only achieve a salute at half-mast? That even a vigorous manual stimulation, which he now applied, could rouse it only to the thickness and length of one of those cigars now imported so freely from the Americas?

It may be that, had she not been thoroughly instructed in what was expected of her, Betsy would have scorned the attentions of so poor a specimen of masculinity, so indifferent an advertisement for the sex. However, to her credit, she showed only interest – and now placed herself on hands and knees, resembling nothing so much as a handsome animal, in order to express what seemed admiration of the pathetic figure before her.

Treglown was, as she had intended, complimented by her interest – no doubt it had been many years since a woman had shown such interest in his person; and took a step towards the bed, at which she left it, and approaching him coiled her body sinuously about his own, a thigh insinuating itself between his own, her hands caressing his back and flaccid haunches, her enticing breasts pressed against his own – for his bosom was only by its pilosity different in shape to that of a woman, though one insufficiently developed for the taste of most men.

There now began a scene of such enticing voluptuousness that it roused my amorous propensities to a degree which equalled that of our victim. Betsy used all her wiles – not to entice a lover, for Treglown needed no encouragement – but to raise him to such heights of goatishness as were positively painful to him. Even his puny dangler was aroused by her attentions to such dimensions as were not entirely disreputable, while that great belly positively panted with desire; and as I saw him stretched upon the bed, his every limb tightened with unalleviated appetite, I was strung between pity and envy.

It was at this point that Betsy, carefully tutored by us, began her questioning; and such was the state to which she had reduced Treglown that the answers to her questions were immediately forthcoming. Careful though she was, I have no doubt that his suspicions were aroused; but his condition made it imperative that his body should be satisfied, and while we could not hear his half-whispered answers, the fact that in a short time she bestrode him (his person being so heavy as to make the superior position desirable as a matter of comfort) and brought him to a climax so keen that a positive wail broke from his lips, convinced us that our ambition had been achieved.

While he was still recovering, Betsy sprung from the bed, and reaching the door was through it, and had closed it behind her. On hearing it close, he roused himself – but reaching the door found it locked, and on opening the shutters found that the room looked out upon a blank quadrangle. As we left our vantage-point, he began to knock upon the door (with intervals during which he began to dress himself); but we had chosen the house with care. He could not be heard, and would only be relieved at our convenience.

Upon the landing, we met and congratulated Betsy – my own embrace being, I must confess, sufficiently keen (the young lady still being unclothed) to rouse Charlie to an uncomfortable though not unfriendly tweaking of my cods, and the reminder that we should attend to business. While she resumed her clothing, Betsy told us what she had discovered: which was the arrival at Dover in two days' time of a young man reputed to be the son of Madame de St Laurent and Prince Edward, Duke of Kent, fourth son of King George III, and father to Victoria. He was to be set forth as a proper heir to the British throne, an alternative to his sister, and an antidote to that dreadful fate, a female monarch! Since this boy had been brought up in France, and much under the influence of the notorious Charles Maurice de Talleyrand, it was hoped by the French that in placing him upon the throne they would have a puppet of their own at the head of the country which they still regard as their greatest rival in Europe.

'And while,' Charlie opined, 'so many of our people share your own prejudice against a female ruler, and since there are no other legitimate sons of George III's children, the plan has a strong chance of success unless it can be forestalled.'

The problem of achieving this was something to which we now turned our attention; and immediately took ourselves off to consult the Viscount Chichley, an old friend upon whose advice we could depend. Treglown, we left to his own devices. He was to remain for the time a prisoner; we had placed, in a cupboard of his comfortable prison, sufficient food and wine to last him for several days; by which time we trusted he could be released – if only to face trial as a traitor.

By the time we reached Chichley's house, I had devised a plan not dissimilar to that which had brought about Treglown's downfall; and Charlie had expressed her support for it, though wondering how it was to be achieved. About that, I had an idea of my own, and Chichley was quick to approve – and was able to inform me of the whereabouts of the person whose assistance was now necessary: my sister and friend Mrs Sophia Nelham.

Chapter Twelve

Sophie's Story

What was my surprise, upon my arrival at Chichley's London home, to find there my old friend Andrew Archer, together with a female friend whom he introduced as Mrs Samuel Treglown, but who goes under the name of Charlotte. She and Andy seemed upon familiar terms, and knowing my boy's delight in the companionship of willing women, I was not amazed, for she is a lady of considerable physical charms, and of just such a spirited nature as to appeal to him.

However, it was not in order to effect that introduction that I had been summoned, for pausing only to order some wine, Chichley explained the reason for my summons. It appears – and he did not explain, for there was not time, the details of the situation – that there was to arrive at Dover upon the following day, from France, a young man who was Pretender to the throne of England, summoned by a cabal of the French and English – the former eager to install here a monarch upon whose loyalty they could count; the latter eager to avoid the disgrace (as they see it) of a woman upon the throne – the present heir being the Princess Victoria.

Chichley's motives in wishing to prevent this were chiefly of a patriotic nature, as were (as I guess) those of my friend; while Mrs Treglown was of my own opinion, that there was at least a chance that a Queen might bring upon the country the same renown as that famous predecessor Elizabeth, whose monarchy was noted neither for weakness nor ineffectuality.

Andy explained to me that it was his plan that I should engage the attentions of the Pretender for a sufficient time to permit Chichley to alert the authorities to the scheme, and to arrest those culpable of it – for should the youth (of whom they know nothing) reach the capital and come into the grasp of the plotters, all may be lost within a very short time.

There were to this plan some objections: not that I was not entirely willing to devote myself body and soul to the country's good, but that we knew not the name of the Pretender, nor precisely when he would arrive; but Andy was convinced that this was no bar to the success of his scheme, and in short, upon my having consented to do what I could in the matter, it proved that he had already commissioned a coach, wherein he, his new friend and myself set out immediately for Dover, leaving Chichley to make contact with those persons in London whose loyalty could be depended upon to destroy any scheme involving a threat to the security of the realm.

On our reaching Dover – a town with which I was then unfamiliar – we found it but a poor fishing village crouched beneath tremendous cliffs of chalk, with only two inns, one of which was in such a condition that no traveller would stay there unless forced to do so. The other, to our great satisfaction, was almost entirely full, and on our making discreet enquiries of the landlord we found that no party had taken rooms for the following evening on behalf of any who might arrive from the continent (this being a less prominent port, for such

arrivals, than Brighthelmstone, further along the coast).
Andy and his friend bespoke the single remaining room
on behalf of Andrew Archer Esq., MP, and Mrs Archer
– and then set about finding lodgings for me and for my
victim, and succeeded in taking a small but decent
cottage on the outskirts of the hamlet; having assured
ourselves that it would suit our purpose, we spent the day
somewhat at ease. After an early dinner Andy and
Charlotte excused themselves on the grounds of an
unconscionable lethargy; the brightness of their eyes
however betrayed rather a desire for carnal congress. I
went to my lonely bed.

Next day we also spent in idleness, but any thought I
might have had of familiarity with my friend, whom I had
not seen for some time, was rendered impossible by his
invariably being in the company of Mrs Treglown, with
whom, on no less than two occasions, he retired to their
room upon one excuse or another – returning some time
later in that state of relaxation which bespeaks physical
contentment. I had never seen my friend so besotted with
a female – but must confess her to be charming enough.

At the hour of eight post meridian, a schooner was due
to arrive from the French port of Le Havre – which,
being the only foreign vessel likely to put in, must contain the traveller in whom we were most interested, and
at this time, we three placed ourselves in the window of
the inn – and to our satisfaction saw three men who
from their appearance were more distinguished than the
gaggle of other travellers who descended the gangway
from the *Petite Marie* (which was the name of the vessel)
approach the place.

On their entering, we saw the trio consisted of two
middle-aged men, one of rougher appearance than the

other, and a young man who was careful to remain as much in the shadow as was possible. Upon enquiry, finding there were no rooms available, the two older men exchanged courtesies in a tone indicative of mingled distress and anger; and one of them, in execrable English, began to enquire as to the possibility of other accommodation, which the landlord denied the existence of (he having been prepared by instruction and payment to do so).

The irritation of the two elder men now became extreme; upon which I rose from my place and approached them.

'Messieurs,' I said (addressing them in their own language, which I had some little knowledge of), 'is it the case that you seek accommodation, and cannot find it?'

They assented – whereupon I offered them the convenience of my humble home – my brother and sister-in-law (with a nod towards Andy and his friend) returning to London within the hour, there were two rooms available, which I was pleased to offer to representatives of that great nation whose recent struggle to relieve herself from the cruel rule of despots I so admired.

The gentlemen were as grateful as they were unsuspicious – indeed, I was almost ashamed at the ease with which I deceived them; and, motioning the younger man to come forward, introduced him as M. le Semblant. A glimpse of his face suggested that the task of making his closer acquaintance would not be a painful one, and his shy smile as he bowed over my hand was one which immediately engaged my sympathy – it was not the face of a villain.

To be short, pausing only for the rougher man (who seemed to be a servant) to pick up the two packages which were their only luggage, the three gentlemen accompanied me to the cottage which we had secured, my having made an ostentatious farewell to Andy and Mrs Treglown.

At the cottage I was for a time fearful that I might be discovered, for though I had explored it as best I might, I was not entirely familiar with its geography; but the travellers were weary, and almost immediately took themselves to their rooms – the two elder men to one at the back of the house, the younger to a room somewhat removed from this.

After allowing a pause of some quarter of an hour or twenty minutes I took a bowl of hot water and knocked softly upon the door of M. le Semblant's room. A gentle voice bade me enter, and doing so I found the young man sitting somewhat melancholy in the window and looking out over the sea towards the coast he had earlier left.

I set the bowl down, with the suggestion that he might wish to refresh himself after the journey; and left the room – pausing for perhaps ten minutes, and then, placing a towel over my arm, returning. This time I entered without knocking, and found the youth – for he was clearly little more – naked to the waist, having blinded himself with soap before assuring himself of a towel, and feeling about him in a state of considerable confusion.

'Monsieur,' I said, 'a thousand pardons! I omitted to provide you with the means to dry yourself!' — and stepping forward handed him the towel, with which he instantly dried his face, while I leaned to take the bowl of water.

Upon his opening his eyes, he found a sight which clearly interested him. I had now changed my formerly modest gown for one which revealed more of my person than perhaps a stranger would count upon discovering except in circumstances of some intimacy. The dress which I now wore was one of those, already out of fashion, which, being of the thinnest cotton, revealed as much as it concealed – and I took care that in picking up the bowl I allowed some of the water to splash upon its front, so that the material clung even more closely to my bosom, from which it was beyond the boy's power to take his eyes.

'M – *madame*,' he stammered, 'all my gratitude . . .'

'But, sir,' I said, 'you look melancholy' – and setting down the bowl reached out a hand and placed it upon his arm; 'you are perhaps sad to leave your home?'

'Ah, *madame*,' he said, 'I am not at liberty to explain the reason, but this is indeed a journey I had rather not make.'

'Yet,' I said, 'this is an hospitable country, in which you will find a warm welcome' – at the same time placing a second hand upon his other arm, in what amounted to an embrace. At this, a mixture of melancholy and the lethargy of the journey (a combination which must weaken the strongest spirits) so attacked him that he seized me about the waist, and in a moment embraced me with a kiss more passionate than I expected from a boy of his years.

The advantage of a French education cannot be too much emphasised where matters of love are concerned. A moment after this first embrace, he drew away, fearful no doubt that he might have offended me; but upon my showing – by the simple act of slipping my dress from my shoulders – that such was not the case, he began to prove the extent to which he excelled any English youth of his age in those arts which best please a lady.

I later learned from him that in preparation for the task he was to face he had been locked away from female company for some months, forced to memorise many facts about the English aristocracy, and in particular the royal family. Previously as accustomed to regular amorous exercise as any Frenchman of his age, his frustration had been considerable; and upon my offering the opportunity of an embrace, he seized it with the greatest enthusiasm.

I am in some difficulty in describing what followed, for to be frank my emotions were soon engaged in so vigorous and persuasive a fashion that I was in a delirium of delight such as I had not known for many months. My constant readers will not be unaware that during my years of adulthood I have been familiar with a number of gentlemen of greater or lesser accomplishment in the arts of love; yet I can say without hesitation that this boy of only nineteen – this Maurice, for that was his name – had a greater knowledge of how to please a female than any other man in my experience.

I should perhaps insert at this point a description of his life, as he later related it to me.

The question whether he is really the son of Madame de St Laurent, let alone of the Duke of Kent, must await discovery; it is what he has been led to believe, and it is clear that from an infant he was raised in the expectation of achieving the English throne. Despite this, however, and all the tuition of that villain Talleyrand, it is an expectation which provoked only melancholy, for he is by no means a person to whom rank and position offers rewards he is eager to acquire.

The reason for this disposition is not difficult to

understand, for from infancy he was treated as a mere vessel for political propaganda; his guardians, bent upon forcing him into their mould, only made themselves representative of a painful tedium. But those responsible for his nurture have been of the lower orders, whose simplicity and good humour seemed infinitely preferable – so that his personal preference was for leading a life of quiet obscurity, and his one ambition to escape the high office others intend him for.

His first memories were of growing up in a farm in Burgundy, where the first fourteen years of his life were entirely free of anxiety; he was treated as one of a family of five children, and though the others were the natural children of the farmer and wife, who played in all respects the part of parents, he was treated with the same kindness as the two boys and two girls who were in every sense except the literal one his brothers and sisters.

He was marked out from them however by being sent for, at the age of five, to the manor house of the area, where he became the pupil of a master who taught him – with the greatest kindness – to read and write excellent French, and to speak English with reasonable fluency. The purpose of this education was not revealed to him until later, and he did not allow his superior knowledge to affect his relationship with his brothers and sisters, which remained extremely close.

Indeed, as seems common with French families, it was in company with them that he made his first explorations of the capabilities of the body; he and his brothers, noting the changes which took place at the time of approaching manhood, were at one in persuading their sisters to reveal whether or not similar changes were occurring with them. They had from the earliest time been used to the differences between the male and female form, having been accustomed to share both bed and bath; and the small appendages which alone marked male from female had seemed to them of little remark. But upon the time coming when these were so enlarged as to occasion comment from their sisters (waking in the morning to the sight of three commanding extensions of their brothers' nether parts) they showed a renewed interest in the girls' persons, finding both curiosity and delight in the fringe of silky hair which now decorated portals which previously had been too naked to command anything other than slight interest.

A natural modesty prevented their doing anything other than look; and in common with other youths, it was in experiment with each other that they discovered the delights conferred by the attention of Mrs Palm and her five daughters, and were soon contesting among themselves as to who could couple the pleasure of emission with its greatest force; a game the girls soon discovered them at, and were keen spectators of.

Upon his attaining the age of sixteen, it was one of those sisters who (and how fortunate that she was not a natural sister, but one in name only!) had seduced Maurice into performing an action which gave him even greater pleasure than that of manual stimulation, and for some time (as he told me with some perturbation) he had run riot through the countryside, discovering that almost every female of his own age welcomed the attentions of his prick, which proved sturdy enough to perform several operations on the same day without diminution either of force or of pleasure.

It was on the occasion of his swiving with a maid at the manor, when he had been left alone for an hour to learn some English phrases, that he was discovered by Madame Lecouvre, the sister of the master of the house, a lady who had for some time been mistress of a gentleman at the court, and was considerably experienced in amatory art.

'She taught me,' he said, 'those skills which best please the sex.' And indeed she had taught him well, for upon the first experience of our coupling, at Dover, he proved the most splendid, efficacious, considerate and compelling of lovers.

I must first say that of all men he was the most beautiful: by which I do not mean in the least effeminate, but the possessor of limbs perfectly shaped, a torso which might have been carved by Michelangelo himself, a noble head crowned with a magnificent mane of blond hair. His hands were not only finely shaped, but admirable in conveying every shade of admiration, ready to respond to desire almost before it had made itself known to the body he caressed.

Indeed, what was astonishing to me was the extent to which the attentions of his hands were arousing – for most men are clumsy to the extent of bruising, handling a woman as they would handle a dog or a horse. Maurice proceeded with much greater care, and while fixing his lips upon my own (occasionally transferring them to the tips of my ears, my eyelids, forehead, chin – even, sometimes, descending to the tips of my breasts) his hands moved with the greatest tenderness over my body, gradually drawing nearer to that goal at which (I assumed) he ultimately aimed.

But there, too, his manners were impeccable: far from thrusting a finger rudely into the aperture, as so many men do, he stroked and caressed my jewel as if indeed it were of a priceless value, stroking first gently up and down the groove; then placing four fingers slightly above, and moving them gently; and finding the boy in the boat, gently but insistently moving his lubricated forefinger around and about, and then upon, that most sensitive zone, until I was almost mad with the pleasure of it, and finally gave way to a spasm of delight so intense that my whole body shook with it.

Yet still he persisted – now with an even more sensitive touch, so that far from making tender the source of my pleasure, he roused me in no short time again almost to the heights – then, as my panting began to signify a second culmination, withdrew his hand and in its stead juxtaposed a machine whose power I was yet ignorant of – though my own fingers had found it of significant size.

To be short about it, he proceeded to demonstrate a style of swiving which was as apprehensive of my pleasure as the preliminaries, for he fell into a regular rocking motion which would have lulled me into sleep had not the friction of his tool within me continued the raising of my spirits. At first content with a shallow penetration, so that his bulb merely stimulated the curtains of my arbour, he gradually pressed deeper, until with a splendid keenness I felt the whole length of his instrument plunging within me, seeming (no doubt through the graduality of his approach) to pierce my very vitals.

Giving myself over entirely to pleasure, and even forgetting the obligations which should have encouraged me to contribute to his enjoyment in the way of such manual caresses as were possible in the situation, I succumbed no less than three more times to convulsions of the utmost agitation before I felt the hot flow of his passion; after which he for some time still continued his movements, though with a slower and less compulsive rhythm, lulling me to the point at which I was not reluctant to permit him to withdraw.

In the light of a moon which had now risen, I could see what I had felt – that his whole body was through his efforts bathed in perspiration, and taking the towel wiped his limbs, which in their relaxed state had a beauty no less than that displayed by his previous excitement. This did not, however, prevent me from my desire to return some of the pleasure he had afforded me (apart from the fact that 'twas my duty); and driven by the ambition to prove myself as considerate and adept a lover as he, I proceeded to exercise upon him those talents which had been sharpened during the years subsequent to my first childish experiences with brother Frank, at our home at Alcovary.

I flatter myself that I was not unsuccessful; and by the time we fell into an exhausted sleep in each other's arms, we had proved to my satisfaction that we were perfectly complementary lovers.

It was with some horror that I awoke, hours later, to find daylight at the window. Opening my eyes, I found not only the sun, but Maurice's eyes, feeding on my body; and indeed on seeing me awake, he reached out as though impelled to discover whether or not the previous night had been a dream. I hastily discouraged him – and now took the great gamble of being honest with him. I have no doubt that Chichley would have been horrified; even Andy might have remonstrated; but I have always had a talent for the estimation of character, and felt in my bones that honesty was in the circumstances the best policy.

I therefore enquired, first, why he was in England; and after some hesitation, he revealed what I already knew – that it was the ambition of that consummate politician Talleyrand to prove him the proper successor to our present King, and for that purpose he was landed in England, to be escorted this day to London and the French Embassy, where a number of gentlemen in and around Parliament and the Court, who were indifferent to the prospect of a female ruler, would be introduced to him and invited to encourage him towards the throne.

And was this his wish, I asked?

Far from it, he replied. The exigencies of high office were a horror to him; all he wished for was a quiet life – and from the embraces he offered me, the company of a pleasant female.

This was my opportunity: relying upon my divination of character, I told him precisely the truth – even to admitting that it had been my intention to seduce him with a view to understanding his plan, specifically in order to frustrate it.

To my pleasure he immediately took my point, even to admitting that not only was he unsure whether his lineage was as had been described to him – but that even if it were so, protesting that he had no desire to pursue the matter! However, it was necessary to escape before the two men who accompanied him were about, for they would undoubtedly (being in the pay and much under the influence of M. Talleyrand) make him accompany them to London, and once at the French Embassy he would willy-nilly be forced to lend his presence to the plot.

We therefore rose speedily, and only pausing to make the most cursory toilet, were within half an hour at the inn and burst in upon Andy and his friend, still twined in each other's arms in a posture suggestive of agreeable concupiscence. Waking them, I explained the situation; and though Andy was clearly suspicious at the ease with which I had converted Maurice, was finally persuaded – not only by his presence but by his modesty and gentlemanlike qualities – of his honesty; while Charlie – whom I should now, in familiarity, address by that somewhat common appellation – at once took my part, immediately grasping the natural attributes of his character.

They rose with equal speed, and pausing only to leave a message for the local Watch, under Chichley's seal, which would result in the Dover magistrate detaining the two Frenchmen *incommunicado* for as long a period as authority deemed necessary, we were upon the road by six o'clock in the morning.

There had been some dispute about our destination. It could certainly not be London – but where else? It was Andy who suggested Alcovary – and once the name had been mentioned, it was clearly the proper place; only Chichley, among our friends, knew of it, and even if by some alchemy my own and Andy's identities were discovered (and it was just possible that M. Foutarque might infer it, though from no hard evidence) my whereabouts would be difficult to apprehend.

Our journey took two days; and we passed through the outskirts of London, pausing for the night at an inn at Greenwich. There, a single room was all that was available; and though Maurice showed some diffidence at sharing a bed with three comparative strangers, upon the landlord agreeing to place a truckle-bed in the room, he assented.

We were by then excessively tired, and stayed awake only long enough to take some refreshment, before taking to our beds in a handsome bow-windowed chamber overlooking the Thames, within a stone's-throw of Mr Wren's magnificent palace. Falling into a deep sleep, I believe that none of us stirred until morning; though waking at first light, at Andy's side, I saw upon his other side the figure of Charlotte, reclining upon one elbow, and regarding Maurice, who in the heat of the night had thrown off the sheet which covered him, and now revealed his figure entirely to the beholder, in utter relaxation, but as beautiful as a carved statue, his limbs perfectly white and perfectly charming.

Catching my eye, Charlotte had the grace to blush; but with a smile I let her know that her admiration was entirely understood by me, and we once more reclined, myself falling again into a slumber from which I was awakened only by the slight motion of the bed which signalled Andy's enjoyment of the body of his mistress (for they must part later that morning). He had slid between her thighs with so quiet a movement that it had not disturbed me, and was moving now with extreme gentleness in order not to wake me. However when, with that mischievousness that had always marked our relationship, I tickled his fundament with an apprehensive finger, he was relieved of the necessity for a caution which must have restricted enjoyment, and the entire mattress was soon bounding with their mutual pleasure – so much so that an uncomfortable (though agreeable) contact with their bodies encouraged me to slip from the bed and to take myself to lie at Maurice's side, who though still asleep now displayed indication of an involuntary but so far unapprehended excitement to which I felt it my duty as well as my pleasure to waken him – for we have not so long on this earth that we can afford to waste the opportunity for pleasure when so strongly evidenced.

That he was not distressed to be drawn from slumber was clear from his immediate reaction to my lips upon his admirably erect tool, which indeed justified that name, formed as it seemed to be in an ideal shape for giving and receiving pleasure. Time was short, and our preliminaries were restricted to confirming that each was ready to accept the caresses of the other – by my sufficiently anointing his instrument, and his at the same time ensuring that my own was sufficiently lubricious to receive it.

This accomplished, he was pleased to turn me upon my face, and lift my hips to address me from the rear, so that while plunging with spirited motion, he was at the same time able to caress with one hand my breasts, and with the other that portion of my inner lips not susceptible to the friction of his weapon.

The emotion resulting from this attention was sufficiently keen to make me screw up my eyes with the sharpness of it; but upon approaching an apogee I opened them to discover that Andy and Charlotte, having accomplished their own pleasure, were finding more in observing us – the latter, I thought, with peculiar appreciation; and upon Maurice courteously lowering me (our passage concluded) to the bed, and for a moment reclining upon me, they applauded us with expressions of admiration.

My lover was at first abashed, but the couple's admiration and approbation was too honest to take offence at, and he relinquished his attempts to cover us with the sheet and permitted me to wipe his body and my own before assuming (as we all did) our clothes.

On our crossing the river Andy now took his leave to make his way to Chichley in London, while Charlotte, Maurice and myself proceeded on the road towards Alcovary, which by dint of travelling all day (with a single break for luncheon) we achieved by two in the morning. It being an extremely warm day, and ourselves being the sole occupants of the coach, we were all to some extent *en dishabille*, Maurice removing his shirt and even (with our permission) his breeches, being then clad only in under-breeches, which it is the habit for gentlemen to wear in France – an uncongenial and even unsalubrious habit which I fear will eventually be assumed in this country. Charlotte and I contented ourselves with opening our clothing to the waist, allowing as much air as possible to cool our bodies, and raising our skirts above our knees.

It could not escape my eye that Charlotte regarded my new friend with an appreciative eye, the more so when he had fallen asleep, and she thought that I also slumbered. Indeed he was a picture worth perusing, and I could not blame her for wishing to study it, though upon observing her hand creep beneath her skirts I wondered whether her appreciation was entirely and singularly aesthetic.

On our reaching Alcovary, we found my brother Frank and my sister-in-law in their beds – but on being roused, as always pleased to welcome us, and keenly interested to greet both my friends and to hear our story – at which they were properly indignant, Frank, somewhat to my surprise, particularly so, for he shared my own view that should the succession fall to the Princess Victoria there was no reason to suppose that she might not prove a proper monarch, under the advice of her counsellors.

We were then allotted our rooms, Frank taking the opportunity to ask me whether I wished to share that of Maurice (for it had been clear to him, who knew me well, that I was not indifferent to the young man). I however preferred us to occupy three separate rooms, for though there was no indication that Maurice would be offended at my presence, I thought it fair that he should feel entirely free, especially in view of his position as a stranger in a strange house.

The next few days were entirely delightful, for a number of reasons. First, it was always a pleasure to be at home at Alcovary, and in halcyon summer weather; then, I had the delight of showing my friends the estate, about which we rode (both my companions being adept riders), and when the heat became oppressive made our way to the lake where Frank, Andy and I had bathed as children, and throwing off our clothes cooled ourselves in the waters, then lying upon the bank as the sun dried the sparkling droplets from our bodies.

I was not altogether surprised when Charlotte took me aside, at the end of our second day, and enquired with much diffidence to what extent I was devoted to Maurice – 'for', she said, 'I find myself strongly attracted to the young man; yet would not wish to make any move of which, as my hostess, you would disapprove.'

'My dear Charlotte,' I replied, 'it has ever been my view that what pleasure a man and woman can enjoy together, they should enjoy without the intervention of profitless jealousy. I have no rights over Maurice's body, and if he would welcome a passage with you – and I have no doubt that so attractive a lady will engage his admiration – then both he and you have my blessing; though I am not sure that my brother would say the same' (for I suspected that Andy admired Charlotte to an extent which she perhaps was not fully aware of).

Having obtained, as it were, my permission, Charlotte was nevertheless concerned not to make any move behind my back; and so it was when we were all lying together in a contented state of nature, after one of our bathes, that she whispered something in Maurice's ear as he lay face downwards upon the grass – underlining the suggestion she made my placing her hand upon his back just at that most sensitive point where the bifurcation of the buttocks offers an invariable trigger of desire.

Maurice's reply was to glance at me; and when inferring the question, I smilingly nodded my permission, he turned to take Charlotte in his arms, transferring to her breast and belly the bright green flecks of grass which had stuck to his wet body.

It was now my turn to admire the manner of their coupling; and while I knew perfectly the extent of his mastery of love-making, I was filled with a new admiration at the mixture of tenderness and insistence, of desire and restraint with which he wooed her body into a feverish eagerness to join with his own. Their mutual pleasure conveyed itself to the watcher not only through observation of their actions – which comprised every known engagement of limb with limb; not only through its prolongment – and an hour at least must have passed while they pleasured each other; but in an apprehension which combined riggishness with tenderness in equal degrees, and marked a mutual affection and respect not less keen than that which had (as I believed) graced my own passages of love with Maurice.

That I should be entirely unmoved by the spectacle was not to be expected; and in the end I was forced (lest I impose my physical presence upon the couple, which they may not have welcomed) to take refuge in the deep and cool waters of the pool, which had the effect of somewhat assuaging my ardour. It was while I was still in the water that they brought their exercises to a final conclusion, and missing my presence, were good enough to express themselves fearful that they had neglected me, and when I issued from the pool greeted me with embraces that were as warm in their emotion as in their physical expression – the apprehension of their heated bodies upon my cool one being as pleasurable, I believe, to them, as to me. While these embraces warmed me again, I was forced to restrain my sentiments, for it was perfectly clear that Maurice was now incapable of responding to them – and while I have from time to time without displeasure been the object of the caresses of another female, such was not my desire upon this occasion.

That I spent a somewhat melancholy evening perhaps need not be said. While I am the least jealous of beings, and have always believed that each individual must be free to bestow affection upon whatever object is pleasing, I had not expected Maurice to transfer his affections so suddenly and so completely to another woman; nor did it seem to me (if I must be truthful) entirely fair to Andy that Mrs Treglown, whatever her feelings towards him, should show so thoroughly the extent to which she found her new lover agreeable (even in the absence of my brother).

Nevertheless, there was nothing to be done; and the

affection shown me by the pair was only restricted by its nature – which did not embrace physical passion; and when at night I heard Maurice's footsteps pass my own door in the direction of Charlotte's, I must make as little of it as I could. Nevertheless, I could not but feel a tear spring to the eye.

Perhaps an hour after falling into the deep sleep which so often accompanies grief, I awoke to feel the familiar but unexpected sensation of an unclothed male body pressed against my own; but upon embracing it felt, rather than the lean body of the Pretender, a fuller – yet by no means obese – figure. The intruder failed to alarm me, being tender in his approaches; and my unspoken question as to whose member was now nuzzling my side was answered by a whispered greeting from Frank, my half-brother, who, recognising my dejection, had left his wife's bed (as I later learned, with her generous approbation) and come to comfort me.

I should perhaps explain that as children we had together explored the parameters of love while, ignorant of the restrictions upon familial intimacy enforced by the Church, we still believed ourselves to be the products of the same parents. Upon our discovery of society's disapproval of incest, we had ceased our pleasant games, not without a certain guilt; only to be delighted at the revelation – through circumstances which I will not now rehearse – that while we shared the same mother, our fathers were two different men. This somewhat alleviated our guilt; and indeed from time to time, when circumstance prompted, we had not hesitated to comfort each other in a manner warmer than might normally have been expected of siblings.

This was just such an occasion; and while we were not

adventurous, our conjugation was perfectly consolatory, and in falling again asleep, this time within the circle of Frank's arms, I did so with a less troubled mind, and certainly a less insatiate body, than hitherto.

I should remark that the Lady Margaret was of such a disposition as positively to welcome her husband's loyalty to an old friend, and her kindness to me at this time was entirely as marked as that of Frank; which enabled me to regard with greater equanimity, if not with entire satisfaction, the degree of preoccupation with which Maurice and Charlotte regarded each other – and to restrain both from recrimination towards the one and coldness towards the other.

More than a week had passed before, one morning, at ten o'clock, a bedraggled figure galloped up to the front door of Alcovary, his horse in a froth of sweat. It was Andy – and with a story which I can only allow him to tell for himself.

Chapter Thirteen

The Adventures of Andy

On my arrival my first action must be to report to Chichley, which I immediately did. He was interested to hear that M. le Semblant had proved sufficiently amiable to be no danger to us once removed from the influence of M. Talleyrand and his associates; and approved our plan of sending him to Alcovary, his confidence in Sophie's good sense being strengthened by his acquaintance with Frank, who though disinclined to politics is a man of some backbone, and entirely trustworthy.

The question now arose what to do about the nefarious influence of Talleyrand's friends in London – notably the Ambassador. That he should merely be instructed to leave the Court, without reason given, would be unsatisfactory, for though His Majesty, informed of the plot, would have no qualms about dismissing him, to do so without excuse would attract much unfavourable comment towards the new Government – while that the plot should be noised abroad would attract equally antagonistic attacks from those who would see it as demonstrating a lamentable lack of prescience among those whose duty it was to prevent such matters.

It was important, then, that the Duc de Laval should be discredited. But in what fashion? I assured Chichley

that I believed that this could be contrived, and having
made my farewells, set out that very night into that part
of London where are chiefly to be found those foreign
women imported into this country for the purpose of
prostitution – for I could not but believe that M.
l'Ambassadeur had his preferences in the matter of sensual enjoyment, and while I did not suppose that he
would prowl the streets of Soho or the pavements of the
Haymarket, it was possible that I might through gossip
hear something to his disadvantage.

I met here in the space of an hour or so Spanish, Italian
and Belgian as well as French women; and by dint of
tipping them (from the liberal purse supplied for the
purpose by Chichley, who insisted that I should not
employ my personal funds for the purpose) was able to
converse with them; but none had so much as heard of
the French Ambassador, either by that title or by his
name. This did not surprise me altogether; he would be
unlikely to use either title or name under the circumstances I envisaged; but a description of his person produced equally negative results.

I then took myself to the accommodation houses of
Oxenden and James Streets, of May Fair, and particularly of Curzon Street, and spoke to those women who
make a handsome living by letting out their premises.
The latter street contains two houses with the best-
known and most luxurious rooms in the whole of
London, those upon the first floors being let for as much
as twenty pounds a night. I knew (through the days when
Frank and I were in something the same business) the
women who kept them; and one gave me some hope. She
had at this moment, she said, a party going forward in
her chief room, at which a foreign gentleman was at

supper with some of her girls, and was sufficiently confident of my discretion to allow me to eavesdrop from the adjoining room (for all these houses have vantage-points from which their guest-rooms may be privately observed – chiefly to prevent disorder or attacks upon the persons of their girls; though sometimes, it must be admitted, upon payment of a few guineas, a gentleman whose pleasure is in looking rather than doing, may command the view).

In this case, I thought at first that I had struck home, for the gentleman whose back was towards me as I looked, seemed certainly to fit the description I had been given of M. le Duc (for, never having seen the gentleman in person, I must rely upon a sketch made for one of the public prints, and upon the fact that the Ambassador has – as Chichley had informed himself by the bribery of a footman – a birthmark upon the front of his right shoulder).

This gentleman was, as might have been expected, unclothed, and was making a good dinner off the bodies of three similarly naked young ladies. I mean, not that he was devouring their bodies (except in the figurative sense), but that upon the breasts and belly of the first were spread various cold meats, neatly garnished; upon the body of the second, a French salad – set out with much ingenuity in the cutting and shaping of the necessaries so that they did not roll from their precarious perch; while the third provided fruits of various kinds – two peaches, skinned, having been hollowed to fit over the points of her breasts, a fine melon, halved, upon her belly, and between her thighs a bunch of grapes, among which the diner was at present dabbling the fingers of one hand, while with the other he gathered the last spoonfuls of a meat sauce which lay about the navel of her friend.

The gentleman, as I have said, had his back to me; and there was no means of discovering a view of his face – but my hopes were dashed immediately by his breaking, through a mouthful of food, into exclamations in the German tongue (and indeed he later proved to be a distant cousin of His Majesty's come from Austria for the Coronation, whose introduction to the pleasures of Curzon Street made him a considerable source of income to the houses there and thereabouts).

I left my vantage-point, shaking my head; whereupon Mrs Blowser (the name of the proprietor of the house) intimated that there was a lady who might be able to help me, and escorting me to another room knocked upon the door, and on receiving an invitation to enter drew me with her into a reception room in which upon a *chaise-longue* reclined a figure which I instantly recognised: it was that of Xanthe, a lady who had been in my employ when with my brother Frank I was supervising our house of pleasure in Brook Street!

She rose immediately, and without reference to Mrs Blowser embraced me with a fervour which could not be mistaken for anything other than friendship.

'Why, Mr Archer!' she said. 'What good fortune brings you to this house! And how long 'tis since we . . .' – giving my cods an appreciative squeeze. Mrs Blowser, observing that we were not strangers to each other, tactfully withdrew; and I must confess that, what with the encouragement of the scene I had just observed, together with Xanthe's throwing off her *négligé* to reveal a body not the least diminished in attractiveness during the three or four years since we had last met, I allowed the question foremost in my mind to be thrust aside for a while, and in short permitted her to assist in the removal of my clothing and to lead me to the bed conveniently placed in the corner of the room, behind a screen which preserved the decencies on occasions when more than one gentleman awaited the attentions of whichever lady occupied the chamber.

Xanthe was good enough to compliment me upon the preservation of my own figure, and (with an appreciative caress) my apparently undiminished vigour; a kindness I was able to return without equivocation, for her slender frame remained as lithe and shapely as I remembered it – which I did in some detail, even to the mole which lay upon the inside of her left thigh, and towards the rear, which I now rediscovered in the course of paying tribute to those portals between which I would shortly take pleasure in slipping.

In parenthesis, I may say that I have always found that despite the considerable number of ladies who have kindly permitted me to admire them, my memory retains a keen approbation of most of them. I can see now, in my mind's eye, the somewhat over-ripe body of Lady Franklyn, Frank's mother (the first woman to show me, to my surprise, that an appetite for love outlasts one's thirtieth year); I remember very keenly the disparity between the bodies of Lady Margaret and Lady Elizabeth Rawby (the former now my friend Frank's wife); while even brief passages with such light skiffs as Mlle Anny, a Parisian lady of pleasure I had encountered but once, or an Arab lady whose extraordinary practices I enjoyed during one brief evening in Cairo, remain in my mind with such clarity that I am sure I would recognise their bodies were I merely to glimpse them without the protective disguise of clothing.

But I digress. Xanthe in the course of the next hour proved that her ability to please had diminished no jot; and her attentions roused me, despite a certain fatigue, to a greater degree of participation in amorous play than I would have believed myself capable of; so that in the end we lay pleasantly exhausted upon the bed, with a bottle of claret between us.

And what was I doing in such a place? she now enquired. Surely I need not purchase the favours of ladies, having always been more than capable of seduction, and being (I quote my friend, and do not assert it myself) impossible to resist, on account (she was kind enough to say) of the freshness of my looks and the enthusiasm of my play?

I explained that I was searching for someone who might have some knowledge of the habits of a gentleman of my acquaintance, a Frenchman; and described, without naming, him.

'Ah, you mean old Laval!' she said.

'You know him?' I exclaimed in delighted surprise.

'Why certainly!' she remarked; 'but not with any pleasure, and not as I know you' (bending to plant a kiss upon my now pliant tool).

My silent questioning then brought forth, without interrogation, the following anecdote:

'You remember George?' Xanthe asked.

Indeed I did: he was a young black man who had been one of the most admired hosts at the house which my sister Sophie had run, in Chiswick, for the delectation of the neglected ladies of the metropolis. The dimensions of that part of his body most admired by ladies were equalled only by his diffidence and charm, and on the winding up of the premises (as the result of a fire, a disaster my sister relates in a chapter of our adventures recorded in *Eros in Town*) he had last been seen in vigorous embrace with the lady whose head now lay engagingly upon my shoulder as she spoke.

'Well,' she continued, 'he has lately been in retirement from the profession, having employed that small fortune he saved while in Mrs Nelham's employ in the purchase of a respectable lodging house in the village of Islington, where from time to time we renew our acquaintance.

'However, his popularity with the ladies is such that he sometimes accepts the invitation of an old friend, and three months ago was sent for to Mrs FitzNott at her house in Knight's Bridge, to participate in a demonstration before a small party of ladies; and was kind enough to invite me upon that occasion to be his partner.

'On arriving at the house, we were drawn aside by Mrs FitzNott, and invited to betray no surprise should we observe anything strange about one of the observers. Nothing more was said – which of course had the effect of making us considerably more curious as to the nature of the audience than we would otherwise have been.

'Nothing at first seemed untoward: there were eight ladies seated upon comfortable chairs arranged in the chief *salon* of the house, and in a candle-light directed more at the cushions piled upon the centre of the floor than upon the faces of the females themselves.

'You will know, Mr Archer, that on such occasions 'tis necessary, especially in the opening passages of a performance, for the gentleman to withdraw attention from any other person than she with whom he is engaging; for should he be more aware of the audience than of his partner, there may be the unfortunate result that he becomes incapable of the act, which results at once in disappointment and the withdrawal of payment, and can even stimulate anger in those who have gathered to witness a performance which is then impossible.

'For the lady, however, the circumstances are not the same; indeed, upon such occasions I have always found it an advantage – however adept my partner in arousing those passions which upon a more private occasion are our particular joy – to detach myself from the proceedings in order to observe their effect upon the persons looking on; indeed, that process is productive not merely of interest and amusement, but sometimes of an inspiriting stimulation.

'On this occasion, after I had discovered to the viewers that part of George's body which invariably engages a rapt attention, and it was his turn to become the active partner, I was enabled by the circumstances, lying back upon the cushions while he grazed with his lips upon my lower body, to turn my eye upon the audience. There, it fell upon a somewhat heavily built lady who, sitting but four or five feet from us, had her eyes fixed most attentively upon George.

'This was not in the least surprising, for, Negroes being a rarity in the city, and scarcely ever to be observed in a state of nature, his body always attracts enthusiastic attention; but this lady was more considerably inspirited than her neighbours – and when again it came to my turn to revolve George's body so that that instrument whose size was the envy of his colleagues was once more revealed, and rendered yet more alert and upstanding by the attentions of my fingers and tongue, I thought the good lady's stays would burst.

'The development of our exhibition now reached the stage at which I must pay more attention to the proceedings, for as you will remember the insertion of George's prick (being of such unusual dimensions) could cause pain to those females insufficiently ready for the operation; however, I have never found it difficult to arouse my passions to a pitch at which liquefaction ensues, and (in short) in a brief time we were joined in that posture which best enables an audience to observe it; that is, with George upon his back, two pillows beneath his arse, and his hips thus elevated to an extent which displayed to advantage the pole upon which I lowered and raised my body.

'Despite the keen sensation always aroused by connection with that most splendid of lovers' (here Xanthe paused, afraid that she might have distressed me by this tribute, and afforded me the pleasure of a kiss) 'I was because of my elevation once more in a line of sight which positively forced me to observe the most prominent member of the audience, the front of whose gown was elevated, at her lap, to a surprising degree, which almost prompted me to suppose . . .'

Here Xanthe paused again; and, smiling at me, drew a finger along the length of my own riding-muscle, which (the picture she drew of the occasion having been sufficiently stimulating) was now if not adamantine, at least engorged to a promising thickness.

'You will no doubt have already guessed the identity of the woman of whom I spoke. Mrs FitzNott, after applause had signalled the end of our show and we had withdrawn, took George aside and asked whether he would be prepared to attend a lady, privately, offering a fee which was sufficiently persuasive. However, in twenty minutes, my friend reappeared in the room where I was taking refreshment, and, without himself pausing to taste anything, whisked me from the room and into a coach. It appears that upon his entering an upstairs bedroom and being embraced by the lady in question (no less than the one I had observed), he had at first been slightly repulsed by that masculine appendage, a slight moustache; yet had been prepared to believe that she suffered from that hirsute growth which can be a distressful trouble to some ladies.

'However, having permitted her to undress him, and even to address herself with enthusiasm to that part which most attracted her, and having accompanied her to the bed and begun to pay her those attentions she seemed to crave, he was puzzled to find that she made no attempt to disrobe; and on his attempting to undo her dress and stays, repulsed him – preferring merely to admire his person, which she did with eyes, hands and lips; then, growing more excited, in a panting motion clutching his body to her own and writhing in a frantic fashion, seemed to expire with such a groan as sometimes accompanies the supreme expression of love.

'Yet more puzzled, George raised himself upon one elbow – to see with embarrassment and even anger, a stain upon the front of the lady's dress which seemed to indicate that she was no lady, but a gentleman in woman's clothes; and – rather to ensure that his suspicion was justified than for any other emotion – thrusting his hand into her breast, produced a piece of cloth which, screwed up and placed there, had counterfeited a not unimpressive bosom.

'Though George has no prejudice against namby-pambies, and indeed would defend their right to take recreation with others of their own persuasion, he has never had carnal connection with one of them; and on this occasion allowed a certain anger at the impertinence of the gentleman concerned to take precedence over his generous nature. Taking up his clothes he strode from the room without even picking up the purse which had been placed for him on the bedside table.

'That the gentleman was none other than the French Ambassador, M. le Duc de Laval, I only discovered upon seeing him pass by to the Coronation, in his nation's official uniform, which nevertheless did not disguise from me his identity – but rather made it clearer, by the full-length old-fashioned wig which he wore on the occasion!'

My pleasure at this story can be imagined! – and I would immediately have leaped from bed and taken myself off to Chichley with the news – even at one o'clock in the morning, which it now was – did not Xanthe claim another passage at arms, which resulted in a sleep from which I awoke only the next morning.

Bidding her an affectionate farewell (having obtained from her news of George's whereabouts, and passing a generous reward to Mrs Blowser, to whom I felt some gratitude – though her part in the affair had been entirely coincidental) I then hurried to Chichley and laid before him the plan which had fixed itself, almost without consideration, in my mind.

The affair was simply organised. His Majesty and his Queen were pleased to accept Chichley's invitation to dine with him (for he was in great favour with the new Administration – and twitted me considerably for being a member of the loyal Opposition); and a small party was arranged, consisting of two or three influential courtiers, and their Excellencies the Ambassadors of Spain, Portugal, Italy, Austria and Russia, all of whom were accompanied by their ladies. There was some small comment on the absence of His Excellency the French Ambassador, but it was assumed that the present cool relations between England and France were responsible, the King having been heard from time to time to express the wish that he could 'blow those d*mn Frenchies out of the water!'

Chichley served a delightful meal, and their Majesties showed that cordiality which permitted them to converse with everyone present on the most friendly terms – the King showing, in especial, a talent for putting the gentlemen at their ease through memoirs of his time at sea.

The ladies were led from the room at the end of the meal, to take their ease in Lady Chichley's drawing-room, while we gentlemen took a pint or so of port apiece; after which Chichley suggested that we should repair to the neighbouring room for a game of cards.

A small procession then formed, led by His Majesty and Chichley, followed by the Ambassadors of Portugal and Russia, and at a signal from the host two footmen threw open the doors and we passed through the intervening drawing-room, and up the stairs to the card-room. Once more, double doors were thrown open, and the party passed inside – to be greeted by the sight of a lady in respectable clothing, kneeling at the feet of a naked black gentleman whose already outstanding equipment she was endeavouring by oral stimulation to rouse to an even more remarkable state of attention.

Hearing a noise behind her, the lady half-turned, and finding herself looking up into the astonished face of the British monarch, lost her balance and falling backwards upon the floor threw her legs into the air, revealing beneath her shirts a pair of white and hairy buttocks which would have seemed expressly unfeminine even without the excited appendages adjacent.

There was a moment's horrified pause, after which His Majesty (whose sense of humour partook of that enthusiastic coarseness which is the mark of Jolly Jack Tar) burst into a roar of laughter – the reaction upon which I had counted, assuming that his years in the Navy would have made amusement, rather than anger, his natural reaction.

The recumbent gentleman sat up, the female wig upon his head slipping over one eye; and to ensure that his identity was clear, Chichley stepped forward and offered his hand, with the words:

'My dear Laval, allow me to assist you!'

But the Duc, now crimson of face, ignored the hand of friendship, and, clambering to his feet, gathered his skirts about him and, making the most perfunctory bow, rushed headlong from the room.

His Majesty guffawed ('tis the only expression). 'Fortunate the ladies were not in attendance, hey, Chichley?' he remarked; but then, with a glance at George, who had retired discreetly to a corner of the room, where he was now standing uncertainly, not sure whether it would be etiquette to begin to resume his clothes in the presence of the King, he added: 'Not but what they might have enjoyed a sight of such remarkable tackle!' – and beckoned to George to approach, which he did with the utmost diffidence.

His Majesty stared for a moment at the now fallen, but still sizeable, apparatus; turned to my friend, and remarked: 'Many a vessel could make use of so substantial a foremast, hey, Chichley? Pity the lad's a sod.'

George would, I am sure, have blushed at this could a

blush have shown itself upon his dark features; but it was impossible to correct His Majesty's impression without revealing our plot; so I merely winked, and supplied some balm to George's honour, later, by providing him with a purse of more than usual weight, together with the news that Xanthe awaited him in one of Chichley's servants' rooms, where they could be pleasant together for as long as they wished.

My task was now done. The hum of conversation among the courtiers and the other Ambassadors would amplify next day to a positive chorus of gossip – and through the ladies (for what husband would not be pleased to regale his wife, upon retiring, with such a rich story?) would soon be known to all London. It was fortunate that my suspicion – that Laval's lust for George's person would be sufficiently strong to attract him to an assignation, proposed in a note conveyed to him through Foutarque – had proved correct.

Chichley having set a watch on the Embassy, it was observed that Laval made immediate preparations to withdraw from London. Unable to do so without making his obeisance at Court, he must face His Majesty once more, to take leave. The Queen being present preserved him from the chaff which would undoubtedly have been his fate; as it was, the King merely tipped him a wink which brought a blush to that cold, white and wrathful face, after which he swept from the Court, from London and from these shores.

The following day, Chichley begged an audience of His Majesty, and in a conversation to which the King alone was privy, told the whole story of the French plot. Naturally aghast, His Majesty was minded to send for le Semblant and bring him immediately to trial for treason.

Chichley at that moment, with permission, summoned me, who was able to persuade the monarch that the Pretender would be no threat to the throne or the succession; and indeed would, I believe, crave of His Majesty the indulgence to remain in England as a refugee, offering whatever securities were at his command to ensure his becoming a decent private citizen, sufficiently removed from public life to render it impossible for Talleyrand or his busybodies to discover him.

At the name of Talleyrand, His Majesty started. Was that gentleman cognizant of the plot? he asked – and on being assured that he was probably its chief perpetrator, the King informed us that the name of that gentleman had just been communicated to him by M. Foutarque, who remained in charge of the Embassy of the French, as that of the man most likely to be appointed Ambassador in Laval's place!

That that became indeed the case, everyone will know; but any narrative of his appointment and what followed should be the prerogative of historians; my concern is in more human matters – and it is a pleasure to record that His Majesty (unable to make any gesture which would make public our part in a plot, knowledge of which was to remain secret) was good enough to offer me his hand and his warm thanks, together with the confident hope of my advancement in my political career, while producing a handsome gold watch which he invited me to present to George as a token of gratitude for his part in the matter, together with his apologies for having cast any aspersion on his manhood (with the muttered aside to the effect that a single glance at his most signal masculine limb should have been sufficient to suggest that it would be the greatest waste should it be devoted to pleasuring any but the female sex). He was also good enough to suggest that should George ever be in need of employment, he should apply to the Lord Chamberlain with the word of His Majesty's interest.

This, I happily conveyed to my friend; and I may digress from the main stream of this narrative sufficiently to record that he did so apply, and in short became a footman at the Court, where he could still be seen forty years hence, a most unusual and commanding figure who filled his uniform with grace and an impressive mein; he became, indeed, a favourite with Her Majesty Queen Victoria, after her accession, who, and whose consort during his lifetime, he served most diligently, never marrying but (as rumour has it) rarely short of female company, drawn from among the minor servants of the royal household and even (it was said) some of its more senior parties – to the great distress of a cocksure Scot, Mr John Brown, who until George's ascendancy had ruled the roost where the seduction of ladies-in-waiting was in question.

Matters having been resolved, it was now my determination to travel to Alcovary, there to assure Maurice le Semblant of the King's agreement to his remaining in the country, and impatient to renew my friendship with Charlotte: an impatience the more eager because I would bear with me the news of her husband's decease – for on travelling to Mrs Jopling's house to release him, I found that he had contrived to open a window at some time during his imprisonment, and in attempting to escape had fallen and broken his neck. To suggest that this gave anyone exceptional cause for mourning would be to suggest what was not so; Mr Treglown was unpopular almost to excess not only with his colleagues in the House, but with his constituents, his election having been achieved only by enormous expenditure in the matter of bribes.

As I rode towards Cambridge at full pelt, I was almost ready to believe that I should propose marriage to the widow (being confident that the unhappiness of one union would not necessarily preclude another pledge of a similar nature). I paused, as was my wont, at the Chequers Inn at Fowlmere, where the landlord, who knew me well, had my usual chamber prepared, which lies over the main room of the inn and has as its only disadvantage the fact that it is a throughway to another room beyond it, this being an ancient house marked by its lack of corridors and passageways, each room leading into the next.

Exhausted by my ride, I partook of a hasty meal, and was not slow in repairing to my four-poster, the curtains of which I drew in order that passers-by should neither disturb my sleep nor enjoy the impertinence of observing me.

To say that I slept soundly would be to understate the matter. Indeed, I did not stir until awaking from a delicious dream of congress with my Charlotte (which I trusted would only be the pre-shadow of an enjoyment to come). I say awaking – but I was rather awakened, by the throwing back of the curtains of the bed and a touch upon my shoulder; on which I opened my eyes to find a well-shaped, dark-haired country girl of perhaps seventeen bending over me and glancing with twinkling eyes at my morning show, which was clearly presented to her through my throwing off the sheets, as is my wont when the nights are close.

That she should then place her hand upon the crux of the matter was, though uninvited by me, something

which was not altogether surprising; for during the five
or six years during which I had stayed at the Chequers,
mine host had become aware of my appetite, which was
usually sufficiently keen to prompt me to enquire
whether there was an acquiescent girl in his employ who
could attend to my corporeal needs – and it had been
latterly his custom, without previously making enquiry,
to send any promising maid to my room with my hot
water in the morning, leaving it to me to decide whether
to engage her in more than a light conversation.

This morning, my looking forward to renewing my
acquaintance with Charlotte, and proving to her my
devotion, would have precluded an interest in any other
female had not circumstances been tempting, in that the
young lady who now sat herself upon the bed at my side
had previously had experience only with the hobble-
dehoys of the village, and was all eagerness to discover
whether a passage of arms with a gentleman would offer
any keener pleasure than with a cow-boy or labourer. To
that end she did not wait for invitation, but immediately
threw her gown over her head, revealing a frame the
delights of which it was beyond my power to ignore –
nor indeed did she give me the opportunity, for in a
moment she was on top of me.

The curious thing was (and from whom she had
learned such a trick it was beyond me to conjecture) that
while the manner of her bestraddling my body and lowering herself upon my prick was not unusual, she did so
while facing my feet! This at first discomfited me; but
then I realised that the disadvantage of being denied the
sight of her breasts, and indeed of the conjunction of our
bodies, was somewhat mitigated by the fact that the posture enabled her to use her fingers in the most stimulating

fashion upon my cods, and that area of my person immediately beneath them, to the stimulation of which I have always been peculiarly susceptible.

That young person, whatever the circumstances of her introduction to the arts of love, had an instinct for them which raised her far above the condition of other fubbsies. Upon the tightening of my person which signalled an approaching paroxysm, for instance, she immediately rose upon her knees, merely stroking my sides and thighs until the urgency – but not the desire – had subsided, then moving backwards so that she could continue with her lips the delightful stimulation while, kneeling astride my chest, she offered to my own lips that fig-like, dark and delightful fissure which I found it impossible not to taste, and which proved as sweet, as comfortable and as tender as that of the handsomest lady of May Fair!

The pleasure of such a posture was sufficiently keen to render me soon once more liable to a sudden culmination; when, sensing it, she again desisted, now merely bending forward to brush gently with dependent breasts my thighs and belly – which proved too much for my impatience, and throwing her sideways upon the bed, without more ado I fucked her in the most attentively violent manner, at which she squeaked with pleasure.

I am not usually given to that melancholy which is said to follow copulation; but on this occasion, as the girl busied herself – without resuming her clothes – in preparing the bath for my ablutions, I could not but remember that it would have better behoved me to retain those juices which had just been expelled for my so-loved Charlotte – and for some time I felt most sad. Yet then, as I stood within the copper vessel and the girl sponged my body, giving particular attention to my male member, and I regarded the delightful prospect offered by each view of her person, I felt yet again that swelling which invariably accompanies my admiration of the female form, and wondered whether it would ever be possible for me with honesty to promise to confine myself to any single female, however charming.

As if to confirm my conjecture, the young lady now dropped the towel with which she had been washing me, and with the most ingratiating smile, turned, and bending forward offered me an open target – which (the reader will guess) I had not the heart to ignore, and taking a step forward, presented myself at the mark and, my hands resting lightly upon the girl's hips, engaged her in gentle play which – the cool air from the open window upon my wet body enabling me to prolong the exercise – led to our being once more satisfied.

The remainder of my journey to Alcovary was slower than that of the previous day; indeed, often I allowed my steed to slow to a walk while I considered the difficulty before me. I was in no doubt that upon Charlotte hearing of her husband's death she would expect an offer from me. Had I the heart to refuse? Yet having accompanied her to the altar, would I be able to remain constant when so common an incident as the maid at an inn offering her body – which was in my experience a matter of course at most public inns – could lead me to stray from the basic conventions of matrimony?

I had still reached no conclusion when I rode through the gates of Alcovary Park and turned up the drive between the elms. Halfway up the drive, I heard voices and laughter from beyond the tall hedge behind which lies the lake: my friends were no doubt enjoying a bathe in the heat of mid-day – and I would be happy to join them. I tethered my steed in the spinney, and disencumbering myself of my clothing walked to the lake – and coming to it saw two figures standing in an embrace, thigh-deep in the water. Frank and his wife, no doubt; or perhaps Sophie and M. le Semblant – for it was not impossible that their obvious infatuation should have lasted this long.

But when, approaching, I called a greeting – what was my surprise (and, I must confess, in the first instance my anger) to discover that the couple who now turned their heads to me, remaining so closely glued together at the waist that one might have been forgiven for supposing that they were fully embraced, were – Charlotte and M. le Semblant!

I turned from them, involuntarily, and began to walk away, ignoring Charlotte's cry; but then I heard her running footsteps soft in the tall grass, and felt her hand upon my shoulder, and in short was made to listen. Her explanation – that she and Maurice (as I will now call him) had discovered a deep attraction, must be accepted by me; for the ways of man and woman do sometimes, and perhaps more often than we may suppose, lead to such engagements. And the nervousness, almost amounting to fear, with which she spoke of it convinced me that it was no insult to me that she should feel thus, but a true compulsion.

Taking her hands from my shoulders, where she had placed them as she spoke, I turned and walked back to the shore of the lake, where Maurice was sitting, his elbows upon his knees and his head in his hands. He must have been remembering that, with my knowledge of the plot in which he had been involved, I had doubtless the power of life and death over him.

Bending to crouch at his side, I placed my arm about his shoulders.

'Fear not, my friend,' I said; 'such an attachment as that of which Mrs Treglown has spoken must take precedence over my warm but less familial feelings. Moreover, should it be your mutual wish, I must tell you that the death of her husband now makes it possible for you to become husband and wife.'

He looked at me in bewildered delight; and at my motion rose and went to Charlie, who had remained at a distance, convinced that even should we resort to fisticuffs it was not her place to intervene. I took to the water to cool my body and, I confess, my emotions, out of the corner of my eye seeing her delight and their embrace – which gave me some pangs, though I knew that I could have done no other than what I had done.

That evening we all dined together, and I regaled the others with the adventures of which I have spoken, and was able to assure Maurice of his safety, and the fact that provided he lived in a decent obscurity every effort would be made to protect him from French agents.

'I would suggest,' I said, 'that you settle in Cornwall; for there the only Frenchmen ever to be seen are the Bretons, who are as uninterested in their national politics as any people could be. That is, if you and Charlie . . .'

Leaning across the table, she took my hand and kissed its fingers.

'How can we reward you for your loving disinterest?' she asked.

The long evening over, passed in conversation, sitting in the drawing-room through whose open windows the scents of summer swam, I took myself off to bed. As I walked down the corridor, I heard footsteps behind me. It was Sophie, who had been peculiarly quiet during the evening. She followed me into my room, where she admitted that her feelings about Maurice had mirrored my own.

'He would, I am convinced, have made an offer,' she said; 'and I am in no doubt that I would have accepted it. Yet are you and I such people as can settle into a routine of dull domesticity, even with those we love?'

I embraced her; the first embrace led to a second; and to be short, within a short time we were in each other's arms, my hands encountering the well-remembered resilience of her still firm breasts, hers reassuring herself that the body she had first excited when we were children together in this same house – indeed, in this same room – was still capable of arousal.

I had just entered her, when the door opened.

We were startled, though not dismayed. No doubt 'twas Frank, come for some purpose or another; and we three had shared the same bed too often for apprehension or shyness.

But the figure which presented itself at the bedside a moment later was a female one: that of Charlie. Sitting beside us, she laid a hand upon my shoulder, and bending forward, whispered something into Sophie's ear.

She had come, it turned out, in order that we two could say our farewells – bringing the request from Maurice that Sophie would offer him for one last time the hospitality of her bed in an adjoining chamber.

I will not detail what followed: the reader will remember what pleasures Mrs Treglown – soon to be Madame le Semblant – and I were capable of offering each other;

but I will say that the knowledge that I was taking a farewell of her body (for I was in no doubt that that was what was occurring, her moral sense being such that once pledged to Maurice she would regard me merely as a friend) sharpened my apprehension of the occasion.

Once more I was plagued with doubts: how many other women gave themselves with such freedom, such complete openness – who offered their bodies to a lover as though it were a landscape through which he would wander without restriction, enjoying in utter freedom the uplands and lowlands, the brakes and rivers, the valleys and hills? How many women explored their lover's person with such attentive admiration – yet at the same time with such a determination to afford to every surface the most signal sigh of a loving attention to the gratification of desire? With how many other women could a lover be so sure that he could make no demand, utter no request that it would not be her immediate pleasure to satisfy?

For my part, I must confess that I took peculiar care, on this occasion, to prove myself equally attentive, delaying again and again that satisfaction she craved; then offering it once more, and once more again – so that in the morning she was so exhausted that I had to leave her in my bed, while I (with a fine pretence of vigour, though truth to tell I was tired almost to fainting) took myself off, having set Maurice a standard which he might have some difficulty – I prided myself – in maintaining.

As I walked along the corridor, I saw a door ajar; and looking in, found sister Sophie abed. I entered, whereat she raised her hand in a lazy salute. I slipped between the sheets, at her side, and laid a hand upon her breast.

'Will you forgive me, sister,' I said, 'if . . .'

'Indeed, brother,' she said, 'I am limper than a dry daffodil; I believe that Maurice was attempting . . .'

'To show what you had lost?' I asked. 'I have attempted the same, I must confess, with Charlie.'

Sophie smiled, lifted my hand, and kissed it.

'Then,' she said, 'let us leave them to renew their vows – if they have the vigour.'

And turning her back upon me, she snuggled into my arms so that we lay together like a set of spoons, and we fell asleep.